Hermaphrodeity

Herma

THE AUTOBIOGRAPHY

 NEW YORK

phrodeity

OF A POET

by Alan Friedman

ALFRED A. KNOPF · 1972

THIS IS A BORZOI BOOK
PUBLISHED BY ALFRED A. KNOPF, INC.

Copyright © 1968, 1970, 1972 by Alan Friedman

All rights reserved under International and Pan-American Copyright Conventions. Published in the United States by Alfred A. Knopf, Inc., New York, and simultaneously in Canada by Random House of Canada Limited, Toronto. Distributed by Random House, Inc., New York.

ISBN: 0–394–47291–8
Library of Congress Catalog Card Number: 77–154910

Portions of this book appeared in *New American Review #2* (1970) and in *Partisan Review* (Summer 1968).

Manufactured in the United States of America

FIRST EDITION

To
EROS

Some do believe hermaphrodeity,
That both do act and suffer.
—BEN JONSON,
The Alchemist

Contents

HOW I CHANGED   3

HOW I CHANGED MY MIND   23

HOW I CHANGED MY BODY   59

HOW I TOOK FIRE   101

HOW I GOT CARRIED AWAY   115

HOW I MADE FRIENDS   125

HOW I BECAME A MYTH   143

HOW I MADE IT   163

HOW I MADE IT BIG   187

HOW I BETRAYED LOVE   231

HOW I MADE LOVE   259

HOW I CAME TO FIGHT   297

HOW I CAME TO TRIAL   317

HOW I DISTRIBUTED MY FLAME   339

HOW I LOST MY LIFE   365

HOW I   423

ALSO BY M. W. NIEMANN

POETRY
Snatches
Towers in a Landscape
Sublunary Lovers
Irrational Numbers
These Bare Bones
The Physical Comedy
Backside of the Moon
The Intelligence Cantos
"The Theban Duet":
  A Cock and a Bull
  Pissoirs of the Heart
God As Spy
Collected Poems
Visions and Revisions
Songs of Degradation

ESSAYS AND BELLES LETTRES
The Poetic Itch
A Bestiary of Motives
The Parliament of Sex
The Whore and the Cyclotron

VERSE DRAMA
Come, Come Now
Hermes and Aphrodite

BIOGRAPHY
A Vested Interest: Memories of B. N. Tieger

LETTERS
E. Carlo Satori and M. W. Niemann:
  A Bitter Exchange

ARCHAEOLOGY AND ETHNOLOGY
Dig!
The Skirts of the God
Climbing Mons Veneris

Hermaphrodeity

How I Changed

TO EROS
You burn me.
—SAPPHO

Coarse? Well, maybe I am. One of the magazines called me a "coarse old lady poet." I won't argue the point. Naturally, I got coarser as I grew older, like most of you. I don't mean only my indecent turn of mind, which comes automatically with age. I mean those mannerisms which even lady poets develop and which never get into print. I can rarely eat without getting food all over my mouth. And these days whenever I eat anything I really enjoy, I make a sharp whining involuntary noise under my chewing. I can hardly control it. And the smell of my feet, which has gotten stronger with age like cheese—well, would it really shock you if I said I like it? I think not, at least not if you've reached my age. But just in case, I want to warn you. Even if you happen to have read some of my verse and thought the sweet-and-sour of it to your taste, prose is another matter. For I think you'll agree with me that it isn't life itself which is coarse, but the way in which it's experienced. And though I wrote about my life in poetry, I experienced it, so to speak, in prose —physically and corruptly.

For example, the first time I wrote a poem I was very troubled by the problem of rhyme and I was scratching my behind all during the composition. I was eight years old and I remember it distinctly because my Uncle Lemmie (dead a long while now. The only thing I remember about him is that he was always pushing a garden wheelbarrow. When other children talked about their fathers' Fords, I used to brag that my Uncle Lemmie pushed me around in a wheelbarrow) saw me scratching and told me that little ladies didn't, not anywhere. He lowered the handles of the wheelbarrow gravely as he said it, sat down on the bench beside me, and began tenderly braiding my hair. "What're you doing, Millie?" he said.

"Writing a poem. What rhymes with fire?"

"Lots of things. Tire, or fire . . ."

"I've already got fire."

"Well, then spire."

We were sitting across the street from my house. Inside through the porch windows I could see my father reading the Sunday paper and I could see my mother playing the piano. Over by the cellar door I could see the smoke which seemed to be coming from the garden where my uncle had been gathering dead leaves and burning them. I had a school copybook on my lap and a pencil in the hand that wasn't scratching. My knees, sticking out beyond the hem of my skirt, were dirty as usual, this time with coal dust. So to cover my knees I moved the copybook cautiously along my skirt with the tip of the pencil while my uncle was busy with my hair. He said, "How come you're writing poetry?"

"Because I've got something extra important to say to Mommy and Daddy. And I can't use spire."

"Well, let me see what you got so far."

> I want to tell you right away
> About a big red fire,
> That if you want the house to stay
> You've got to

His breath smelled while he pondered the verse over my shoulder. "That's not bad," he said. "What about in-spire?"

I gave it some thought and shook my head.

"Per-spire?"

"Uncle Lemmie," I rebuked him, "this is serious. I was down in the cellar before, and if they don't call the fire engines soon, we won't have a house. There's a whole pile of Daddy's old newspapers caught fire from the stove."

What with Daddy running with water buckets in a minute or two and Mommy screaming and Uncle Lemmie and my brother breaking the fire alarm box and calling the fire engines, and the firemen pulling hoses all over the porch, the poem never got finished. But when the firemen, chopping and dousing away, had saved about three-quarters of the house, Daddy said, "What the hell was she writing poetry for?" And Mother hit me hysterically in the back of the head and said, "Why didn't you tell us?" But even after Uncle Lemmie had explained about the rhyme, they didn't understand.

Now I believe that the act of poetry is always utilitarian. For them, of course, my wanting to communicate in poetry at all, and my searching so hard for the perfect rhyme to do it with, remained —forever—a purpose mysterious, rankling, insolubly perverse. But that was because I never told them that it was I who had set the fire.

I was a fat little girl—wretchedly fat. In the photographs I have (Plate I), I look blonde, bloated, and worried. There was so much of me that I thought I was a freak, and I was preoccupied with my physical being—in fact, my earliest memories are not of people at all, but of sensations. A deeply buried excitement as of a smaller body within my own body, gradually expanding to giant proportions —that's the earliest. It happened only during absolute darkness, silence, rest, probably as I was falling asleep in my crib, and came of itself, like grace. Something within me formed and grew—swelling, swelling out of all belief, doubling, tripling the limits of my already puffed tiny body as I lay overpowered and rigid, exulting unpardonably in my size but helpless with the fear that any moment I would burst.

Another—a burning sensation which began in the mouth and ran quickly through the rest of me, inside and out as though I were on fire—happened only once, I think, in infancy, but recurred often in later life in moments of feared passion, usually as a prelude to lovemaking. According to my mother it can be traced back to my first summer, to the time my father drew the water for my bath. He had boiled the water on the stove and added it to the basin, assuming my mother would add cold as needed. She assumed that he had already adjusted the temperature, and proceeded to add me, instead. I screamed in time as my heel went in, and the result was a kind of topsy-turvy Achilles' heel, a blister which became a permanent tough scar. (I was to prove almost impervious there.) But in my own opinion this episode can't account for the flaming sensation I remember, and later on have experienced again, since this always begins in the mouth.

My father was a lawyer, a tiny man with a mustache that looked phony and big ears with tufts of hair growing in them. People who heard his loud voice for the first time, only a few words of trivial conversation, were invariably shocked: that out of such a tiny man, under the suddenly arched lip and mustache, broke a voice like an overloaded loudspeaker, metallic, compelling, and deeply annoying. Perhaps that was why his legal successes were cerebral ones, triumphs of the office rather than the court. Still, he believed with passion in forensic skill and he began training my older brother Sander from early childhood in public speaking—heading him for the bar and, I suppose, Congress. He used to have Sandy stand up at the table after dinner every night to speak extemporaneously for five minutes to all of us—though Mother usually left in obvious boredom—on whatever topic my father chose. These were usually matters of childhood interest although later, as Sandy grew older, they became wider in scope, political or philosophical. Often, however, they were topics of mere absurdity. Indeed my father claimed that for practice, the best subjects in the world on which to sharpen the teeth of logic and persuasion were those to which no reasonable man could listen. They would serve Sandy later, he claimed, like the weights carried by the Spartans or the stones in Demosthenes' mouth.

I recall in particular one of the absurd topics on which Daddy insisted Sandy speak, because it made at the time an almost mystical impression on me. I was four years old and Sandy was nine and he spoke with all the eloquence he could muster (which by that time was plenty) on the proposition that the sun was really the moon. I listened with my cheek on the table. Sandy stood by his chair as usual, alternately leaning on the table with curled fingers and standing back from it, pushing the blond hair off his forehead, squinting one eye sometimes while he spoke, blowing his nose once or twice and picking it, and pointing a subtle finger at the moon. "You say you can see for yourself. But how good are your eyes? At that distance anyone could make a mistake, couldn't they? The evidence is suspicious right off. Even if every one of you thinks it's the sun, in China they all think they're standing on top of the world. And the earth looks flat, doesn't it? What we need is people with an open mind because the cards are stacked—"

"Facts," Daddy coached loudly, motioning with his toothpick at Sandy's pocket. "I have here."

"I have here reports from ten top scientists, disagreeing with each other about what the sun is made out of, and if those scientists can't agree, it's up to us. They say they have to look at it in an eclipse. Well, we ought to bring the thing down and have it looked at in broad daylight. And we could, too, if they weren't spending all our money and keeping us cooling our heels out here in the outfield, trying to tell us what to do—"

"Drive it home!"

"It's up to every one of you to decide in his own heart. That poor moon might be up there all this time, every day, and everybody thinking it was the sun."

"No good," Daddy carped. "You missed the point: the sun is the moon."

I was shivering with attention and overwhelmed by what I had heard. Were they seriously proposing that the sun was the moon? I longed to find out, I yearned to go up there. Or were they proposing that the two ought to be changed, could be changed? I lay with my cheek on the table, rigid with wonder.

Though not the first, this was one of my earliest exposures to the idea of transformation, which as the critics have noted, recurs often in my poetry, and without which I would never have risked the daring realism of utterly transforming myself into what otherwise —for all the hacks and quacks around—would have remained only potential in me for a lifetime. "It's all relative" is the cant phrase you hear now even in grocery stores or on park benches. And "It's all in your point of view"—far too easy, isn't it, and any honest man, if pushed, will admit it's not *quite* true. One's point of view—the eyes of the beholder—can't really transform a thing. An additional step, a tougher and solider adventure is needed before you can have transmutation, or wealth, or poetry.

In any case, for years Sandy used to practice a rhetoric of sophistication and deceit (the kind he later used so successfully to have his way with me), while I listened, rapt with admiration and jealous of his skill and intelligence. I never managed to realize that the five years' difference in our ages, by which he kept exactly the same distance ahead of me all the time, had anything at all to do with it. He seemed unreachably brilliant and beautiful: his sharp features, his freckles, his skinny boy's body. I wanted his mind and body for my own. I raged and desired him unconditionally. And certainly no little girl's wishes were ever answered so unconditionally.

"You never know what's underneath," my father said to quiet me. It's the very earliest memory I have of him. He had taken me to the matinee at a local theater one Saturday—a kind of vaudeville performance for children. On stage a troupe of dancing animals snarled back at the trainer's whip, and the audience of children was uneasy. "You never know," my father said, his hand on the back of my neck, soothingly. I was three and a half. When the biggest animal of all came down off the stage—a lion, I suppose, though to me he was only Animal—and began to climb through the theater over the empty rows up front, the children panicked. From where I sat toward the side, he seemed to be climbing over the audience, his paws on their heads. Still, I kept quiet. He came fourfootedly up the center aisle and paused, the audience shrieking and backing away. To calm them, he sat back on his haunches and proceeded to slit his throat, from his furry chin down—out came a man's head: I screamed—down to his groin—a man's body: I screamed louder.

What terrified me then and always has is not the beast in man, but the man in the beast. Look at the person nearest you this moment and you'll see what I mean. The emergence of man from animal is always half complete: I see him standing there, cheap actor, one leg out of the fur forever. Our history only repeats the first man's history. When he stepped out completely and shook the dead golden rag on the floor, I went wild. I screamed hysterically for almost ten minutes, my father trying to stop me in the lobby with loud, reasonable arguments. And let me mention that, later on, one of the most soul-terrifying moments I've ever had (the resultant short poem, "Boy, You Theban Beast," is one of my most celebrated) came to me when I looked at my brother, then grown old, and saw that in fact he was not a beast.

My brother, five years more interested than I was in "what's underneath," took me under the bed one day when I was four and he was nine to find out. "Let's swap," he said. "You look, I look." I had no particular objection, but he added, "Give and take, that's the way the world works." In the midst of a very thorough exploration, he announced himself disappointed. "What a gyp! This is no trade— there's nothing here."

I got used to this sort of examination in childhood. I underwent a number of them, and reactions were always the same. I remained passive and uninterested myself. It was only the last, performed by a gynecologist when I was sixteen, that—as the reader will see—excited me, as Keats said of Cortez, with a wild surmise.

One smart aleck offered in trade his really long appendicitis scar and I accepted. A group of robber barons stopped me in the park and offered to gouge and club me with the blades of their iceskates if I didn't immediately lift up my skirt and take down my pants. Their enthusiasm puzzled me. I considered refusing, because it was already getting dark, a late winter afternoon, and I was afraid I might be cold. But I recognized them. The bushes into which I had been pushed were on the grounds of the Children's Museum, where I had gone with friends after school. After the others had left I had stayed behind to see an exhibition of sculpture and lantern slides about the facts of birth and anatomy, entitled "Nature's Miracle." I had seen the same group of boys with iceskates in the auditorium. And though their approach was blunt, the idea of being asked to take my small part in the exhibition of a miracle seemed reasonable. Patiently, I complied. One of the young toughs said wearily, "See, what'd I tell ya."

Mother raised a great cry when I told her. "Eight years old!" she wailed. She called Daddy at the office, but he wasn't in. Then she took me around the corner to the police station and raised a great cry there. I was staggered when we were given a patrol car and two policemen to search for the boys. We toured the neighborhood. I had been at ease in the park but I was frightened in the patrol car. We slowed up past every group of boys on the streets, especially those with iceskates, and I began to think it would soothe everybody if I merely pointed my finger at no matter whom. The policeman kept saying, "There, kid?" and Mother kept threatening, "When I get my hands on them . . ." But looking closely, I saw that her eyes were shut, and this disturbed me. The odd part of this ride was that we actually did come across the boys—I recognized in particular the one who had insulted me by being bored with my miracle. But something about Mother's eyes being closed, as though upon her own private version of the deed, warned me and stopped me. I said nothing at all.

It was a habit of hers. She had large eyes, and she kept them closed a lot of the time, when she was playing the piano, or when she was just sitting, and under the taut lids you could see her eyeballs moving. I felt she was never of this moment or in this room. And then the upper surfaces of her forearms were covered with fine black hair; I used to struggle when she hugged me, as though I were being dragged backward in time against my will. Hugging me, she would tell me long stories of the slums in which she had lived as a girl until Daddy found her, of the nuns who gave cocoa and graham crackers to the girls every Wednesday, of the pitiful dresses she had had to wear. (She made lovely dresses for me, of taffeta and embroidered cotton, with crinoline slips often, and little aprons, of which I was very proud, partly because I thought they helped hide my stout shape.) And we laughed regularly and immoderately together whenever she told how she once spit from the third-floor landing of a great marble library staircase onto the glittering bald pate of a gentleman in the lobby, because she admired his gleam so. At the "splat" of the hit, which sound she imitated, we shrieked.

There was a strange absence of logic in Mother, or the presence of a personal anti-logic, which appealed to me when I was extremely young, but which began to disturb me even by the time I was seven. Once, I recall, she was washing the dishes with her eyes closed and broke a plate. She walked across the room to where Sandy was quietly reading, and slapped him hard, telling him he talked too much—which was certainly true.

I pondered Mother a long while, and more as I grew older. Father and Sandy trying with their arguments to sew up our daily life with the threads of persuasion; Father trying with his law practice to spin the affairs of men generally, and crime in particular, into a cocoon of rules and consequences; and Mother, with her eyes closed and a flick of her hand, destroying their webs. I have always pretended, even to myself, to be of Father's and Sandy's party, trying to trap life in the nets of my own reason and expression—especially in my early poetry, but also in talking to friends, and even in thinking alone —but I see now that I have been deeply and upsettingly committed to Mother all along. When I wrote my first poem of warning and kept searching for the rhyme, I was only pretending to be on their side. I was on her side when I set fire to the house. But I'm not proud to admit it—because whenever I try to remember Mother, I see her in the patrol car, her eyelids gripped on revenge.

On the street all the way home from the police station she kept hugging me, every few feet. She kept it up even after we got home until I began to think that without knowing it I had really been injured in some way which she wouldn't tell me about. I began to cry. I was still crying when Daddy came home and we told him. He got incensed for a while, but then relaxed into, "So they were checking on science, were they?" and finally concluded, "Boys will be boys." Mother was shocked. She wanted to alert the school authorities and the papers. Daddy kept the calmer view. "Boys!" he boomed vastly, blotting out with that loud monosyllable all questions of right and wrong, blame or tears.

"Kid stuff!" Sandy mimicked intensely, studying me.

It was about this time that I began to get a bit thinner—more boyish, I felt with immense pleasure—and began to chase in desperate tomboy style after Sandy and his friends. Most of the time they managed to elude me, or they teased me with games that demanded feats physically impossible for me. One summer day with me at the tag end, Sandy led the pack on a chase of Follow-the-Leader. Jumping from high walls, swinging from trees, climbing over barbed-wire fences. On the last of these I tore both the hem of my skirt and my calf—a ragged, bloody cut behind and below the knee. I still have that scar, too. He took me back to the house and treated the wound with cotton and iodine while I sat and writhed in a chair in the living room. There was no one else at home. I still remember how dark the living room was with the blinds drawn, and the smell of the iodine which I thought was the smell of my blood, and Sandy's blue hat which he had debonairly tossed under the piano after wiping his fingers all over it to get the blood off them. I was crying. To quiet me (I thought), he said anxiously, "Would you like me to show you what grownups do at night?"

I must have sensed that there was something wrong because I immediately began crying louder, quite deliberately. Obviously, however, he had already given his plans much thought. He replied as if I had raised an anticipated objection. Resourcefully, he began drying my eyes with my braids. "There, there. You're never too young to learn. You're a clever girl, but you lack initiative."

He was almost fourteen years old, and the power of his rhetoric by now was formidable. I made no attempt to engage in debate. I adjusted my skirt, which he had raised much too high to treat my leg (I suddenly noticed), and started putting on the sock and shoe which he had removed because they were wet with blood. "I want to go out again and play," I said.

"That's the trouble with you girls. You want to grow up to be wives and mothers without the responsibilities of training for a profession. No wonder so many of you fail. Until the day you marry, you refuse to start practicing. It's all play with you, isn't it? You've got to take your responsibilities more seriously."

The best I could manage was the childish, "You think you're so smart, don't you!" But it was I who thought it, and a lot more: radiant with his messy blond hair tufted over his ears, enviably slender, and manly, and graceful, and above all earnest and sensitive —with shadowy eyes and encyclopedic lips. "My leg still hurts," I said.

Single-mindedly, he continued, "Where do you expect to learn—" this said scornfully—"from books, from hygiene classes, from pajama-party bull sessions? There's no substitute, I tell you, for the school of hard knocks. Experience is the best teacher, and practice makes perfect."

"Let go," I complained, because by now he had his hand under my skirt, and I began to have the first clear idea of what we had been talking about. I got up.

"All right, Millie," he said gravely, "let's be realistic. How do you want to learn about this? From Mommy and Daddy?"

The thought was embarrassing. "I'm going out to play," I repeated.

"And when? Do you want to have to wait till you're my age to find out?" That really gave me pause: waiting five years seemed an unimaginable strain.

"And then do you want to have to learn from strangers?" He had obviously saved his trump for last. I thought of all the little boys of my acquaintance. "What do I have to do?" I said cautiously.

But for all his brave arguments, he had only the mistiest ideas (I realized much later). In the darkness of the living room, standing and gyrating and hopping forward across the rug, we performed together a weird and ritualistic dance, based on his strenuous imagination and the observation of dogs. This way and that he turned me, making certain pistonlike motions of his own, which frightened me and left him confused, but pleased at his daring. Finally he tied my shoelace for me and picked up his hat and we went out to play Follow-the-Leader again with his friends.

That evening while Mother changed the Band-Aid he stayed in the room listening to see if I would say a word about what had happened, and we were both flushed the whole time. Still frightened, I said nothing. After dinner, at Daddy's suggestion, Sandy delivered a fervent oration on the topic, "Firecrackers in the Hands of Children."

Gradually from that day on I began to hate Mommy and Daddy for making no attempt to interfere with us or stop us. I never allowed myself to realize that it was I who prevented them with my utter silence— How could they expect me to tell them? I thought. The only attempt I did make to tell occurred the next morning: I set fire to the house—and more, I tried words too, the very best words I knew:

> I want to tell you right away
> About a big red fire,
> That if you want the house to stay
> You've got to

but nobody understood. So I abandoned poetry, and didn't try again until my teens.

And so, from that rude beginning in the living room grew a strange and unexpected vine: a slow, childish, and extremely delicate courtship.   CHICK-
       "MIL-

            lie's

                        en," he would singsong. And "I'm not," I would reply with reasonable calm and dignity.

"Millie, facts are stronger than fiction. I refer of course," he said, using one of Father's favorite phrases, "to the facts of life. Are you interested in biology?"

I returned to Hans Christian Andersen and "The Goose That Laid the Golden Egg."

Looking over my shoulder, he asked, "Which is worth more, a million dollars or a Golden Egg?"

A riddle? "A Golden Egg," I guessed.

"Little goose," he said fondly, "which came first, the chicken or the egg?"

"The chicken," I tried.

He shook his head.

"The egg?"

He shook his head. "Facts," he said. "Millie, do you realize that you already have in your body all the hundreds of eggs you'll ever lay, maybe five hundred?" he calculated.

"I'm a girl, not a chicken, and girls don't—"

"Sure, eggs, one a month, biological fact of life."

I suspected he was making all this up, but I couldn't be sure. "You're lying."

"Am I?" He went out into the kitchen, calling back, "I'll show you." We were alone in the house and the moment he was out of the room I missed him. He came back with his hands behind his back. "If you like fairy tales, bet you like magic. I'm a sort of magician. Magic hands. Watch."

He showed me his hands. One was empty, one held a handkerchief. I determined not to take my eyes off his hands. But he was up my skirt in no time and I backed away, slapping his face, so that I took my eyes off his hands, so that I missed the trick. "You keep your—"

"No sense of humor. Don't you like tricks? Go on. Look in your pants."

I had already felt the egg in there, cold from the refrigerator, and I looked in, a trifle hysterical. Sandy looked, too. There it was, right inside my underwear. I laughed, panicked. Sandy laughed, too, in his earnest way. He reached inside my pants. Gingerly, he removed the egg—he was a gentleman—without touching me.

"Now why did I do that?" he asked me. "Guess."

I had no idea but I was scared. "Why?"

"Because you're a chicken," he said.

I put my hands inside my pants to warm me up. "Do girls lay eggs? Honestly?" The one he held in his hands had rusty brown stains at one end, marbled blood.

"Honestly. When they grow up."

I snatched it. And before his shocked eyes I let it drop to the wooden floor where it smashed. The yolk ran, a spurt of golden love and white fear. I sat down on the floor, hunched over it, frightened of Sandy, of the egg, of what we'd done. I watched the yolk spreading. And then, adding to my fright, Father came in the door.

He said, "What have you two kids been up to?" I tightened my legs. I sat up straight. I thought salvation had come.

"Monkey business," Sandy replied with anthropoid eyes, wiping up the egg with his handkerchief. Salvation was unmentionable.

At the end of the day's business Father was often disheartened, uninterested in our answers to his questions. He loosened his collar and tie and the phlegm in his throat. "How's business?" Sandy queried.

"Law's a profession," Father responded irritably, "it isn't business. Do you know where I'd be today if I'd gone into business?—believe you me, I'd be right up there in seventh heaven. This fellow I was moonlighting for once asked me did I want to come in with him, this nobody. This shyster. He'd just got his hands on a General Motors franchise. But no, not me, I was fresh out of law school, I wanted to practice law, I told him, hell no. Today he's got that dealership on the Parkway, do you know how much he's worth?" The sum was unmentionable.

"A million bucks?" Sandy guessed.

A golden egg, I thought.

Father sighed. "If I'd gone into business, I'd be sitting pretty today."

I'd go into business, I decided. I remember that, I remember hoping for it and wishing for it, I longed to be sitting pretty, it was all I wanted.

Sandy, sensing my resistance, became hesitant in his attempts, almost meditative, as though considering my age and our relationship. ("Wouldn't it be easy for me, Millie," he said, "to abuse the trust of my little sister? We have to keep this on the highest plane.") Though I found his interest in me repulsive, his words distracted me. Did they not ring out with the authority I associated with Daddy at the dinner table? The serpentine logic, the fluent nonsense confused me. Once when I protested his unbuttoning the back of my dress, he said bewilderingly, "Silence is the golden rule, remember? Do unto others. Silently." It seemed to me that I did remember something like that. Still I screamed—at half-volume—until he desisted, commenting, "The exception proves the rule." It was all over my head.

But little by little as I realized the power I had over him, my ancient, poignant desire to have his sinuous mind and thin freckled body for my own, and thus to triumph over him, seemed within reach. Though I was frightened, he was offering them to me, always tactful and considerate—"your respect, Millie, has to come first"—

until I began both to want him and to love him as the World's Treasure. Yet so slow were we that we did not actually consummate our feelings for two years, until I was eleven, and even then it was a most gentle consummation, and certainly not a real penetration, partly because Sandy could never quite figure out how to manage, and partly because of my physical abnormality—of which more later.

Generally we waited until we were alone at home in the evening, which happened occasionally, and then I would shower or bathe and Sandy would wash me. Or sometimes even when our parents were home I would go into his room and sit next to him while he studied his Latin or mathematics. You may doubt me when I say that he really studied, but he had great powers of concentration and won all sorts of school prizes in both Latin and mathematics, possibly because I encouraged his love for them. I came to marvel at his capacity for simultaneous interest, the daring heights to which his intellectual and sexual excitement could hurl itself at both extremes, brain and groin (Quem ad finem sese effrenata iactabit audacia?). When in my later poetry or the few essays I've had occasion to write, I speak of "completing the man" or of

slipping on the easy sweet of the banana split

I think back to those evenings with Sandy. Searching in his clothes with love, I felt that I helped to create, at least in its more godly aspect, his sexual tool. Even today, I don't think I was really wrong about that. Some of the bewildering enigmas about how things get created—in the universe of physics, in human prehistory, in art— later seemed clearer to me: the tense forces released in the approach and separation of opposites; the paralyzed shimmering when they are put unstably together. But for the reader who may remain shocked, despite all philosophical reflection, by the story of my brother and me, I'll add—for your most serious consideration—that it was precisely these years of incest which in the long run kept me from the terrible perversions of homosexuality.

During this period, my face thinned, my features became clear and delicate, my body lengthened. Unreasonably, I suspected that I owed all of these changes to Sandy, as though by his attentions he had given me a new physical being. My gratitude was inwardly slavish. I thought of very little else except him. I was utterly uninterested in school, other girls, boys. Only the things Sandy said to

me seemed important, though I must admit that that was partly because they seemed mysterious. Once he rattled off: "Politics makes
strange bedfellows too. And there's something comforting in that
because we need the illusion of democracy, even if it's only a question
of whether we're going to be ruled by the same few or a changing
few." He was tucking me in for the night at the time. I didn't sleep
for hours, puzzling over what he meant.

Another evening, while he was working away at his biology
assignment, I remember that he commented, "We're just the beginning, you and I, the single cell. We're the binary fission of ourselves,
out of which will later come more highly developed forms of life
and reproduction."

I never forgave him for going away to college. I was desolate.
But the night before he left he sneaked into my room. My mouth
glowed on his and flames spread down through my body. For the
first time we spent the entire night cushioned together, like two
Egyptian brother-sister princelings in a temple over the Nile, watching the river of clouds through my window—tearless and serious
and dignified at parting, as befits royalty. "Since I'm going away,"
Sandy mused out loud in his endless peroration, "let's make it an
entering wedge. Paradise is over. It has to stop sometime—"

"Does it? There'll be summers."

"No. It has to stop. Millie, you're going to become a woman—"

"Will I?" I said wistfully. I was almost thirteen.

"Of course. We'll be man and woman, grown and separate. I
suppose we'll be embarrassed when we look back, but let's not have
regrets. After all, we made the choice. Now we've got to make
other choices—"

"Create other choices," I corrected him ironically—the first time
it had ever entered my head to correct him, or to be ironical. I was
awed at myself. There *were* no other choices. But I would invent
them.

Desperately, I began writing verse again—filled a whole year's
diary with girlish love poems, pleading with him for his affection.
Impatiently I kept waiting for his first summer vacation. But he was
as good as his word and when he did come back, he remained irre-
proachable, unapproachable. After he left again for the second year,
I succumbed to endless nighttime imaginings of his presence in my
bed.

With a good deal less interest I kept waiting to become a woman,
as a kind of consolation, never forgetting that Sandy had promised

it to me. I was already rather pretty, blonde and graceful, and as thin as a young girl should be. But I was worried because by that time I should also have been adolescent. I began to think that nature was spitefully withholding my maturity from me on account of my precocious adventures with my brother. I was already fourteen and terribly conscious whenever I undressed with the other girls during swimming periods at school that I was childishly hairless and flat-chested. It seemed to me that for purely physical and therefore unfair reasons the other girls were automatically relegating me to the position of social failure; I resented it.

When Sandy came home the second summer, I consulted him, hoping also to tempt him by making him touch me where I was flat. Mocking me goodnaturedly, he said, "Let's create a choice for you, Millie." So he carved a pair of sponges into the proper shape, and when school came round again in the fall, on his advice I dropped swimming classes and began wearing my womanhood inside a bras-siere. The result was immediate and it shocked me: I had more in-vitations than I could accept. Since except for Sandy, I wanted to keep the boys at a distance but at the same time wanted the appear-ance of social success, the solution was painless. Of course whenever I was taken to the movies I was dreadfully afraid of detection all the time and went so far as to dip the points of the sponges into a bit of mucilage, which then soaked up and hardened inside the sponge like nipples. Although the imitation was hardly accurate, the boys, in their ignorance, accepted it gladly, and in the darkness they pressed and compressed my sponges until they exhausted themselves, while I enjoyed the evening in perfect freedom, sensationless. When a hand strayed to my leg, an occasional slap on the wrist was all that was needed; they returned happily to what I was willing to give. In that way for some time I enjoyed my triumph—as word spread among the boys at school—without yielding one breath of my devotion to Sandy.

In fact, I was well over sixteen before my breasts began to come up naturally—small and soft and perfect, just as they should have been, I supposed—but at the same time a fine blonde down began to come out on my face. At first it was only on the upper lip, then later on the cheeks and chin, but I began to have visions of becoming the bearded lady of the circus as my earliest fears of being a freak were revived. I wanted to shave off the down; but Mother said that that would only encourage it, and sent me to a doctor. The doctor said it might pass of itself, but if it didn't, he could take the hairs out electrically. At first I refused to consider that. But when my voice began to get distinctly hoarse and a bit foggy, so that I began to be noticed with laughter at school and even Daddy made fun of me sometimes, booming out at me with that exploding voice of his, I went into virtual seclusion for a time, trying to decide. Mortified, I pleaded the onset of painful menstruation—which was utterly untrue. But with a little modest artifice here, too, I even convinced Mother.

I stayed in my bedroom for almost seven days, meditating and deciphering. It seemed to me clear that nature was at last completing its vendetta against incest, and that I had been selected as the object of a monstrous sexual revenge. The more I thought, the more certain it seemed. But I determined to consult a specialist.

Pleading continued illness, I persuaded Mother to make an appointment with a gynecologist. In order to go alone, I called the doctor secretly, changed the time of the appointment from afternoon to morning. When Mother was out, I dressed, trying to make myself look as mature and feminine as possible. I chose my most daring dress, I put on silk stockings and heels, I pinned up my hair, and I wore a little hat of Mother's with a blue dotted veil.

At the doctor's I was earnest and decorous, confident of the effect of my clothes. At first, the doctor himself struck me as a dapper salesman, too smooth to trust; later, during the examination, he struck me as a brute. Without the slightest consideration for the embarrassed feelings of a sixteen-year-old girl in her first pelvic examination, he treated me as he would have treated any other patient. But when I was ready, reclining on the table with my knees wide, I realized that there could be no mistake, and the thought comforted me with the promise of finality. The doctor was saying, "Nothing to worry about if a girl matures late . . . yes, there is some underdevelopment here . . . arrested uterus . . ."

He sat down suddenly and put his hand to his heart.

"Am I all right, doctor?" I said, afraid to move. "Or am I a boy?" It was more than a question—it was a chorus of conviction.

"Don't move, miss," he said, short of breath, as if he thought I were going to fade like a miracle. And in a moment he was back to the examination, palpating my abdomen.

Doctors all over the country soon became familiar with the details of my case, since several studies of my anatomy subsequently appeared in the *Journal* of the American Medical Association as well as other medical publications in Britain and America. Briefly, the medical picture was this: not only did I have the female organs with which I had been born, still in an infantile condition; I also had, re-tracted and sealed in vaginal tissue, the organs of the male sex, by now fully adolescent and, so to speak, trapped. As the doctor himself put it, moments after he had finished examining me, "You're not a boy, miss," and he was sweating when he said it. "You're also a boy."

For weeks, specialists examined my "miracle." I was, they told me, a true hermaphrodite, a "genetic accident," not only known to the annals of modern science, but known from the testimonies of archaeology and ethnology, ancient art and literature, to have appeared now and again throughout history and all over the world. But today, they said, it was another matter. In our society hermaphroditism was a condition that could be treated and corrected. The two possibilities were clear. Would I like to have my newfound male organs cut away surgically, and my female organs brought to full maturity with hor-mones? Or conversely: would I like to have my manly parts released to their normal position, and my uterus and ovaries cut away? "It's up to you, Millie." Me? "You or your parents," they said. "Take your choice—male or female."

Although the full complexities of choice were not clear to me for weeks, still, even in those first ten minutes after I learned the truth, I realized that I was a lot less confused than the doctor; all my experience had made it possible for me to grasp without vertigo the news of my sexual fusion. I had the uncanny impression that I had actually transformed myself—into a freak, if you will—by an alchemy of illicit desire. I was a changeling. I had substituted myself for my brother. And now, hopelessly triumphant, I was to be deprived of Sandy forever. Getting dressed again in the doctor's office, fixing the garters to my silk stockings and slipping my heels back on, I began to search for a way back.

That same night, I discussed the doctor's visit with my shaken parents for five difficult hours. Daddy's voice seemed to lose its spring; his steeltrap mind opened limply. "Millie darling," he whis-pered, "you won't let them . . . alter you . . . would you?" I vowed in a horrified baritone that I wouldn't let them take my womb. Fiercely, Mother kept sobbing, "We'll sue the doctor." They phoned. They hung up. Unanimously and desperately they pleaded with me to remain their daughter. But I will say this to their credit: they left the choice to me.

I said goodnight—for the first time without kissing them—and went to bed. I sat on the edge. I had equaled Sandy, and in doing so, lost him. But it wasn't irreversible. I slipped off my heels—unhooked my garters—pulled down one stocking—and instead of going to sleep, took up a pencil. The words, the lines, seemed to force themselves lovingly on me, as if I had to hold my twin self visibly at arm's length on paper to decide. It was the work of a sixteen-year-old girlboy, addressed to her lost-and-found brother.

> I turned with you as you withdrew
> Because I thought the sun was proud.
> Whose orbit brought me to this birth?
> O still my moon revolves for you,
>
> Not earth, and splits itself in two.
> All settled now, my dust has vowed
> To bring your squeaky man on earth.
> Yours the heat, the flame, the mirth.
>
> Coldly I unwind a shroud.

It was almost light when I woke up. I read the lines over several times, and saw what I had decided. I had chosen to become a poet. With the blessings of surgery I could parade my hard-won maleness. But for the sake of poetry I would keep my double sex physically intact. A public man with a private womb. My transmutation, my twinning—I would not give up one iota.

How I
Changed
My Mind

Every man knows by experience that there
are parts that often move, stand up, and
lie down, without his leave. Now these
passions which touch only the rind of
us cannot be called ours. To make them ours,
the man as a whole must be involved.

—MONTAIGNE

The destiny that followed—the happily obsessed career of bodily passion and spiritual realization I embraced with a will—in a single volume? Hardly. No . . . no matter how thick this book, if I can cram half my lifetime into its pages I'll be satisfied, believe me.

Sentimentally, I've kept a bulging manila envelope full of pictures from that far-off time. Candid-camera shots of me. Smirking on the porch. Gobbling at Thanksgiving dinner. Trying out my new boy's bike. Every time I pull the rubberband off the envelope I experience an unpleasant twinge in my groin. There I stand with a skirt on—in several photos you can see the beginnings of my girlshape under my blouse. In others taken only months later I'm wearing pants and a tie, looking skinny and afraid. There's one eloquent photograph: it's a group picture and it tells the story (Plate II). We're all standing there. Mother's fists and eyes are grimly clenched. Father's tongue is proudly flexing his mustache. And my brother Sandy's fingers are gingerly clasping my shoulder. I'm the blond sixteen-year-old lad up front, the one with the bright embarrassed teeth.

Anatomy is destiny, we hear from Freud by way of Napoleon. To comprehend the course of my destiny, you really ought to see the before-and-after shots of my operation. The medical close-ups of my naked saddle—these are fascinating. Caught during and after surgery, every detail of my genitals shows with clarity in this expert series of stills depicting my transition from girlhood to manhood. It's almost too graphic for words: below my mons veneris emerges first the glans of my penis, then gradually the shaft; then in the place of my girl-lips appear (photographed in four stages of emergence) my testicles. The successful procedure adopted by the surgeon was at once featured in medical journals here and abroad (Plates III–VIII). One way or another I have always caused a stir. Those medical plates were my first published work, and not, as is generally supposed, the astonishing group of tongue-twisters that appeared in *Poetry*. I may add that although it was hard for my folks to understand what had happened, and although over the years it's been difficult for everyone, my readers and enemies alike, that's only because no one takes poetry seriously.

Yet beforehand, I must admit, I'd had my doubts too. "Are you kidding?" I giggled once. "Life is real! Life is earnest—"

"Miss—" the surgeon scrutinized my face—"this is not a matter for jokes or a time for poetry." He made an indelicate pun about Longfellow, which I won't bother to repeat. "You will be able to function well and normally. Still, what you don't or won't understand is that even after I've completed your first operation, you'll still have the gonads of both sexes—ovaries and testes—unless I operate *further*. Now I've explained this twice to your father and mother—I will not take responsibility for the case otherwise—I refuse to help you out of your remarkable situation until I have obtained your consent to a second operation, miss. And to avoid the possibility of doubts . . . ambiguities . . ."—he leaned forward and placed a stubby fingertip on the belly of the slacks I was wearing—"and shadows, I want to remove your ovaries."

Medical science is clearheaded. He tapped. He showed me firmly where he wanted to go in. He frightened me . . . of course he did . . . but I didn't lose my wits. I could be firm too, and just as clearheaded. What did he expect me to do? To succumb to the firmly tapping index finger of science and certainties? I didn't want to be a Longfellow. Essential and equivocal tension was what I wanted, the impossible tug-o'-war, the powerful silent accumulation of negative and positive in body and mind that causes the lightning tongue to speak out loud in illuminations.

I was sixteen and stubborn about my body. And passionately patient. I explained to the blunt-fingered surgeon, to the rest of the medical world, and to my baffled parents how enormously grateful, how glad, I'd be to become male—physically, mentally, emotionally —the works—a banana split sundae with nuts, whipped cream, and cherries. There, you see? I cried out, I didn't want to have my ovaries and womb touched, cut out—good God! they were *my body*— couldn't they understand that?—I wanted them left where they were, only sealed off, made impossible for legal purposes (Father's idea) and impassable for other purposes (Mother's). Thoroughly unusable, sure, but *there*, not taken away. To my folks I even explained why. "For black and white, for silver and gold, for sun and moon."

Father had a good mind, but he was no help at all. He flushed, controlling his anger and confusion. "There's not going to be any grey in this house, no girlish boys in *my* family, you get that straight right now, once for all. For sixteen years we thought you were a girl. Okay. Anyone can make a mistake. Then out of the blue this lousy gynecologist discovers you're a genetic marvel. Well, grin and bear it—hermaphrodite—who even knew how to spell it. And now you turn around and tell us you'd rather be a boy—okay. It's your choice. So far, so good. But take your choice and abide by it: black or white. Even biological accidents have to be straightened out, Millie . . . an open-and-shut case." And suddenly without warning he broke down, "I can't stand it!" and he roared, "Either/or! You hear me? You can't be both!"

"I am both."

"Then cut it out, you hear! You just cut this funny business out!"

For the first time, the only time, he hit me—a swinging blow to the side of my head. I didn't believe the pain or where it had come from. My head heated up and I stared. The tears came.

Mother intervened, clasping me to her breast.

To Father she said, "You moron." To me she said for solace, "Pay no attention to him and his noise. No matter what you decide, you'll always be my girl."

I unzipped my way out of her arms.

I was staggered. She hadn't even grasped my decision yet. Or else she had grasped it fully, more deeply than anyone else.

She drew me aside into the kitchen and whispered, "You're a little double-crosser, darling, but don't you double-cross me. Wise up, Millie, this is your chance. Who'd marry you now? You'll never be able to get married. But you can fox them good."

I tried to explain again, "On the outside, Mom—"

She cut me short. "Look at me." She shook her head sadly. "In my little finger I had more brains than you'll ever have, and more talent than your father, and what happened to me? S-E-X—that's what. Do you think I wanted a house and a husband and kids? Get smart, and you'll be able to dodge the whole marriage-and-kids business."

Father shouted at us from the living room, "The shilly-shallying is over! It's elementary logic! Either! Or!"

"Neither," Mother winked.

"Both," I argued.

"Same thing!" she insisted. She closed her dark-lidded eyes over my argument.

Families never understand. That didn't matter in the long run, though somewhere in the bottom story of my mind where the old floor is never mopped and nothing makes neat sense I guess I've never managed to stop thinking of myself as a double-crosser.

Even my gynecologist was kinder. "Millie dear, no one's going to force you against your will, but why don't you give in? Don't you see that this misunderstanding, this extraordinary stubbornness of yours, is pure fright—hysteria in every sense of the word? It's true that you were born hermaphroditic. That's not your fault. And it's true that if you absolutely insist, we can leave your womb intact.

But it's going to atrophy anyway. After the second operation, your entire female system is going to waste away even if we don't touch it. Wither. Poof! Gone anyhow. You're going to be a boy, Millie."

In fact, as I soon came to realize, I held the trumps. The one trump. It was in me. None of the doctors who were brought into the case could tolerate the thought of simply leaving me as I was. Their minds boggled at it—letting me remain a girl, sexually infantile? —when right there, buried behind a tiny wall of tissue and growing every day, I had an adult male phallus?

"Easier than a nose job," the surgeon assured me, cheering me on while the nurses who had just prepped me wheeled me through the corridors onto the elevator. In the operating room I had a few moments of paralyzing doubt and terror: bending over me, the surgeon winked.

"A stiff upper lip, kid," he said next morning, winking past on his hospital rounds. "I'll see you again in a couple of months for the rest of the work."

For a time I was dizzy, sick from the aftereffects of anaesthesia and feverish with a sense of anticipation. It must have been the second day when Father came to visit and cried, putting his head on the foot of my bed. The third or fourth day, as soon as the ache in my groin was bearable, I stood up, without the nurse's permission, staggered gingerly into the bathroom, and locked myself in. Half a week after the operation, the bandages had been partially loosened: cautiously, I took them aside completely and—with my heart doing little scared squirrel jumps between my two tiny fluttery breasts—I examined myself.

There! God Almighty! There it hung! My swinger! Frankly, I'll admit to you I'd expected something, well, heavier, wealthier, more muscular, more dramatic. (I'd always seen Sandy's grand organ erected.) This tool of mine looked a trifle on the unambitious side. Still, even a hungry, skinny tool was a grand tool, I decided optimistically. And right there underneath . . . yes, that funny little fleshy sac of testicles. Only then did I come to appreciate the surgical skill that had made my miracle a reality: when my goldenbrown hair grew in again, my curls would conceal the stitches; underneath, my familiar cleft was thoroughly blocked and hidden by the folds of the brave new sac. Only a scar was visible there. I satisfied myself that I was unenterable and undetectable unless you were a doctor who knew in advance the mystery of my locked compartment.

You know what I did next? I swung. I swung myself for the

pure innocent unexampled pleasure of seeing my own tiny majesty swing. Then I commanded him to RISE! He wouldn't of course. Well, no matter. When I got back into bed I was giggling with happiness.

All in all, I made a goodlooking boy. A scrawny blue-eyed blond kid. My hands and feet were kind of small for a boy and I was medium height . . . how peculiar that felt . . . for years I'd thought of myself as a tall girl! At home, under hormone treatment, in a matter of only a few weeks my little breasts (which Mother and I called my "boobles," private talk somewhere between boobies and baubles) dwindled like two swollen bruises and soon receded altogether into my chest. I was deeply impressed by the mysteries of chemistry. Scissors, shears, knives—cutting my hair, clipping my nails, learning to play mumbletypeg, snipping loose threads from my underwear, which had to be perfect. I felt peculiar, pulling myself into boys' underwear.

I was under doctors' orders not to stimulate myself. Don't fret, they explained. Several months would have to elapse before the supporting tissues where the internal sutures had been placed would be fully healed, strong enough and secure enough to withstand certain natural strains. If erection occurred while I was asleep (it never did) or occurred by itself somehow (it simply wouldn't), I was not to worry. But under no circumstances was I to masturbate. Well, naturally I got impatient, naturally I worried, inevitably I fretted. Why no stirrings down below? Why no life, no quickening? Was it because I was too small? *Was* I too small? It wasn't that I wanted to masturbate. No—but I wanted to grow. I pinched and I pushed and I pulled and *once*, once I got my limp member, my absurdly pink delicate resisting flesh, out to a maximum extension of two inches. I could claim no special knowledge of the field, but my two flaccid inches struck me as undersized. Was I wrong? Was I greedy?

One afternoon I took the *World Almanac* boldly down from the shelf in Father's study. I sat manfully at his desk. Having copied what I needed, I made for my guidance a precise chart on heavy white cardboard to hang on the wall over my bed. I set myself a series of interim objectives to shoot for, exactly the way an enterprising company projects its estimates for growth and expansion. I suppose you imagine I was unrealistic. Not at all. I was humble, yet I faced the future with willpower and determination. It was obvious to me that a former teenage girl had a social obligation to be reasonable even about her erections. Six inches, I'd heard from Sandy, was standard: "One in the hand equals two to the foot." With this in mind, I established a table of guidelines and goals.

$$.17 \text{ feet} = 2 \text{ inches}$$
$$.083 \text{ yards} = 3 \text{ inches}$$
$$.00006 \text{ miles} = 4 \text{ inches}$$
$$.006315 \text{ chains} = 5 \text{ inches}$$
$$1,500,000,000,000 \text{ milliangstroms} = 6 \text{ inches}$$

Not many people are familiar with milliangstroms. But what vast pleasure it gave me to know that my two inches of sex already equaled five hundred billion of them. Reassured, I calculated, I made long-range plans. And the constant nagging sense of penis-inferiority that resulted has been of immeasurable aid in all my ambitions.

I was reasonably confident. I hid in the garage. To measure my progress accurately, I took my notebook with me and a yardstick. And I can't tell you how tragic I felt when, no matter how I tried, I didn't, I couldn't, it wouldn't. The garage was a good place, dim, quiet, and exciting. Father's car was gone, but the air still had the stimulating smell of gasoline, oil, rust. There were tools, sparkplugs, a vise. How? In God's name, how? I rubbed, I massaged, I jumped . . . how did one make it rise? . . . surely by some physical means. Or maybe by thought? Do you believe in making physical things rise by thought? I didn't, but I knew I had to be open-minded in a field where a girl's experience was irrelevant. All right—levitation, then. I tried thinking about women. I tried movie actresses, I confess I even tried my mother, I tried the bodies of the girls down the block. No good, no use, no luck. Well, after all, I knew logically that after sixteen years of being a girl I'd stand a greater chance of success if I thought of boys, or if I remembered precisely how it had been in bed with my brother Sandy kissing and holding me, but I absolutely *would* not, good Lord! I'd resolved to become a boy, a normal boy. Not even for the purpose of masturbation could I entertain for one minute the idea of homosexual incest.

Funereally, head hanging, everything hanging, I returned to my bedroom. Some people might have been permanently flattened by a disaster like this. Not me. I've always had that saving streak, that old American stick-to-itiveness.

I cut up another sheet of heavy cardboard. I made six big white squares, and on those squares I printed in darkest India ink the indelible letters of my lost name, my ineradicable name—

MILLIE

—one letter to a square. I spaced those six squares along the wall, tacking them in a row over my bed.

Grit and determination, especially self-determination, it's to those personal qualities more than anything else (love excepted) that I owe my success in art, business, archaeology, and the rest of it: I have been often, and sometimes easily, crushed in life . . . but never permanently . . . not even when I was indicted for treason by the United States government. It was Booker T. Washington, I think, who said wisely that you should judge a man, not by the heights to which he has risen, but by the depths from which he has come.

Out into the kitchen I went and from the top of the refrigerator I took down the wishbone—drying there since the Sunday before my operation. And I broke it with Mother. I used Sandy's trick, the upper thumb. So I won. Mother muttered, "I suppose you think you're going to get out of washing the dishes."

Ignoring her, I locked my bedroom door, hid the larger jagged piece of the wishbone under my pillow, and stood in front of my mystic sign, hands clasped over my newfound jagged sexual organ. I shut my eyes and wished, wished harder, harder. With my right hand I reached for the wall while, according to plan, with my left hand I rubbed my organ zealously—it wouldn't grow or rise, I knew, but it tingled—I rubbed until I felt the wall in front of me vibrating with my own impassioned energy and essence. I concentrated all my force. Then I flicked and spun my first letter. I'd taken care to tack it loosely, the better to spin it. I opened my eyes. Round and round my letter spun. I watched—sure of it—

WILLIE

—there I was!

Seven out of ten times I came up "W." Rubbing while spinning did certainly seem to help.

After that I called myself Willie. Sometimes Billy. But when Mother came into my room and took one look at my wall, she called me Willy-Nilly.

. . .

Every day I traveled by trolleycar across the city to a new school—
it was a sensible arrangement, Father's idea. He was all for being
positive and thoroughgoing about change. And unlike Mother, he
accepted me immediately in his positivistic fashion. My sensitive
nostalgia, my holding on to a few of my old inner organs, remained
a mystery to him; still, I'd chosen to become a boy, I'd jumped the
fence. He jumped with me and began thumping me on the back
the way he used to thump Sandy. "Let 'em know who you are," he'd
say every morning as I left for school. But I was just as glad that
nobody knew me and nobody cared (only the principal had been
informed). To the teachers, to the other pupils, I was just another
nuisance—a boy who'd somehow got transferred in the middle of the
term—a new, pale, scared kid in the lower senior class.

I was scared because from the start I was physically intimidated.
The involuted psychological warfare by which girls maintain their
power circles may be crueler than the direct approach of boys, but
the latter scared me half out of my wits. The first afternoon as I was
leaving school, a lanky boy with eyes that were watering under his
glasses took me aside and told me confidentially in my ear, "Whitey's
boss here." As he said it, he shoved me sideways as hard as he could
so that I hit the wall and fell. As I fell, he jammed his elbow into my
ribs. I had a raspberry on my shoulder and a black-and-blue mark
on my ribs for the next week. I was so paralyzed with fright I didn't
even cry.

"I'm leaving school," I wailed to Father when he came home that
evening. "I can't stand it." I told him what had happened.

"Good," he said. "A little fast, but it's the lesson you've got to
learn."

Furious with him, I started to walk out of the room—but he held
on to my arm. "You've got to stand up to them."

Mother screeched, "Fight back? My Billie? I don't want her
fighting with boys."

I gave her a dirty look for the pronoun, but I felt the same way
myself. "I'm not fighting with anyone."

"You don't have to fight if you know how to stand up to them."

"All I want is to be treated with a little consideration."

"Then you should have stayed a girl."

"Boys are animals," I shouted. "I'm not, and I'm not going to
become one."

But Father had already begun looking up jujitsu in the classified
telephone directory.

At first the shock of physical combat with a man—the instructor, a balding Japanese perfectionist named Haidu—actually made me cry. I wept, but instead of pausing to console me, he bounded into the air, coming at me with both feet forward: I was so shocked I defended myself. "No that way. You this way," he said, holding me upright with his feet, then sitting up like a bolt and seesawing me across his forearm. When I made a mistake, he hissed.

For over a month, Haidu's jack-in-the-box tactics, the smell and clumsiness of his pupils, the constant touch of the sweating half-naked struggling bodies of the other boys in the class, revolted and horrified me. But I was mesmerized by a motive, an idea, that would never have occurred to Father. Physical prowess—confidence in my body—would, I thought, soon tighten the psychic springs—the springs that caused a member to grow taut and potent.

I wanted to learn. I used to watch with awe at the very beginning of every class for the first sight of Haidu coming through the door like a tubby Oriental Superman, his kimono billowing behind him and his tights too tight. He looked funny but in motion his body was ferocious. It frightened me until I discovered that no matter how violent or stunning his gymnastics, his face preserved a kindly, doll-gentle, distant look. So I tried to concentrate on his face, to see nothing but that gentle look of his even when he was springing at me, and this maneuver actually helped me. Slowly, and with practice, my timing became perfect. I began to get at least the elementary exercises and responses down pat—provided I was working out with Haidu himself. The moment he paired me with one of the sweaty boys in the class, I fumbled badly.

One evening Haidu detained me after class. "Too much restraint," he said, hissing. I had no idea what he meant, but I felt miserable. "Woman is restraint," he continued. "Man is energy." Observing the bright, babylike look in his eyes, I had the tearful impulse to confide in him. But I restrained the impulse and stood there hesitating for words. He waited for me to speak. When I said nothing, he repeated, "Too much restraint," and walked out of the room.

For weeks thereafter I worked like a demon. I would become Energy Incarnate. It went so far that Haidu suddenly had to hiss at me, with a wink, "More restraint, Hishi." Had he discovered something? He began using the new nickname, always with a wink, and taking special care with my progress. It was as if he had adopted me as his protégé. I complained to him that I was too light; he showed me how to use a stronger or heavier opponent's power as though it were my own, by pivoting against it to change its direction and adding its new direction to my own. "Take care, Hishi," he said, winking, "and you will become perfect instrument. You have secret already in own body. What is art of judo? It is balance point of restraint and energy. Shift balance suddenly, and you have attacked. Remove restraint, and attacker's energy will lose force."

Once, when I ended someone's knife charge too abruptly by knocking the rubber knife out of his hand instead of seizing his wrist, Haidu reproved me, shrilling, "Do not try to win, Hishi. Judo must be dance, not struggle, even when attacker thinks it is struggle. There is no opponent, only partner. Follow partner, and you will have the victory without the trying."

But on this score I was a bad pupil. I kept trying. I *wanted* to win. When I realized that a good intuitive sense of timing (which I had) was more important than strength, I learned to throw boys twice my weight, and the power to pinion a boy or to make him wheel over my arm or around me as a matador controls the bull had a tonic effect. I began to enjoy dominating boys, and—less frequently—being dominated. Partly this was because I never quite got over the feeling that I was a kind of star girl-athlete, the kind which I personally have always detested. I couldn't help feeling that I was only play-acting the part of a boy, that under my trousers or gym shorts my doggy genitals were only sewed onto my crotch. To overcome my uneasiness, I used to force myself to parade naked in the locker room. This was almost unbearably difficult for me.

Father, of course, was delighted with my progress. "Aren't you glad you began jujitsu?" he beamed, strutting up and down the living room.

"Golly, I sure am!"

His face changed sternly. "You've still got a lot to learn," he said, "a hell of a lot more. How to swear, for instance, and how to walk like a boy, and . . ."

"And what?" I thought I might ask him for advice about self-stimulation. But there was no telling how he'd take it. I hesitated.

"Forget it . . . start with swearing," he said.

"Teach me."

The top of his forehead turned a dark red. "A boy doesn't ask his old man to teach him to swear. What you do is keep your ears wide open, you'll pick it up."

"Okay." I couldn't see why he was so grudging about it. But anything with words I could probably manage to learn by myself.

"What else?" I asked. He hesitated, thinking, which made his mustache tremble. I wondered if I should grow a mustache.

"It's not a question of *what else*, Billy—there isn't any next. It's all in your mental attitude. Being a man comes from inside you."

"Right." I made a mental note. "But you could try to be more helpful, Father. After all, I'm a late bloomer."

"Stop calling me Father," his mustache twitched again. Was he going to laugh or cry? "Call me Pop."

"Okay, but I could use a few hints. What else?"

"Pop," he insisted.

"What *else, please!*" How could he expect me to call him Pop? Pop?

"Lots of things. Lots, kid. Most important, you got to learn . . ." He paused. He twitched.

I guessed. Squeezing my knees together hard, I forced it out. I said it, I was so proud of myself. "To jerk off, Pop?"

His perpetually open mouth slowly glided to a stern and appraising slit. "No. That's not on the docket and don't you be wise with me. First things first. Listen, Billy . . ." it was very hard for him, "Billy, have you ever felt—maybe you already know what I mean—a certain attraction for the girls?"

It was hard for both of us.

I blushed and balked.

He twitched and twisted. "Attraction comes first."

I studied attraction.

At school I sat in class studying girls. (My grades were lower than usual that year, except for French.) I hadn't the slightest idea how to begin. I suppose attraction does come first, but most boys begin very early with their mothers. In my case, considering how undependable she was, that was out of the question. I even felt panicky about the few girls in my neighborhood who'd once been vague girlfriends of mine. But now, what with zipping up my trousers every morning, eating hormones with my cereal, and trekking to the big school where there were hundreds of new junior and senior girls around me, I figured I had a chance. I sat through history, math, English, study hall, lunch, biology, French, physics, picking different girls to stare at, trying out different positions in my seat, waiting for it to happen. Even an itch inside when I examined a girl's hemline would have felt like progress. But how? But when? The gynecologist and the clinical psychologist kept on claiming that there was nothing wrong with me organically; the problem, they said, was mental.

Naturally, I asked the doctors questions. By now, they said, tumescence should be a distinct possibility. Had I had any wet dreams as yet? Had I experienced any waking urges? There was no hurry, they said. But there was. I asked every doctor I saw (and on routine check-up visits to the hospital I saw plenty) the most elementary questions. What was desire? What caused erection? And I got plenty of answers, elementary and complex: instinct, procreation, love, and sphincters. None of the answers helped a bit. The trouble down below was up above: there was a roadblock in my head. I tried to unblock.

"Ssss!" There was a stocky boy named Dave who used to sit in front of me in history. Practically every day halfway through the class, I began to notice, he'd shift around in his seat, he'd nudge his friend—"Ssss!"—and motion slyly with his eyes only—"Ssss!"—to the back of the room. She wasn't especially goodlooking. But whenever this Dave would signal, she'd be sitting there with her skirt up and her knees apart. It was the repetition that upset me. That young men of my own age should remain interested, every day and day after day, in the insides of a girl's thighs struck me as offensive and highly immature.

Still and all, transformation was possible, no one knew that better than I. To move beyond the reach of sexual doubts, I saw that I might have to become not only daring and energetic, but perhaps (to be absolutely safe) coarse. I determined to bend my whole will to the effort.

No one who has been only a boy can appreciate the enormous concentration with which I went about this monkey-imitation—how much it meant to me—and how nearly perfectly I succeeded. *Not* perfectly, no, but it was a fine job on the surface. I hung around mainly on the school steps and in the candy store a block away. Every day I practiced smoking a cigarette while I played the pinball machine, I read the comics, and I listened. I memorized every slang phrase and item of dirt I heard. I wrote everything down afterward, right away, and I made sure by practice that I could use every bit. I studied. The lingo, the gift of slow gab, the art of keeping a cigarette stuck to one lip, the sullenness, the blinking—a bit soft in the voice and skin, a trifle "boyish"—but it was hard to tell me from the real thing. Tough?—I looked as if I *might* be, there on the outside. A sort of pallid-complexioned, too goodlooking, maybe even slightly feminine-looking punk was the effect I was aiming at. It was all I dared hope for as yet—I hardly dared to believe that I was getting coarse on the inside. Yet sometimes it did seem to me that I scared some of my teachers when I entered a room just the right number of seconds late, slinked into a corner seat, and practiced staring at the radiator for forty minutes. But I couldn't be sure—maybe they were only worried about me.

After school, standing in the center safety strip of the big boulevard in our neighborhood, I practiced swearing. I swore at unsuspecting drivers, passed, passing, and to come. I felt I had to put on the power of strong language like the damned, ripped, bleeding muscles of the god Man. But my tongue at first absolutely refused to produce the necessary sounds. They disgusted me and rendered me tongue-tied. So I had to limber up on tongue-twisters at the beginning of each session. "Thelonious Throstle, the Thessalonian thistle-sifter, sifted thistles with his thick thumbs." Tongue-twisters solved my problem. With my tongue still leaping, I found myself able to say, "She smells pee smells by the wee whore," and I could soon take a running jump into the most horrendous filth. "How much ass would a dumb shmuck suck if a dumb shmuck could fuck twat?" Did I know how vulgar these practices were? Of course I did. In fact the principal obstacle in the way of my steady progress was an incessant, burning desire to go wash my mouth out with soap and warm water. Nevertheless I exercised constantly. And concentration on technique got me over the problem of content. Inventing the most complex dirt daily, I became increasingly dexterous in techniques of linked syllables, alliterative rhythms, assonance and dissonance. "Peter Piper pecked his pick of speckled peckers"—I soiled my tongue but I polished my art.

Nowhere is it clearer than here that my whole life—like everyone else's—is a crystallization of the development of the century. My mature poetics—both theory and practice—had its roots in this sowing of wild dirt. I was still young, still vulnerable. But art has peculiar necessities. And this account would be dishonest, neither enlightening nor complete, if I scrupled to trace the storm of poetry back to the breaths and voids that blew it into being.

I tried everything. I tried pornography. In my day pornography was unavailable in English, all I could manage to get hold of were French pamphlets. The cartoons inside were absurd, and the text— well, I discovered that French is simply not exciting. I buckled down hard to the problems posed by translation, but every time she'd open her *cuisses*, I'd have to start turning the pages of the dictionary. This is unnatural and distracting. She'd undo his buttons and take his strong round white throbbing *cou* in both her hands and I'd race hopefully over to the *c*'s, down the columns, turn the page, and for Godsake. His neck?! Besides, you know how it is: the crucial words weren't even defined by the dictionaries I could get hold of. You had to be a past master of the French language to have an erection.

I even tried dating. Only once. I asked a girl in my French class out to a movie. I'd been to the movies with girls before when I'd been a girl (and with boys), but it gave me palpitations to do it again the new way. By now, however, I was desperate enough to try anything. In the flickering dark of the theater I tried everything. *"Mamelles, tétons,"* I whispered. She didn't respond. *"Pine,"* I murmured. I was unsure of certain distinctions, but I tried them all. *"Con, cul, queue, cou, cuisses, couillons."* My entire repertory. She was a very unresponsive girl.

I began to doubt that she knew much French. But I didn't give up easily. I considered the possibility of tickling her arm, but thought I'd better work myself up into some semblance of desire first. I put one finger tentatively on the vegetable structure of her ear. And then, possessed by a suicidal heroism, forcing my courage by an exercise of willpower, shutting my eyes tight, I reached out and did what you were supposed to do, I seized her by the breast. I held on manfully. I was sure she'd resist, but she didn't, she cooperated, it was awful. She moved toward me, settling lower in her seat, so I was left with this entire breast resting on my hand. Through the next few minutes I suffered. Her bosom was huge, resilient. Unwilling to be guilty of cowardice, I kept my fingers active, and all the while I sat there squirming with the intense pangs of jealousy—a throwback to the time I'd resented all breasts because I was flat-chested.

I tried walking. After school one day I took a good square look at myself in the mirror, the large gold-framed mirror we had in the living room. There was no doubt about it. The reflection—the past in the present imperfect—depressed me. Those big eyes, owlish and frightened. A bird in a log, a girl's hanky soul in a boy's lanky body. I tried thumbing my nose at myself, but my eyes never got less sad. I tried walking around. It was true, as Pop said, my walk was wrong. All this paraphernalia of mine—my boy's haircut, collar, tie, belt, fly, crease, cuffs—only made my familiar girlish walk look worse. But I was determined, I was highly motivated. A proper boy's walk, I imagined, produced a natural stimulus: all day long his organ swung gently back and forth, constantly stirring his desire without resort to pornography. I took incredible pains to get it right, first in the living room, then by means of outside research. Sitting on school steps and park benches, analyzing various types of male and female strides, I decided that Father was right. I decided that although each boy had a different rhythm and energy, all had one thing in common: the splendid bright play of their shoulders, wrists, and knees came from inside out, from the center, the swinging pendulum of their manhood.

Later when with a maturer eye I came to study the walk of the other sex, I saw that, despite her rocking appearance, one part of a woman's body does remain at rest with respect to the line of motion —her womb moves forward in an unbroken straight line while all her other parts, so to speak, go forward and back, or swing or rock, round the still, unmoving center. But this distinction should be made: the pendulum is not the clock, not the clockworks. In a woman the energy of her movement is an inward rhythm, establishing time (birth, lifetime, periods, moon), while in a man it travels out, establishing space (flesh, matter, light, cosmos). These lifelong observations provided the thematic principle, the unstated but basic groundwork of metaphor for my *Backside of the Moon*, the book-length poem for which I was awarded a Pulitzer prize. That award of course created a scandal at the time, about which I have till now maintained silence. But it may be appropriate to comment here at last that it was precisely by means of filth that I solved the problem of the once vast and seemingly unbridgeable gap between poet and audience, between poetry isolated and poetry for society. In a sense those verses written much later in life were begun in high school by the struggle for a modality of existence, and a method of movement, opposed to my own.

All these efforts, observations, and workouts taught me the value of discipline. They strengthened my resolve, unlimbered my joints, and unlocked my throat. Pretty soon I could walk like a trooper and swear a mound of dung. In a couple of months I'd outstripped Father's wildest hopes for me. So when Sandy came home from Harvard for Thanksgiving, I was immensely excited. I hurried home from the big boulevard that afternoon and came bounding upstairs to shake his hand, proud to be able to greet him with genuine masculine warmth and brotherly affection. "Sandy, you bastard, welcome home goddamnittohell, you look just great, you sonofabitch prick, you're a sight for sore eyes, no kidding, it's great to have you back, you farting cocksucker, what's new with you, kiddo, now don't you go slipandpissinapailofshit, pal, just put 'er there, boy, and shake, man, shake it till it shakes your ass off or so help me, Sandy, I'll shove it right up your shittytittystickyprickyluckyfuckysnottyclottybirdturdwhackoffjackoffjerkofffuckoffsuckoffasshole, you motherfucking fuck you."

He was impressed. After I'd finished, he regarded me thoughtfully, cool grey eyes tightening, nostrils flaring, deliberating for one instant before he threw a swift punch at my jaw.

I've never been so surprised in my life. I was almost seventeen and he was over twenty-one, and I believe this is the only time we ever tangled physically (that is, fighting) as brothers normally do in the course of growing up. His fist only grazed my chin since I was already moving like a reflex with the punch. I caught his wrist. I jerked it forward in the direction it was coming. He followed it across the room, caromed off a chest of drawers, and bruised himself on a magazine rack.

"God *damn* you, Millie," he yelled, fetching up on the base of a floor lamp.

"Up yours, kid," I said.

"I'm sorry. I meant Willie."

"Then say so."

I could see he meant it, so I forgave him at once. I helped him up, straightening out his sweater, repressing with all my might a feeling of love, experiencing an uncomfortable desire to touch him gently on the cheek and ask him if he'd got hurt. I wondered of course what *he* felt about *me*. But it was not the kind of thing we could discuss any more. It wasn't entirely clear to me either why he'd been such a poor sport about my greeting, or why he'd tried to hit me. But I wouldn't ask; it was manlier not to.

He recovered his sense of humor with his breath. "New skills, Willie. Where've you been practicing *that?*"

"Oh that? Tongue-twisters, you see, if you practice tongue-twisters . . ."

"No, *that.*"

"Oh. Haidu. School of Judo."

"Pretty fancy"—rubbing his cheekbone.

"Balls. That's nothing."

We shook hands warmly; he winced. My fingers, wrists, and forearms had been getting a workout in judo exercises, three times a week in class, daily at home. Zipped into my black leather jacket and moving with my well-oiled, muted glide, I slipped into the living room and leaned against the bookshelves on one elbow, one thumb pulling at one pocket, and looked my brother over solemnly.

He said, "Hey, what's with the new jacket?"

"Cut wrong for the Ivy League?" I asked with cool sarcasm, appraising him. He looked so dignified it was almost funny. The pointed chin and cheeks—long cheeks—and sharp fuzzless ears were what did it. His blond hair looked even paler, and just a bit on the bushy side, the tufts still as messy as ever. He seemed to have picked up a new habit of listening with his hands placed behind his head, both elbows fanning out like a pair of elephant ears. His changeless grey eyes, I discovered, did change. They varied during the course of that evening from frostpane remoteness to unexpected slow thaws of tenderness. And there, etched alongside his eyes, were tiny lines that moved as if he'd just seen something funny but wouldn't say what. I *liked* him, I decided. From my new vantage point as a boy, I thought maybe we could be friends.

During Thanksgiving dinner my knee kept bouncing, I remember—another method I had devised to stimulate myself. I suppose it was the excitement of having Sandy around again, or maybe only a sensation of rivalry or jealousy. Anyhow, my leg wouldn't stop, I kept thinking I was about to produce the desired result at last. As a result, I nearly missed the big announcement.

Sandy announced (standing up to do so) a career for himself. Medicine. He began to "dissect" the turkey. Sandy a doctor? I thought of my gynecologist and decided my brother must be joking. I'd always been told he was doing brilliant work in physics, but now he was completing all his remaining premed requirements, and Father was worried. How was he going to put Sander through medical school? He was still paying off my hospital and surgical expenses. (Hermaphoditism, I might note in passing, is a possibility too little considered by Blue Cross–Blue Shield. Father remained in debt for years while wrangling in a legal suit to crush their allegations of cosmetic surgery.)

They began to talk about premed entrance requirements. My knee was still bouncing under the table. But *why?* Father queried and objected. Physics was the biggest thing, wide open, help yourself to gravy, wave of the future. Pumpkin, sweet potatoes? And Sandy, Father argued, was especially gifted in it. Cranberry sauce? Sure. Stuffing, too. Sandy explained that he felt more interested in medicine. But why? It had something to do with me. Celery. This whole thing, my operation, had hit him hard. My experience had in a way been partly his. No thanks, Mother. Father, peas? Body, mind, mystery, candied carrots, in one's own family, please. Not an exact science, but more human, the study of the body. Stop talking, doctor, and chew your food.

I ate my breast reflectively, making my knee bounce up and down, seeing if I could get an answering quiver in my groin. No luck. Sandy wanted to know why I wasn't being sent to see a psychiatrist. I threw him a dirty look. Pop claimed that he distrusted the whole tribe on professional grounds—their testimony in court always irritated him by its pompous vagueness. But Mother explained the real reason. "Look at her, a boy now! Body, mind, never mind. Who *paid* for Billie?"

I had given up trying to transform Mother.

After dinner who had to wash the dishes? As always, me. Mother cleared, I washed, Sandy dried, Father phoned. To make me feel better, pretty soon Sander wrapped a big dishtowel around his waist, shoved me aside, and continued with the dishwashing. So I just dried.

Father went out to play poker. Mother lay down for a nap.

I beckoned. I took Sandy into Father's study and went rummaging in the bottom drawer of the big desk. I asked Sandy if he wanted a glass of the stuff. He said, "Listen, put it back. I'll buy you some."

"Don't get me wrong, only a taste for me, that's all I ever take," I explained, "whenever he goes out for poker. I've got to get used to it somehow."

He made me put it back. We settled down in his old bedroom. I almost never went in there any more. I shook a cigarette loose from a crushed pack and held it out. I flipped the match and slung my feet up across one corner of his old desk, crossing my ankles.

"Willie, what's going on with you, you're trying too hard."

"I've got to catch up."

"You've got to relax."

I shook my head. "I've got to try harder."

"You've got to *stop* trying." He put his hands behind his head.

"Advice is cheap. Listen, Sandy," I said, unslinging my ankles and leaning forward quickly. I pointed a slender finger at him. "I don't know a single other person in this country who's got problems like mine."

I could see that this touched him, even though that was all I said. He got up and walked round the room, then went to the window and looked out. That was all he did, but it was dark, there was nothing to see, and he stayed there looking out a long time, so I knew he remembered—and still felt some of the power of the old days. I wondered if I could tell him what was giving me my newest nightmares. If I couldn't be open and honest with Sandy, of all people, with whom . . . so . . . I told him. He pulled his head in from the window, shocked. "The doctors say the trouble spot isn't behind my fly, it's up behind the eyes. So what I want to know is just one thing. What happens inside a guy's head? What turns his switch ON and makes it go up, up, up?"

"That's a hell of a thing for you to ask me."

"I *have* to ask."

"I don't believe it. You already know."

"What d'you mean, I know? You mean all that malarkey the doctors hand out about desire, instinct, intercourse, sphincters? I *know* all that, premed—but what makes it work? That I don't know. What makes it really go? What makes it *go, go, GO!*"

He stared at me. Remote.

"All right," I said, "be superior."

"I'm not being superior. That's not fair."

Was he embarrassed, then? He was acting very strangely. The wings of his nose were pulsing. I inquired, "What made it go for us?" I corrected myself: "For you."

He smiled and hummed abruptly—this absurd casual stance of his only revealing his embarrassment.

I said, "Don't be a jackass, please, we *can talk* about this." His laugh-wrinkles made his eyes almost tear. As for me, talking openly about our past gave me a sense of freedom from it, and yet preserved our intimacy. "Stop hemming and humming with me. Older brothers are supposed to tell their kid brothers things like this."

Amused? Yes, he was. Was I so funny? Why? Lying down on his bed, arms behind his head, he began to preach, "Willie, it's love—"

"That makes the world go round?" I suggested. "Please don't be soupy with me," I warned him. "I've heard enough of that crap already."

Obligingly, he changed his tune, "Well, then, it's hate. It's hate that makes the world go round. It's love that makes it square."

I hadn't any idea whether he was being on the level with me. But I doubted it. "Sandy," I tried, "I hate-love Mom and I love-hate Pop. And neither one of them turns my switch."

"You're talking nonsense, Millie."

I burned red, then paled to white. I told him, "I know a jujitsu pressure point that will paralyze half your body."

"Sorry, Willie. Relax." He closed his eyes.

"Okay. But *tell* me! What makes it go up?"

He opened his eyes. He put out his cigarette. He got off his bed, slumped down in his chair, closed his eyes. And finally he answered me with one blunt word.

I thought I was going to have a fit, but I held on carefully. I said in a low, reasonable mutter, "Are you going to sit there and tell me that an *opening* is exciting?" All I could think of was where and how I used to pee. It was futile to hope I could ever get very excited about that, of all the goddamn things. "Are you going to sit there and tell me that everyone alive today in this country got procreated because labia are exciting?"

"What? You're not serious . . . everyone in the country . . ." His ears began to move by themselves, involuntarily trembling; this talk was evidently a strain for him. Yet the hidden tension in the center showed only at the edges, the sides and corners. "As you say, there's procreation, there's evolution, it's all those things, and love, and instinct, and secondary sex characteristics."

I took a long breath. "What?"

"Lots of things about a woman—her pretty face, a pair of legs, even pretty clothing—but the central thing is—" He didn't repeat it.

I thought of the raised skirt, the daily thighs. "But that's for kids, isn't it?"

He shook his head.

The whole thing struck me as preposterous. I simply didn't believe Sander's theory, I confess, not a word of it. Just that one extra hole? There had to be more than that to the enigma of procreation and instinct. I came to the conclusion that no one in the country understood the mystery—a rash conclusion, but I was approximately correct. Sandy of course was merely wrong, but he was young, his mistake was excusable, he changed his mind in after years. As for me, it took me the effort of a lifetime to find the answer to this elementary riddle.

Desire, love, hate, sex—the overheated cauldron of instincts—up from the impassive scrotums of the world issue billions of billions of sperm screaming with pleasure, screaming for help, down out of their ovarian caves drop millions of millions of eggs weeping with ecstasy, weeping for life, and everywhere and always wanders the self-sufficient, coldblooded, and oversexed snail, needing no other snail

to procreate, restless hermaphrodite, searching with antennae unfurling, searching before the final cracking of the shell . . . before
nothing at all . . . for nothing at all. . . .

A day later Sandy sat, staring and thinking. There were plenty of
seats on the subway, but I preferred to stand, strap-hanging and practicing my grip. At the storefront studio that Haidu called his school,
my brother watched our class go through the usual ascending series
of defensive and offensive drills. But the memorable thing about that
Friday afternoon was that after class he actually managed to get
Haidu to work out with him, and that made me jealous. By the time
I got out of the locker room they were already at it.

They sat on the floor and they both looked preposterous—both
cross-legged on a straw mat, facing each other—Sandy in his Harvard
striped tie and Argyle socks, button-down collar and patched-up
elbows, and Haidu with his Superjap costume, big in the gut, with
his stubby arms resting on his knees. Laughing to myself, I lounged
on the floor. Myself, I had on my usual rig: thick black belt, heavy-
knit blue T-shirt with a leather thong high up on my chest, and low
black boots. A Japanese woman appeared; unintroduced, she sidled
in and served us sake. It was hot, without much taste to it. I pulled
over one of the sweaty exercise pads and lay on my back, slinging
my bluejeans up over a bench.

I watched Sandy maneuvering. He moved in for a grip. He said,
"For the spirit, okay, I see that. Spiritually I see that there can be no
comparison with wrestling. But why should it be superior as a sport,
physically?"

Haidu pivoted. "Distinction is foolish, no? Spiritual, physical, not
exist this distinction—artificial."

"It does exist."

Haidu bent and tasted his sake, almost a bow, without replying.

Sandy said, "Even if the distinction doesn't exist, then still you
ought to be able to explain to me about jujitsu in plain physical terms,
why it's superior physically to wrestling."

"Oh yes, sure, this possible. Jujitsu superior due to superior understanding of physical principles of cause and effect."

I said to Sandy, "Like if an arm comes shooting at you, which is
the cause, now if you twist it or block it, you come up against it so
you lose Energy. But instead, you can just add more of the same
cause to it, if you know what you're doing, and change the effect

like crazy, because you can cause it to cause itself to wrench itself all by itself right out of its socket or even make an arm tear its own muscles in back of the shoulder. Yesterday afternoon, for instance, I had to be careful how I handled you. Haidu is teaching me Restraint."

I found out later that Haidu had already learned from Sandy about our encounter. They heard me out without interrupting me, and I thought maybe I'd take part in the conversation, but right after this they went out of my depth. It was the technique of the art that interested me, not the spiritual part. But not my brother. You could see that Sandy would never enroll in a jujitsu course, for example: he was after theory, principles. I began to wonder what was going on with him at Harvard. College seemed to be changing him for the worse—adding new causes in the direction of old ones.

"Well, if it's scientific," Sandy said, "training a person automatically to apply his scientific knowledge of cause and effect, where does the spirit-angle come in? You said—"

"Please you listen, is higher level of spirit, but same principle as physical, on higher level master of art of jujitsu understand more. Understand and use what he understand. Cause one thing with effect. One thing. In combat is not this force against that force. Is one force. In combat is never this man against that man. Is one man. He win. This spiritual skill which master know."

"So spiritual is identical with physical and cause is the same as effect?" Sandy smiled and mulled this information over dubiously, and added, "But that's just a way of talking."

"Not so. Way of knowing."

"Well," Sandy compromised, "let's say it's a *way* of knowing. But it isn't real, it's not reality."

Haidu was quiet for a while. He lifted his puffy eyes and looked at me. I grinned and made a skeptical chin-jerk toward Sandy. Haidu merely continued to look at me seriously, then he smiled and turned to smile at Sandy. "In same moment a bird leave the nest he learn to fly. Hishi has most intelligent brother, but not ready to leave the nest. Listen you listen now. At highest level the great master knows that he who knows is same with what he knows. This is difficult for me, highest level is here," he said, gesturing over his head, "and Haidu sits here—on floor. He who knows, what he knows, and knowing are one thing. I sit here, you sit by me, but host and guest are same as hospitable act. Lover and person loved are same as act of loving."

It was at this point that he caught my full attention. I sat up and said, "You're *not* going to tell me that male and female are the same, too?"

He stared at me without speaking. I paled.

"Then if they're the same," I said nervously, "what causes the male to be excited by the female, answer me *that!*"

Haidu looked at Sandy, who swallowed. Haidu looked at me, fumbled for the English word, and answered in a word, a single blunt word.

Sandy tried to catch my glance. He sat there, but I couldn't, I walked out. I tried to relax. Soon Sandy came out. We walked to the subway, busy with our separate thoughts. But if male and female were one? That was the problem, then. The others each had one part . . . I had both . . . I could suddenly put the pieces together, see them whole, and make sense of them. They each had one: hence desire. I had both: hence? What Haidu had said to Sandy went round again in my ears. The same, the same—here, surely, if anywhere, lay nothing less than the first sexual secret I was looking for—how the mystery worked: the identity of spirit with body, of cause with effect, of process with agent—yes, the secret was there, and I was crushed. For if I'd got it right, sexual excitement and potency in my binary state were in fact not possible for me. Out of the question.

I couldn't believe it . . . my intuition misgave me . . . I resisted with all my might a conclusion so discouraging.

Haidu shook me up that night. (But not until many years later did I come to realize the lifelong tugging influence that that one evening of wrestling with Haidu had on my brother.) Was I hopeless then? Even if Haidu and Sandy both thought so, they might both be wrong. If there was any hope left for me, it might lie in raw experience alone: the untheoretical gross experience of being a boy among boys. Maybe I could pick up desire by being exposed to it, the way one picks up a cold or a case of German measles.

I'd seen the pale flicker of Whitey's hair rarely, always at a distance. For months I'd been handing over bag lunches and copies of my homework. I had let Whitey's "Rattlers" look over my shoulder during exams, given up choice seats for school movies, brought glasses of water to Rattlers who asked for them and occasionally to their girls, taken the blame once for a broken ceiling light, and generally been only mildly humiliated by managing to keep out of the way . . . until I decided to resist.

My behavior in this entire episode, I begin to see as I come to set it down, runs parallel to many of my adventurous achievements in later life. My inward desperation, the methodical risks I took, the limits I placed on risk, and the limits I placed on success—the parallels with my career will be obvious to those friends who have known me well. Even for them this boyhood tale may help illustrate the development in me of that combination of traits—tranquil innocence with cunning sagacity, an angelic willingness to rush in like a fool but not foolishly, the rash and defiant creation of confidence by forcing myself forward where I felt least confident—which accounts not only for my financial success, but for that more crucial human success early in life with men more gifted and knowledgeable than myself.

In a large and difficult school Whitey—Captain of the School Guards since his third year—had by now created a remarkable double system: within the official school monitors, the Guards, he maintained an unofficial inner corps, the Rattlers. The Guards in general kept order in the halls, stairs, washrooms, gym, entrances . . . they did the job well, too, by means of beatings administered by hard-core Rattlers. With Captain Whitey's consent, one or two Rattlers at a time were able to leave school during certain hours; all Rattlers could move about freely in the halls; and they had one washroom and a large adjoining janitor's room to themselves on the top floor where they could smoke. It was said that every once in a while school authorities had tried to do away with the gang's influence, usually after such outrages as an attack on a girl in the corridors or an open game of craps at the school entrance. But Whitey, after accepting his defeat with a goodnatured smile, and everyone was unanimous about his smile, would organize a riot in the lunchroom —an enormous, densely crowded place, difficult to control except from the inside—or wanton terror on the way home from school— until he was called in again to keep the peace, which he did.

Whitey's smile invariably charmed. For a long while it puzzled me that people could be so deceived. But there was no deception in this. No one was taken in; everyone knew his character. I've discovered that people are always willing to trust or follow a known villain who does his job and doesn't offend visibly.

"Whitey eats today." That was the signal. On an average of once every two weeks I had sacrificed my lunch. I had simply yielded. I had so far accepted the situation I found, while trying to improve myself—outwardly by jujitsu, inwardly by walking, talking, and thinking like a boy . . . until I made up my mind. When I made up my mind, I aimed for the Rattlers, not the Guards.

Like other kids, I suppose I must have seen too many Western and gangland movies. But I was careful. I adopted Pop's sound advice about using a show of strength to avoid a fight. One day immediately after my lunch had been taken again without any unusual murmur of protest from me which might have aroused suspicion, I simply went up to the top floor to join up. The washroom was deserted, as I knew it would be. I had investigated beforehand; in fact, I had meticulously planned every detail of what I had to do. I walked right through to the inner sanctum. A dozen boys were eating sandwiches and playing cards, mostly on the floor, some on benches. They stopped playing when I came in; some continued eating, which struck me as the most menacing thing they could have done. I kept my hands in my black leather pockets, partly to seem unaggressive, partly to comfort myself. I didn't see Whitey at first because I was much too tense. Besides, I was looking for someone else, the watery-eyed kid who had attacked me the very first day. By now I knew he'd risen to the "left hand"—that is, third-in-command. I'd considered for a while challenging the "right hand" kid, but I had sense enough to realize that between Whitey and his second-in-command, ties of loyalty would make my challenge a little too direct. So I looked round for Smiley—nicknamed that way so far as I could tell because, though his eyes teared, his upper lip had a tic. I saw him immediately on the bench in the corner. I pointed to him and said, before anyone else could speak, "He called my motherfucker a mother." It was a slip of the tongue. You can't *imagine* how many hundreds of times I'd practiced that small speech, over and over, and *still*, in the strain of the moment, I slipped up. I turned pale, I must have, when I realized I'd stumbled right at the outset. But they didn't seem to notice the slip, they must have been too surprised; they got the point right anyway. I'd picked that particular phrase deliberately because I'd overheard, analyzed, and concluded, after months of attentiveness in the lunchroom, school yard, judo locker rooms, bike shop, and everywhere boys were more or less out of earshot of anyone except other boys, that the only unforgivable insult to a boy is the insult to his mother. Insults to oneself, one's friends, one's girlfriend, sister, father, all had to be avenged, but not suicidally—and I had entered suicidally, as though determined on revenge or extermination. Note that I did not insult Smiley's mother, which would have been a mistake in tactics. By mentioning my mother I had their sentimentality on my side, and for that moment they let me alone.

Smiley stood up, baffled and hunched like a question mark. He might have called me a liar and sworn he'd never said a single word about my mother, but he couldn't because it would have made him sound weak.

"Take off your glasses," I said to him. I knew it was unfair: if he took off his glasses, he wouldn't even see me; but I thought it was what one had to say.

Smiley's lip went up. "You little fuck," he said.

He came across the room slowly. But when he reached me, he made a sudden jab with his leg—just a feint—and brought both his hands up and forward in a lunge. I went back with him as if I were part of him, and when he was over my arm I took his glasses off.

It was quite a show, and brought some admiring laughs. I turned to put his glasses down, but he came at me again so unexpectedly that to save them from ruin, I had to go down on my back under his attack—the glasses on my stomach. The force of his lunge was terrific, so all I had to do was help him over my head with my feet; he hit the wall.

I got up and, for the effect, nudged him in the behind with my toes. This trite vaudeville, though it brought another laugh in my favor, almost cost me my victory. The stricken Smiley grabbed for my stable foot, the only one on which I was standing. I hopped up and came down on his wrist.

There was a moment of silence, the decisive moment. The others were waiting for Whitey to pass the word. I said as quickly as I could, "What this gang needs is a hearse." The word meant car. I had already learned that nothing stops motion in a group of boys like the word "car"; it can be relied on.

One dull kid said, lowering, "Whitey eats kids like you." But he had no seconds.

Whitey was looking at me. I caught sight, for the first time close up, of his sumptuous head of hair, neither white nor yellow but somewhere in between, a ghostly moonpale unkempt radiance that looked as if thousands of threadlike hairs were individually transparent. He was sitting on a bench with several other boys, his feet stretched evenly to a second bench. What struck me most was the crease in his trousers, quite immaculate, and also his clean wrinkleless socks with the fine silkthreaded design—probably because this was the type of thing I had noticed in boys for the first sixteen years of my life. Later I noticed that Whitey always dressed neatly; not with a dandy's care—he was never obtrusive—but with modest elegance. He was modest in all things. Even his features, large and potentially dragon-cruel, were generally relaxed into a totally different focus, a disarming, friendly, boy's grin. He said to me in his most amiable way, "I had a friend who thought the same thing. He's got a private room up in boys' town now." Boys' town meant the state reformatory thirty miles up the Hudson. (The girls' reformatory, by the way, wasn't called girls' town, but the hen house.)

"Then he should have stuck with hubcaps," I pointed out breathlessly. This was a trifle too bold, but it had a good ring to it because the "friend"—Whitey's predecessor, as the whole school knew—had specialized until his demise in the resale of hubcaps removed at night; it was Whitey who had added wipers, mirrors, aerials, and radiator emblems. These were often snapped in broad daylight from moving cars—a breathtaking sport, invented by Whitey and far more popular than the merely lucrative venture of hubcaps.

But I was proposing the whole car again, and he demurred.

"Where's my lunch?" I said. My body, still taut from the combat with Smiley, had begun to waver. Self-conscious, I thought it might look girlish, and I wanted to sit down.

Whitey motioned, and the boy who had taken my lunch threw it to me. It had barely been started. I sat down on a bench and reached into the bag.

"Who said you could eat?" Whitey said.

"Who's eating?" I said. I took out the two cents I had wrapped in a bit of paper, opened the paper, got up and put the pennies down on the bench near Whitey. Even Smiley was watching me. "I couldn't take on the whole gang of you," I said, "could I? So here's my contribution to the hearse right now." The sight of my two pitiful pennies on the bench—what with the substantial-looking pile of nickels and dimes on the floor in the card game— brought another laugh, this time against me.

But Whitey, among others, didn't laugh. "You ain't a dummy, are you? And I thought you was a dummy."

And so began the system of collections for "protection" which ultimately brought the gang its hearse—and brought Whitey, too, I might add, to his own room in boys' town. As soon as Whitey understood, he cut my figure in half. "A penny a day's enough. Take us longer that way, you got a point, but we got to avoid too many complaints, or it's no hearse for us. A dime a week's just asking for trouble. We settle for a nickel, that way we cut down on beatings, save ourselves time, get around to more kids. The trick is quantity—

how many hundreds can we take on every day? What d'you say, Shark?"

Shark was Whitey's right. "I give you a hundred."

"That's because you don't see it the way I see it. Everything takes setup. And we got setup. We get every little pisser on his way into school. Squeeze 'em on the way in, tap 'em on the way out. See it now?"

And then to me: "What's your name, kid?"

"Billy."

"Is that right?" he said. Then he put back his head and laughed. "You got a big billy?"

It startled me. But he only meant to be friendly, to welcome me to the gang. And though I hadn't realized it, that was the signal of acceptance: comic reference to the male genitals. In fact, it took me much longer to understand—as a rough but handy rule-of-thumb—that among boys any mention of the male genitals, even in an angry tone, was meant to have a friendly ring; any mention of the female genitals, even casually, was intended as a form of insult. (And when in after years I founded a commercial empire of my own on not much more than a penny per pisser per day, it was—and still is—my boast that I helped stem and turn this ancient tide of abuse.)

I was made a Guard—Whitey submitted my name to the Dean of Boys. I was given an armband and a post on the stairs, and became an official Rattler. Within days the system of secret collections for "protection" was instituted and it had, as I had thought it would, a calming effect on school life. Everyone paid his surreptitious mite, and Whitey felt obliged to see to it that peace reigned. The system of collection was at stake—there was too much to lose if it came out into the open. Deliberate beatings became rare, wanton attacks almost unknown. Of course at the beginning, a few assaults had to be made against recalcitrants, for example's sake. For these, no matter how hard I tried to persuade myself that the overall effect of the "protection" was good, I felt personally guilty. I wanted to withdraw from the Rattlers a dozen times just after I had been accepted. But I never did. Being one of them meant too much to me. Over the months I learned to smoke dope, to play cards, to shoot craps, to pretend I liked the taste of liquor, and to talk a fairly good game of any sport you care to name. I learned jokes about all the things that could get lost between a woman's legs, like explorers, wagon trains, motorcycles. And I learned that a fast, menacing feint at somebody's groin to make him wince was the friendliest form of salutation—none of them ever tired of it. (I was admired because, lacking the reflex, I never winced.) Of course there were things I just couldn't manage, couldn't stomach. One was to "bloody up" on a kid. The most I ever managed to do was to scare him with a heavy judo fall—a skill which fortunately was so envied that I was never forced by the gang to do more.

But every month I had to witness things—petty cruelties, nasty stupidities—which sickened me more than the outright brutalities. Once a fellow who had refused, one time only, to make an extra copy of his homework was chased into a basement alleyway, cornered, and forced to tear out every page of every book he was carrying—one by one, it took him almost an hour, and I had the feeling he must have loved those books—while the gang sat around playing cards and insisting he do it slowly, only one page at a time. Another time a boy who had asked Whitey's girl for a date, and whose chest was covered with a gorilla's growth of hair—he was a really big guy —was held down by about ten Rattlers while Shark, with soap, brush, and razor, cut a swath through his hair in the shape of an "R." I wasn't only sickened of course when I watched these depredations; I must admit they also excited me. I used to experience a kind of heart-thundering relief—let me even call it joy—realizing that it wasn't happening to me. And I think every one of the gang experienced the same fear-soothing relief. They looked forward to crucial moments when they could come to grips with panic by seeing it come true in others. I remember the first time this thought came into my head. After an hour of rough flirting with about half a dozen girls on an empty lot a few blocks from school, among patches of dry grass, garbage, ashes, newspapers, and rusting tin cans, the gang caught a younger boy, about fifteen, sat on him, and began to give him a "pink belly," a continual tap-slapping of the stomach till it turns a bright pink. But because there were girls nearby, after the first two minutes of slapping the gang decided to remove his pants and underwear. The poor fellow writhed and flapped like a fish, and screamed piercingly, especially when the girls—who at first kept their distance out of modesty—came to tease. And I remember how after a while, the first time I had ever seen it happen, the boys in a sort of glad, appeased exhaustion actually let him get up and go before they were through with him, his stomach only half reddened.

"Keep 'em sharpening their claws they're happy," Whitey said. "Busy, happy guys. A boy's got a long claw, he's got to keep it sharp." He was lying on the ground on a mound of stones, a cigarette at the

side of his mouth, his crystal-white teeth showing at the opposite
corner.

I was sitting nearby. "You shouldn't have let him go," I said. I
had learned generally to say the opposite of what I felt; it was safer.

He laughed and shook his elegant white head, his eyes closed.
"You don't see it like I do. Next year that kid's going to join my
gang, he will now, you'll see, he's had it just enough, and he'll beg me
to get in as soon as he's old enough just so he can see it happen."
His tongue pushed a tobacco flake out onto his upper lip, where it
stayed. "Like you."

"Me!" I was suddenly very worried. "Where do you get that
shit?"

"Take it easy," he said, "and quit playing dumb."

"I'm not playing dumb, it's just I don't like to hear a guy come
out with wrong ideas." He used to talk his ideas out loud with me
more than he did with the others, maybe because he sensed how much
I wanted to learn.

"You know, kid, you got brains, and you got crust, like me, but
you couldn't run this gang. You lack drive, you stop too soon. One
flipflop and you've had it."

"Me? I never stop," I protested. "Didn't I say you let him go too
soon?"

But all he did was open his eyes and look at me. Then he sat up
and nudged me with his toe. "What'd Napoleon want, and Genghis
Khan? Tell me that, kid."

"I don't know. Empires, I guess."

"I don't care a fart what they *did*, kid. What'd they *want?*"

"Don't know," I said. "How do I know?"

"Feel it, that's all. You got to feel it."

"I don't feel it."

He shook his head, disappointed in me. Then he flashed that
disarming grin of his and gave me the answer in one blunt word.

Nights, the Rattlers used to go on long peeping-tomcat expeditions, skulking about for hours on the rooftops, scouting houses for
the most promising lights. It was a neighborhood of garbage cans in
a maze of alleyways, garages, and fences, ominous smelly apartment
houses with great pebbly roofs conveniently overtopping small flat-
roofed close-packed houses. I liked the rooftop work—the silent
climbing, jumping, swinging, and running—it used to remind me of
games of Follow-the-Leader with Sandy. But the ultimate reward
always bored me.

"Je-e-e-sus!" whispered Sacky's unbelieving, patient voice in the darkness. "Look at the size of them."

"O-o-o-oh!" sighed the Fatman.

And bucktoothed Mickey on my left breathed, "O-h-h-h-h."

Personally, I think she knew we were out there. I wondered if Juliet knew that Romeo was out there.

"Off," pleaded Shark.

"Off," exulted Smiley softly to the night air.

We were leaning over a metal fire escape and it was shaking—you could feel the vibrations as the gang wiggled against the bars like small caged animals. As usual I felt inferior, annoyed, and a little sleepy with the dull wait. To pass the time I strained my fingers on the highest fire-escape bar, strengthening my wrists while the others strained their eyes and their anatomy.

"Pretty little pussy. Pretty little pussy," Whitey purred.

"If you don't take 'em off . . ." threatened Shark.

And then she raised her hand and out went the light.

The silence on the fire escape was black. "We gotta win," Whitey said. "We gotta. What about the girls' locker room?"

"There ain't no windows in there, Whitey," Shark said. He put an arm consolingly around Khan-Napoleon-Romeo's shoulders.

"We put a hole through."

"Where to where?" said Shark, and spat down the dark alley. We padded off the fire escape like cats, and sat on the curb under a ring of light.

Were Haidu and Sandy right, after all? I mulled it over. "The locker room might be an idea," I said casually. I thought I saw a chance to end these interminable night waits.

"No, Shark's right, kid, forget it," Whitey said. "You got to know the layout."

"All right, so we go in and case it," I said, lighting a cigarette.

Shark was impressed but worried. "You going in there?"

"Us," I said. "In dresses. What about it? How many of you guys got the guts to go in with me?" There was a moment of cowardly thought.

"Not me," said Mickey.

"They'd spot us," said the Fatman. "We'd get in but we'd never get out."

I made a noise between my teeth to indicate my disgust. "All it takes is one kid with steady nerves," I said.

Smiley chimed in hopefully. "You get caught, champ, you're

through." His position in the Rattlers had deteriorated since my advent. But since I had made a firm point of being on good terms with everyone in the gang, I'd never challenged him again.

Still, for a moment I was uncertain about him. "I'm not *going* to get caught," I said, "—unless maybe you squeal." The threat was apparent to everyone listening, and as it turned out, it stuck.

I must have been feeling pretty confident of myself by then, because the next day I showed up carrying in a parcel my mother's dress—the same one I had worn to the gynecologist's office almost a year earlier. The gang helped me get ready in the top-floor washroom—a red and yellow kerchief over my head. There were a few wisecracks, but on the whole the gang was tense and very serious: the stakes, they sensed, were high.

Actually, my performance was almost effortless. I went in at the change of class periods, among a couple of hundred girls of various sizes and shapes. (During my archaeological excavations I've had occasion to be impressed, remembering the ingenuity of the early procedure I adopted.) Through the commotion of zippers and sneakers, I made a seemingly casual but careful circuit of the labyrinthine locker rooms. The "layout" was far more complicated than I had imagined, and for a while I thought I would have to make an architect's drawing. But then I hit on the ingenious idea of following the water pipes in the shower room, located down half a flight of steps, which led to the swimming pool. The place was so full of vapor from the showers, with girls milling about and towels slung all over the pipes, that it was hard to get the design of the pipes straight. I left, traced the same route in the corridor outside, went back through to the shower room to check the layout again, and then reported to Whitey.

I would have been a hero even if the plan hadn't worked. The upstairs washroom was loud with cheers. Still, I had made one staggering mistake. "But what'd you *see?*" they pleaded with me. "For Chrissake what'd you *see!*"

See? I decided to tell the truth. Why not? I hadn't noticed that part of the business anyhow.

They were suspicious. "You didn't notice?"

I shrugged. "I was too busy figuring, and the goddamn place was full of steam."

Luckily, they were ready to forgive me almost anything.

But their desperate disbelief, their impassioned will to believe I'd observed more than floor plans and corridors and conduits forced me to believe finally. The female body . . . who in his right mind could ever have imagined . . . ? Reluctantly, I was forced to admit it. Doubting, I no longer dared to deny it. Still doubting, I had to accept it—with question-mark belief, so to speak. The incredible source of all that motive power of male desire? How unpleasant. How paltry. How funny—a joke that might be laughed at a single time if the mood was right—but how fundamentally uninteresting and irritating. Did I *have* to bother my head learning to master the riddle of desire if that was all it came to? Dante, I later read, speaks of love first entering through the eyes. But that sex should enter through the eyes and from there pull the bodily strings and make that little naked unseen puppet rise and dance before its mistress seemed an unworthy image for poetry and a low image of life. Yet in adolescence I was forced to face the low facts of American sex life into which I'd been initiated, by my own choice, by my own doing, over these past weeks and months. Beauty —I hardly need to say it—had nothing to do with it: it was flesh for flesh's sake.

The water pipes, as it turned out, came out through the wall of an unused janitor's closet in the basement storage area below the gym. Shark jimmied the lock. Within three days Fatman, whose father was a plumber, had cleared the masonry through the wall over the sink. Just under the ceiling, Whitey, who had a fine hand with a steel bit, drilled the final wee opening—so that nothing fell through at all. A mere pinprick must have been visible on the other side. We covered the excavation on our side, when not in use, with a mirror surmounted by the school banner.

Triumphant shower-watching, standing on the sink, at first replaced all other sports and diversions. One at a time, backs were arched to the hole and necks stretched. But because of the position of the girls' shower room, the angle of vision never reached higher than the girls' shoulders, and usually only to the navel. They were so close, we couldn't see their faces.

So all day long in corridors and classes the gang tried to memorize figures: only to discover how impossible it was to identify the same figures unclothed. Day after day the boys took down the mirror and pressed themselves to the small hole in paroxysms of hope, longing to recognize their conquests—in vain. Just on the other side of the pinpoint opening—hundreds and hundreds every day—flitted wet soapy nameless bellies, red impersonal knees, breasts without owners, indifferently busy washcloths and fingers. Do you think the onlookers minded the impersonality, the lack of particularity? Do you imagine that pelvis without person, groin without a name or subject, ever palled? The boys kept at it for months, mesmerized by the flesh until they were numbed by it. One day Whitey said, "Let's cat it again, what d'you say?" And that night we all took to the roofs again—"for a little excitement," Shark admitted to me with relief. We had to break the routine . . . but the tedium could not be broken, never. It was only for more of the same, I discovered. Only for the sake of added physical exercise and a greater variety of the same blunt word.

Something . . . the woman still in me? . . . my gorge? . . . rose in mutiny. In my head I heard one word echoing with all the bewildering accents of my experience: a male experience that I could now see was to be never-ending.

Of course it didn't escape me that perhaps this was only a stage . . . that these young men would grow older, become the fathers of families, and so change . . . grow to find the motivation for sexual love in something less gross than this single unengrossing, rather plain item. But I doubted it. I looked at them and I doubted; and when I looked at myself, something misgave me there, too. If I *had* to become a man this way, and what other way was there, how would I emerge from the process? Their way? Another way?

Their way . . . willy-nilly. Their way . . . more or less. I knew it. I foresaw it. Sure, to this day I remain molded by that experience. But even then I couldn't help seeing that unless something changed I'd come to *enjoy* the very attitudes that sickened me.

Manhood? On these terms manhood wasn't worth it. I returned to the gynecologist, the surgeon. It wasn't bravery, it was only clarity. I had no choice. Forward, then. Begin again with the body of love, the eye of the hurricane, the tail of the comet. The song, the sweep, the star, the silences of desire had been too long postponed, might never be mine. They were shocked to hear my request. "It's too late," they chorused. But it's never too late. And it's never too soon either. "Make me a girl," I announced. I requested nothing. I announced. "I don't want to lose my male organ, you understand. It's mine, God knows. But sew me up. Seal it in. Completely." They goggled, they laughed, they gagged, they drew diagrams, they offered scientific arguments, they launched personal attacks on me and on the imbecility, to say nothing of the unfeasibility, of my surgical desires. And over and over they wanted to know why: "Why?"

I tried to tell them. The male attitude toward my primordial womb was treason. What attitude? they wanted to know. I coughed and despaired of explanation. Nevertheless I replied that I had to escape from the pestilence of error before it was too late. What pestilence of error? they demanded. The part for the whole, I answered. I rejected the stifling male equation, lock, stock, and barrel. "Why? What?" I gave the simplest possible answer at last. And though they claimed not to believe me, though every man jack of them pretended to deny my reasoning, I'm sure they understood me when I told them bluntly, "Cunt."

How I Changed My Body

And such as knew he was a man would say,
"Leander, thou art made for amorous play;
Why art thou not in love, and loved of all?"
—MARLOWE

My college education is in essence the story of how I managed to become a woman. As such it signals those later successes of adult life based in each case on willpower and free enterprise. But the reader, no matter how sympathetic he may be with the cause of womanhood, must be forewarned: my male phallus, hanging in the way of logic, will appall him. My initiative, I trust, will earn his warmest commendations. But my methods may strike him as questionable, unethical, even piratical.

Yet I beg him to remember two things in my defense. One: hard facts and biological circumstance were against me. Two: all logical, reasonable, moral, and scientific avenues were closed to me. How—by what means short, that is, of castration—could I become a woman? I mean a woman. Not a transvestite, not a fairy, not an effeminate compromise. I *mean* a woman. I had to follow peculiar underground channels of my own, often not knowing myself the pressures of these forces that were leading me by roundabout ways to my existential goal.

The Dean of Boys called me into his office. He closed the door and made me sit. "Willie, tell me, how'd you ever make it," he bent closer, "an average like yours, come on, tell me."

I wet my lips and tried to give him a smile as fluorescent as Whitey's. "Me average?"

He nodded. "You going to go up there dressed like a cowboy?" he said. Then as if absent-mindedly picking up a ruler from his desk, he pointed it at the crotch of my jeans—slowly, not jabbing—and said, "You think I don't know?"

Had this happened a couple of months earlier, I'd have gone frigid with anxiety and hot with embarrassment . . . but not now. I'd learned a lot, mixing with Rattlers. I tried to hold my smile, but no, I couldn't quite manage that. It came down into a grin of hate. Hardly moving, I put one finger on the tip of his ruler and shoved it slowly, very slowly, aside. "What you know is your business," I told him. "I don't want to know what you know."

"It's all here in black and white," he insisted. "Here—these came into my office—look at these—" and he pushed a file of papers in front of me, my letter of acceptance, the medical records and transcripts—"that's you—your history—you're a Harvard man!" He laughed. "Punk." He tapped the file. "Harvard punk! Congratulations."

Father was ecstatic. "A scholarship! Research! The key to the future!" He punched me affectionately in the shoulder, a little harder than was necessary. (I didn't find out why until later that night.) "You've always made the right decisions, Willie. Attaboy! What made you apply to Harvard? A writ of mandamus, chalk up another for the old family, two out of two, we score again! Harvard!" He undulated round the living room. "What a school! First my Sandy, then my Willie. Habeas corpus and up you go!" He beamed.

I tapped the side of my temple. "I had this idea I'd get in," I said, lying. "I'm special. It all figures." In fact, I'd grasped at a straw, hoping to tag after Sandy.

"Just listen to this," Father said, strutting, coughing ritually, and reading aloud to Mother from the letter, " '. . . recognition of exceptional creativity . . . physical and emotional handicaps . . . resourcefulness and ingenuity . . . the courage to overcome the impossible.' " He smiled fondly at me.

"I had to adjust," I observed modestly. "You always have to adjust."

"You zany!" Mother said. "You wiseacre!"

"Ma!" I said warningly. "Watch it!"

"Mr. Tough," she sneered. "Tomboy!"

I walked out of the room. I sat in the kitchen, strengthening my muscles by trying to lift the sink with the flats of my palms.

Father followed me. "Like a football scholarship," he winked. "You're carrying the ball." He grinned, the cave of his mouth amplifying his syllables. "The Crimson forever! Three cheers for Harvard!"

But that night I overheard their honest reactions. Harsh tones and high voices came tempting me, drifting in from behind their bedroom door; catlike, I tiptoed closer. ". . . not again! Out of the blue. Every few years! It's a blow," Father was saying, "it's a real blow! Free tuition! Grand. And how am I going to pay for the rest? And what's wrong with City College? He could live with us. How much more can I shell out, for Godsake?"

Mother, not far from the mark, consoled him with, "Don't blame the wrong one. It's all her brother's fault, you mark my words, *he* put the little gypsy up to this."

But Sandy, as it turned out, solved everything.

To be precise, I'd received a Harvard University Research Grant. Not that Harvard expected me to engage in research; they were going to do the research on me. The Harvard Institute for Research in Endocrinology lusted after my body—or, as HIRE put it in a letter, my glandular situation was of exceptional significance for college students everywhere in the country. If I would permit my-self to be studied in depth over a four-year period, I'd be eligible for free tuition as a Special Student.

Higher education: it took me twice that many years to see the prostitution in it. For years it didn't even occur to me to ask who had masterminded my lucky break, who had recommended me to HIRE, who had cheerfully suggested they look into me.

Sandy of course.

Me in the great temple of Grand Central Station—all that air enclosed above for no earthly reason, and grey people fluttering like pigeons across the pavement to the ticket windows. The station looked to me like a cross between the Parthenon and the Taj Mahal. I thought it would all collapse over me when Father kissed me good-bye.

Mother shook a bent finger. "Keep away from the boys!"

For once we were in complete agreement. I was overjoyed to be going away to Cambridge because I was sure the specialists I had so far seen had blindly opposed my will out of prejudice and lack of ingenuity. I took the train optimistically because I was sure the foremost endocrinologists in the country would be open-minded. They would possess the needed know-how. They'd make me a woman again.

I spent the first night at Sandy's. He was living in an apartment across the river from Cambridge then. He'd completed premed work over the summer and was just beginning his first year at the Harvard School of Medicine. This time when we shook hands there was no rough stuff. I was at college now, and I resolved to act differently. He took my suitcase and offered me congratulations. I looked around. On the wall hung Oriental prints of a man driving a bull; on the table lay sticks of incense—black sticks in bright red paper, gold stamped. He lighted the remnant of a stick of incense in an incense burner and dropped the match inside. On the floor nearby a plump black pillow rested on a black mat. (I didn't think at the time to make the connection with the pillows and mats of Haidu.) And his bookcases—there were so many books—they worried me and I said so. He turned and asked with a serious smile of penetrating in-terest, "Willie, what do you want out of Harvard?"

"Money," I said.

"That's all?"

"A million bucks," I quipped.

"That's all?"

It wasn't all. Peculiar things snapped into my mind. Everything I could think of all at once began with "M." Motion. Magnificence. Mankind. Monuments. But with half of creation crackling in my ears and making my eyes pop, I couldn't open my lips to let it out. I didn't answer.

He put a drink in my hand. "What's the matter? You've gone limp."

Glass in hand, I shifted awkwardly in his living room, staring anxiously at his bookcases—the new swollen medical volumes mingled with the slimmer texts and journals of physics. On the floor by his chair lay an anatomy textbook, a thousand pages flung open to a blood-red diagram. He said, "I think I've got a place for you to stay."

I didn't follow. "I'm living in the dorms," I explained, and I started to pull out the letter with "Wigglesworth something-or-other—"

He shook his head. "I know. But you're a Special Student." That was true.

"We'll arrange it," he assured me. "It'll save the old man money."

"How much money?"

"Free."

"No shit. How come?"

But I didn't find out until the following day.

And the following day, which introduced me to Cambridge and Harvard, remains undimmed in memory because it was the occasion of my first tumescence.

While the credit for erecting me must go to Harvard in general, it belongs in a narrower sense to the Radiation Lab. In the end it took not only a woman but a six-billion-electron-volt cyclotron—operating simultaneously—to stimulate me. Here the reader, exhausted, may throw up his hands. Will he not be astounded to learn that during this period of inward revulsion against masculinity, when I longed hopelessly day and night to return to my girlhood, when I sincerely wished to abandon the struggle for potency, my giddy sexual organ should suddenly take it into its head to defy the law of gravity? But I must remind the understanding reader of other laws, those of human nature, for instance. My inner upheaval was strictly in accord with the laws of probability.

Sandy and I took the bus together through the rain across the river. We walked down a wet tree-lined mall. We came to a glistening raindrop fence skirting a complex of dripping buildings. It was Saturday, hardly anyone in sight except a uniformed guard. Waving his umbrella, he came out of his booth to stop us at the checkpoint. He made a phonecall. "You know the way?" His umbrella waved us on.

How absurd that decades later, under vicious indictment for treason, I was to be asked by defense counsel to describe to the jury the events of this dizzy afternoon. But I had plenty of reason to recall it exactly, with anguish. In the dryness of the building a hum of fluorescent lights, rising and fading, played tag with us along corridors. It was not unlike the eerie hum, signaling the start of the cyclotron, which I was soon to hear. We turned right. Down three steps, through double doors.

Abruptly it was dark. Colored lights flickered on and off. Except for the dimness, the place looked like a Coney Island penny arcade. Slot machines and pinball machines around the walls. A girl, seated in front of one of the big ones, playing it intently, held a button and threw a lever. Sandy motioned, "Watch." I was already watching. On the deck and panel of the pinball machine, lights began to jitter and burst—a jazz syncopation of flares, a percussion of sharp clicking. Bright zooming. Flare-shine-flicker-flit, rat-a-tat-clickety-zing. Zing. "What's she doing?"

"That's Frankenstein," he said in my ear. The girl? (But Frankenstein turned out to be the machine.) "My supervisor—last year," he whispered. "Did my honors thesis on negative particles under her—with her help—she even taught me to run this monster. She's quite a trick till you get the hang of her."

Machine? girl? "How does she work," I said.

"Frankenstein?"

I nodded. It was peculiar. That whole afternoon we drifted through confusions like these, recurring unwished-for, obeying the laws of probability.

"Well, essentially she records bubble-chamber tracks. The tracks are put on film. The film is run off here. Frankenstein clicks off coordinates. The coordinates are picked up on magnetic tape. The tape gets fed to the computers."

Maybe you understand. I didn't. I stopped asking questions. On a screen glowing in the gloom, I watched a dark arrow pick its way along a black-and-white network of gyrating swirls and darting sparks. Zing. Zing, zing. And then suddenly a burglar alarm. Jackpot? Eureka? Fire in the boiler room? I still don't know. She stopped the bell, stood up abruptly—I guessed it must have signaled some error—and suddenly she noticed us watching her. But it wasn't *she* who was startled, it was me. The woman looked like me!

Now remember, I had a crewcut. But in the half-light I could make out the same Byronic chin, the same bony long perfect nose, the same tense bow of the lips. And with the glow of the screen directly behind her, I thought she was fair. But when she switched on the lights, I could see that her hair, cut almost as short as mine, was dark. She was older, too, of course, though I wasn't sure how much. "This is my kid brother Willie," Sandy said. "Willie, meet Flaminia."

She stood in her stocking feet—she had slipped off her shoes while working—and she extended her arm to shake hands. I've never had my arm (not just my hand) pumped so hard by a woman: she leaned into a handshake with her shoulder, like pushing open a stuck door to friendship.

I said, "Glad to meet you, Miss Frankenstein."

This, Flaminia took to be a witticism. She laughed—and again I saw myself mirror-image—except of course for the fullness of flesh and the darkness of hair—and nobody said a thing about it. Sandy was making inquiries instead. "Do you think Satori would be willing to put the kid up?"

"He does not look to me a trouble."

Italian? Her accent lilted. She sat down again to put on her heels.

We went on toward the cyclotron, Flaminia clicking ahead of us. "Flaminia is in the high-energy group," Sandy explained.

This made me uncomfortable, but remembering my high school training, I made up my mind not to ask questions. He said to her, "Let's have a look at the bubble chamber. Willie, would you like to see it?"

I nodded. I thought it must be a bathtub.

She made a funny clucking noise with her mouth and shrugged. "They have it apart to clean." Her accent was pleasant. Ease and music in it. "Never mind, we try." She swayed charmingly along on her heels, very sure of herself. It struck me how *unlike* we were. Mentally she seemed so securely a man, physically so securely a woman. Of course with the passage of time, as now I know, Flaminia was to be fulfilled in me. That's why she so excited me in the long run. What I saw in her, what Sandy did not see, was not myself, but a point in future time toward which my self was racing.

The cyclotron was housed in an enormous amphitheater—all

high air and black struts and overhead lights—and from the catwalk up there, where Flaminia took us, you could look down on the giant itself. It looked exactly like a circular hallway; round and round it went, meeting itself, going nowhere, sealed off, and wrapped like a parcel. "Even a small leak of radiation," Flaminia remarked as she picked her way carefully in her high heels down the wooden steps of the catwalk, "at high speeds like this, why, I—so!—could tear a hole through a man's body."

The idea of Flaminia tearing a hole through a man's body upset me for a while and I began to miss some of the explanations Sandy was relaying into my ear—about particles pulsing into the bubble chamber—"Then the pressure drops, the bubbles ping, the film snaps—"

"Listen," I interrupted, "about the apartment, please—"

"Not an apartment. Flaminia lives with her father-in-law, it's a big house, there's plenty of room if they want to put you up. Flaminia—"

He turned to her, but we had just reached the bubble chamber, and, "Look this," she said. I noticed this was the second time she'd avoided answering Sandy's question—noncommittal about me still—avoided it by either accident or skill. "You see," she said, "it is quite open. This I never see before."

It lay in two pieces on the floor, and though it was probably made of dark-grey cast metal, it looked hewn out of dark stone, like a stone bathtub fit for an emperor, with a great slab of a cover alongside it. Flaminia bent one knee on the edge, poking her head down. "Look these reflecting surfaces inside." She appeared ready to hop in for a bath. The outer walls of the tub were about two feet thick—the kind of dead weight only a crane could lift—but though bigger outside, the inside hollow was a perfect bathtub size, six feet long.

Trying to say something intelligent, I said, "How come you've never seen the inside of a bubble chamber before if you work with it all the time?"

"I work from instruments," Flaminia explained, straightening. "You study at Harvard?"

"She gets opened only for inspection and cleaning," Sandy remarked, peering at the surfaces.

Shocked, I must have turned color. Flaminia stared at me attentively for the first time. "You do not interest yourself in physics?"

My lip held tight between my teeth, I shook my head.

We went on. "This is my shack where I do most my work,"

Flaminia said, ushering me into her "shack." And in fact, situated directly under the amphitheater, she had a small wooden cabin with a rough wooden door—about the size of a bathroom, but filled like an airplane cockpit with instruments—dials, dials, and dials, a dozen dozen meters, rheostatic switches whose function she explained, and a couple of small screens. "So I can look what is happening in the bubble chamber, but I do not, it is now not important, because we have it now on the film. What will he study?" This last to Sandy, who had guided me into a seat.

He didn't answer. Instead, he said to me (or to her?), "Flaminia was the best boss I've ever had," with the merest firefly of a grin.

I looked at her for confirmation. "I was supervisor the work for his thesis, however, he was having two supervisors, it is not important. Well, so you think you would live with us? My father-in-law is Satori, you know him?"

I imagine half the civilized world by that time may have heard of at least the *name* Satori for his work on Minos, but as for me, it rang no bell. "*Professor* Satori?" I guessed. It was a good guess.

But as a result I learned no more. Flaminia nodded. She looked at Sandy, she looked at me, and closing her eyes slowly, slowly said, "I think it is not a good thing."

Sandy said, "Flaminia, don't be difficult." When she kept her eyes closed, he said, "For Godsake!"

I got up, pretending to examine one of the meters near the door, and sidled out without a word. I was embarrassed, confused, and annoyed: it was as if they had exposed themselves with deliberate intent to embarrass, confuse, and annoy me. I stood in the amphitheater, looking across the neon expanse to where a barn door seemed to be opening. Gradually as the door opened, the air took on the blue-yellow tint of sunlight and I could see wet trees and ivy and the nearest buildings. One just doesn't say to one's supervisor . . . unless one . . . "Flaminia, don't be difficult" . . . he might just as well have said to her in my presence, "Flaminia, lie down" . . . but that was not the chief thing that ached in the pit of my groin. Together they evidently could and did inhabit an intellectual kingdom I could not enter. Physics. Science, not just sex; research and discovery, not just woman and man. From that moment the trite phrase "physical love" took on a new dimension for me. Cyclotronic. Parity. She and he whirled together with all their electrons and pions on collision course, brain and body in their bubble chamber.

Readers of my verse will remember

> My cunt knows physics.
> Her degree's from the moon.
> But for my mind exists
> No physic. None.

and, recalling the government's persecution and my trial for treason, will be aware that I became interested in physics later on in my own way. The recent interview in the *Paris Review* quotes me at elaborate length on the subject of that appalling trial, as well as on the long-standing critical argument about my *Physical Comedy*. And I will not enter again into this nauseating dispute. I'll say only this. Everyone grants that the phenomenal world can be divided into physics and psyche. And psyche, one easily assumes, especially from what the Canadian surgeon Penfield has by now demonstrated indisputably about the nature of brain tissue, may be regarded certainly as a function of physics: great mind is a function of grey matter. But there is a catch to all this. Everything Einstein has told us about relativity makes it clear that by a mere shift—a quite legitimate shift—of our system or "frame," it makes absolutely the same sense to say either that mind is a function of matter or that matter is a function of mind. Of course today there is enormous resistance against adopting the latter "frame." To ask any scientist of one's acquaintance to see—even to conceive theoretically, only for the sake of argument—that matter is a function of mind is to ask for trouble. And further, it is probable that the grim and widespread refusal to regard phenomena in this way is not sheer pigheadedness at all. More likely it represents, for the time being, simply the far more fruitful approach to scientific investigation. Still, as a poet, I would insist—and have insisted—that the far more fruitful approach to poetic investigation is precisely the opposed view, the opposite system or "frame": psyche creates the world, at least in poetry. (But a world, yes, a hard physical world, it must in fact create.) There is "soul verse" and there is "thing verse," but in a great poem every line is both soul and thing and you cannot separate them. Psyche and physics.

I returned to Flaminia's shed, expecting to find them making love, backed up against switches and meters, causing short circuits in the baffled cyclotron. I even took the precaution of peeping through the tiny reinforced-glass window in the door before pushing it circumspectly open. Still arguing about me? Very obviously they were in the midst of something disturbing. Arm raised, Sandy was shaking his elbow and curling his index finger. His yellow dandelion hair had shaken loose, the way I'd once loved, over his smooth temples. And strong-willed Dr. Satori (as I learned later Flaminia was called at the lab: she was married to old Satori's son) was shaking her cleft chin firmly from side to side, though you could see she was amused at him—and I thought, God, what the hell do I care if she doesn't want me to live with her, and why does Sandy want me to anyway, and I don't want him discussing my problems with her. I really think I was about to shout, "Don't argue with her about me," as I opened the door, but what I heard was something along these lines.

". . . theoretically—"

Flaminia, waggling her chin with much amusement: "No!"

With a spurt of his elbow: "Yes!"

Her chin: "No!"

He drew her to a little table and began writing a neat ladder of equations running down a pad of graph paper. Controlling himself, he said utterly without excitement, "Theoretically, in a negative four-dimensional Riemann space—so—a particle—an anti-muon, let's say, with mass y and left-hand spin—would intersect the system of coordinates along an axis running—"

"But why a *negative* Riemann?"

"That's just *it*. At intersection point P, particles would scatter inversely along the negative square of the axis."

She bent to examine the equations.

Sandy said, "It's worth a try."

I went out. They had noticed me, but hadn't even stopped talking, stopped arguing, stopped loving each other.

The big barn door had been closed. From far across the cyclotron structure I could hear men's voices. I wondered how many women physicists there were in the world. I wandered back to the bubble chamber. It was quiet there. And this time as I looked at the heavy grey oblong chamber, with its heavy grey cover open at its side, it reminded me not of a bathtub, but of a sarcophagus, one of those monumental Egyptian relics I had seen in museums. I stared. It was very still. Someday this bubble chamber, too, would be a relic, as I would. And then, half-hypnotized, I got in and I lay down flat inside. I waited for Sandy to come and find me there, perhaps to "bawl me out" for crawling in where I didn't belong, God how I wanted to pick a quarrel with him, and after a second or two I recognized a familiar burning sensation in my mouth and knew I was seething with double jealousy, my entire body humming with the force of that feeling.

I became aware of a vibration at first—all along my tense body and then in my ears, a profound noise that I could more easily feel than hear, pulsing into my flesh from the inside surfaces of the bubble chamber itself. The cyclotron, I thought, good God—get out. Up. I was terrified (though in fact I was in no danger). Paralyzed by my terror, I lay still, realizing, no, it's me, it's me *pulsing*. My entire physical being was vibrating from within, shimmering with a blur of fear and envy. I was surprised and ashamed of myself, but it was true. I envied Flaminia for possessing Sandy in a way I never could since I'd become a boy. Irrationally, I was also jealous of Sandy for possessing her—someone who visibly excited him and invisibly gratified him, a woman who was me and was not me, but who should have been me. I wanted her because I wanted to be Sandy, to have her, to be him, and so to possess myself.

Unable to budge, I imagined Sandy cupped between her nuclear knees, Flaminia rising to the pressure of his magnetic thighs. The eerie electronic hum spread—upward from the nails of my toes to the back of my neck and down again to my fingernails. I saw her opening her negative four-dimensional space for him, I pictured him entering with mass y and left-hand spin, his entire system of co-ordinates running along her axis until he and she intersected at point P, perfectly, magnificently, all their particles inversely scattering. The drone, the pervasive resonance within me: something was happening, something had changed. I put my hand down, I touched myself between the legs.

No, I wasn't stiff. But almost. I was pulsing at the core. I was half-erect—both soft and hard—and curved like a vine.

"Congratulations!" We were on our way back when I told him what had happened to me. He clapped me on the back. "That's the way!"

"Who needs it?" I grumbled, disappointed.

"That's half the battle!"

"Half a hard-on? So? So what?" It was still with me in my pants, semi-secret, semi-erect, uncomfortable. "What do I do with it now? Does it show?"

"Shut up, just shut up." He shook my shoulder with brotherly tenderness. "This calls for a celebration!" He ducked into a package store, pulling me after him.

"Yesterday we celebrated—"

"That was for getting into Harvard. This is an erection."

He found the clerk. "A bottle of chilled champagne," he ordered. We brought it back to his place. "And a fat joint. You're on your way!" he said, rolling it. I'd already smoked with the Rattlers a few heavy times, but grass and champagne? He put down the finished joint and picked up the chilled bottle. "A magnificent prognosis. And when you come, when you finally climax, may it be like this." He popped the cork. It bounced with the stunning violence of a double explosion—out of the bottle and off the skylight—the white fumes gushed, the bubbling liquid rushed out of the narrow throat of the bottle, it wouldn't stop coming, we held our glasses and we tried to catch as much of it as we could, but a continuing, eddying stream of it soaked the floor. Sandy drank to my health. "Happy days!"

Impressed, I drank. (Nowadays the ejaculate always has for me the festive bubbliness of champagne.) But I had reservations. "Maybe it was an accident."

He tilted his glass, he shook his head. "A fascinating experiment. So you sneaked back to the bubble chamber . . ."

"But not for that. Look, it just *happened*, Sandy."

"Just happened?"

"A fluke."

"Not a chance." He finished his glass and leaned forward, passing me the lighted joint. After he exhaled, he said, "The conditions were perfect. It supports my theory of the physics of personality. Into the bubble chamber and—phoom!—a new man. Medicine is still in its infancy, just as much as psychiatry. Both of them now imagine they're advanced because they're moving in the direction of chemistry. Biochemistry, virus states, mind drugs, psychopharmacology— but it's mere child's play still. The final direction will be physics. That's how I'm beginning to look at it. Molecular physics in medicine. Subatomic physics in psychiatry. Character? Organic structure? Disease, health, every conceivable order and disorder of soma and personality, they're all going to be viewed as fluctuations in fields of force. All medicine and all psychiatry will be founded in the study of particle physics. And all treatment will be a refinement of what you experienced today. That's my theory."

I passed it back to him. "Look, Sandy, you're way off base." How could I tell him? And should I risk it? "I was lying there jealous of you and Flaminia, that's all, so I was lying there—"

"Precisely. All emotional states are physical states—it was pure physics."

I gave up arguing. "Anyhow, believe me, I didn't want it."

"The hell you didn't. You did."

I closed my eyes and downed my glass. "No. It was pure fluke. I've changed, Sandy. I've changed my mind completely. Flipflop."

"Polarities, mass, and vectors in your brain cells shifted and—whoops!"

He worried me. "Sandy, you don't get it. I've reversed my field, I've switched my bets, I've thrown in the towel—"

"Come on, come on—" He poured me a second glass. He began rolling a second joint.

I worried some more. He was right. I was caught in my own contradiction. Caught, I stammered insistently, "The last couple of months I've pissed blood, I had to swallow such a pile of crap—" No, that was too sweaty, too strong, it had a stink of masculinity about it, I tried saying it differently. "—don't you understand, I've come to *see* things, so clearly, so—altogether freshly, my origins and my true needs, by witnessing such gross unnecessary stupidities—" No, that was too curled and well brushed, demanding and at the same time delicate, it had a curl of femininity about it. I gave up trying to explain myself. "I'm just going to ask the doctors here to make me over again into a girl."

He coughed. He spilled his champagne. He bent, picked up the joint, and dried the floor with his handkerchief. "Willie," he coughed and coughed. He couldn't speak.

I was their prize. Harvard's only genuine hermaphrodite. I received every attention. I saw physicians and physiologists of every description: internists, biochemists, radiologists, urologists, gynecologists, psychiatrists, anatomists, geneticists, and of course endocrinologists. And from the very first, from the morning of my initial visit to HIRE, my situation became transparent to me. If anyone was going to solve my sexual problem, it would have to be me.

Room after room was stacked with monstrous equipment: X-ray machines that dangled from runways in the ceiling over metal "beds" that rose, pivoted, and stretched on invisible command; three-dimensional steel frames, calibrated in centimeters, into which the entire human body or any part thereof—the head, the foot, the thigh, the phallus, the pinky—could be speedily locked, immobilized, measured, recorded, and photographed; electrograph tables from whose edges arched thin wires and delicate plates, flexibly formed to fit the scalp, wrists, chest, labia and/or scrotum, soles, tongue, eyelids—

one at a time or all at once—and from beneath which a thick cable ran to an instrument panel of windowed meters, inked pentips and rolling graphs. All of this so touched me with respect that I bowed to it mentally even when I was merely giving blood or filling out questionnaires. One afternoon, waiting for one of the clinicians, I wrote the verse that follows:

> On a run his heart has stitched
> Ink prances. Deaf and dumb
> Roll the drum for pianola dances.

—and students of my work will recognize in these unimportant but interesting lines the germ of that later effort of mine, "Whoever Picks My Lock" (from *God As Spy*), which opens with the bolder

> My mystery cracks,
> My secrets leak.

Years afterward in collating manuscript copy for an edition of my collected poems I noticed that even in the earlier verse I had attempted to register the feeling that clear categories and exact measurements were deaf-and-dumb distortions of nature. Opaquely expressed, the feeling was there in the early piece because it was everywhere implicit in my experience and contact with HIRE.

I grew accustomed to probing questions and probing in general—not only of my genitalia, but of every bodily organ and function (I had not realized how many I had)—my gums, my joints, my lymph, my nails, my uvula, my scalp, my muscles, my sacrum, my tibia, my body hair, and even on occasion my blisters became the objects of scrutiny. Did I mind? Not at all. To be measured and defined was pleasing. It fed my vanity. It was a source of satisfaction to relax while calipers were applied to my hips; to engage the orthopedist in polite questions-and-answers while my X-rays were illuminated before us, vast and authoritative; to yield my tears and urine to the lab technician (a sweet girl who took whatever I gave, exuviae or effluvia, body hairs, blood, or excrement, took them always with the same private, gratified smile); to offer generously for electron microscopy copious quantities of skin scrapings, smears, and spittle. I always made it a point to give considerably more than was asked, in gratitude for the grant which made my Harvard education possible.

"I guess it's a case of poetic justice," I complained to the specialist who examined me first. "I'll never be able to make it through Harvard now."

"Lots of young men your age, Mr. Niemann—"

"Willie, please—" Other college boys gradually resign themselves to being addressed as men. Not me. I always suffered the "mister."

"Why doesn't it go down?" I got the feeling he was awfully damn proprietary about *my* flesh and blood. I could hardly stomach the professional snoopiness in his manner.

"Nothing remarkable about tumescence—" he palpated.

"Except—" he manipulated.

"Unless—" he rotated. "How long have you had this?"

I told him, grumbling and sputtering, "Of all the lousy times to get excited, during freshman orientation week."

"Can you feel anything?" he irritated.

"I'll have to sneak into classes—"

"Any discomfort?" he elevated.

"I'll be unable to concentrate. I'll be—"

"Splendid," he congratulated.

"My ass."

"A splendid intersexual condition, Mr. Niemann! You're just out of high school, but you're even *more* interesting than we expected."

He really rubbed me the wrong way. "Stop testing the thing," I muttered. "Just fix it."

He continued rapping and tapping, inserting and hurting, exploring away. "By golly! By golly it *is!* Fascinating!"

"Is what?"

"Priapism. A distinct case of priapism, do you realize how rare that is?"

I eyed him coolly. I'd always been considered unusual, but I thought his enthusiasm vulgar in the extreme. "Why don't you just get rid of it," I suggested.

"Get rid of it, son?" He took his eyes off my new burden reluctantly. He wobbled his head slowly. "There's no known cure for priapism, Mr. Niemann. Your sphincters are partly contracted, so naturally the blood vessels retain the supply of blood. The tissues in the organ are naturally elastic, and so naturally you have what we might call a semi-erection. It's nothing to worry about. Get dressed."

I sat up so that the blood left my brain. For a few seconds I was dizzy and couldn't see. I thought I was only impatient with him. Annoyed, I clenched the edge of the table. "Doctor—look—" I tried to think of something threatening to say, some warning, but I discovered I was numb with anxiety. "Everything that goes up . . ."

He shook his head. "Sorry, Mr. Niemann."

"But there must be a way."

He shook it again. "The only known remedies are extremely harmful, a good deal worse than the disease, so to speak. Unless complications develop, I wouldn't advise them. No doctor would."

I gazed helplessly at him.

Gradually, however, as I began to get dressed, my vision cleared. "Frankly," I told him bitterly, glaring and stuffing my tie down into my pocket, "I don't believe you."

He shrugged. "Does it interfere with your sleep?"

"That isn't the point."

"Does it hurt when you walk?"

"That isn't the point either."

"Then what's the problem? You're halfway there. I'll bet it feels good. Damn good."

"Now look," I lost my patience, "the problem is I don't want it at all, I'm neither here nor there, and I don't want to be *there*. I want to be female. I want your help. I started as a girl and that's where I belong." I'd finally blurted it out.

His head was long, equine, but thick-jowled like a cart horse or a mule, with rubbery insensitive lips and open wrinkled nostrils and heavily lidded eyes. He narrowed his rheumy eyes and smiled. He put his hoofs into the pockets of his white coat. "We're not surgeons here," he said. "We're endocrinologists."

"I don't want surgery."

"But you want to be a woman. How?"

I stared back at his twitching nose. Was he amused? Did he have flies?

"How?" he repeated, snickering maddeningly.

"I don't know how. But I've made up my mind."

"The evidence to the contrary notwithstanding?" He pointed crudely and smiled openly.

"That's my *body*," I insisted. "Don't you see? I'm not *that*. From the start, from the very beginning, I—me—my identity—was female."

"That's an interesting theory. But our plan here at Harvard is not to tinker around, patch you up, or alter you according to anyone's theory, yours or ours, until we know a lot more about you than we do." He explained mulishly that one of the prime aims of the Institute's four-year program would be to study the relative stability and balance of the masculine and feminine in me—not only hormonally, but structurally, psychologically, cellularly, and genetically. "When we know enough, we might be able to help you."

"In four years!" I couldn't believe it. If they wouldn't do it, I'd have to make myself a woman. Somehow. "Four years?"

He nodded. He *must* have known I couldn't wait four years. I pointed to the evidence: "And meanwhile?"

"Meanwhile, keep it tucked in."

"Commander" was what Flaminia generally called him when they were speaking Italian—"*Comandante*." Commander of what? He seemed to have other titles whose significance puzzled me too. One was "*l'Onorevole*," The Honorable: in what? for what? Flaminia said, introducing me, "Comandante, quest' è il fratello." I remember feeling uneasy. Was I tucked in properly?

He had been reading in a leather chair in the living room as we came in. Scratching the back and top of his head, he slid his brown hornrimmed glasses (which he always wore attached round his collar by a black ribbon) down his nose and let them fall, but he didn't look at me, he looked at Flaminia. In Italian, the next minutes escaped me: I couldn't even tell who was asking questions and who was answering, but it was peculiarly intense on both sides. Talk stopped abruptly. Satori felt with his knuckly fingers for his knuckly glasses, adjusted them and began reading again. He hadn't looked at me.

Now even at that time I was unwilling to stand for this sort of treatment. To remain *unnoticed* filled me with reckless rage. I said, "Professor Satori, my name is Willie Niemann. You're going to hear more of that name one of these days."

Walruslike in his chair, he vented a few groans, unastonished, but he did not look up. I felt like hitting him.

I left the room, following Flaminia out into the hallway, and in her presence I felt mortified, unable to move further. "I show your room," Flaminia said.

I shook my head. I had three choices—none of which included going to see my room. One was to lean against her stupidly and sob—that was what I felt most like doing; another was to walk out of the house—which would have been the simplest and yet least satisfying; and the third was to go back and actually attack the old man physically—the most improbable. Even as I turned back into the living room, I sensed that it was because it was improbable that I had to do it.

"You shithead," I began as coolly as I could, "I'm telling it to you, so get it straight. That's right, *you*, fuckface, I want you to know—"

"I know it already," he said. He looked up. His eyes were a mottled yellow with brownish streaks like the marbles Sandy used to play with—and as I stared, the profanity drained out of me, and I knew, too. I knew that he knew what I wanted him to know.

His hand slowly traveled down his shirt front, idly inserting his glasses under his half-open vest, his eyes not following the movement. And at the same moment I became aware of the special light of the man.

I lived with him long ago, but so intensely that his image vibrates still in memory. I see him in many rooms, at many hours, in many countries. I see his heavy head with its shag rug of yellow-white hair, I see his ugly nose (enormous—more than a facial feature, it was a trademark), I see the thick dirty nails with which he scraped walls and dirt and powdery clay and spidery coral, I see the tender raw scar where he'd had his foreskin removed (I'll explain this later) and the purple varicose bumps on his testicles which I enjoyed nibbling (any obscene thoughts the reader may entertain at this suggestion are irresponsible and unjustified), I see the white hair crawling up out of his collar, I see those awful old-man's glisteny silk ties he wore, I see the charcoal eyebrows and ash wrinkles around his eager gentle yellow eyes. And all these details, as I said, shimmer, they twinkle with vitality. Yet none of them, none of them, gives any idea of the man's extraordinary force, his uncanniness.

He had an aura which in my own mind I can only call discovery. One normally thinks of discovery as an event—something that happens or something one does, an accomplishment—but with Satori it was a light, the luminousness of the man himself. People give off heat, sweat, yes, even light. Satori emanated discovery. The shine was in the man, not merely in his accomplishments. I knew next to nothing about him as I stood before him in his living room, and yet *I* discovered something with him, for he had the knack of communicating to others the motive spring and tension of his being. What I discovered was myself.

"Will I?" I said. No voice had spoken; it was not a matter of telepathy. But I knew he had discovered me.

"Oh yes," he said, nodding.

"That's impossible." I was only slightly alarmed, wondering how he knew. "It'll never work."

"They'll work together. For example, shit and head. Or for that matter, fuck and face. Study etymology. Get down into the roots of things. Do. That's where the real tangles show up."

Caught off guard, pretending a sudden need to scratch the side of my thigh, I ran my hand inobtrusively across the front of my trousers. A slight telltale sign. A trace. So that was how he knew. Still, it was remarkable how he could proceed in this fashion from the merest shadows of evidence. I asked, "And then?"

He smiled. "Oh yes," he said, nodding, "very great. Magnificent. You will be formidable. But—patience . . . you must grow . . . how shall I say—" he had only the slightest accent, and what little accent there was, was far more British than Italian—"less rich with your eyes, more of a beggar, less fingers and more palms, you know, don't scratch, don't try to make a scene. Only adore the scenery."

It was something like that, and I didn't grasp it all, though I know now exactly what he meant. But more than my goal, more than my wished-for greatness, had penetrated; I'd seen—and obvious as it may be, I'd never *seen* it till then—that it was not to be attained by direct means, but only by beggars and worshippers and other light-fingered people. When I left the room, I noticed that, ignoring his own admonition, he'd already begun scratching himself under his belt. Perhaps he was glad to be rid of me.

Flaminia was waiting. I must have looked peculiar. When she smiled, the bow of her lips arched with amusement, I found her mirth not unpleasant. She motioned me to follow her. I murmured, "Something else, isn't he?"

"He has sixty-two," she said, without the slightest relevancy that I could make out. "Here is your room."

A high white bed, white curtains, an old secretary, a stained mahogany dresser.

Very dignified, very formal, she said, "I want that you stay with us here and that you pass here a very happy time." She reached for my hand and shook it—I didn't expect a handshake since she was about to leave—she pumped my arm with that characteristic force, her womanly energy coming from her elbow, leaning into the shake with genuine style and genuine welcome. And that's what she said. "Welcome, Willie. I am pleased for you." Such frankness, such kindness: before relinquishing my hand, she gave it a warm squeeze.

I held on. She was a godsend.

Her fingers fluttered for release, then relaxed in my grip. She examined my face quizzically, a parenthesis appeared at one corner of her lips, her lips fluttered, too, second by second they were more amused—our handshake, protracted, was no longer a handshake, not at least for me. Slowly her eyes fell. They fell further. And the fluttering succulent stem in my underwear rose toward her sunny smile like a heliotrope.

She laughed, she couldn't help it, and those breast-deep distant gunshot cries of amusement, her tactfully withheld, finally forthcoming laughter, filled me again with gunshy adolescent desire. Once more she'd touched me unwittingly at my hitherto paralyzed core. And this time—whether or not she was in some sense myself, whether or not she was in any sense Sandy's—I made up my mind to possess her. Was it possible that I could be excited only by some version of myself? If so, the discovery was crucial. I made up my mind—someday—with my own erectile God-given priapism—to enter flamingly into Flaminia herself.

But how?· How to arrange a seduction? Like all other college men, I was obsessed with one thing. I can no longer recall anything I learned in the courses I took, any of my professors, any of my books. Yet I can still recall vividly the half-tumescent phallus I had to take along everywhere I went—to lunch, to the library, to all my classes. So much for the first year of Harvard education.

I learned to insulate my electric organ—its negative despair and its positive ambition—behind a jock. I learned to walk non-magnetically, attracting no attention in the Widener reading room despite thousands of eyes. I learned to study anywhere, sitting or standing, despite occasional trills on my instrument, musical semi-hemi-demi-quavers down below. I never became fond of it; only tolerant. It was a cross, yet I intended to make it a tool, an instrument of seduction.

But how? Surely one had to proceed to bed by cunningly gradual degrees, by a slow, sly intimacy in things of the mind, through common interests privately shared. Sandy had physics. And I? . . . had an inspiration: Italian. Excited by the chance to converse at home with Flaminia and her father-in-law, stimulated by the large number of books and periodicals in Italian lying around, I registered for an intensive course in the language and made exceptional progress. I parroted Flaminia's accent, as indeed I parroted her in every way.

Alone, I spent most of my time with one finger in her Italian-English dictionary.

Flaminia made simple conversation with me in my new language as often as I requested. Mostly we spoke English—but even so, I ate and drank in Italian. Sometimes before dinner she'd serve me a liqueur—she liked Strega, which I detested; I liked Campari best, since she said it was mostly for men—and she would chat with me. Pursuing her cunningly, I asked if there were many girl physicists in Italy —or for that matter in the United States.

"There are proportionately in Italy more," she told me, speaking rapidly, "many more. You see, for women are quite few professions possible in my country besides to teach. On the other hand, atomic physics is a recent material, a new career, which is not already sealed in a tradition, so results that the women may enter it freely as the men. *There* is less prejudice than in medicine, for example, as a woman, but that is not so true here."

She spoke with quick-as-flit, simple earnestness which (because I was unused to it) struck me as both comical and impressive.

"What will you choose to make, Willie," she said, "for your life?"

Money? "Physics maybe. Why not?" College was the time to decide on a professional career; to hell with money, I saw how to decide: another interest shared, it wouldn't hurt. I slumped down on a leather chair. "What made *you* want—"

"I had very early some talent for the mathematics. In physics were the opportunities more high, well, in sum, more money was in physics."

"More money!"

"Yes, certainly, I had not so much, it is difficult for a girl, and in the university the Commander Satori was a large help to me, for many years, with money, with friends, for the sake of his son."

I started to ask how long she'd been married when abruptly she sat on the sofa, spreading her skirt over her knees with a quick motion and patting the cushion alongside her, "Come, sit here to me," she said—and I rose to sit by her—and she added, "and sit *so*, with your legs *so*, like *so*."

Did she know something? It seemed a very odd thing to say— as if she were talking to a girl. I reassured myself at once that maybe she was only changing the subject in order to distract me . . . be- cause I'd asked about her husband. But God, do I remember all those *so*'s and how I flushed sudden blood in my cheeks as I flipped my legs up under me any which way. There were only two possible explanations. Either she'd heard from Sandy that I'd once been a girl, or else she'd seen a telltale trace of my demiurge. I said crudely, "In this country a guy can sit any damn way he pleases."

She sipped her yellow drink. "So." She looked upset, too. "I'm sorry." She stroked my cheek. Her eyes were wide, wet with the liqueur of sympathy.

"Okay," I said. "So you know." I was irritated and writhing.

She shrugged, a careless, friendly shrug. "Willie, you have heard perhaps in physics of the Indeterminacy?"

I said nothing. Of course I hadn't. And further, I wasn't sure I wanted to.

She said, "In quantum theory, is possible only to measure of a particle *either* the position accurately, listen, or the velocity accurately. But not both. Not both in once. I am thinking of you, Willie. If more we know one, so less we may know the other. This is the uncertainty always. And it cannot be changed."

I was still writhing. "So?"

"Or of the principle of Complementarity?"

I shook my head. But I was becoming interested.

"By this physics has told to us that of a given system we may always have two descriptions, each contradictory, each mutually exclusive, but both correct. *Because* that they are contradictory, thus are they mutually complementary."

I didn't understand and I said so. But I felt better. Already.

She sighed. "Without the mathematics I cannot explain you very well. But a necessary thing for every formulation of a system must be the incomplete knowledge."

I forgave her at once. I didn't know precisely why. My knowledge remained incomplete. But I forgave her freely.

The Commander came down to dinner. He drank a Punt e Mes. And I didn't find out about her husband either.

Table conversation was about three-fourths Italian, at first I missed three-fourths of what was said. I had to guess or imagine what was in the air—stimulating, but sometimes uncomfortable. Satori would sit at the table with his huge white napkin tucked into his collar, his Adam's apple working away, putting forkfuls of spaghetti with his favorite green sauce, *pasta al pesto*, into the gold recesses of his mouth, while from out of that busy treasury spewed mouthfuls of lore. He had known Schliemann's widow. He had once found an underground tomb by following a lizard. He had taken Isadora

Duncan to see the ruins of Mycenae. She had insisted on dancing there, under a hot sun, on the very spot she resolutely claimed had been Agamemnon's bathroom—she had located the bath itself—a puddle of water still drying on the ridged floor, with the blood still visible in it after three millennia. (" 'Rust,' I explain, 'my dear Isadora, rust, iron oxide.' . . . 'Blood!' she stammers, terrified, 'blood, blood, blood on the floor, blood in the bath!' Terrified. She was an extraordinary woman.") Arab diggers were more careful workmen than Greek diggers. Radiocarbon dating was already a thing of the past—the newer chemical techniques were subtler. He himself did not believe much in aerial prospecting for sites. Everything said for my benefit was spoken in English. Satori was amused by the rough, calf-like, unlicked intensity with which I listened, and he would switch from chitchat in Italian to archaeology in English, just to see me stop eating and look at him with a sudden rapture of attention. He couldn't, however, remain entirely amused for very long. I discovered that all I had to do was to listen to him, really to listen: and precisely because my listening was genuine, my fascination unfeigned, well— even the humor with which he pretended to despise my awed servility slowly broke down, and he became, in a sense, subject to me, the reverse of his captive audience.

Flaminia knew all this, and suddenly she would skip into Italian, taking her father-in-law by the arm, so to speak, away from me, and the air would grow tense with the machine-gun rippling of Romance language. What were they saying? Why did Flaminia look so amused suddenly? Why did Satori's eyelids come down and darken to an almost purple color—was that anger or boredom or nothing at all?—as with practiced ease he scooped the marrow out of his shankbone with the tip of his knife. What did he answer her? Why was she now hysterical, refilling his wineglass? He brushed the shaggy hair behind his neck with his quick fat hand and said something *sotto voce* which made Flaminia even more shrill. I had never seen her so affected, so gay, so un-self-possessed before, she leaned her low vibrant bosom over the table, turning to me as if to include me in their gaiety while knowing perfectly well I couldn't understand it at all, patting my wrist and almost sniffing at me, the loveliness in her throat palpitating strangely. I became aware that it was she who was angry, he who was amused. He didn't laugh; but the lowered veindark lids, the haired nostrils crinkling together in his sunburned dreadful nose, the coming and going and coming together again of the heavy furrows in his cheeks, where as he drank, needlepoints of sweat (his pleasure in his food) showed and vanished—all this was laughter, laughter at her expense. Suddenly their talk exploded again, on and on they tick-tick-ticked and rat-a-tat-tatted.

I imagined what they were saying. Of course. I wasn't going to sit there bored and deprived. I made up whole conversations.

"You're warm tonight, my dear Flaminia, one may be permitted to observe that you are melting with appetite."

"Delightful marrow. And why not, Commander? In my village there is a saying, 'A girl without love is like a hole without marrow.'"

"Yes, but how feverishly you attack that little bone. A bit more restraint. Permit me." He raised the wine.

"Thank you. Of course. But you don't, I notice, fill the boy's glass. No doubt you're afraid it might go to his head?"

"A great deal depends, it's true, on where it goes."

"To whose bone, to whose marrow?"

"You are warm, Flaminia, you are delightfully obscene this eve-ning."

"Your presence—"

"His surely. But what bony little wrists the boy has, compared to his brother's, eh? Hardly any marrow."

"You find him thin? Perhaps. But he has an innocent grace—"

"—common in an American lad, my dear, but alas! rare, most rare, in Italian women. Haven't you observed?"

"I think, Commander, you are an old fool, but that perhaps the child over there hasn't yet observed *you* well." She reached for her wine.

I shuddered. I tried to recover, reminding myself that that was all imaginary. I touched my wine-soiled, giddy lips with the linen of my napkin. Was I far wrong in my invention, was I entirely mis-guided in the play of my imagination on the glint of appearances? But those witty, malevolent looks they gave each other! And the arch bitterness of those machine-gun exchanges! How far wrong could I be? I brought more wine to my lips in a studied imitation of nonchalance—wine was still too new for me to be casual about it. Over the rim of my glass I looked at Flaminia, hoping that my youth-ful eyes looked naïve and seductive. She of course was glaring at the Commander. Satori was totally absorbed in finishing the remains of his salad; his eyes were wet with undiminishable appetite; his lips were oily with dressing. What was he saying? He was picking at his salad.

"There's a hair in the lettuce."

"Whose?"

"It's a pubic hair, how very interesting." He seemed pleased.

"Perhaps it's hers." Grammatically impossible as it was, it seemed to me that I'd heard that Italian pronoun.

"It could be anyone's—mine, yours, his, hers, its, ours, yours, theirs."

Incredible table talk. Hers? Life, however, proved more embarrassing than my imagination's meager grammar. Why did they never mention Flaminia's husband to me? I invented that, too. Unimpeded by language, I was diligent. I was energetic.

"There's no fool—"

"In my village, dear Flaminia, there is a saying: 'It is less foolish to make a fool of yourself than to be fooled by others.' Need I explain?"

"You'd better explain yourself at once."

"Your young guest's magnetism runs in the family. You're making a fool of my son."

"With this child?"

"And with the brother. Between the two of them there's a family resemblance, yes, but your appetite is unseemly."

"Remember, it was your son who left *me*, Commander, not vice versa. Where is he now, eh? does he write to you? Not a word in three years. He is in Rome, so they say—but with whom, with which one of his many whores, does he write and tell you? And I, meanwhile, I am to remain single here, and careful, and seemly, and without—the very marrow of love? Is that your idea, your plan for your daughter-in-law, *Onorevole*, while your own stomach grows full and taut and hard for my friend's sister, this little bitch?"

"Calm down—my son will certainly come back to you. We will go back together to him in a few years, to Rome, don't be upset, calm yourself, you will have money, he will have money—calm yourself!"

"And *I* brought her here! I *brought* her! Her brother, a former student of mine, asks me, I am happy to do my friend a favor, and then night after night I have to sit here and watch you caressing her with your eyes and your tongue and then listen to you tell me *I* am unseemly—*I* am unseemly—because I'm fond of her brother. It is too much, too much, too unspeakably much, you should be ashamed, all of you should be ashamed."

They hadn't said a word of this, but I *was* ashamed—especially because I'd invented it all.

I was waiting for Flaminia to pick me up on Brattle Street to drive me home as she did every Friday afternoon; Sandy arrived instead. He was driving Flaminia's car. "Get in, climb aboard," he said.

I wondered if I could consult him about my progress in seducing his woman. But it seemed to me that I might be pushing brotherly love too far. Still, there's something about one person's driving another person's car that suggests intimacy to me, I sense complete possession in the act, and before I knew it I'd blurted out, "Sandy, you and Flaminia, you're making it together, aren't you?"

The cobbled street gave way to a tar surface. Then he said, "That's a pretty crude question, isn't it? How long have you been in Cambridge?"

We crossed the Charles. I counted the number of license plates on the bridge that had "M" or "W" in them; there were more with "W." I rephrased it. "After a certain age, if people are going out together all the time, in our subculture doesn't that pretty much always imply that they're sleeping with each other?"

He swung left and passed a car.

"That's a more civilized way of putting it," he said. We followed the edge of the river's curve. "Yes," he said.

We were on our way to Sandy's place. He slowed as the light turned orange, made the turn anyway. He said, "She's getting dressed. We're going to pick her up, she ought to be done." All that he told me. "By now," he added.

I said, "Would you teach *me* to drive?" I wondered—would he understand?

"Ask Flaminia." He slowed again. "It's her car." Perhaps he'd understood.

She was standing out front, dressed; she waved and signaled her happiness. She had on an ivory-white dress which I knew she'd made herself. In Italy, she'd told me, she had made all her clothes. Now there was less time and more money and nothing fit her as well. She had just put it on—she could scarcely, I realized, have been at work in that dress—and I pondered all the things I was learning. She and Sandy could hardly have had fifteen minutes together after leaving the lab. She got in alongside me, very leggy and bosomy in her glitter of ivory (but all perfectly smooth under the dress, as she slid inside the car—how did she manage her slide so neatly at that velocity?), and she kissed me and patted me and smiled out the windshield—at what?—some image in her mind.

So that was how it was done. I said, "Flaminia, would you teach me to drive?"

"It is all right," she said.

I had picked the right moment to ask. "Tomorrow?" I ventured.

"It may be." She smiled to herself.

I was talking in symbols of course—a way I had which came to me so naturally that sometimes I vaguely assumed that everybody else must be doing the same thing. Flaminia, who was not given to symbolic utterance, did not understand me yet.

I tried later to explain to Sandy how it happened. Not to apologize, only to explain; but I found that a very difficult thing to do. Love had more to do with flies and birds, that first time, than with sex. It had almost nothing to do with sex.

Saturday was an unseasonably warmish day. I was apprehensive, of course, in fact I was keyed to a pitch of fever-and-chills tension. All night long, in and out of sleep, I'd pondered the imponderable: seduction. By morning I confessed to myself that I had no idea how to proceed, any more than I knew how to drive. Yet just as surely did I know that my hour had come round. And since lovemaking was, *must* be, a natural process, rather than a mechanical one, it must certainly be simpler than learning to drive.

We packed a box lunch in the kitchen. We worked on it together, hardboiled eggs, sandwiches, cheese, wine; and we set out for our lesson late in the morning.

It was sunny, so Flaminia put the convertible top back. She drove out somewhere near Walden and found a back road, a country road, quite straight—and I took the wheel there. I made the usual mistakes at first—the car lurched, I accelerated, it bucked, I braked, we stalled —and so on, *da capo*. Flaminia was remarkably patient, a good teacher. "Pull here," she said, meaning pull over—I braked, stalled, and let a car pass. But I improved rapidly. I discovered that if I pretended I was Sandy, I got better at once—I simply imagined my brother was at the wheel and the car seemed to drive itself. "Stop!" Flaminia cried as we approached a bicycle, but I passed the cyclist with a gentle swing and room to spare. The convertible, as it were, swung out and back. We came to the sedan that had passed us before, sitting empty now in front of a country house, and I tried learning to park behind it. "But you are *grand!*" my teacher exclaimed, as the convertible, quite of its own accord, so it seemed to me, slipped backward into position behind the empty sedan. How I did it, I don't know. I put it into gear, decided I was Sandy, and the car parked.

I suggested the secret of my success to Flaminia. "*Pazzo*," she laughed.

"*Pazzo?*" I queried. "What's that?"

"Crazy." On we went. "Pull here." I stopped with only a slight jerk by the edge of a field. We followed a footpath, found ourselves some trees. It was an isolated spot, overhung with sagging branches. We spread out a blanket, and had our lunch. The eggs were still warm. The moment was propitious. But how? What next? She was eating . . . slowly. She was wearing a dark Italian print, and with her dark hair cut much shorter recently she looked lovely—her eyes were so black—I actually wished Sandy were there to see her. And I said so.

"I meet him after," she said.

That stimulated me. My mouth went dry. My arms were trembling. But I showed no sign of tension. I salted the remainder of my egg. "Are you in love with him?"

"Hush!" she murmured. (What she actually murmured was more like "sssSS!")

"Why? It's all right. You could get a divorce." I liked the mature sound of that.

"In Italy, for all practical purpose, divorce is still limited."

We drank our wine. I let it roll around my tongue as Satori had taught me at the dinner table, tasting it rather than drinking it. Flaminia put down the bitten half of her half of a sandwich and stopped eating. She just sat.

I said, "How *long* have you been in love with my brother?"

She smiled at me. "I have been now happy three months, most four. Not more. It is a too long time, such happiness, and I will pay it with years of misery. I know."

From experience I'd learned she didn't like to talk about her husband; nevertheless, I hinted, "You could divorce him in America." My mind was very clear, very cunning. "You're dedicated to your marriage?" I suggested.

She breathed long and audibly before answering. "No, to my work," she said, and then she added, "I am thirty-one."

"So?"

Flaminia lay down on the blanket. Flies gathered on the cheese. My mouth was on fire and I drank more wine. She looked very beautiful, her eyes closed. I leaned forward and a tiny electric spark flared at the tip of my penis. Risk it now? Was the timing right? Was it absolutely right?

I went back to the car and made the hood go forward for shade. Getting in, I concentrated on the problem. What if someday Sandy and Flaminia were going to be married? I rested my chin on the wheel and pondered, giddy with wine, warm, confused—but not unhappy, it seemed to me; not so sad as Flaminia. Probably Sandy had no such intention. He was young, he had years of medical school ahead, their future was unpredictable; God knows, *I* knew Sandy could be difficult—a charmer, agreeable, no one sweeter, but unpredictable, as full of turns as a country road. The shade of the car was hot. I went back for more wine. I went back with the fear that Flaminia wouldn't be there.

She was lying on her side, eyes open; she didn't look up. I lay down alongside her, resting on one elbow. I focused on how pretty and womanly she was, and yet how manly, just the girl for me. I focused until my groin began to hum and my mind started to develop pins-and-needles. I leaned over her. She nodded. "We go back?" She blew a fly from her cheek, turning up her lip. "You will drive more?"

I shrugged. The sun was hot. In my trousers my mounting penis seemed to have begun a peculiar ticking motion, pulsing like clockwork. Was the alarm going to go off suddenly? Now or never. I lay down completely and I actually embraced her and kissed her lip. She took my hands away from her breasts. "SSsss," she said. She took my hands away from her hips and she shook her head. "SSsss." The flies made noises, too. One landed on my eye, but I just closed my eye and let it walk there. The ticking sensation in my loins was beginning to hurt, the constant pulse of it almost made me wince. How was I supposed to concentrate on lovemaking if the ache continued much longer?

I tried concentrating on Flaminia. "He'll marry you," I said, "you'll see." The fly walked down my nose like a teardrop, but I wasn't unhappy. I stroked a fold of her dress where it rested against the blanket and where there wasn't any of her body inside, just the material and the sun's heat. And now? What next? "I'm not used to this," I said.

"*This* I know." From her tone I thought she must be laughing at me and I opened my eyes quickly. But she looked as lost in thought, as mournful as ever.

"I mean I—"

"I *know.*"

"Everything?"

"Of course sure. Lie still."

Overhead on the lowest branch of the tree a comic woodpecker ticked against the bark. In my pants my own pecker ticked against my fly. I absolutely had to take my mind off the latter. I thought it would help if I could keep my mind exclusively on the one up there with wings instead. It was spotted, with a chisel beak, pale back, tinged underparts. A small bill: a hairy woodpecker? A downy woodpecker? Its throat pulsed. Its beak darted. It was eager. "Flaminia, you're the only—"

"I know this."

A yellow-bellied red-breasted sapsucker?

I turned my head. "Well for God's sake," I demanded, "can't you *do* something about it then?"

Even then she didn't smile. If I recall correctly what happened next, I only touched her mouth with my mouth—gently, not a peck, but it seemed to me that she distinctly gave back a little pressure there, smiling finally against my lips. And after a while, yes, her warm tongue came helpfully into my mouth. For a few seconds the bird up above spread its wings, watching us, suddenly wary of us. A red-shafted flicker? But we hardly moved. Flitting circumspectly to one side, it stayed on the treetrunk. A tilted lean body, a red patch on its head. She stroked my crewcut hair slowly. Nervously, the hairy woodpecker kept flickering its wings.

She began to loosen my clothing. She loosened mine, then hers. She did all the work I should have done, and the nearest leaves ran vibrating away from us while the breeze went through their stems until abruptly they stopped and only one leaf was still vibrant. And how had she managed in six seconds flat to get my nakedness against hers? Mine? The sun was going up, I noticed, but that was impossible in the middle of the day. I kept one eye on the feet of the bird, they were black and splayed, they seemed to slip sideways, but I kept my lips against hers. The moment had come.

I put both my hands around the back of her hips, molding them. She arched her back. Her belly slid against mine, against the one-eyed head of the woodpecker. It throbbed, it turned, hungry for ants, for flies. My ankles twitched and my palms drifted on the small of her back. Harder. Her belly played. It pressed and held me. The wary bird circled clockwise, ticking, tocking against her arching belly. It darted to another tree, inches away. Hunting, my hands turned in her branches, feeding on her breasts one at a time. Her green leaves rippled in the blue air, forming a web of light, and so between my legs I was as hard as a treetrunk now, and I could feel every tick of the beak of the woodpecker as it dipped, glaring with its single eye, and hopped down her navel, over her bark, into the cave in the wood.

Her fingers held me all together, all my astonishing parts, but she was unastonished to find them on me. She folded them slowly between her serene, indifferent hands and then—unbelievable—impatient legs. Good God! The breeze had caught one tree, a tall one with slender leaves. It was sinking into her. It ignited against the impossible glare of the sun, distracting me, uprooted and unbearable now since she held me inside her while the rapidly throbbing head of the big bird swooped to the base of the trunk and paused in mid-flight and settled and Sandy was loud, cawing, bird-singing inside her wood. The hot strong chirp, peck, ran, I was Sandy and there were red leaves. But that was me, too, forcing something she had opened open. The heat of her, the lips of her, she who circled me with her lips, puckered to hold my peeled branch stem prick throat trunk to the smoldering sun, surrounded by leaves, by hair, by her unfurling blue burning waterfall, over the edge I went playing and screaming, backward, long. Circling the white sun a yellow-white band, distinct, blinding. Signaling an oncoming hurricane of light.

The leaves flew away. The woodpecker disintegrated. Feathers against sunlight. One eye, two eyes, three eyes. And the rest of me followed. The long thrust of the living spout went straight, straight, straight to the quickening storm. The winds spent themselves. They tore me, they shredded her, they discarded us.

Five or ten minutes later, Flaminia stroked my chest. We sat up. Hurriedly I adjusted all my clothes—shirttails, underwear, zipper, belt —it would go away later, I thought. Together we put together all the picnic leftovers and headed back along the tiny path to the car. I walked very close to Flaminia, touching arms. It wasn't until we were on the path back to the car that I had the first inkling that something might be seriously wrong. It hadn't gone away. I was protruding half a foot in front.

I got behind the wheel, but I sat there motionless, thinking. I put it into reverse. She corrected me, holding my hand as she moved both my hand and the gearshift into first. "So," she said. "Go."

I drove down the road maybe about two hundred yards to where it curved left and I went off the road going at about twenty miles an hour and hit a tree.

I was white all the way back, white and cold. "It is all right, never mind, only the bumper lies bent," Flaminia reassured me.

I swallowed. I was in a panic.

"What is the matter? You can drive more, everyone makes an incident some time in his life, I trust you, you want right now I let you drive, Willie?" She stopped. Traffic went by. "Here." She tried to put my hand on the wheel, but I drew my hand away. I wouldn't let her touch me. She blushed faintly, and moved her lips without saying anything. She drove again, but now she looked worried.

I couldn't speak.

"Willie, it is all right. Nobody is hurt." I felt hurt. She said, "It was only a bumper."

I nodded. I couldn't look at her. She said, "You go to the library now? I take you."

I tried to think. I couldn't go to the library in this condition. Hadn't she noticed? What did she expect? I couldn't go anywhere. She kept pressing me—the library—a little work would do me good —hadn't I said I had some studying to do when we got back? In a burst of nervous anger I told her for Chrissake to lay off, I had no work to do today, anyhow, so she could drop me off at home. Only —the moment I'd said it, I realized I'd said it in Italian. It was the first time I'd spoken the language unconsciously, utterly without trying, "Porca miseria, non rompermi le scatole, non ci ho niente da fare, lasciami a casa." Effortless. Was *that* how one learned a language? Was I becoming Flaminia, too? But that was the least of my worries now.

As soon as we got home, I hurried out of the car and concentrated on the real issue. I went to my room, closed the door, and uncovered myself. There was no doubt about it. It was Sandy's I had, an unreasonably self-confident, unreasonably accurate facsimile of Sandy's horn, a regular poker, his piston, his hand brake, I was monstrous, I'd had no idea even from my previous condition that I was going to be so conceited when full-blown. My eyes were still staring at myself, aghast, when Flaminia knocked. "You are okay?" she called in. "Willie? You feel well?" She knocked again, anxiously. "Answer to me."

I let her in. Of course I'd more or less covered myself, but there was no hiding the problem. She could see for herself why I was worried.

"Still?" she inquired.

"It's worse. Priapism. A perfect case."

"How? What is that?"

"It began in the cyclotron. It's incurable."

For a moment she looked grave. "Now you stop to worry. Is nothing incurable, Willie. Calm."

"Sandy's." I took it out and showed her. "Look, don't you see? It's his."

She looked, all right, but though scientifically inclined, she couldn't maintain her seriousness, and pretty soon her soft bosom was shaking, each springy breast separately—stop-and-go, sad, explosive, choked laughter.

I regarded her clinically. She struck me as either rude or quite insane. "Can't you stop that?" I requested. She didn't. "Stop giggling!"

She shook her head, holding her torso, holding her waist, uncontrollable. "How can I stop," she cried, gulping for air, "when you are right? That is absolutely his."

"Sandy's gearshift," I nodded.

She murmured, "His what?"

I said, "Organ. Penis."

"Cock," she corrected me. "Do I teach to you your language? His cock."

"Cock," I pronounced.

"In Italian, *cazzo*."

"Plural, *cazzi*."

She grasped it in her hand. She bent and licked it with her tongue. Then while it was still wet, she pulled and raised. I felt as if it were some sort of self-starter. Then—and that was something— an extraordinary sensation—linguistic and automotive—she pulled me across the room, sliding her fingers. It was as if I were a chassis, connected to that drive shaft. I was taken on a tour. Then, still tickled by my melancholy amazement, she pulled it to her and held me against her. "Identity!" she agreed.

I felt I had no hands, no legs, only what she held in her grip. I looked at that wide-eyed, cleft-chinned laughing face of hers and recognized myself. What I'd once been or might soon have become, she was Millie and she'd *said* there was nothing incurable. She'd told me what I'd known once, better than my medicine men. She was me, she was right, I was Sandy, I was sure.

Confident at last, though weak in almost every limb, I slumped into the soft chair nearby and pulled Flaminia down with me. Deliberately. She was startled. It didn't matter to me. Nothing mattered to me.

But she objected. "Willie—"

"Damn it, I want to try again, a person has got to persevere if—"

"But is enough for today, Willie."

"You can't leave me like this, you just can't," I insisted.

She bent her eyes—puzzled—and breathed deeply, a long, confused breath.

Having once learned how, I seemed to know the way. She had a slight odor of oil and gasoline, I thought, but I didn't let that bother me. I smiled and stroked her hair. I'd been so uncertain before, so lacking in masculine initiative, that she was startled. I even surprised myself: my assurance was phenomenal, my actions graceful. But I knew exactly through what simple means I'd learned the manly art of driving. And I was determined now to apply them to sex as well, the primary art. The most important thing was to keep in mind that I had Sandy's. Thoughtfully, I moved my hand on her brows, sweeping smoothly from side to side.

I turned her a bit on my lap. Did she seem slow, cold, unresponsive? Well, I didn't allow it to worry me. The key, I recalled, was the ignition. Knowledgeably, my hands found their way and undid her bra. Everything seemed to be in working order . . . her generator, oil pressure, tachometer . . . to the slightest touch, her jittery meters darted with an unerring delicacy of response. But her idling speed? I listened carefully to the way she breathed and murmured as she kissed me. A slight adjustment, I decided. Nothing simpler. I loosened her knees and reached in under the hood. She leaned forward to help me, but this time I was on my own.

As soon as she was warm and charging properly, I released her emergency. I clutched her. A sensation of power swept through my veins as we moved ahead without the slightest bucking or stalling. I opened her up. "Go easy, slow," she said. But I was too excited to slow down. I held her hips. I put her in second. The sense of all that reserve power was exhilarating. I slipped into third, we turned a corner—too fast, I was going too fast, I jammed on the brakes, pale, and we lurched as her rear end swerved. "That's enough," Flaminia said, her fingers white on my arm.

But it wasn't enough, and I showed her. I looked down and shook my head. Stubborn, inflexible, rigid—not me—Sandy's drive-shaft—the thing was exactly as it had been all along. She sighed. She got up. She undressed, all the while shaking her head sadly. She said, "Now for this time follow me please precisely. I tell you how." She lay back on the bed, nude, and motioned me to come over.

She looked absolutely nothing like a car. But my case was desperate. I concentrated.

Lying on her back, she bent her legs up. I lay down precisely on her cushioning thighs, with her calves kicking air over my shoulders. "No," she shook her patient head, shifting under me. "Go there."

Suddenly I was comfortable and very warm. She had a new reassuring feel, her steering had just the right amount of free play. Idling, I was inspired.

"Willie—"

"Sh." I knew what I was doing. Her turning radius was small, accurate, and tight. I enjoyed slipping her clutch. I practiced gunning her. I braked sharply. She never pulled. Her marvelously designed body was under me and in front of me—firing evenly—so beautifully tuned she was! There was nothing she wouldn't do perfectly. I came to a full stop, kissed her, and took off again, masterfully. "You see?" I said.

She nodded, pleased. "To the left a little. Hold *there*, no— THERE!—yes!"

She was absolutely right. When I took her to the left, I could feel the difference. She handled superbly.

I speeded up. "Please." There was a hill ahead. Flaminia tapped me on the arm. "This do gently."

Around the uphill curve I changed lanes. Flaminia paled. "Signal WHEN, *before*. Is important."

The joy, the marvelous energy behind her. I understood now. Not just the pleasure of driving, but the sense of nearly unlimited freedom, the softness of power, the smooth springing thrust of the ride: I leaned as we swung and surged. "Willie, be careful," Flaminia begged, grasping me with momentary fright, turning her lips against my ear, nervous at my confidence but obviously pleased as we took the astonishing hill effortlessly . . . all the way . . . we crested it.

That sweet accelerating ease as we darted, soaring, swinging faster and faster ahead. Losing my head, I floored her.

"Willie!"

"I love you!"

"Slow!"

But I couldn't.

"Willie!"

I saw it coming but I couldn't stop.

She screamed. "Willie-e-e-ee!" She was still screaming. Was that *me* screaming?—the collision shattered glass into our faces. And we kept right on traveling—unstoppable, out through the front of the machine, an arc through space, bones smashed against bedposts, blood reddening the wallpaper, with our own shrieking momentum hurtling ahead while the machine—its front end bashed, its hood crumpled, its engine useless—stood stock-still behind us—destroyed, watching our joy, our flight.

I ached all over.

Five minutes later I still felt struck down—pierced—drained—split—gored.

Flaminia held my hand. "Is over, is all right, Willie. Is okay. Willie?"

I looked down. Where was it? My priapism had disappeared. My hand brake was released. My penis, thank the lord, was normal again.

I got over it gradually. Ten minutes later I had almost recovered. I ached mildly, pleasantly, hypnotically.

Flaminia kissed me as she left, fully dressed, adjusting her skirt. Something, I noticed, was wrong with her alignment, but I was too tired to care now.

I waited for the pins-and-needles sensation in my groin to go away. I wasn't sure what to think. I'd had so little experience. But I guessed that some tingling, some pain, must be normal after such recklessness.

So I stayed in bed, aching. It was a pleasure to stay in bed with a normal penis after all these months. To my extraordinary relief it had come to rest at last, curled up and tucked away, smaller now than I'd ever seen it, nesting in the sac of my scrotum as if it had pulled the covers up over its throat for warmth, breathing serenely, sleeping, dreaming. With Flaminia's help, I'd done the trick. What medical science had been powerless to exorcise, I had put to rest myself. Hurting happily, I slept, too.

· · ·

Hours later I awoke with a vague ache. Stomach cramps? It was lower. I put my hand down, I felt my scrotum. My testes? Where? . . . the slippery little marbles . . . they were pulled up against my groin. Hernia? Overwork? Strain? Vacation? Should I call for medical help at two in the morning? I was groggy with an immense longing to sleep; my discomfort was only slight. Surely it could all wait till 8 A.M., when I could drop in at the clinic like a reasonable, unfrightened person.

But every two or three hours that night I woke up, and each time the situation was a little different. I got scared when I found I could no longer feel my wandering testes: they'd evidently drifted somewhere underneath my pubic bone. My becalmed penis was no longer merely furled; snail-like, it had virtually drawn its head inside the now vacant sac. The sac itself, enclosing my penis like a foreskin, was no longer chubby and relaxed. It was wrinkled and hard against my crotch as though a spring, fastened inside my abdomen, were exerting a steady, stubborn, irresistible pull on the entire genital system. My vagina? I felt underneath my scrotum for my ancient trapdoor, now a knot of hard lips as indrawn as my navel. But the sealed entrance must have been jolted and loosened, or even torn open a bit, because by God! I was no longer impenetrable! For the first time since my high school operation I could actually get my pinky into the opening. I worked it around inside, shocked, chilled, carsick. Then I stopped, afraid to explore further. But I thought of the great portal in the Radiation Lab, sliding open like a barn door. And it seemed to me that my testicles and penis, the tiny cyclotron and linear accelerator of my manhood, were being sucked upward by the vacuum in my pelvic floor.

I switched on the light when I had that thought. I examined myself. Then I sat there, considering. It was getting on toward dawn. Had I . . . was I becoming . . . ? At 7:45 I looked down. Where was it? Where were they?

At eight sharp I was outside the clinic doors. I waited, only slightly uncomfortable. I saw two physicians at HIRE that memorable morning, I told them in detail of my fulfillment as a boy, and I observed that both men were impressed: whatever irrepressible stimulus had kept my organ for all these months on the verge of erection was now discharged. Fired.

"Well?" I inquired proudly. Were they alarmed? I looked from one face to the other. There was no doubt from their stunned expressions that they were not as happy with me as they should have been.

After thorough investigation they informed me—in fact they told me off irritably—that my original surgical operation had proved unequal to the strain. Evidently the tension of my relations with Flaminia, both natural and mechanical, had been extraordinary. The internal stress had proved to be more than the artificial one-sex structure of an irresponsible (their word) hermaphrodite could be expected to withstand. Couldn't I have used my head! Didn't I have any sense, any restraint? ("Woman is restraint," I recalled.) The internal tissues and muscles built up around the sutures had been overworked, they charged. Overworked, I mocked, or inadequate in the first place? But they refused to accept any of the blame, for themselves or the medical profession in general. They pinned the blame on me and on reflex. The muscular reflex resulting from the strain, as in the case of the trauma that causes infantile hernia, had drawn my depleted and deflated testes and penis up again toward my abdomen. And my male valuables were now once more deposited in the safe deposit box inside the vault from which the masked surgeons had once freed them. For the time being, until the trauma to the tissues had been alleviated, another operation of the same kind was out of the question. To save everything and allow my organs to heal, my reluctant medical men—outflanked and outraged—were obliged to place new stitches to secure my pelvis against further strain—in effect sewing my male organs back inside me . . . as I had wished.

There was some uncertainty, they warned me in obscure technical terms, about the morphological results. I was only human (they granted), nevertheless *no more sex*. I promised. But God only knew (they confessed) what might happen next. It was agreed on all hands, human, technological, and divine, to watch my condition with care.

I remained entirely at ease about all this. I was confident. Not so my physicians. They clucked over me, they pulled long faces, they put me under intensive care. But my seesaw glands now refused to yield anything like normal results. It was during this fervent week of uncertainty that I remember myself sitting gleefully in a padded chair with my arms strapped. One bottle was upside down on a rod over my head, futilely feeding me by controlled drops through a plastic tube into my left arm. Another smaller bottle was vainly emptying its secretions into my right thigh. My right wrist was making a needle twitter and skip to my two-step pulse. It had been over half a year now since I'd begun volunteering my thyroid, pineal, and suprarenal glands; I'd offered up my lymph glands and sweat glands; I'd let them work away at the glands under my jaw, in my stomach, in my armpits, under my tongue. Somewhat unwillingly, I'd even let them fool around with those intriguing glands behind the ears which register and govern excitement. But that day, I recall, it was the emperor. "Every gland is a feudal baron," my physician leaned over me to explain, "with a bodily territory all its own, which it rules by means of hormones. But each baron owes allegiance to the emperor, the tiny pituitary gland who rules them all. And rules you, too."

I asked, "And you're trying to take control of my pituitary?"

He smiled . . . he tutted me . . . without taking his eyes off my twittering needle. "If we could control the pituitary, we could control not only what a person is, but probably even what he wishes to be."

My needle started jumping and swooping. *Watch out* EASY *now* CUT *that out* he said, watching the needle, not me, muttering, "Stop thinking."

I was wishing.

I was confident. I was sure. For days and weeks I'd been elated and anxious, nervous and nauseated, uncomfortable and clairvoyant, day and night. The day came.

I noticed my endocrinologist eyeing me suspiciously as I walked into his office. I remained close to the door. "Sit down," he suggested. But I remained standing. "I don't want to shock you," he murmured. But I remained unastonished, even when he waved the lab report. He whispered, "Son, do you realize you're pregnant?"

I nodded modestly.

But just as later in my trial for treason, my doctor of course—all my doctors—flatly disbelieved my story about Flaminia. Unwilling or unable to take the leap of faith with me, they accused me of moral turpitude.

"Don't you think," my gland-man preached, "don't you honestly think it was a goddamn stupid thing to do?"

"Getting knocked up?"

"No, boy, I mean having relations with a man."

"Either your mind or your logic is suspect," I said. "It was a woman I—"

All I got was a horse laugh.

"Don't you believe me?" I demanded.

His cart horse lips went up over his flat and yellow teeth. "With a woman!" he whinnied. "Are you too ashamed to admit the truth? Here." He handed over one copy of the report he'd required for medical confirmation.

His insensitivity, his antagonism, his morality, his sardonic humor were wasted on me. I clasped the report like the hand of a bosom friend. "You couldn't do it," I told him. "So I had to do it. I've made myself a woman."

He looked at me as if I were out of my mind. "Poppycock," he sniffed.

I found it hard to hold on to my temper. "Are you trying to tell me that self-impregnation is impossible? In a case like mine?"

"No," he neighed, cynical and superior. He enjoyed his toothy laugh. "But let's say highly unlikely, Mr. Niemann. Highly unlikely."

"Not so highly unlikely," I insisted with heat, "since that's what happened."

"Balls," he snorted. "Now let's have it straight. Who was the man?"

I flushed.

"Me."

He shook his mane and finally came out with, "Horse manure."

I lost patience with him. "Forget it." I perused the lab report. It seemed to me I held my diploma, and I informed him, "This is what I wanted. I'm a woman."

"The hell you say."

I waved the report at him. "I'm pregnant—I'm a woman—do you deny the mind-body identity?"

His brows moved up, rippling. A fly had landed—he was puzzled —he had just seen my nightmare.

But I've often wondered at the issue. The statistics of probability are baffling. It's always seemed to me unmathematical, and somehow touching, that one out of millions of sperm, and that dauntless one my very own, should have probed my womb for an egg and struck the spark of life. Later, millions upon millions from other men, swarming like minnows through a grotto, entered me and found nothing. All this strikes me as cause for reflection. Surely even probability cannot be accident. It cannot be accident that a double-barreled two-timing creature whose lust destined her to poetry should at this early age "accidentally" have impregnated herself. By such chances poems have been invented, civilizations have been declared lost and found, paper has been stamped legal tender, and men have loved God.

How I Took Fire

Poca favilla gran fiamma seconda.
—DANTE

A great flame follows a little spark.

And so began my lifelong servitude, my obsession with hetero-sexual passion—the pursuit of the taint of Eros which has stuck to the legend of my life and the text of my poems like a colorful mold. I drove myself, I admit. I had to prove myself. I had to keep reassuring myself for the rest of my life that I was female. A life of meaningful excess.

> Galeotto fu il libro e chi lo scrisse:
> quel giorno più non vi legemmo avante.

Dante was still too hard for me. I studied in the living room that night, sitting on the sofa, looking up *Galeotto*.

> questi, che mai da me non fia diviso,
> la bocca mi baciò tutto tremante.

That was Sandy, all right, I thought.

Across the room from me the Commander sat in front of two maps. One was an elevation map of the island of Sardinia, the land of his birth, and it was tacked to the wall. He was going back soon, and I could sense how much it moved him. The second was larger and he held it spread out before him on a desk. It showed various levels of excavation of some site or other—he often studied charts and maps after dinner. From time to time he made marks on the excavation plan. In the light of the lamp I noticed the hair on the backs of his fleshy hands. They were two small animals, those hairy hands.

After a long while he folded the map and said, "Here, Mr. Niemann" (he still preserved the formalities, Oxonian Italian) "here somewhere which defies our direct detection, but close, you may be sure we are very close, lies a mound, perhaps intact, perhaps Cartha-ginian, perhaps nuragic, buried but waiting." He turned off the light.

He left the room. So he, too, talked in signs and code, suggestive, but irritatingly opaque. Mound? Had he discovered my news already?

Upstairs I could hear him pacing. After a while I could smell the unmistakable stench of one of his Tuscan cigars; the stink of it must have come down right through the floorboards.

Flaminia was out. Probably spending the evening with my brother. The stench, the mess: free of conventional moral feeling as I necessarily was—given the fleshy facts of my ontogeny—neverthe-less I couldn't escape the moral sense that there was something sordid about all of us. It was true she'd only tried to be helpful in making love with me. One afternoon of first aid and kindness. We kept our distance now. But this evening she was with Sandy. And in only a matter of months I was going to have our child. And it was not even hers. I tried to bring the swirling dusty haze into focus. What in the world was I going to do then? What was I going to do meanwhile? Abortion was out of the question now that I had my passport to womanhood in my womb, almost in reach, almost in sight. How many months till I showed? I had to get away somewhere. Anywhere. Anywhere but here in Cambridge.

And in the middle of that night I saw where. I had the sensation that a great wind was rising, was blowing through my room, was blowing leaves and oil-rags and exam-papers and other debris through my windows, and I woke very slowly. It came to me. I perceived a luminous answer, a graceful exit, a way out of the sordid mess. To Sardinia with Satori. He would take me along. I'd become his mistress. In the morning I'd ask him, I'd persuade him. There were shouts somewhere in the house. Satori's voice, then Flaminia's—the shouting was violent. It was prolonged. Quiet came abruptly. I listened. I expected to hear tears. Instead, I began to hear whispering—insanely raucous whispering, followed by screams from Flaminia—pause— then Satori's deep acid voice—insults? curses? sarcasm? I made out one repeated phrase very clearly. *"Pazza di cazzi, pazza di cazzi."*

In the morning I lost my nerve. I slept late, by the time I got down for breakfast he was gone, and a sense of the ludicrous reality of my situation overcame me. It was days, it was weeks, before I gained sufficient courage to ask him, and then only in a state of half-insane desperation. My mind kept denying my body's identity.

Now speaking frankly, all questions of morality aside, the idea— at least when I was fully awake—the very *idea* of my having sexual contact with a man, no matter how healthy it would have been for me, for weeks remained intolerable, insupportable, menacing. It threatened me—and indeed it very nearly overwhelmed me—with mental catastrophe. Yet it was urgent. And as everyone knows, I succeeded—I succeeded brilliantly and sanely. I even succeeded heterosexually. It has therefore always been a minor nuisance to me that certain minor voices, dubiously idealistic, have been pleased to condemn my success as depraved. Yes of course depraved. But what else? And whose sexuality permits decency? Given the physical arrangements of my life, not so very different from those of anyone else's except in the arrangement of a few centimeters of tissue and flesh, no other course but indecency was open to me. Heterosexuality was the best available substitute for purity and poetry. Would they, I wonder, have preferred it, those murmuring minor voices, if, having found myself as a woman again, I had continued to indulge myself in relations only with women? (But such voices are best ignored.)

In these memoirs I cannot, for reasons of space, treat all the liaisons of my life, all those passages of exploration and possession— for reasons of artistic economy alone—even if I could remember all of them. Drawing an honorable line between Apologia and Confessions, I can assure the reader that I intend to treat only those entangling alliances which influenced my development as a poet.

When I knew Satori in Cambridge, he was sixty-two, and his achievements on the island of Minos were then already eight years in the past. The Minos excavations were his best-known work, and they were monumental. He had established beyond question the identity of Minoan and Cretan cultures by uncovering the labyrinth of Daedalus, formerly thought to be the Cretan maze at Knossos. He had also excavated the most extensive early Hellenic civilization known, the city and palace of Hellen surrounding the great stone of Pelops. At the time of the excavations photographs of the palace and stone appeared in every major newspaper and news magazine in the world. Many of my readers will remember the monstrous stone Gate of the Griffins, and the sagging wall of Hellen with its alternating wide and narrow gates crumbling out of the hillside. (I omit here the very recent argument over the validity of attributing the palace and city to the legendary Hellen himself. Still, to keep the record accurate, one should note that the conifex script upon which the first possibility of a positive identification of "King Hellen" was originally based has since been reworked by the brilliant young scholar Pach in Zurich, indicating that the translation "the palace of the Hellenes" may be correct, rather than "the palace of the King Hellenos"— all of which is admittedly rather less exciting.) Though I was only a child then and had no interest in archaeology, I had seen the color reproductions in *Life* of the staggering Gate of the Griffins. Naturally, I'd paid no attention at the time to the name of the archaeologist who had unearthed the city.

The ruins on Minos were his most celebrated discoveries, partly for their intrinsic value, partly for the light they shed on the origins of Greek culture, and partly for the dramatic circumstances surrounding the three-year dig: the revolution which had threatened the work, the Turkish intervention, the theft and recovery of the trove of beaten-gold necklaces. But among archaeologists Satori's reputation rested not merely on this peculiarly spectacular achievement, but on his steadier lifelong dedication to research in the Dardanelles and on various Mediterranean islands. He'd always worked carefully, he'd preserved patiently, he'd usually written his monographs directly *in situ*, and his published studies had been considered illuminating.

His professorship at Harvard was new. (He had previously been associated with the Istituto di Studii Orientali at Naples, the University of Rome, and later with the British Museum.) In Cambridge the year I met him he had been training a group at the Harvard Museum of Man in preparation for another Mediterranean field expedition, this time a new attempt at his native Sardinia, a two-year dig to be financed jointly by Harvard, the Smithsonian, and the Ford Foundation. How simple I thought it would be to join their party, to explore my new world in their company, to relearn—with Satori to guide me—the whole sexual universe. Hadn't I done so once already? And how much more complex and disturbing in fact this second time turned out to be.

Not even HIRE could help me adequately. I had presented the staff there with a medical *fait accompli*. Their response was curious. They decided—albeit reluctantly—to recommend abortion to me: a legal abortion on psychological and medical grounds. Naturally when I learned of this suggestion, I turned it down with moral indignation. I spurned it; I rebuked them.

At a second, emergency meeting it was decided to follow me, rather than oppose me. (To follow Nature, they should have seen, rather than oppose her.) A few members of the urological staff, so I heard, remained disconsolate. But the endocrine majority were pleased—a golden opportunity—I'd opened a new area for research.

They began treating me with massive doses of female hormones. These were administered intravenously, twice daily, and they had two preliminary purposes: to make sure I didn't lose the fetus and to help me through my period of sexual transition.

Anxiously I awaited the inevitable glandular changes. Sometimes when I reported for morning and evening injections I'd remember nostalgically my first arrival, hot, impatient, muscular in a flat-chested T-shirt, clutching modestly in front of my palpitating fly the letter with the address and hour of my appointment clearly marked. And now . . . my forgotten breasts, my bony hips, my abandoned vagina . . . perhaps you can imagine. I took measurements, I kept records. I put on flesh over my stomach (though I didn't actually "show" for months). My gynecological system developed under the healthy stimulus of pregnancy and the beneficent shower of hormones. In fact my uterus, the doctors said, would probably bear the strain of full-term; even my immature vagina was coming along wonderfully. My figure was a leafy bud opening at the behest of chemical nutrients. But my mind . . .

What I mainly remember about the next few weeks of hormone treatment was a great heat. Spring that year, it's true, was abnormally warm. But the heat I experienced was behind the temples and in front of the eyes. It caused a shifting, haunting sense of unreality and a peculiar sense of expectancy. I remember the broken rung in the chair I kicked once, the ashtray in which I burned my mail from home. Desperately, I began to copy Flaminia more intensively than ever now. In all things—her way of keeping her legs together, for instance, sliding when getting into or out of a car; her way of pumping hands, of course; her way of reaching nonchalantly for her wineglass. When surprised, I tried never to narrow my eyes, I learned to widen them; I learned how to let them grow wet with tears of sympathy, should an occasion for sympathy ever arise. But the first time I put on one of her dresses, I made a mistake. Deliberately and reasonably, I chose the one I had first possessed her in, I chose it with intention, and yet when I saw myself in the mirror, I promptly threw up.

I had to conceal my transition from everyone except my doctors. I was as careful as I could be. When no one was at home, I raided Flaminia's closet. Piece by piece I went through her wardrobe. I sat and studied in her clothes, Italian and American: fifteen minutes the first day, thirty minutes the second day, forty-five minutes the third day, and so on, beginning with her slacks and working up through her less exciting skirts and blouses. I adjusted finally, but I didn't grow entirely calloused, entirely unaroused by what I was wearing. (In this respect as in so many others, my responses were already quite healthy and normal for a girl without my knowing it or acknowledging it for years.) From the bottom of the pile, I borrowed one of Flaminia's nightgowns. Once only. I couldn't sleep. It was a long time before I had the nerve to go out and buy my own things, or for that matter to walk outside the house dressed as a girl. The first time I tried it, I combed my hair down in bangs and tried to do something interesting with the unkempt tufts overgrown at my ears. I put on lipstick and then rubbed it off so that it hardly showed. I hid my

new soufflé breasts under a bulky sweater. From the skin out I was
wearing, in the following order, a sanitary napkin in case of spotting;
a jock for old times' sake, to hold my Kotex in place; a garter-belt
and stockings; Argyle socks over my stockings; pedal pushers; a
corduroy skirt over that; and torn sneakers. I couldn't make it out the
door. I resorted to a neutral, unrevealing raincoat to cover my embarrassment. Dressed like that, I strolled from the Commander's house
to the cemetery on Mt. Auburn Street.

The sky began to rain in sympathy. The rain relaxed me. I took
a long wet walk back toward the Yard. On Massachusetts Avenue
I slipped into a coffee shop. On my napkin with a pencil I started
sketching the faces and figures of "other girls" sipping coffee and
munching brownies. They stared back—my blond hair too short for
a girl's, my deadpan lips too pink for a boy's, my sexless raincoat
buttoned way up to my throat—but I didn't give a damn what they
thought—I was disturbed by all the faces I'd drawn: they looked
masculine. It was petty, spiteful consolation to imagine that that
was only because they were Radcliffe girls.

(Ultimately, the solution to my clothing problems was the no-
nonsense fashion favored at Radcliffe—a man's white shirt with a
button-down collar and men's bluejeans with a zipper-up fly. Indeed,
I recall wanting very much to remain unnoticed at the staff meetings
for the Sardinian expedition, and succeeding: by adopting the simple
expedient of wearing bluejeans, heavy boots, a sweatshirt, and a red
kerchief on my head. My presence at these meetings was not required
—since I was to be entered on the payroll only later on, and only in
the capacity of a clerk. But I remember going and I remember my
inobtrusiveness—silence—reticence—the more clearly because when
I came to accept myself as a girl, within a matter of weeks, I took a
far more articulate role in the work of the expedition than anyone
could possibly have imagined beforehand. Indeed, I became officious
—not merely to make up for being a girl, but for being only eighteen
and only a clerk.)

That same afternoon it stopped raining and, like the man in the
story, I took off my raincoat as the sun emerged and I managed to
make it a few feet into Harvard Yard. I entered through a familiar
gate bearing an inscription that Sandy had once translated for me, the
first time he took me to see the Yard. Sandy and his Latin and our
childhood, unregretted. Reading it overhead this time brought tears
to my eyes.

Felices ter et amplius
quos inrupta tenet copula nec malis
divolsus querimoniis
suprema citius solvet amor die.

I could barely get through that gate.

But on succeeding afternoons I managed to traverse the Yard from end to end, first in pedal pushers (which might have been mistaken for Bermuda shorts), then in a skirt, then in a dress. Though my eyes were open, I stared hypnotically ahead while I walked: it felt like a high-wire trapeze stunt every time. Harvard men—well, those who didn't know me at all tried to pick me up, and of course I ignored them, and of course they persisted. It wasn't only hard on me. It must have been very trying for *them* since within weeks of the onset of pregnancy and hormone-intensification, I was already becoming a willowy blonde, small-breasted but high, with a porcelain face and a faraway nightmare in my eyes, a short-haired Renaissance madonna ripe for seduction. As for those who knew me from classes, they were invariably pesky. They recognized me vaguely, took me for my own sister, or asked me pointedly hadn't they met me somewhere before, then suddenly became confused by my smooth denials and invited me to come have coffee. Coffee? It filled me with disgust. I tried to get over it, I tried to consider myself female. Yet I was hounded by that horror of the coffee date which still pursues me. Absurd? Not in a case like mine.

Following the dictates of its own uncontrollable logic, my mind refused to cooperate. I *felt* like a boy in drag. Full transformation, genuine transformation, I knew in the privacy of my room and the queasiness of my heart, would remain closed to me, elusive, unachievable until I met it head on: on openly sexual grounds. But a lover? Copulation? I couldn't. (Again, in this respect, I was already a reasonably adjusted freshman coed without knowing it.) I thought about it continually.

One day I attempted to push my transformation over the brink by shoving it exactly where it clutched the edge and hesitated. A single, shy, but well-aimed push. Alone, I smoked one of the joints Sandy had given me months ago. I smoked another. Then in a trance of modest resolution, I found and stimulated my first love, my primordial sex, with my idle fingers.

The results were immediate and they were startling. I was alone in my room, sitting with a book on my lap, but concentrating on the real issues. I was wearing my raincoat, buttoned high and tight. Underneath I was naked: my supply of underwear had long ago been exhausted in my stop-and-go, forward-and-back effort to cross the great divide. And—Lord!—I thought I'd succeeded. I actually managed to excite myself, with my finger fully sheathed and moving in the opening between my legs—but in that same instant I developed a terrific case of stage fright: the walls of my room began to ripple and sway like canvas, as if they weren't walls but the painted props for a stage set. Had someone unseen entered and slammed my door? The trees outside my window shook, melted, and flowed. Painted on canvas, too. I desisted. I stopped that crucial funny business and went about my other daily business. But my wall-to-wall stage fright didn't stop, my sense of root-and-branch unreality persisted—unexpectedly frightening me while I was putting on lipstick, or urinating, or turning a page. My lipstick image in the mirror receded—the bathroom darkened—my book was blank, had never been printed. The room around me shook with heat like fuel in a fire, but with no sign of burning . . . curling at the edges, crisping, browning, charring . . . and no flames. A stanza came back to me.

> I want to tell you right away
> About a big red fire,
> That if you want the house to stay
> You've got to

what? . . . The old fire frightened me. A match seemed to flare at the core of my head, an exactly focused pinpoint. Light without heat. It was light so intense it seared by radiance alone and I couldn't stop it. And then came a whole sea of dancing flames. I saw tidal waves of flame—I couldn't believe it! At first they appeared to be infinitely far off, yet circling me, surrounding my charred head, surrounding the crisped room, the curling earth outside and all the crackling galaxies. Was it a nightmare, had I lost my mind? I was shivering, watching, fighting to get away. Both these radiances, pinpoint and ocean, rapidly approached and penetrated each other, the inexhaustible effulgence outside *became* the pinpoint inside my head. All of a sudden my head was on fire and so vast I thought I was destroyed, I blazed up into a cosmos and greater than that, I or It had created the blaze, the whole flaming Creation was smaller than the inside of my head, impossible, unendurable.

I tried to think my way out—to somewhere a lot cooler, smaller, darker. Who was I, was I anyone? Was I, was I at all, was there an It outside me? I could feel that a connecting thread had been pulled. I fought with all my might to wind my self back in. The dazzling of the lights dwindled and went out and I was grateful. But my mind—where was that? It hovered overhead. Free-floating, attached to my body by an invisible thread, by sheer loyalty and habit, and these had been strained. I tugged at the thread. I put my jeans back on. I ran water into the sink, I was in my own room, I took a deep breath, I tried doing my laundry again, I knew I had to concentrate on something practical and sensible.

I stared at the soft, smelly heap—my athletic socks and nylon mesh stockings, my absurd jockey shorts and atrocious black panties, my T-shirts and padded bras—and suddenly I stuffed the senseless mess of it sopping wet back into my laundry bag and took it all downstairs. I walked. I hardly knew where I was going, the fabric of the world still had that wavy smoky look. The trees in the Yard were praying to God, that's what I couldn't help thinking it looked like, all their twigs and leaves were praying, every tree was curling in the flame I had seen but couldn't see now, and the paths kept sinking under my heels like a crazy quilt. Carrying my laundry bag, I crept past Memorial Church. You can imagine what gyrations its thin white spire was up to. But it was the haze of the steps that gripped my attention: there in one corner, where there ought to have been blur, the steps were sharp, crystalline, like the teeth on a saw. Sandy was sitting there. He was sitting motionless, pinning down the world for several feet around him. Was he waiting for Flaminia? He seemed to be staring right at me. But as I paused, stopped in my tracks, I observed that his eyes were like the large eyeball-less eyes in sculpture, the sockets filled to bulging and unstaring at me. His absolute immobility and the absolute immobility of the white stairs for several feet in all directions around him filled me with an electric anticipation bordering on seizure, as if I were on the verge of either a mystical revelation of the meaning of the flames or a sick hallucination.

I wanted to speak but couldn't, I absolutely couldn't. I stood there quivering, only a few yards away at the foot of the stairs, and didn't move.

It wasn't until years afterward that I was able to discover the significance of this vision. At the time, in confusion and deep fatigue, I made my way at last to a self-service laundromat. But I couldn't enter. I stood there, I just stood there, still shaking, before I knew what I had to do.

Satori's office was in the Harvard Museum of Man. I found his office number in the registry and took the stairs, searching. I followed numbers. I spiraled dizzily around level after level of display cases—bones, plaster casts, spears, shields, cups, crusted stones—they seemed to pour in through his door as I entered without knocking, neat piles of cups and casts, bones and stones, on the floor of his office, on chairs, on the desk in front of him, a flood that went into the man.

"*Onorevole!*" I practically shouted, relieved to find him.

"*Caspita!*" he muttered, and then breaking into his Oxford manner, said, "Here, what's this, a visit? From the home front? Sit down." He didn't get up.

"*Comandante, sono—sono—*" but I could never get through it in Italian.

He sniffed suspiciously, "What's all that laundry?"

"*Mi . . . fa . . . schifo—*"

He said, "Do speak English, boy, I expect it will calm your nerves, you look exceedingly pale."

"Commander," I quieted momentarily. "I have something to tell you. Every time you refer to me as a boy—"

"But I know that already. I knew it from the start. What did you expect?" His heavy cheeks nodded. "I don't wish to be unkind, but I'm generally rather busy at the museum these days, and I must say I really find your sexual nature neither extremely interesting nor entirely extraordinary. Come here."

I had rarely heard him speak like that before—so cool, so brusque —nor had I ever seen him look so uneasy. Ill at ease with me? Why? Above his puffy, leathery cheeks his eyes were bloodshot.

He motioned me to a case of metal statuettes—bronze, gaunt, twisted, elongated, popeyed figurines. "These are from my native Sardinia," he informed me, "a Mediterranean culture which, however unique, is not particularly unusual in its objects of worship. This was found by a shepherd," he said, handing me a figure only the thickness of a twig, only about six inches high, "and it is *not* especially rare."

I was dumbfounded. I held it in my hand. I stared. It was not only an unmistakable hermaphrodite—with breasts as round as earrings and a penis like the tip of a matchstick—but it was also pregnant. A huge belly, a rounded belly. A belly like a twig that had swallowed a plum.

"Well?" he inquired. The wings of his bulbous nose went in and out with otherwise unexpressed humor.

I was aghast. I was speechless.

"So?" he demanded.

So he knew. Everything. He'd discovered it.

I turned away from the case of statuettes weakly, and then turned back. "Take me!" I cried. I'm afraid I had a sense of the drama of the moment and exclaimed "Take me!" with the desolate, commanding air of a tragedienne.

He was startled. "Sit down!" he bellowed. "And put that bronze down before you drop it and injure it!"

I did as he said. "Please," I cried, extending my arms dramatically, but also sobbing in genuine anguish, genuine desire, "take me!"

"Close the door."

I closed it.

"I am not in the habit, Mr. or Miss Niemann," he said, still much too loud, and his voice rose, "of debauching young persons of either sex." He turned livid, a reddish-purple suffused his cheeks, he brought his palms down on a great leatherbound volume with a thunderclap, and he shouted, "Who has given you these ideas? These presumptions! Who?"

"Flaminia and Sandy." I meant of course that it had all started with them. Satori, however, understood something quite different. He grew suddenly cautious and intent, and regarded me quietly. I chattered on. "It's not their fault," I explained, "if a kind of ticking hum goes through me. It's not Flaminia's fault that when I see her shift, I grab for the emergency. You see, her car drives me."

And despite my general incoherence, I managed to make it pretty clear at last about Flaminia and myself. Satori could hardly have grasped all I was saying, but when he got the half of it, when he got the gist of our lesson, "Flaminia!" he hissed, getting up, cursing her in Italian, his tongue showing in his teeth. "Gran fija de mignotta —" he began to pace—"è 'na bocchinara, 'na sgallettata, 'na leccona! Rottinculo! Magnacazzi! Leccacazzi! È 'na troia!" And so on—the room was too small for the stagger of his pace, and as I backed away from him, unable to understand his dialect, I couldn't help continuing myself, "—has a mind of its own, turns left, swerves right, it backs into position," I rattled nervously. "All I have to do is imagine I'm Sandy—"

"Shut up! Do shut up!" He turned on me. I thought he was

going to hit me. The white jealousy in his face was so vivid, it made the freckles stand out—how could I not have realized it before, how could I not have seen it? There it was in his face, staring at me.

I said confidently, "You shouldn't be surprised, Commander. You shouldn't even be disturbed. After all, Flaminia is half your age, exactly half, she's barely thirty-one."

He stood meditating, silent, enraged.

I wet my lips and added, "Besides, she's dedicated to her husband and her work and in Italy divorce is limited."

"What else did she tell you?" he said quietly.

"Nothing," I said, but I said it as if it were a lie, gritting my teeth. Naturally he assumed I knew a great deal. "She told me nothing. But I figured it out for myself, you see, I'm eighteen, and Flaminia is half your age, or seventy-five percent older than I am, which makes you exactly sixty-two, or exactly three hundred and fifty percent older than I am."

Perhaps it was unkind. It set him off again. "Did she also happen to tell you how long she has been your brother's mistress?"

"Three or four weeks," I lied. "Not more."

That was evidently what he wanted to know. His face grew— well, how shall I say it?—kinder, rather than relieved: his eyes grew moist and yellow with kindness.

He said, "Did she tell you everything?"

"Everything." I nodded with compassion. "Take me."

He advanced on me. Unexpectedly grabbing my chin, he forced my head back, twisted my neck painfully, and mouthed at me with grossly amused contempt, "Even if you *were* a young woman, young man, I would *still* be three-and-a-half times your age. Now remember that, do, do you hear? And behave. Behave like a man."

But I couldn't. "I can't," I explained. "Not any more. How can I, now that I'm pregnant?"

He looked at me. Letting up on my head, he sat down clumsily. His big fingers felt absent-mindedly for his glasses, which were hanging on that crinkled ribbon only halfway down his chest, but he couldn't find them. He sagged. He breathed. He looked at me skeptically. He looked at me critically. Did he doubt my word?

"It's true," I said. And I pointed to the pregnant figurine. He looked at it, he looked at me. I nodded reassuringly.

So he hadn't known after all.

When even his own science failed to persuade him, I fished around in my pockets for my wallet, and in it I found the lab report. I handed the paper over. I pointed convincingly to the word "Positive."

He studied it. "No! This is quite out of the question. It's utterly fantastic—"

I agreed. "A fantastic opportunity—"

"A pregnant boy—"

"Not exactly—"

"Here," he handed the lab report back to me, "nonsense."

I shrugged. So? So. I burned it disconsolately in the ashtray while he fingered his eyelids. He looked exhausted, feverish. He'd had a difficult afternoon. I said, "Anyhow, would you take me to Sardinia?"

"Where? What?"

"It's not uncommon in American education. The junior year abroad."

"You're only a freshman—"

"I've got to get away. Lots of girls—"

He put on his hornrimmed glasses and stared at me as if I were a specimen.

"That's normal," I insisted. "I—"

"You're not pregnant."

"Time will tell," I assured him.

He looked at my stomach. He picked up the figurine.

"I—"

"Sss." He was concentrating. He scratched his head, top and back. He scratched his lip and looked at me point-blank. "Who?"

"Who?"

"*Who is the father?*" he bellowed so loud I thought his glasses would drop.

Well, what should I have said? Flaminia? I couldn't name Flaminia.

"Who?" he repeated, more self-controlled, more firmly.

Myself? Self-incrimination?

I *had* to fib. It came to me all at once. "My brother," I said. That was exactly what he wanted to hear. He practically cooked.

How I Got Carried Away

And I remain despairing of the port.
—WYATT

En route to the island, passing Gibraltar, it was hot, the Italian sailors, most of them mere boys, took off their jackets, they wore their white shirts unbuttoned halfway to their trousers. The sight of their smooth sweating chests, some lightly tanned, some darkly toasted, under the whiteness of their spread collars loosened a few remaining springs in me. They moved gracefully, they smiled graciously, it was all surprisingly simple, suddenly natural, unexpectedly interesting. I wanted a sailor. Any one of them would have satisfied me in that mood. There can be no doubt this was due to my continuing pregnancy—enduring, expanding secretly. (It was June and still . . . maddeningly . . . I didn't show.) It was *not* only a question of hormones, it was my pride in motherhood. I gazed after them as they passed, the Rock a blur in my eyes, my focus closer, dizzyingly close. The saliva on their salt-tongued grins made me feel faint. The suggestion of knuckly ribs, as the wind whipped their shirts, made me grin weakly back. And something new happened to me. Wearing shorts and a halter, leaning on my shuffleboard stick to keep my balance, I felt my flesh flush hot beneath my stomach, and there without any assistance from me for the first time in the vessel between my thighs I became moist.

Of course I did nothing. With strangers? Hardly.

When we put in at Naples but weren't permitted ashore, I was immensely disappointed. Weren't we even going to set foot on the mainland of Italy? My usual nausea and morning sickness had just about passed by the time the customs officials came aboard to check our passports. Satori assembled our party in a small room off the lounge and explained to us that he had just received word of trouble —a flare-up of violence in Cagliari, the capital of Sardinia, over certain "political issues": regional autonomy versus independence. There was some talk, the customs officers had said, of restricting transportation in and out of Cagliari until the trouble was over. In any event, Satori advised us, it would be best if we all stayed right where we were, aboard ship. If we ventured ashore now in Naples, we might be detained there by the exceedingly nervous (in Satori's opinion, unduly nervous) mainland authorities. Everyone looked grave. I was furious. As the youngest member of the party, I spoke up fearlessly. I always did now. "You haven't made the slightest attempt to check," I pointed out. "It may only be a stupid rumor. Why worry about their holding you on shore when they can hold you right here on your floating ass!"

The Commander smiled patiently. It was obvious to me that he was enchanted by my outburst, rather than interested in what I had to say. I became more angry and petulant than ever. In the middle of his reply, which was some cant to the effect that singly or as a group, once ashore, we could be delayed for a matter of weeks on the mainland, and that he could not afford to spare any of us, least of all a member of the weaker sex—I walked out.

In disgust.

I went out on deck with the notion of sneaking or swimming ashore and leaned over the railings and saw the dockhands and police scurrying and swarming down below on the pier and I hated politics: I hated that "flare-up of violence," whatever it was, purely and only because it had been responsible for denying me my small personal pleasure. Self-determination? Autonomy? Liberation? As inauspicious as this was my first brush with Sardinian political issues. I fumed in annoyance at the riotous grey crumble of Naples and the tar-and-oil slick of her allegedly blue bay. Above the cone of Vesuvius: was it only a cloud? was it smoke from the guts of the world? I thought about all the volcanoes I'd ever heard tell of, Etna, Stromboli, Mauna Loa, Fuji, and decided that the earth had a bad case of indigestion, had spewed from its stinking holes the hot nasty matter which gave rise to "political issues."

No, I went nowhere, I didn't jump ship. I went below to my cabin.

(It may be worth a moment to note that Satori, though politically indifferent himself, was to that day remembered and disliked by certain radical factions on his native island because long ago he had not once attempted to resist Il Duce's unprincipled attempt to manipulate Sardinian archaeology. Mussolini's interest in archaeology may surprise you, but you will remember how absurdly crucial it seemed to the Fascist leadership to exhume and embellish ancient Roman grandeur in order to deck modern Italy in the toga of Augustus Caesar—pride, conquest, power, money—a lot of black magic was at stake. And Satori, young director then of Cagliari's Museum of Antiquities, had taken no stand against the Fascist Ministry's attempt to make archaeological science a tool of the State, to interfere with its work and control its findings. In Sardinia, Carthaginian and even nuragic ruins had been at times falsely declared to be Roman.)

It puzzles me a bit to remember how often in my disconcerting life water has played the obbligato to love. I stayed below deck all day. That night the Commander and I consummated our slow entanglement.

The salty ocean. During the course of the voyage I had been importuned openly or slyly by every member of our party—except for Mrs. Hackett of course—by joking George Nicolopolos, by Vincent whose last name I've forgotten, even by little rickety Ted Palmer, the Smithsonian curator whose ears I'll never forget. None of them knew anything about my androgynous make-up. But from the moment Satori had put me on the staff, they'd suspected other things: that I was his little girl, that he'd knocked me up, and that he'd troubled to announce my pregnancy in advance in order to avoid surprises later. As for myself, not once in my secret heart had I blamed them for trying to make me—one and all. But I hadn't responded. The harder they'd tried, the more relaxed I'd become, the more it had helped to dispel the persistent, annoying feeling that my pregnancy was unreal, neurotic, hysterical; and that in reality I was only a confused and effeminate young man. Besides, I liked them: especially George for his unfailing humor, and for the fact that once he actually proposed to me—my first proposal—by moonlight, high on the boat deck; and Palmer for his tiny ears—like rolled anchovies. But I saw that I was becoming psychologically dependent on their flirtation, in order to believe in my own identity, and that worried me. I solved the problem by discouraging them while I encouraged myself. Playing chess, reading archaeological texts daily, reclining in a deck chair, I exposed myself to the general view in a brief orange sunsuit or a trim blue swimsuit with a peekaboo bodice and a pleated skirt. And I told myself that when I ran barefoot to the pool I caused a sensation. I was more womanly these days—evidently. My stomach had still not arched, but its curve and the swelling of my breasts had become more opulent. I dived, and it gave me a rush of pleasure to know that however masculine, neuter, or vegetable I sometimes felt to myself, others found me sexy and feminine. I felt the continual stir of attention around me. Sailorboys and archaeologists, young and old, first class and third. But—perhaps because I was young—out of loyalty to the Commander I'd resolved I wouldn't yield to anyone else in our party.

I had special problems, God knows, problems of belief, problems of self-confidence, problems of anatomy—a sexual chess game that I'd been trying to mastermind ever since we'd set sail. So completely did I wish to become a typical, trite sophomore coed by the time—a year from now—I returned to Radcliffe that, though I was all for sex, I actually wanted to remain a virgin until I married.

"But . . . " you will say. No buts. That was how I felt—my pregnancy, my experiences with Sandy and Flaminia to the contrary notwithstanding. I'd changed since those thinblooded years as a girl, since those fullblooded months as a boy. I'd become a young woman . . . and misunderstanding the nature of desire in general and of coeds in particular, I proposed for the future to dabble more cautiously, to sit calmly but squarely blocking the entrance to the cave of sex, to seal a high hymen across the low threshold of desire. I wanted to be *virgina intacta* when I married. And yet I needed the reassurance of premarital sex. It was a problem.

All that day and through the evening, I remained out of sight, sulking in my cabin. During dinner, which I ate lying in my bed, we began to put on steam for Sardinia. A band was playing in the lounge, George informed me, knocking on my door after dinner. Didn't I want to—? I did not. A gypsy band. I didn't give one damn about their ethnic heritage. Moonlight. I didn't answer. He left. The ship reverberated, screwing its way through the deep. At half-hour intervals after George, the others came, even dour Lou Hackett. I remained unmoved, I remained in what, when I was a little girl, Mother used to call a pet. Finally the Commander rapped. He grunted something.

"Stay out."

It was unlocked; he came in. I was lying on my stomach, fully dressed for cocktails or dancing—a velvet skirt and a plunging top, in case somebody could persuade me, with a book under my chin, pretending to read. He said heavily, "If you are to remain of any use to me as a member of my staff, you will have to reform your manners. I can't very well allow you—"

I turned a page.

"You are intolerable," he assured me. "You have become atrocious."

"What does 'nuragic' actually mean?" I asked without looking up.

"Will you kindly close that book?"

I closed it. I put my forehead on the bedspread. "What does '*troia*' mean? What does '*cazzi*' mean?" I knew.

He was silent.

Eyes closed, I said, "I overheard an argument. What I'm trying to say is, what was the relation, what was going on, between you and Flaminia?"

"That has nothing to do with the subject at hand, which is your impertinence and bad temper."

"It does so." It was clear he didn't know how I worked. I said, "We're approximately three thousand miles from Cambridge now. Is there any reason not to tell me approximately?"

"If you're feeling unwell, I'll be merciful and leave you alone to recover."

He waited for a reply. He didn't know anything about my feelings. I was asking questions only in order to appease him.

I can't simply continue, not about everything. But I discovered in the next few minutes what I'd wanted to know. He succeeded in filling up the void of my uncertainties, in hushing the bark of my ill temper, in erasing the smudges of my poor confidence, in soothing all that had made me so irritable earlier in the day. He sat on the edge of my bed. The cabin rolled. I let the book drop. He picked it up and looked at it. It was one of his. "Tell me," I asked.

He stroked my head. So while the cabin rocked and vibrated, I learned in effect what I'd come to suspect. I learned from Satori's at times amused mutter that Flaminia had been the archaeologist's mistress in Rome—while she'd still been at the university there. He had taken care of her: fed her, kept her, introduced her to the right people, to all the right people, he assured me, smiling sourly. It was to him, whatever her intelligence, that she owed the rapidity of her advancement, to his connections and influence her present job in Cambridge, to him her passage, her visa, her welcome. There was no husband.

"But her name—Satori—" I sat up. I kept my legs crossed. I widened my eyes.

"It is a false name, not too difficult a matter to arrange, you know, somewhat easier in Italy than in your country because it is somewhat more essential in Italy. I simply, well, adopted her, as it were."

I widened my eyes further. "Then you haven't got a son?"

"Yes of course, but when my son left her—"

"Yes?" He stood up, about to leave. How had I failed? "Yes?" I repeated. "Your son?"

"On her account my son and I have been, shall we say, at odds since then. Estranged." With some distaste he grunted, "A lawyer and a petty politician. Still in Cagliari, I'm told, though I hear he will soon be working for the American Embassy in Rome. Next year, I understand."

"You could look him up when we get to Cagliari—"

"I'll thank you not to meddle. Will you come upstairs to dance?"

I needed more persuasion than that. It was hard to get adequate persuasion. I tried, "Why did he leave her?"

He laughed. "Carlo?" He shrugged. "Carlo." He nodded. "It is sufficient explanation."

I racked my brain for a way. There must be a way. I made my eyes grow slowly wet with sympathy. "And now she's left you for my brother."

"With whom, without a doubt, she will find greater satisfaction." And as he said it, he did something odd with the creases in his face, but I couldn't catch the expression: some emotion, some complex of emotions, which he brought under control.

"Will she?" I said, only slightly jealous.

He nodded tensely. "You see, after Flaminia and my son separated she was quite unreasonably distraught. Miserable. It was bad for her work. I saw that, almost immediately. I took her on a holiday to clear her mind. The mountains did it, the lake, Lago di Garda. I learned that she was willing to make love to me—"

Willing to. Merely willing to—that was the frugal, unassuming phrase he used. She herself had remained without "satisfaction." Privacy is here strained, but, in effect, she had learned to make love to him in the one way that could arouse and satisfy him at all.

Knowing Flaminia as I did, I was aghast. But it was here that I triumphed, here that I saw the next move in the tense game I had to play, check and mate in a single move. It was to precisely this mystery play that my lips were introduced that evening while the ship hummed, pitched, pulsed, and rolled—to self-sacrifice in the worship of the phallic god—to a liturgy of blessings I can still recite. I kneeled before him: I wanted to be taken as a woman, I wanted to be a woman to someone. But I wanted to remain chaste in memory of my brother. All this was granted me.

Of course I don't deny that there was a certain element of vulgarity in all of this, especially in my decision to remain chaste. Vulgarity was inherent in the moment, as in my life. In fact, it was intrinsic in my body, just as it is in yours—and not merely in the phenomenon of sex, nor merely in our minds, but in the noumenon of consciousness in general. Yet though I admit vulgarity, I deny categorically that there was anything the least bit homoerotic in our encounter. Possibly you may find that difficult to believe. You may doubt that when I unzippered the Commander's nautical trousers, and even when I had his ancient knotty testicles in my lips, my affection for him remained utterly heterosexual. But I tell you it was more, it was filial—a tenderness and sense of obligation that was daughterly.

My lingering disbelief was finally resolved the moment I sensed where in my ding-dang yin-yang anatomy I was becoming aroused. I had no further doubts. I had moist facts. I had physical evidence. From that time forward, no matter how heated we became, Satori's way of love caused me no anxieties: I had no fear that our closeness and fondness might lead to a wrong turn in the tricky route of my sexual organs. Awed, flirtatious, hesitant, modest, anxious to please— I was invariably illumined by the least touch of his interest in me: a father, yes, if you please, a grandfather, hence a man absolutely beyond me, for whom I saw that I was indeed, was necessarily, was reassuringly, a very young girl. No doubt that's why I've often been attracted to older men—Satori was not the last—whether or not sexual communion was ever in question. Invariably they soothed (while they did not ever answer) the harsh question in the fissures of my loins and the furrows of my mind, the issue of my final self-creation.

That evening I took the sanctity of the god. I moaned faintly, a humming cry. The fire of my tongue ran to my palate, swept down my throat, and coursed through my being till I burned. Satori uncovered and discovered, he caressed the perspiring crown of my head, he blessed my mouth with his sacred sex, while with my nervous, prayerful lips and the service of a full heart, I embraced and discovered him on my knees until he stood appeased finally, holding me tenderly before him.

But whatever you may happen to think privately, for myself, it has always been very hard to separate divinity from dirt. Perhaps you'd be more sympathetic if I said it was difficult for me to separate physical things from spiritual things. But my first way of putting it is more accurate. And for precisely this reason, this accuracy of mine, the mystical strain in my poetry has been genuine from the start. No one has ever doubted the sincerity of my sonnet on fellatio, "How May a Man Rise?" with its celebrated final pentameter,

Pumping pollen, gouts of Jahweh's juice.

I was clumsy. The Commander was vigorous. The ship was pitching and tossing. He splashed the survey map of Sardinia that I'd taped to the wall of my cabin, not far either from the spot our expedition was heading for. He stained the snapshot of Sandy I had on my nightstand. He clouded the glass of my porthole. And yet for all that, the climax was beautiful. Think what you like. So beautiful that—while still barely aroused sexually myself—I began to whisper through my teeth, to pray, to weep, to cry with awe at the grand energy of the created and creating universe. And that immodest, impure tête-à-tête has remained, to my way of thinking, one—only one—in a series of encounters, a chain of apprehension, that led me through sex and politics to divinity.

Often, later, I've tried to evoke and paint again this incongruous arrival of mine in Italy, for the amusement of friends or to accomplish the customary preliminary throat-clearing noises of an after-dinner speech—a little story always greeted with smiles of sympathy. Well, I didn't recognize my destiny. How many do at eighteen? Political struggle? No, sir, no, I craved sex, I craved poetry, I was bored by politics, I was indifferent to oppression, I was indignant only at not being permitted to have a go at Naples.

After it was over, after the Commander had left, I was depressed. It seemed unaccountable at the time. I remained below in my cabin. But I consoled myself for everything, for everything, by reading out loud to myself from my beloved Leopardi—that ultimate poem of his quiet ferocity in which, considering the inhuman trunk and lava-seared flanks of Vesuvius, he cries out:

> *Dall'utero tonante*
> *Scagliata al ciel profondo,*
> *Di ceneri e di pomici e di sassi*
> *Notte e ruina.*

All that night we steamed for the island through a heavy sea. I was sick.

And still feeling sick a little after dawn, watching the shoulders of Sardinia lift into the sunlight like a cloud massing, I remembered that my love-child was to be born there and taken from me there. Wakeful in the suck and chop of the sea, at the earliest hint of day I pulled myself onto the forward deck to catch my first sight . . . ragged cliffs . . . a vast island. Deceptively, the land mass beckoned and gleamed, extending a mineral welcome. Hello as hard as mica. A little later the port of Cagliari rose at its southern end. The capital city. Seacliffs left and right, both sides of the port, sidled toward me on the prow like the giant claws of a lobster reaching for my unborn infant, and I distrusted the place from that moment. My spirit rushed out, I leaned over the railing. A primitive reflex. Away, quickly away, into the preserving sea, lifted on a pure wave, swirled my revulsion. Gone. As a result I've always regarded Sardinia as a second home—a homeland. This may at first seem remarkable. But is it not opposition, an early powerful revulsion for one's country, that calls forth in the ensuing vacuum of soul a love so profound that it refuses to answer the questions put to it by doubt, and which creates precisely that overplus of feeling we call patriotism?

Nothing less was my experience of Sardinia after vomiting.

And a few hours later I was busy helping with an inventory check as we unloaded the ship. Today the old waterfront is no longer the same. Partly at my direction, in the intervening years a number of dock structures as well as the rail terminal in the port sector of the city were reduced to char and rubble by bombs.

How I
Made
Friends

Ogni tanto si fermava a guardare il poderetto
tutto verde fra le due muraglie di fichi d'India
. . . . Appunto come un uccello che emigra:
sentiva di lasciar lassú la parte
migliore di sé stesso.

—DELEDDA

Every once in a while he paused to look up at
the little farm, all green between two walls
of cactus pears. . . . Just like a migrating
bird: he felt he was leaving up there the best
part of himself.

The preselected target for our dig was a plateau about fifteen miles below Nuoro, a town in the central mountains of the island. It was there, within view of the whalelike massif of Gennargentu which rears a silver-black hulk, seemingly wet, skyward out of the other mountains, that Satori proposed to begin. He took me out to see: the site was a remarkable elevation that looked like a choppy ocean solidified—a foam of briar on a wildly eroded soil. It was there that the shepherd, Mungianeddu Puddu, had turned up the pregnant nuragic statue I'd seen in Cambridge.

Puddu's stone tower was three thousand years old, a small, crumbling exemplar of the mysterious gutted towers of prehistoric Sardinia that dot the fields and cliffs of the island from end to end. There are over six thousand of them. They are not rare, they are not lovely, only serviceable once—and now mysterious. What service they once performed is the mystery: at present they are used as shepherds' huts and/or sheepcotes, or unused, except the big ones that have been dedicated by the government as monuments. Monuments to whom? Where did the builders come from; where did they go? Their towers, built over a period of roughly a thousand years, though they vary in size, are all on the same architectural design—a thousand-year, unique civilization that vanished without a howl into thin historical air some time between 500 B.C. and perhaps 300 B.C. Not an iota of their culture was absorbed into that of the Carthaginian colonists who conquered them, nor by the Romans who drove out the Carthaginians. A people with only a name, a people named only for their towers—nuraghi.

The stones of which the bases of these towers are formed are large enough to cause some wonder, but not nearly so large as those of the Egyptian pyramids; nor do even the largest of the nuraghi begin to compare with the staggering piles of Egypt, Knossos, or Sumer. Inside, a large one will have a circular vaulted chamber several stories high. These central vaults slope inward toward a round opening at the top, somewhat like immense versions of Hindu stupas or giant lime kilns. Between the vault and the outer wall, the thick structure of the tower itself is honeycombed with passages and window slits, spiral staircases, niches, rooms, and curved cells. Were these Bronze Age buildings used as fortresses? temples? silos? palaces? signal towers? all of these?

Signal towers, at least in part, they must surely have been. On an elevation projection map once during the Sardinian Independence struggle I had occasion to work out the location of every known tower on the island—we were using them as arsenals then—and I discovered an interesting phenomenon. I had placed little wooden picks on the map grids (pins being then unavailable, the shepherds had cut a quantity of splinterlike pegs) at each location of our network of towers. Examining these, I was not slow to realize that though the scattering of pegs seemed wildly uneven—the distance between them varying from sometimes half a mile to stretches of some twenty-eight miles—the summit of each tower would in fact have been visible from the next (an observation that could not be readily made in the field because in all cases but a few hundred of the six thousand towers extant, only the base remains intact). Slope and declivity thus proved to be the key: the uneven distribution of the wooden pegs corresponded with almost perfect accuracy to the unevenness of the terrain. That is, a mountainous territory might not have, as at first I expected, *more* towers, but often fewer, provided that an accessible area for building could command a long canyon view to the next turning in the geological formation. (All the exceptions—for there were missing links in this chain of visibility—are in the region of the massif; it must be assumed that the "exceptions" have been buried in landslips or, if standing, have not yet been found.) Thus it became evident that in the familiar prehistoric event of invasion by sea, the life-or-death alarm could at once have been relayed—smoke by day, fire by night. So the Promethean brag of Greek Clytemnestra, that she had had a chain of beacons erected to signal instantaneously to her in Mycenae the far-off fall of Troy, a technological feat which many have been led to take merely as a portrait of her character, had here on Sardinia once in the Bronze Age actually been matched. In the face of the unremitting terror—the piracy, conquest, and colonization to which all island civilizations in the Mediterranean succumbed one by one—a shout of fire could have been relayed among the ancient Sards to every garrison on their island network, even to the innermost ring of defense, the citadel Satori unearthed in the mountain fastness of the interior.

A tiny stricken citadel: one additional layer down, several centuries of silt, shale, mica, and dust beneath the fallen and buried temples of their Roman and Carthaginian conquerors, he unearthed still another and startling find—the hivelike complex of a small nuragic city.

Nothing of this was visible when we began the dig . . . only two half-human things, one a glimmer in the obscure distance like a gold tooth in the maw of the mountains: a solitary and ghostlike tower. And another stiff grey phallic form in the cactus nearby, a tower never very large and now half-ruined, fouled by sheep and shepherds for centuries. Puddu's. It was on a slight ridge just over our site; it used to turn different colors at different hours of the day—silver to yellow-green to greenish-purple to purplish-black—as the variegated blisters of its dead and living lichen refracted the shifting light of the sun.

Satori introduced me to him the evening we arrived. We'd wound down from Nuoro, taking the tiny road past Nieddu as far as the cars could go and then following the banks of the Locoe in carts and on donkeys, Mrs. Hackett and Satori, Nicolopolos and myself, Palmer, and a local guide on horseback, plus a half-dozen men on donkeys. (Later we employed over fifty workers from three villages nearby, almost a hundred during the heaviest work of moving the earth.) We passed small herds of sheep grazing at a distance in the rock-strewn uplands. The tower was our landmark. In the almost barren pasturage below it we at once set up our camp—tents at first, in later weeks shacks and small stone buildings for the winter—and that same evening we saw Puddu arriving. Or rather we saw his sheep and goats come over the ridge—his dog, too—the shepherd was inconspicuous somewhere beyond that moving woolly mass of dirty tawny fur—and I had the sense that we'd invaded his isolation, his perfect kingdom, however barren.

Our tents were up. Satori, remembering the twisted, two-sexed, big-bellied figurine I'd had such an interest in, called me over, and together we went out to meet its finder and talk to him. I was immensely curious of course, but so apologetic for our presence on the plateau that at first I hung back reticently and watched his sheep, his dog, his boots. . . . The Commander asked all sorts of questions. Would the shepherd take him tomorrow to the exact spot? . . . Puddu shrugged. . . . Could the shepherd show him anything else he'd found? . . . Nothing else. . . . The replies came out briefly through that frondlike mustache which concealed his lips. Finally the Commander brought him over—neither of us had been invited into the tower—Puddu didn't speak to me, but shook hands gently, very seriously, as if to confer a serious dignity on me. He wore a black cap, a sheepskin jacket, white leggings, rock-heavy boots. He was young—not much older than I was. And he was very short—knotty, muscular calves and arms—large hands. He let go my hand and stood waiting, half-amused, half in sorrow. His steady knotted focused sorrowing eyes were extraordinary—was that sorrow for himself? for me?—his grief-eyes and grief-smile were confusing, but on the whole attractive. Ill at ease, I asked him questions. (I spoke Italian well by now; and all Sardinians, though they have an island language of their own, closer to Latin than Italian is, also speak the national language.) I asked about his village—his family—his work. His answers remained brief, but they were curiously friendly, his look unfailingly direct. There was a touch of manly eloquence in his tone. He spoke without flirtation. And I had the impression that he talked to me as he would talk to a man. That made me terribly uncomfortable of course.

I was dead wrong. I discovered my error in the following weeks, and the truth was more startling and more depressing. I wandered up to his tower once in the stifling hours of an early red evening. He was milking goats outside—milk for our party. Nearby, his herd of sheep looked disreputable to me, even the lambs looked shifty-eyed and seedy. The ewes had stupid, triangular faces, knobby knees, flies. Behind, they had dung on their wool. I remember noticing their udders—nothing at all like a cow's—these were narrow, long, and pointed. They weren't a bit female, they looked like curved monstrous penises, obscene satires of the dangling dork in the human male. I saw no rams. It's an odd fact, but I never remember seeing a ram around. I asked Puddu hesitantly if he would teach me to milk. He asked by way of reply whether I found my occupation difficult. I wondered if he had the slightest idea what my occupation was.

"Not too easy." I smiled. "My first job."

The young shepherd nodded, bent over, very small, jangling the pail tinnily with fine squirts that seemed to issue from his thick fingers. He said, "It will be easier in the spring."

I mumbled something about the heat.

He remarked idly, sympathetically: "It will be easier when you are not carrying a child."

I looked out to the craggy red tilt of the horizon, said something—about cactus, cabbages, flying fish—what, I have no idea. The squeeze and spurt of the timpani went on.

I'm sure I didn't show. No moon face, no crescent stomach. Later on I came to understand the affinity Sardinians feel with motherhood.

He stood up. He brought the pail and a dipper. I sipped some milk. I thanked him and said goodnight. Just as I was leaving, he touched me, casually and seriously, a touch quite as casual and serious as his remark had been—he put the flat of his heavy palm against the soft side of my breast.

It's hard to describe the gesture. It was neither hesitant nor bold, there was nothing erotic, nothing seductive in the least about the way this smelly, stone-featured, mustachioed shepherd touched my breast. He didn't caress, he didn't squeeze, he didn't feel, he didn't weigh, he didn't test me for pregnancy, he didn't fondle or pat me —though of all these, his touch came closest to a pat. It was a kind of tap of appreciation and acknowledgment.

I learned a lot from Puddu . . . though never as much as I wanted. One afternoon, almost smiling through a pall of smoke as he puffed on what appeared to be half of a rough cigar, he told me that he was about to leave to visit his "betrothed." A formal contract of betrothal had been drawn up. He was to be married next year to a widow in Nuoro, the capital of the mountain province. She was wealthy, he informed me slyly. Older, considerably older than he was—he insisted deliberately on this . . . "mature," he called her, examining seriously the stub he was smoking. He was going to bring her a present of wild game. Outside his tower the stillness was broken only occasionally by the bleating of a sheep. But inside, he said, a young boar was roasting. This, when done, he would soon be taking to her. I asked to see the boar, but it was buried in stones and myrtle leaves, completely buried in the earth under the fire. There was nothing to see, and nothing to smell, except Puddu and what he was smoking.

He continued about marriage, noting with incredibly persistent interest (morbid, I thought, in a young man about to take a wife) that there was a certain amount of infidelity among Sardinian women —but only after they were married—because it was safer then— safer at least for the woman herself. If found out, the most she generally got was a beating, sometimes not even that, sometimes not even contempt. He explained, "If a stranger takes a married woman, that woman is like a sheep or a goat which has been stolen by a thief. It is natural that the owner will try to recover his sheep. And yet he would be a fool to beat the animal when he gets her back. He locks her up. But if he can, if he *dares*, he kills the thief."

He was smoking a short cigar—a thick brown stumpy twisted thing—it was almost black—and it looked like a piece of live wood broken from a crooked branch. He offered me one but I refused. These were the so-called "shepherds"—a kind of cigar. From the workmen I'd already heard about them. They were filled with a mixture of cigarette tobacco and specially treated cactus—an inexpensive local mixture whose effect was reputed to be mildly stimulating and even aphrodisiac.

"There must be many dead thieves," I said, half as a question.

He shrugged.

"It is sometimes hard," he said quietly, "for a thief to resist, especially at a certain time." It was sometimes hard for me to take Puddu seriously because of his slight stature and his floppy, melancholy mustache. I gave that remark scant attention, I assumed he meant that adultery was most common in the spring of the year. Even by then I should have guessed that the time he meant was the period of a woman's pregnancy. (I might note that in the mountain regions of Sardinia a pregnant woman is often kept literally in confinement, a prisoner during her last two months.)

Probably by now it's occurred to you that Mungianeddu Puddu and I . . . not at all. You don't understand me if that's what you think. I was the Commander's. Indeed, on the site my principal responsibilities had turned out to be not simply and purely those of a recorder, the position for which I'd been formally employed; my occupation turned out to be pure Satori. Generally no mention is made of this position in personnel assignments in archaeology, but for work in isolated areas, the importance of there being at least one female member of the party cannot be too strongly emphasized. In the case of an intuitive genius like the Commander I was essential. (It would be supererogatory and an invasion of privacy to speculate on Mrs. Hackett's ministrations to the rest of our party. In any event, experienced as she was, she could hardly have been more effective than I was.) Mostly it was field work I did. I followed the Commander about everywhere, I took my job seriously, it wasn't easy. It was both more trying and more interesting to be near him now than it had been in Cambridge. When the Commander was in the field, everything excited him. He was insatiable. He'd sense a find— a bronze fragment, shards, a chipped knife—often when he was yards away from it. And immediately his full attention was aroused—I worked directly under him, and he was incredible. "My God, it operates like a divining rod," I teased him, watching his sleeping virility come slowly to life and point, twitching and alert, in the direction of his gaze.

"Mm-m-m," he pondered, stroking my head gratefully, while, thoroughly absorbed, I caressed his blue-veined membrane. Slowly he remarked, "Yes . . . I'm sure of it." He glanced down at me. His sex looked double-chinned, red-eyed, perspiring in that heat, and irritable. "Please, no nonsense. It has nothing to do with divination, my dear girl. Nothing whatever. Strictly a matter of logic and a reasonably good eye for detail," he said. "You see, don't you, that faint depression where the erosion line changes direction? I'll venture the wall turns there—precisely there."

From where I was sitting anyhow it looked like divination. Responsive to every promise of the landscape, his local genius pulsed attentively. Science? Well, maybe. But there's no denying that unconscious elements played a large part in his calculation and, indeed, normally do in the work of any successful archaeologist.

I dwell on these particulars in self-defense, perhaps more than good taste entirely warrants, because in later years my work has often been attacked as mere accident, the familiar triumph of the amateur. By jealous, niggish academicians, my findings have been impugned on the grounds of my inadequate credentials! I don't mean to dismiss the virtues of graduate degrees and formal academic discipline. But there can be no substitute for direct one-to-one contact with a great teacher, and in the field I had intimate, well-nigh continuous connection with Satori. I intend no jest when I say that he aroused my passion for archaeology. It is always difficult for the layman to accept the perfectly evident fact that there is a direct, even reciprocal relationship between Eros and genius. The cock crows, the mind glows. And vice versa. That this is as true in science as in the arts is sometimes hard for scientists themselves to accept. Satori knew. Despite the heat, despite the terrain, I discharged my duties faithfully. But I don't pretend that I always satisfied the Commander. On the contrary. Some years earlier he had undergone an operation to have his foreskin removed, hoping thereby to increase his waning sensitivity—an operation attended by only small success. Despite my lip service, often he merely underwent an earthquake of pride at being sexually worshipped by a nineteen-year-old child. Magnificent man as he was for his advancing age, he was frequently forced to sublimate his tremors in his work. From all this he profited. But I profited more. During this apprenticeship of mine, cross-fertilization between his talent and my own was inevitable. I absorbed more than knowledge. I learned more than when to make soundings and where to place level tags, I learned more than petroglyph data and the Wheeler method. And even if, despite my unremitting effort to retain the seeds of his genius, drops of his seminal fluid touched the ground, for me that bit of uterine earth was hallowed.

I remained therefore quite impervious to Puddu's carnal intentions. For of course that was what my shepherd had in his bachelor's mind, even when he gave me to taste of his milk, to eat of his boar, or to judge of his smoke. I knew it, and let me tell you, I was therefore bowled over, I gaped with astonishment at the first and only four-letter word I heard from him. So casual! Could I believe him?

He handed me one of those crude dark substitutes for cigars. Not a stogie. It was small. Homemade, he said, and hand-rolled. It had a savor that was hard to explain—an ineffably pleasant taste like a cigarette, but different—it twisted all down my throat to my lungs in a tantalizing, almost electrical way. "*What's* it called?" I demanded again, incredulous.

"Sometimes it is called *fica*," he told me.

Naturally—since *fica* means "cunt"—I was thunderstruck. I mulled over that "sometimes," too. I realized a moment or two later that given the rumored stimulus, *fica* was the inevitable nickname— the natural pun on *fichi*—cactus pears. The Italians call the succulent fruit of the cactus *fichi d'India*. And the cactus filler for the twisted hand-rolled little cigars known to others as "shepherds," or *pastori*, came from a local variety of tall and very sharply barbed cactus, *Carnegiea spinosa nuorensis*. The shepherds themselves of course rarely called their own cigars "shepherds." For them the more common expression was indeed *fica* and it was used without satire, without a smile. For Puddu, cunt was the name, no more. (I should add that *abba ardente*, Sardinia's specialty liquor and the favorite drink on the island, was sometimes made from the same versatile cactus. On the site the workmen, who called it *filu ferru*, or barbed wire, actually drank it for breakfast! But in moderation. Never did I see anyone take more than two fingers.)

As we talked I enjoyed the cigar—a cigar only in its shape since it wasn't rolled from leaves, and since when inhaled it was milder than a cigarette. I remember feeling buoyant, but only delicately so. Sexual? It wasn't. Not really. Not precisely. Sensual, maybe that's what it was . . . but I suspected it was all imaginary. After all, knowing what to look for, I'd experienced the effect . . . it was predictable . . . my flesh seemed to be developing unaccustomed sensations everywhere—a kind of "presence." But it was very slight. My mind was the same, normally clear, nothing in any way out of the ordinary, no "high" at all . . . but something else—my body—seemed to be clearer than usual, that's all . . . a kind of pleasant "low"—it struck me that I was experiencing my fleshly, animal self in an unusually sustained and resonant way—clear-bodied. I became aware of my skin, that thin contact between me and the rest of the world. My elbow, touching a rock, felt ticklish, and even the touch of my clothes made me tingle.

Imaginary? I wasn't sure. But it was delightful.

Would he teach me to make those cactus cigars? Impressed by my interest, he volunteered to teach me how—and even promised me an invitation to dinner when I'd learned. It was a simple process, although it took a couple of weeks of patience and care. We cut down some of the nearby cactus and dragged it back in burlap. He showed me how to trim off the outside of the plant, reserving the spines for later use. Chopping up the heads and hearts, we cooked them to a juicy pulp. He showed me how to flavor the residue ever so faintly with the pungent little seeds of a plant known as "grains of paradise." Then he had me turn out this mash into a flat wooden container he kept in the tower, a long board with low sides. We set the thickening pulp out to ferment and dry in the sun slowly, every day at sundown cutting and shredding it further as it hardened, both to aid in the slow drying and to produce the final coarse-cut texture. The spines, ground to a powder in a stone mortar and pestle, were added near the end when the mixture had begun to look like greenish-brown dried herbs. And then we mixed the fibrous stuff with tobacco and rolled it in heavy brown papers, twisted like Tuscan cigars. I got the hang of rolling them at once. The finished twiglike cheroots, when lighted, had that same virtually flavorless, yet seraphic bouquet.

We smoked them as the prelude to our feast.

Only a couple. Again the delightfully clearheaded, clearskinned sensation. I imagined I could taste with my skin. And I did with my mouth of course . . . that suckling pig—so small it was only the size of Mungianeddu's boot—its baby snout still bloodied, its ribs crucified on a crisscross of wooden skewers, and its crackling skin coated with an exquisite cactus-lemon-and-blood sauce. Puddu gave me the recipe. He had made it, he said, in a few minutes, from the same cactus mash we had prepared together. Another attempt to arouse me? If one could believe him (and I did), the sauce was superb on chicken and spring lamb, and had to contain, besides lemon and honey, a few drops of blood from one's own thumb.

The violent gentleness in him. A boyhood of frustration—he had wanted to stay in school and been unable to continue beyond sixth grade; the penury of his family—he had begun to herd sheep for a living when he was eleven; the period he had spent in prison—together with two older brothers, now dead, Mungianeddu at fourteen had burned to the ground the farm of a wealthy landlord and committed certain sexual atrocities against the landlord's cattle, a vendetta for some unrevealed offense to their sister. He was out on parole.

Since he told me all this with hardly a tremor of feeling, I never understood until a good deal later how much he had come to hate the police by now, the present system, and in fact mainland Italy—he hated even Satori, whom he regarded as a Sardinian defector. Nor of course did I guess that he had already violated his parole by becoming secretly implicated in the island's sporadic agitation against Italy.

(I remember that on the first day of our arrival in the port of Cagliari, the Commander had gone off to a private dinner of reconciliation with his son Carlo. I had wandered up the street from our hotel, alone, and on a great retaining wall there I'd seen slogans scrawled:

No Ai Militari, No Ai Padroni, No All'Italia
La Sardegna È La Nostra
Rivoluzione E Indipendenza

But I saw not a trace of revolution in Sardinia. Nowhere, not once during my stay. The secessionist violence we'd heard about aboard ship in Naples had been put down, and apparently it stayed put.)

In a roundabout manner, however, something of Puddu's political feelings did come out that evening—despite his guarded manner—I was to remember this in after years with surprised chagrin at my own unperceptiveness.

I was licking my fingertips and telling him—alas, with condescension—about Satori's work and I mentioned Homer and the discovery of Troy. He stopped me dead in the middle of what I was saying and seized me by the upper arm. Holding me almost painfully, to my dizzy disbelief he proceeded to inform me that the so-called sardonic smile of Ulysses, which Homer himself calls sardonic, did not mean, could not mean, a Sardinian smile even though the ancient Greeks called the islanders *Sardi*. The similarity in words must have been an accident. To smile in a sardonic way—what was that?—a man must have guile. But the Sardinians were the most straightforward undesigning people, always.

Did he read Greek? No, of course not, he had read *about* all that, but it was an argument that interested him greatly. Greatly. Letting his fingers slide, he grabbed my elbow and informed me pointedly, with grievance, that in the passage where Cicero speaks of the notoriously corrupt Sardinians, he could not have meant the corruption of Sardinians themselves, but of their government. Government officials.

Who were—? Romans of course, corrupt administrators sent over from the mainland. It was almost the same story now as then, wasn't it? With this one difference: Now, he said, we are going to kick them out.

To this determination of his I paid too little attention. But I had my reasons. I suppose I was too aware of another determination he had, with respect to me. (His desire then and my reluctance, despite the stimulation of his cigars and his sauce—how painful and shameful to remember that later on, when his dedication to his homeland came uppermost, our relations became utterly reversed.) The double stone walls of every nuragic tower enclose a spiral of rooms. In the ruined state the dome at the top is open to the stars. "Please—" I remonstrated with him that night, wanting him to remain my friend.

"*Here.*"

"No."

"Come on then." Smaller than me, he started to pull . . . gently. "Up there."

"No."

"Outside?"

"No. I can't," I told him.

"A vow?"

"Yes." It was close to the truth, close enough.

"Sit down then," he said, "if it can't be helped. Stay here. Watch the fire. I'm not calm. I'm going outside."

But I didn't watch the fire. There was a fire in my mouth and I was afraid. I didn't sit. He had disappeared.

Where? Puddu moved quickly. Though small of stature or perhaps because of that, he had a controlled, forceful way of moving—a tense energy in his legs like the dignified strength in his head and glance. Gone suddenly.

Where to?

I went round quietly behind the tower. The moon was curved like a sheep's udder. I looked over to where the sheep were penned. They were watching, too. I rather doubt it would have bothered Puddu to know I was watching. I'm sure it hadn't even occurred to him that I'd do anything other than watch a fire I'd been instructed to watch. What I saw was Puddu with one of his least attractive and, in my judgment, least respectable ewes. He was with her, he was on her, he was in her, he was too busy to hear me approach, he was calming himself. There was energy in what they were up to, I suppose. But nothing you could condemn as lust. There was heat and vigor—something that passed for sentiment even. But no passion. He calmed himself inside that extraordinarily docile beast.

And *she* looked round: I'm certain that that knobby-kneed, bug-eyed ewe did see me.

I returned to the fire—irritated, amused, outraged, and a great deal more at ease about remaining in the tower with Puddu. The fire in my mouth had gone out.

When he returned, he was entirely serene, altogether relaxed. His inclinations, his needs, his cocky sureness, his gritty eloquence, his wealth of information on every subject . . . Puddu, except for his mustache, was ugly, but he was not repellent to me, I assure you. I took him for what he was, a part of his landscape. And I admired his intelligence. But God knows he stank. Even from where I was sitting I could perceive him vividly when he came striding back in through the opening. Sitting cross-legged with him on the dirt floor of his tower while the flames of his odorless cooking crackled and smoked through the open cone above, I listened to all his theories and explanations. "It is because you are not Sardinian," he said with that perpetual look of dark grinning wistful interest which remained just this side of a smile, "that you must refuse. When a Sardinian woman is great with child, the men who see her all rejoice and are happy to take her if they can because then there is no chance that she will present her husband with a false child." It was a very sorrowful smile he gave me under his mustache. "If the Commander were—"

"I'm not married to him."

I could see the fellow bristle. His calf flexed abruptly. His boot shoved a brand further into the fire. He did not easily brook interruption from a girl or woman, married or unmarried. But then for him I was perhaps neither—nothing at all in the usual sense. No Sardinian woman was blonde, wore pants, wandered around by herself, walked alone among men, had dinner with Puddu in his tower, or said proudly, as I did, "I'm unmarried. You told me there were *no* infidelities—"

"Among girls I said," he came back at me angrily, "because the father must sell them for their drop of blood."

I gave him my quizzical look, my head cocked to one side. I speculated, was he thinking of widows?

His cheeks rose at both sides in that expression that never passed the planning for a glum laugh. And then he shifted position uncomfortably. Could one talk to a female in this way? I could practically see him wondering. Well, to me he could continue because I wore jeans. "The dowry the father gives with the girl. But we say that he sells his daughter at the wedding for the drop of blood he gets in return. After the ceremony, her father and all the wedding guests remain, they remain in the living room, drinking and singing at night, while the new couple goes to bed. Everyone stays until the bridegroom reappears. He must reappear from the bedroom, alone with the bridal sheet in his hand, showing the drop of blood, which he presents to her father in payment."

I grew heated. "But not every girl—"

He grew overheated. "Every girl." He kicked the fire irritably, he kicked it again.

"Some of your newlyweds must cut their thumbs."

He softened, he *almost* smiled. And when Mungianeddu Puddu's knotted eyes and cheeks relaxed and brightened, he became—no, not handsome, but prodigious, as if a worn rock should suddenly manifest a sense of humor.

I had a lot to learn—about archaeology—and about Sardinians. The plateau we were digging into was as hot as an oven, hemmed in by radiant crags and cliffs that seemed to act as reflecting surfaces focusing the sun on us. It was cooler down in the trench of the excavation itself, where the men and donkeys were continually pulling out soil, but since most of my work was up above, I found the long daily heat insufferable. No matter what the temperature, the Sardinians wore their black stocking-caps and white knicker-pants. The rest of us had to resort to sun helmets and shorts. I dressed more or less like the others: at night jeans or jodhpurs and a shirt, during the day khaki shorts and a white halter.

The traditional Sardinian dress for women covers the body from a woman's Adam's apple to her ankles, long billowing black dresses for workdays, multicolored gowns like birds of paradise on holidays. To the local men, most of whom were shepherds when they could find employment, I must have looked half-naked. Their reactions speeded our work.

When I wasn't serving as Satori's understudy, I worked outside Puddu's tower near the foreman's tent as a liaison between our Sardinian foreman, Urru, and the archaeologists. I kept the Small Finds Index, I recorded our daily progress in the Site Notebook, and I acted as a kind of checker for the work gangs. So, to catch a good look at my exposed body, the men (sometimes smoking *pastori* cheroots) drove their donkeys, loaded with double bags of soil and rubble, eagerly up out of the ditch to pause at my checkstand. There was no doubt that I was popular. A trail of men and donkeys wound past me into the heat, climbing along the cactus ridges to dump their loads, then gladly back to me again.

I refused all their offers of cigars. I did accept the prickly succulent little cactus pears they brought. And sometimes I went with them, walking or riding. Sardinian donkeys are pygmy-size. If you want to ride, you have to ride with your feet almost scraping the ground. It was fun, but I took the precaution of being always in the company of at least two men. Until I learned to do that, there had been dozens of incidents like the one with Puddu. The men were nothing but gentle with me, but they couldn't seem to keep their hands off, one spot or another, usually my belly. Several of them even kissed me there, or on the sides of my breasts, and though I enjoyed their appreciative soft nuzzling of my expanding mound, I wasn't quite sure about the other one, or whether I should feel insulted, or where international friendship might lead.

As my pregnancy advanced, the archaeologists to a man grew more solicitous for my welfare, it's true, but shockingly indifferent to my engorged body. Even Satori. The coldness in his warm concern gave me gooseflesh: did I repel him? Did I repel all of them? Gradually, I got so big that letting out my shorts didn't work; I had to borrow first Mrs. Hackett's, then the Commander's. But no matter how big I got, interest among the workmen persisted, appreciation of my shape waxed stronger as I grew larger. Enthusiasm was general and, I thought, intense. "Round, very round. A good fine belly."

"Thank you, good day to you, much luck to you."

"Like the belly of a donkey, miss."

"Thank you, hurry back now." By this time they all knew I was unmarried, but they seemed untroubled by the fact. Did they regard me as a slut? That wasn't at all the way they sounded. Perhaps they thought of me as peculiar, eccentric, incomprehensible—undressed, unmarried, unashamed.

"The right time of the year, you'll give birth with the sheep." Laughter—at my expense? It was too genial to be anything but merriment, hilarity, pleasure. I was admired. I was sought after. It was as if the plumpness at my middle were a lodestone; I had a magnet that drew them around me. They responded to me: I responded to them. They appreciated my fertility: I appreciated their appreciation. And I began to experience the kind of indiscriminate and sweeping desire I had experienced on shipboard. I wanted them, almost any one of them, as I had wanted almost any sailor aboard, any gentle, sardonic, appreciative Sardinian at all. But which one? Puddu was too cocksure, too irritable, too impatient. Well, there was Urarti, with a mustache thicker than Puddu's and wider, Urarti with whom I had once rubbed cheeks and whose old, unlined face was as comfortable and aromatic as a tobacco pouch. Or there was young Carrus, closer to my own age, whose nose had nostrils like a donkey's, nostrils that expanded whenever he sniffed round me lecherously, but whose genuine shyness and sweetness trembled in his long eyelashes with every voyeuristic glimpse of my belly he stole. The two Gonnosfanadigo boys? Unpronounceable sons of an unpronounceable father, the Gonnosfanadigo lads, both in their middle forties, carried a pick and a shovel respectfully, flatfooting it in polite, if skin-deep awe behind their tough-skinned whisker-white old man who wielded the family spade and never gave them a word that wasn't an order. And yet it did my heart good to see the three of them approach me on an equal footing, their eyes glistening equally, their mouths watering equally. Or the tiny army of hard-fingered small-haunched bump-shouldered young men who lingered a moment near me in gratitude and then sweated on: past the obliging *americana*, their well of lust, their shade of love, the single exfoliate denuded fruit-bearing palm tree in their desert. A dozen or more young men in their teens and twenties, a couple of dozen more in their thirties, sunburned and thirsty, hardened but desirous. "A strong healthy woman," I heard literally dozens of times, "is more beautiful than the most beautiful of horses," a confession often accompanied by the fondest of pats, "as the child is more beautiful than the foal."

"Thank you, it's always a pleasure to talk to you, come back with more." I meant it, every word of it.

Satori scratched the top of his head. "If you persist, you're going to start a new fertility cult, more popular than the ancient one," he chuckled.

"Tell me about the ancient one," I demanded.

But he went on chuckling—hiding his annoyance, guarding his arcane learning, twitting me about the obvious position of leadership I now enjoyed by virtue of my fleshly charisma. No, I hadn't exactly supplanted him. At least not yet. But I got more work out of the men than either he or the foreman did. And as for fertility cults, well, I wouldn't have minded. I encouraged their proverbs, I confessed their faith, I worshipped their worship. But which one, which of my many lusty adorers? Which of my open, dedicated, votive lovers?

Which of my rock-faced, bone-muscled, glaze-fired, ingot-toothed, four-handled, trilingual, wide-lipped, stêle-browed, bronze-flanked fertility-lovers would I love in return? Which one? Marinaru, S'Adde, or Anghelu Ruju? Priu, or Mannu, or Bonnanaro? Accocci, Birori, or Nuraxinieddu? Concas, Sa Perda, Ilixi, Silanus, Is Paras, Paddaggiu, Rebeccu, Utu? Su Lamarzu, Orcosu? Baunei, Bultei? Gerrei, Sulcei? Cicicu Creccu? Or little sandstone, blockheaded, bull-necked, eneolithic Ba Shardan, with an irregular squarish hole for a mouth, probably an import from North Africa, and even shorter than Puddu? No. How could I choose? Not a single one of them would have served the purpose sufficiently. No one of them could have satisfied the adulation they had all aroused. I wanted not one of them, I wanted all of them. Every last one of them. With the baby in my belly, I felt I had come into my power as a woman.

> I want to tell you right away
> About a big red fire

But the attitude of the men toward me did not persist, it changed subtly near the beginning of my seventh month. It seemed to happen almost overnight . . . they still flocked round me, but they no longer treated me with the old fond, if rough, familiarity; they still watched me, but they stopped the warmth, the pleasantries. A distance stretched between them and me: and I couldn't make it out. Suddenly I found it hard to talk to them. Mungianeddu Puddu would tell me nothing. He was mysterious. Baffled, I put the whole thing down to the physical grossness of advanced pregnancy—I had become ungainly, unsightly, unattractive . . . to everyone now.

Of course I was wrong, I know now what had happened, there was no mystery about it. I should have guessed. A week or so earlier, toward the end of my sixth month, Satori had insisted—over my continuing objections—that I had to go see a doctor and have monthly check-ups from now to the end. Well, I went—George and Mrs. Hackett drove me into Nuoro one day—and exactly what I knew would happen, happened. Damn it, but what else was I supposed to do? The doctor insisted on giving me a pelvic. He was an ancient frail bald white-bearded doll-like man who looked about seventy, he tottered to the examining table like a starving goat. I was sure he was going to have a heart attack. I tried to warn him, I tried to explain, "You see—" I apologized, "I'm sorry, I—" But he was too quick for me.

He was surprised of course, but not all *that* surprised. He bent. "Magnificent," he said, working his gums and his eyes energetically. He almost grinned. It was totally unlike my first examination.

"I was born—"

"*Zitto!*" He had his fingers in me and he worked them around expertly, examining his find like an appraiser working on a jewel. "Unbelievable!"

"When I was sixteen—"

"Miraculous."

"I'm sorry."

"Don't be silly."

"I should have warned you."

"You forget," he shook his head—ancient, cherry-lipped, benevolent—in a hurry he poured himself an overflowing thimbleful of *abba ardente*—"in pagan times—" he muttered briefly—and downed his ounce. He capped the bottle and his mouth. All he would say was, "You forget, you forget, this is Sardinia."

How I
Became
A Myth

The hidden manna I do eat,
The word of life it is my meat.
—ANNE BRADSTREET

The history of my stay in Sardinia is largely the story of my pregnancy. It's true that in the short time I was there many astounding things happened to me. I discovered a new country, I contracted a fever called archaeology, I fell in love with a shepherd, I was kidnapped, lost, and raped, I was even deified as the local goddess. But none of these phenomenal happenings was nearly so astounding or crucial as the phenomenon of pregnancy itself—the great single event. And what was most amazing of all was its apparent or at least seeming normalness—its really cheeky confidence in its development. It took me over; it became the center.

It became the point around which everything else in the world revolved. Did the cliffs form an oven, reflecting heat on our site? Then my womb was the center of that oven, the focus of the rays from the sun, and the child in my belly was a kind of supreme bread, manna in mannish form, rising and baking, rising and baking. Were the villagers intrigued by the unaccustomed exposure of my fertile shape and flesh? Did I excite, did I stimulate, did I titillate them? Well, then, not because I was female or imprudent, but because I was a firefly, a spark by day in the blackness of their lust, a visible fire that ignited their dark enthusiasm for generation. I would soon open a door for them, I was a warder, I was the keeper of their imagination. Did our excavation on the plateau grow deeper each week, did it reach into history, into the earth, into death? I reached deeper each week, into the past, too, but beyond history into something unrealized, beyond the crust of earthly soil into something unearthly, even beyond the possibility of dying, though he/she would die in time.

As our excavation deepened, my hill rose, and my excitement and awareness shifted gradually from archaeology to genesis. It no longer seemed to me that I *was* my body, or even that I was *in* it, but that it had been borrowed and stuck temporarily outside and below me where I could keep my eye on it perfectly. I studied its progress. I appropriated one of the tapes used for marking and recording in our journals the exact positions of finds. In my own journal, I marked and recorded, in both inches and centimeters, the gradual swell of my belly. Never since the time I used to fuss about my penis had I been so avid for measurement. I was amazing: not only my girth fascinated me, not only my breasts, plumper, heavier, more tender, more swollen, like soft gourds. But my nipples budded like berries, and like berries they turned darker every month. I could hardly recognize me. From where I looked, my breasts appeared to rest on a shelf, my abdomen. The skin there developed the tough texture of animal hide while preserving the gloss of fine parchment. My belly was a drum to finger, a gourd to rattle, a hill to run on, a moon to gape at, a package to not open before Christmas. And when my knotty belly button popped, I began to laugh at the show.

It occurred to me that I was witnessing not merely a clever spectacle and a farce, but a trick, an illusion, a delusion. Me—Millie —pregnant? Me—Millie-Willie—pregnant? It didn't matter at all which name I named. An undertow—disbelief—which had been tugging at me from the beginning of my affair with Flaminia, despite my assurance, set in, set in ever more strongly as the tide of pregnancy advanced, until I couldn't deny that it had caught me. Me, of all people. Yes, I still hoped, maybe even believed—but I became gradually, terribly aware that I'd been skeptical from way back. My doubts became enormous; bit by bit, week by week, my suspicions grew with my shape.

For one thing, I was only human: I was convinced that my own body did not have the know-how and resources to create another one. Second, it struck me that I might after all be sick rather than pregnant: I was growing a tumor in there instead of a fetus. Third, there simply wasn't enough room, not inside me there wasn't. Before the end of the fifth month I saw that the available space was gone; by the end of the sixth I canceled all plans for expansion; by the end of the seventh my continuing inflation made me hysterical, I walked around gingerly, watching for splinters, ready to burst. Fourth, the more I thought about it, the less likely it seemed that I could have impregnated myself anyhow; and parthenogenesis had been written off the books along with spontaneous generation; the whole thing was a hoax. Fifth, the very idea that my own sperm or anyone else's could be responsible for initiating such total changes—not just a new contour under my clothes, but a new life, a new soul—consciousness, desire, joy, fear, and suffering—who could believe it? It defied credence. Sixth, if I *myself* was a freak, if I was pregnant and pregnancy *itself* was freakish, it followed that any conceivable child of that condition would turn out to be, as I had been, a sport, a bent link, a joke of nature, and, likely as not, another hermaphrodite. I was prepared for the worst.

I didn't only ponder these matters; my pregnancy produced poetry as well. I scribbled fragments of verse, whenever and wherever I could, sometimes on the bottom of our burial reports.

Please.
Don't push.
Give me time.
It gives me the chills.
Just give me a fish in my womb
To catch, a milkloving fish to nurse
Till he swims, an adorable fish with gills
For brains, and I'm the whale that spermed him.

But I soon saw that my jottings, lyrical as they were, fell wide of the mark. They failed to achieve the kind of poetic intensity and intention that results only from extension: in breadth and in depth. I hadn't much time to think about these matters during the day, but at night, while the others played cards or chess, I studied my fragments under a kerosene lamp. My weaknesses were apparent. And oddly, one night, the reason presented itself clearly, presented itself between one high yellow flicker, so to speak, and the next blue guttering of my short wick's flame. I've quoted the lines above not as an example, but because they were the very scrawl that pointed to the path I needed to take. The materials for a poetic breakthrough, I realized with an awe reserved for the apprehension of miracles, were everywhere at hand—all around me. By chance? By accident? Miracles cannot be accidents.

The path was out in the night and in the inner darkness. It was in my body and in the pit we were digging, not in the one, not in the other, but in both seen as a single process. The birth of the future and the exhumation of the past. To produce the living child whose rhythmic heart would pulse pentameters of the spirit, forward as long as life lasted, and forward again in yet another child of its own creation—to produce *that*, my body had reached back beyond me into the flickerings of protoplasm: the very beat and rhythm by which the primal cells had danced the first dance under the meter of the cold tide. Backward in time equals forward in time. As Satori and the shepherds and the rest of us unearthed the pillars and lintels, the coals and bracelets, the funeral urns and pisspots of a civilization withered nearly beyond recall, we brought that delicate and dust-clogged death out into sweaty day and fresh acknowledgment. Backward in time, forward in time. In poetry no less was true. Time was my clue. A poem entered the future by the wedge of the past. And the key was at hand: the myth, the mythic substratum, the silted layers, the fish in my womb, the poetic artifact that reaches backward to pulse forward.

Others before me of course had adopted myths—had *employed* them—to order and extend poetic meanings. But my conception was altogether in another dimension. I was not going to use myth, I was going to become one: I would "mythicize" myself, the poet, not the poem. Damn the poem!—I suddenly realized—if the author were mythic and wrote out of that myth, the poem could take care of itself. Would.

Now remember, it isn't easy to make yourself into a myth; that's not one of your everyday problems, the kind that can be solved. Try it and see. Self-mythification is a two-finger exercise for fools. The ancient texts are lucid and unanimous. Leda became a myth by the violence of the gods, Helen by the terrible suffrage of men, and Medea by the tears and acid of circumstance. In my own case a sticky little web formed of all three strands—the divine, the human, and the circumstantial—caught me when I fell and supported me through the ordeal of apotheosis. Yes, mythmaking was something that happened to me, something I stumbled into, I admit I couldn't have pulled myself into the stars by my own bootstraps. And yet, and yet. It wasn't until I bent to tie my laces that I tripped, fell, and could rise again.

Toward the end of my pregnancy I sank into a heavy melancholy, a tired resentment the very reverse of that serenity, that joyful confidence, which usually accompanies the last weeks before childbirth. I'm not entirely sure how to account for my depression. Partly it was Palmer's death. In October he'd been sick, yellow jaundice, and we had got used to doing without him. Then he seemed to be getting better. And then he got lost. And then in November he was found dead one morning in a back street of the village of Mamoiada, miles from our site, wrapped in a sack, with a shotgun bullet through his head. It was ear to ear. I didn't see him, but I was told it was a single clean shot. And that was about all that could be said: it may have been his peculiar ears, it may have been a senseless killing. The police were baffled and blocked at every turn. Political motives were ruled out, since he was a foreigner. There were bandits in the hills, but Palmer hadn't been robbed. There had been no evidence of kidnapping, no demand for ransom. Vendetta killings were common, but not against foreigners, nor did anyone really know what code or custom Palmer could conceivably have broken. Sardinian villagers in the mountains are tight-lipped and clannish about talking to the police. No one admitted having seen him in Mamoiada. Why had he gone there in the first place; or had he been merely deposited there? The investigation went on futilely into December. We never found out anything.

So I suppose it was Palmer's death in part. But partly it was the landscape, too—so cruel, so fantastically inhuman, devoid of interest in us and yet presiding over us. And partly it was the excavation, the daily disemboweling of time. Stratified: we were digging up always a deeper, a more ancient death—the lost, the well lost, too, a disintegration for which no one sorrowed. Below me, the pit smelled as I thought Palmer's corpse must have smelled by the time it was found. It was no place for a new birth, the earth seemed inhospitable, it was going to be like giving birth in a moon crater. If Sandy had been with me, I knew it would have been different. He'd have held my hand and talked brilliantly, cynically, and made me feel a sentimental fool and I'd have been happy . . . expectant . . . laughing a little at myself.

How *was* he? I'd had only one little postcard from him in all this time. I'd sent him a snapshot of me in my explorer's sun helmet and jodhpurs, showing me kneeling in a trench at the south end of the temple (Plate IX), chipping away the soil around a half-exposed clay tablet and frowning earnestly. I hadn't been in the least bit sentimental in that letter. I'd wished him lots of luck in his second year at medical school; I'd asked whether he was hoping for a boy or a girl and if he had any suggestions for a name. He wrote back mentioning the synthesis of a new hormone which he thought might someday be of use to me (but which later came to nothing); wondered how tight my jodhpurs were; specified that he preferred a child of both sexes ("I want a girl just like the girl that"). And there, squeezed in at the bottom of his card, were two rows of names, Mabel, Susan, Jane, Irma—Marvin, Sam, Joe, Ike—something on that order. I thought of burying the card in the fresh-dug tomb of Noragugume, but instead I fed it spitefully to one of the diminutive asses that happened to be passing by with a load of dirt.

Noragugume's dirt. Manured by skin and calcined with teeth. It was no time for a new birth. That was late November or early December. By then we had already unearthed pretty much the entire base of a fair-sized Punic temple and were trying to sort and order the fragments of walls, architraves, and fallen pillars—the fat short pock-marked columns of Carthage. The cellars of the temple and the burial vaults adjoining it now yielded, to the patient work of the diggers, new excitements daily: metalwork, worn tablets, sewers, tools, carbonized bones, toothless skulls, and two emblazoned thrones.

The work became delicate and slow; the Commander himself was apt to dig with a trowel or knife for hours in a few inches of soil. I ought to mention that although I myself left after a year, the job of excavation continued not only into a second, but into a third, unplanned year because it was not until the latter part of the second year that Satori found what he'd been persistently hunting for: the nuragic subsegment. Getting to it threatened the entire Carthaginian remains above and proved a hair-raising feat. Until I managed to return to the island years later, I saw only pictures of these prehistoric ruins: an irregular wall with parapets that looked like giants' toes with rotten toenails; a long embankment of presumably military cells; streets, huts, wells, two temples, and a circle of squat hives—fortresses in approximately the moundlike construction of nuraghi, unevenly arranged to protect a central stronghold or miniature "palace."

The dig went on. The morning rains had come, softening the soil, and though it was colder now, it was quite tolerable to work outdoors in the sunny afternoons. I sat and watched and checked and counted, heavier day by day, and everyone was helpful to me, cheerful, very cheerful, Satori, the digger teams, Lou, and I couldn't bear their solicitude. By the year's end, as I approached full term, I was in the grip of a peculiar combination of anger and lethargy from which no one could pry me loose. For above everything else, what hurt me most and depressed me most was precisely that Satori and the rest took it for granted that the wisest course . . . the perfect thing . . . was that I should bring my baby into being and just give the creature away. *Was* that immutable? necessary? healthy? I thought back and forth about keeping the child, I began to imagine trite lives for unwed mothers, perhaps I could run away to Rome and work as a housemaid to support the baby and me, or I could marry Nicco (who'd stopped pursuing me, but would again after it was over, I knew) and live in Greece, or I could stay here in Sardinia to work alongside Mungianeddu, not a bad life. But impossible. I saw it. Impossible because the vastly ambitious drive of my life, the whole desire of my being, would not permit it. In the field once, poking fun at my earnestness and my pride, the Commander had teased me, "I'll wager that one of these days someone will come along and solve the riddle of the origins of human civilization for us, and when I look round it will turn out to be you." I vowed then and there to oblige him. I *was* proud. And my needs were more imperative than the usual fantasies of the college girl. I felt I *could* become a great archaeologist if I stuck at it, Satori had become ever more encouraging in these months, he was taking me almost seriously now, I thought, in an almost professional way—I had another three years of college to go, it was true—but if I wanted to get on in archaeology, my education—surely I had to finish—and then? There was so much ahead, so much to *do*—and with a baby? I was only nineteen. If I wanted a career, my own exciting life, the exacting challenge to *achieve* something . . . well yes, I did want that. There seemed no way out.

So gradually I formed another plan, seemingly of itself, or rather, a "solution" took shape and it grew in me like the baby, a poetic notion, filling me with satisfying, staggering urgency. It is difficult to explain it even to myself now—what I did—though when I remember the desolate insulting silver glare of Gennargentu and the corpselike smell (*had* Palmer smelled like that?) of the deepening excavation and my longing for Sandy, I can come close to it. I can understand, that is, the young confusion of feelings. The action, however, I can only attribute to the dramatic giddiness of a very boyish girl.

My idea, my mythmaking gesture, was to give birth in just the fiercely forlorn way I really felt about the whole thing. I would go away as lonely as a wild animal, alone in my pains when my time came round. I would find some spot on this island where I could expose my shuddering big belly naked on an open rock or maybe hidden away in a clump of giant cactus, any spot would do between the high sun and the core of the earth that was isolated and cruel enough for my ritual. I would dedicate him or her to the gods of Sardinia—to the old hard gods of the pit. Whoever they were, wherever they were under the terrible moldy earth, they rotted, and I would present the child formally to their powers and presences and ask their blessings on the infant's head.

Away in the distance, rust and orange in the falling of the sun, the tower of Barbagia sos Nidos looked as likely a place as any.

It was a damn fool thing to do.

They said later that the tower was twenty kilometers away. My due date was the twenty-fifth of January, but I was sure the baby was going to be born on New Year's Eve or New Year's Day. I watched for the contractions—the *contorsioni*—but New Year's Eve came and New Year's Day went and I was still just heavy and depressed.

It began with an invitation. The mayor of Cagliari, a personal friend of Satori's, invited our entire party to be guests of his city for the Feast of the Epiphany—that is, Twelfth Night. The Commander was opposed; he didn't want to lose half a week's work; it was hard enough now with Palmer gone. But he knew from experience that it would be difficult to continue through the holidays. Most of the men would not show up for work at all during the feast days, and the festival would be worth seeing, a period of processions, dances, acrobatics, horse combats, high-spirited drunken foolery. In remote parts of the island, it was said, some celebrations lasted for days, with obscure and primitive rituals that were far from Christian—and kept well hidden from strangers since the Church disapproved. The celebration in the island's capital was more civilized. (While he was there the Commander also planned to consult his son about the disposition of my child and to ask him to take care of the legalities of an adoption. I did not know about this until years later: he kept it from me to spare me any unnecessary concern.) But in any event, the mayor's invitation brought only frustration to me: I was nearly nine months pregnant and quite unable to undergo the long rough automobile journey over dirt roads down to the capital.

Neither could I be left alone. Mrs. Hackett?—she wanted to see the festivities, too. So I was packed off to Nuoro to await their return. It was quite safe. You can imagine how I felt: just in case my baby might be a bit earlier than expected, everything was arranged. I was to stay in the house of the very midwife whose services had been previously contracted. No trouble. Convenient. I felt abandoned, miserable, and cheated. Sullen, I said nothing. We all drove carefully up the valley, zigzag into Nuoro one early morning—Satori shook a thick-fingered *ciao* out of the window as he pulled away, *ciao, pazienza, auguri,* and the rest of it—and I was left standing on the steep steps of the doctor's house a little after 8 A.M. I saw the doctor, he saw me. At 8:30 I left his house to walk the three cobblestone blocks to the midwife's house. I never got there.

I had time. I decided instead to have a look at the monument I'd heard about, a memorial to Grazia Deledda, the Sardinian novelist, one of the first women to receive the Nobel Prize in Literature. I've often found it strange to think that my adventure began with that step, however incomplete. (The visit to her monument described in my Stockholm acceptance speech took place years later. But let me take the opportunity to reiterate here, echoing Hemingway, that despite my accomplishments, the extraordinary Isak Dinesen deserved to receive the Nobel award long before I did.) I started to walk, uncertain of my direction. Rattling down the street toward me was a donkey cart drawn by two stiff-legged rickety donkeys. I recognized the cart that regularly delivered the mail to our camp and made the daily circuit of all the mountain villages. I recognized the driver, too, and I thumbed a ride with him in the general direction of the Deledda monument. Probably he understood not a word I said; later he claimed that he thought I said I wanted a ride back to the site, a protestation of his innocence which may or may not have been true. There's no telling. But that's the direction he took me in—back to camp. I got in, and pretty soon I saw that we were leaving Nuoro, clumsily rolling back down into the cactus valley. Far in the brightening distance I saw the silver snout of Gennargentu and the tiny golden glare of the nuragic tower beneath its summit.

I began to feel them as the cart jolted over the ruts. I felt them, I felt them again, I felt them again, and I decided—quite incorrectly— that I was entering labor. Contractions. My golden tower. I'd manage, I would get there somehow, deliver the baby myself, dedicate the wrinkled primitive child to the wrinkled primitive gods—well, utter nonsense, of course. And wide, wide of the mark as it turned out. What happened was beyond my power to arrange.

The road we were on skirted the ridges of cliffs—down, then up again. My tower disappeared, became visible, and remained visible in the peaks for miles. When the donkeys had pulled to a point in the road which I judged to be perhaps the closest point, I asked the driver to stop. I told him that I'd changed my mind, that I was going back to Nuoro—I was going to go with the others to Cagliari after all, to the Feast of the Epiphany. He showed no surprise. What did he think? Well, Sardinian women who are pregnant are confined to the house; an American woman can walk where she likes. I don't know what he thought—he was an old man with a long white beard, wearing the puffy white pants and the long black stocking-cap—but he put me down at the side of the road as I requested. Later at Orgosolo, his first stop, he reported that the *pazza americana* had changed her mind and gone off to Cagliari with the others. That much we substantiated afterward.

I had no idea of course that I was being tracked as I made my way climbing across the landscape. I felt I was walking in utter isolation across the imposing expanse of a crater on the moon. But I had probably been watched from the time I left the doctor's, perhaps earlier, and had probably given the watchers some surprise when I got into the cart. I may be paranoid about the issue, but I can't help suspecting forethought. My doctor was a sweet old man and a competent village physician, but it's certain he was also a senile village gossip and a loose bladder-mouth. Almost two months had elapsed since he'd first examined me. Out there where the landscape is rugged and few write letters for the mail cart to deliver, word of mouth is fleet of foot and short of breath. By now, if not everyone in Sardinia, at least everyone in the mountains must have heard of the American mother-to-be whose packed cavernous womb contained a question mark and an exclamation point. The organs of generation of both sexes. A marvel: a sign of something or other, no doubt about it.

So I suspect. In any event they intercepted me about half an hour after I'd begun my walk. My contractions had stopped long before, but I was far from comfortable on my cross-country hike, I felt almost as bruised by the brightness of the sun as by the rocks underfoot, I had trouble keeping my tower in view, and I was glad of company. They hailed me from a distance. I was crossing one of the small dirt roads that intersected my straight line of march. What I saw was a trail of men and donkeys—no carts—a long procession winding casually downhill toward me.

They all wore the familiar white knee-pants, short jackets, and black drooping hats. Some mustachioed, some shaven, all sunburned. Short, sad men—my fellow workers on the dig plus a fair sprinkling of men I didn't recognize. Anghelu Ruju was there, of course, and Ba Shardan. I greeted with pleasure S'Adde and Is Paras, Su Lamarzu and Sa Perda. I waved with delight at the Gonnosfanadigo men, young and old, at nosy teenage Carrus, aromatic Urarti, and ancient sway-backed Marinaru. I saluted them all, Mannu, Orcosu, Priu, Sulcei, Silanus, Accocci, Bonnanaro, Gerrei, Birori, Bultei, Ilixi, Utu, Baunei, Cicicu, Rebeccu, Paddaggiu, Concas, and Nuraxinieddu. They were all there, they crowded round me as they came up, friendly, polite, quiet in a formal way. "Good day, signorina, a warm morning!"

"Good day! Very warm! A fine warm day for a holiday!"

"You've lost your way?"

I assured them I had not.

"You've lost your way," they insisted. They milled around me. Most of them had been walking. A few who'd been riding stepped backward off their midget donkeys and came to jostle and whisper. There was nothing offensive in any of this: they were anxious as always to have a closer look, and nowadays a long stare. "Will you drink some wine?" someone suggested. "Wine!" A dozen wickered jugs were lifted from the belly-bags of the nearest donkeys. Their animals, I noticed, were loaded with all manner of gear.

The invitation to drink was casual only on the surface. It is not merely impolite, it is insulting and dangerous in Sardinia to refuse an offer of wine made under seemingly casual circumstances like these. I drank. There was a pause, then a moment of distinct change, a loosening, and the sadness in the air took a distinct turn toward gaiety. Everyone drank.

Bread was offered, quite as casually, quite as formally as the wine, with the same ritual implication: it was a terribly hard crust they produced. I bit into it. It was passed around; everyone bit; it disappeared; more was found; more was eaten.

"We were on our way," someone who looked a little like Puddu (the little shepherd himself wasn't there)—a man smaller than the others, someone who might have been Mungianeddu's father or brother in a long sheepskin jacket that was almost a shawl—announced with sudden amiability, "to celebrate the Feast of the Epiphany."

Join them! But would they take me? The idea of going with them came to me immediately, it was too good to be believed, I gave up mythmaking without regret. Here I was—abandoned—while the others had all gone down to the public pompous rites in the capital, and I—I had stumbled by luck on the primitive ceremonies of the shepherds themselves.

Join them? Could I? I asked. They answered. I did. It wasn't for half a day that I realized that I had "joined" the strategy of a kidnapping. I was immediately presented with a gourd of *abba ardente* from which I could sip and given the seat of honor on the back of the lead donkey.

It was far more comfortable than the bumpy cart had been. I rode bareback and sideways of course. My donkey's gait was slow, his seat was wide, our girths were roughly the same, and the warmth of his tough furry hide was pleasant under my own seat. I grew drowsy and very nearly napped part of the time, my chin bobbing, my lips trying to smile at occasional shouts of this or that pleasantry, the sounds shimmeringly perceived like light through dust, my eyes closing and opening as the peak of Gennargentu vanished.

I was wakened by the sound of sheep bells. Restless sheep, rattling their bells. For a moment I thought I could also make out the bass muttering of voices under the tin treble of clappers.

It was clear that I was certainly in a tower, either Barbagia sos Nidos or another one. They were all very much alike. I could even more or less recognize the kind of room I was in, a second-story hexagonal chamber that was often considered to have been a prison cell, mostly because it had to be entered on hands and knees: I was familiar with the design of the chamber from Puddu's tower and others. But whether or not I was in the nuraghe I'd been heading for . . . I felt heavy. I felt almost too tired and too vast to move. How long had I been asleep? How had they got me in here without waking me? Why was I alone? I was cranky. I was groggy. The men had vanished, my contractions had vanished—for both of which I was sleepily grateful.

Sheep bells again.

The window hole. It was light out, very bright. It must have been afternoon. I wasn't frightened of course, there was no occasion for fright. I could crawl out easily. I got to my feet and decided to trundle myself down through the tunnel when a fresh sound of bells, coming now through the deep slit that served as a window, changed my mind.

I looked out. I saw it, but I didn't believe it. Down below, squeezing through the defile and up the trail toward the tower—no, it wasn't possible, it was sheer hallucination—I saw a herd of sheep riding on donkeys.

Men of course. Dressed up as sheep. The pelts they wore shook as they rode. They were too far away for me to make out their faces, and they circled round to the rear of the tower, dismounting out of sight. In a few moments the muttering I'd heard down below me in the tower became human, it became almost intelligible, it doubled and trebled—greetings, enthusiasm, grunts of welcome and, I detected, of bickering. My nerves were now on edge. Walk down calmly and present myself? Down there? To what? I hesitated. In with the muted, tin-can dragging of bells came new thuds of stomping. The smell of smoke, cactus cigars. Then hilarity. Then silence.

I was going to crawl out hurriedly when a sharp peal of sound hit me—like a wave breaking with the noise of a gigantic tambourine—it rippled through my body like a contraction. I got to the window as soon as I realized that whatever it was, it was outside the tower, not inside me. They were out there. The beast-men. And except for one funny detail the scene I saw was eerie: the detail, in its absolute absurdity, was more unexpected than the grimness of the spectacle. Down below me, whatever they were—beasts or men—over their heads and tied under their chins, they were all wearing pretty kerchiefs. Damned if they weren't!

This ludicrous detail kept my nerves in order. But let me put it in perspective. They were leaping heavily—slowly and jerkily bounding round the tower in a long double file—there must have been forty or fifty men all told, and the rhythm of their shaky march triggered the bells they were wearing. All this ominous timed leaping produced a weird, precise music. They were probably naked under their furs from the waist down, but except for their calves, which were pale, knotty, and bare, their bodies were swaddled in rough fur—rich, shaggy, thick-piled brown ram pelts probably. And the pelts themselves were half-obscured by another covering. Back and front, chest and shoulders, they wore nets of bells, bronze and iron bells, about a hundred per ram, I judged, bulky bells and tiny bells, sheep bells of all sizes. They must have weighed considerable, and the high-pitched crashing pealing music they made was unbelievably loud even from my perch. On the line of march it must have been head-shattering. Clean, bright bell-thunder, not constant rippling: in unison, they moved ahead, swinging one shoulder sharply and falling on a single foot. They bent their heads. Then the other shoulder jerked, opposite foot stamped. And without warning, the entire line of beasts in three slow leaps began to swing round and reverse direction, coming at me now, and I saw that where their familiar faces should have been were masks. Full-face wooden masks, with slits for eyes, surmounted by those silly kerchiefs.

The closest I can come to describing the grotesqueness of their masks is to say that they resembled the subhuman ugliness Picasso was fond of inflicting on his Cubist faces. The garish features were frighteningly twisted right or left, and they were gaudily painted— partly human, partly animal, and somehow distinctly female. The female touches were demonic—peaked eyebrows, rouged cheeks round as polka dots, splinters of black hair at the temples, and open puffy-lipped mouths set into the wood vertically like gaping vulvas.

Understandably, I was paralyzed. The whole herd, two by two, advanced toward me, stamping on their bare legs and ferociously shaking four thousand to five thousand bells in unison as they swung their furry shoulders. The brilliance of the racket touched me to the bone. They had almost reached the tower again when it occurred to me that of course they knew I was up there watching. The menace of the bells and the intensity of their approach made me pull back behind the slot of the window, a turtle's beak pulling back behind its shell.

They seemed to be coming . . . at me? For me? But I wanted to *see;* through a crack between the stones I watched more cautiously. Without any signal I could make out, the herd pivoted, reversing its field, and moved off again diagonally away from me.

Their appearance was beyond belief, but even more so was their endurance. The energetic dancing went on for hours. Irregularly, however, about once every twenty minutes, it came to an abrupt stop as the beasts paused, sat down like the friendly men I remembered, and passed refreshments. Wineskins, gourds of *abba ardente, pastori* cheroots, and dried cactus pears or cactus buttons—I couldn't tell which from a distance. On that plateau, under that sun, dancing under their weight of bells for hours, they must have needed refreshment. And gradually as they drank, smoked, and chewed, the course of their bizarre march became more and more disorderly. Each time they picked up the rhythm again after each break for a swig of wine, a puff of smoke, or a gulp of *abba ardente*, it looked less rhythmical, less controlled—wilder and wilder. The form of a line disappeared by midafternoon—the herd broke into groups of frenetic dancers— the bright heaving of bells drifted into uneven jerky shuffling. And I began to suspect they were appealing to me—to their foreign mascot and marvel, the carefully chosen, subtly kidnapped, and privileged stranger, the strange male mother up in the tower—double-sexed, but desirable, and quite possibly divine—to come down. My imagination? My vanity? My fears? They bobbed drunkenly in the great open rocky space, circled especially round a black rock in the middle, trailed off brokenly underneath my window, came closer, raised their hideously female features, shook their furred flanks, and danced off. Others came, repeating, beseeching, appealing.

Appealing for what? Did I dare, I wondered—did I have the coolness of nerve to go down there? Was there anything to fear really? Violence? Assault? They had always been gentle with me, they had never offered the slightest violence before, they knew I was up there watching, and they were certainly making no effort to oblige me to come down. Still I hesitated, uncertain, unwilling to find out.

It was getting on toward sunset when a herd of sheep—real sheep —pregnant sheep—returned to the tower, trooping unevenly, slowly, with a dog behind them. I thought they might be Puddu's. All of them were swollen with young, all of them were confused, suspicious, wandering, circling warily around the drunken beast-dancers. They paused stupidly, stiffly, straightening their black knees, swaying their engorged bellies and udders. Their bells, their bleats, were inaudible in the harsh jangling. Stimulated by the presence of the sheep, the dancers rippled their own bells with new energy.

And it was in that din that I heard the clanging behind me. I turned. One of the beast-men, ferociously masked and comically kerchiefed, was crawling through the miniature doorway on all fours, waddling and jingling as he came. I didn't scream. I thought I recognized him. Raising one hand, he beckoned. Despite the slotted wood over his face and the shaggy rugs on his torso, I guessed. Mungianeddu Puddu. With relief I imagined that knotted, sardonic smile of woe under his mask, under his mustache, under his tense eyes. I crawled out with him. Me first.

I still have no idea why I didn't expect what finally occurred. When I waddled out and hurried down, I expected they'd give me a couple of sheepskins to throw over me, I thought they'd fasten bells on my shoulders, I thought they'd teach me the step. But no. Puddu led me to the center of the circle, where the black rock was. The rock was littered here and there with small fibrous cactus buttons. Except for their momentary crescendo of jangling, which was no greater when I appeared than when the sheep had sidled in, the dance continued almost exactly as before. But the dancers circled non-stop now. No drinking. No smoking or chewing. The sun burned redder. Puddu danced in front of me, behind me. Was it Puddu? He was wordless, he was fearsome, he was funny. His familiar tense masterful way of moving his legs, his head, his arms, soothed me and aroused me and tickled me. Trembling on the verge of nervous giggling hysteria, I almost laughed, it's true, but I also loved him. Slowly, I was overwhelmed. For that hour I was even grateful that I could smell him, the fecal sweated sheep-musk odor trapped under his shag rug. Massive in my body, massive in apprehension, unworried and unable to understand why, I adored him.

And then I saw what was happening, what was beginning to take place all around me as the sun touched the horizon. Milking and mating. Some of the beast-men milked while others, clasping the huge-bellied sheep from behind by grabbing fistfuls of wool, mounted the skittish, shitten ewes. Not all at once. Most of the masked beasts shook their shoulders in the dance while a few, taking turns, coupled with the scared yet stolid, louring, baaing animals.

I had few questions when Puddu, still capering, motioned me to him. I was ecstatic. But lie down first? Standing, I looked round uncertainly. It was a sight both mysterious and revolting, both spectacular and oppressive; it was a vision for the nostrils. Everywhere on the circle of rocks surrounding the tower, thin jets of sweet-smelling milk flowed in puddles, and the fitful stink and frenzy of copulation extended itself until it disappeared over a dip or around a bend—beast-men impregnating their pregnant beasts.

I lay down, I leaned back. Puddu—his atrocious agony-grin more comprehensible to me now—began gesturing obscenely over me, and as soon as I understood what was expected of me, I accepted. I got down on all fours.

He milked me first, though I didn't flow. Then he mounted me. He clasped my enormous belly and pulled that sagging rotundity of womb toward him. When he entered me, I felt wounded, cauterized, assaulted, cured, paralyzed, and sanctified. The power of his thrust did all of those things to me, one by one.

Then one by one the human rams separated themselves from their animal mothers, pried themselves from the sexual dance, and came to start a new one with me. Down on my knees on the black stone— well, I gave up trying to see the faces of the creatures who took me from behind—but I couldn't help occasionally seeing those who stood in front of me, shaking their bells in rhythm with the thrusts penetrating my grand swaying flesh, their jagged faces changing from hideous to serene as I darted my glance from left to right, from right to left. I have no idea how many of them milked me and took me in that ecstatic agony of trance, melting into the black stone. Perhaps all of them, perhaps not. Each of them seemed larger than the last, more searing, more unendurable—the penetration was awesome. And the dance continued. The pealing of the bells in my ears as I bent my head to the rock kept shattering the insides of my head. The pelts shook before my eyes. My eyes burned. My teats ached. Insofar as flesh is flesh, the dance was cruel. And yet from the overweening penetration of that cruelty emerged the truth of my flesh.

I clawed the earth with my fingernails, that enormous mother earth, a stony soil unwilling to become jealous or aroused by my sacrifice, and I shared the animal act and divine conjunction in which all of us were caught as man-made bells rattled over my humped back to the pumping of their loins. There was nothing further to be asked, no act of the body so inexplicable, so stupid, so utterly obscene as this mass venomous rutting outside the tower, and no further question about my childbearing. I was woman, I was animal, I understood.

· · ·

I lay there after they left me, my back to the rock-torn earth, my face to the stars finally, watching the jitters of those firebits and firemist with such ecstatic concentration that I seemed to discern motion —not just passage, but motion—across the top of the universe—hearing the crickets fiddling in the cactus, smelling the odor of sheep dung, tasting sheep sweat on my tongue and teeth, learning the beck and call of vermin in my crotch—and knowing that it had come round for me. I reached out in the pitch black.

Was I in pain during the dancing, or afterward, lying there? I suppose so, but the pain of dancing was utterly obliterated by the incomparably more painful exultation and anguish of childbirth.

I was exhausted, but conscious, when he carried me back into the tower. God be thanked, he'd come back. I was conscious, but exhausted, when he began to rub my wrists.

While I moaned and clutched and perspired, he stroked my hand and turned me on my side and rubbed my back until—

"You will be patient."

I screamed.

"You will have a fat boy."

My thin little girl was born quickly. Puddu delivered the child by the light of a lantern in the filthiest, most unsanitary conditions. The tiny doll cried weakly, suddenly brought forth a single bell-like scream, followed by an ear-splitting racket of cries like bells, and she lived and was a healthy, whole baby girl. She was just a girl, exactly a girl—I sobbed louder than she did, exhausted as I was—nor did she turn out to be a monster like her mother.

But of course Puddu had seen the peculiar facts of my anatomy. His reaction always struck me as odd. He'd known . . . but he'd never seen. Hadn't he believed? Was seeing so different from believing? I know exactly when he noticed: he looked up at me from between my legs—a sharp moment of embarrassment—then he bent to his work again. Not a word, not a question, not a pause. I've never forgotten his look, his sudden decision that no matter what, he'd go on working.

When I was lying in a heavy wooden bed in Nuoro—wearing the robe Lou Hackett had brought for me—with my present spread out on the blanket in front of me, the Sardinian dress, heavy with gold brocade and ornate embroidery, which the doctor had given me and I'd accepted with pride—and the Commander and Nicco and everyone had finished playing with my little baby's hands and chuckling over her prehensile toes and serious blue gaze, Mungianeddu Puddu remained behind. His grieving smile: I know now that he loved the child, if not the mother. "Look." He showed me something in confidence. From inside his pocket. Another small figurine, something like the one I'd seen in Satori's office, but tinier, slightly cracked and dirtier. The ancient Sardinian god-goddess of fertility. So he'd been holding out on the Commander after all. I remember thinking that I'd served the ritual of fertility and birth at the tower better than any five-inch figurine.

I must admit that for the first day or two the baby held no interest for me. I was so wan and washed out, I seemed to be still gyrating in the spell of that sickening selflessness, or it may have been the deep paroxysm of labor, the exposure and the lack of food. I knew where I was—but at times barely. And I wasn't sure I'd be able to hold my own, or where I'd find the strength.

I was not myself again for months afterward, the entire time I was in Sardinia. Something had happened to me for which there are no words; it is my suspicion—a hunch which I am unable to confirm because words, mine and other women's, fail us here—that something of what happened to me in Barbagia sos Nidos happens to every woman in the slow climax to the last quickening uncontrollable moments of gestation. I believe it must overtake all of us, except if we are anaesthetized, perhaps even then, but that in time most of us fight it out of awareness, shove it down and out as quick as we can. We must. For in the very act of life we learn that we are *not* alive, not as we thought we were. At the heights of sensation and panic, the exact sequence of anguish and pain passes to the center of one's emotional and physical being and then leads step by step to an inevitable abandonment of the self—it is a climax of non-existence. It is more lonely and more forbidding than orgasm not *only* because extreme pain rather than extreme pleasure forces it into being. In the mounting ecstasy of sexual love, the self seems to disappear, too, but it vanishes (or seems to) in company with that of the lover and so seems to vanish into that other self; and it returns—if all goes well—reinforced by his. But in the terror of creation, like that of death, there can be no company—all relationship is sundered, identity is meaningless, sex and the difference of the sexes cease to exist, will counts for less than nothing, there is no past, no future, and no one in the present, only cataclysm and creation—the self, will it come back? did it ever exist? does one wish for it again?—and when it does return, *must* one make an effort to care, it is not hard, it is not easy, you just put it around you like an old bathrobe—you only put it around you because people will not recognize you or even talk to you otherwise—and you discover in a day or two that something essential is missing—the old robe hasn't got a drawstring, no belt, nothing to tie it to you—it hangs remarkably loose, it is not you, it is a necessary robe. Where has the missing essential element, the tie-string, gone? Into the baby, of course! One had almost forgotten about the baby. *There's* the new life, there's the new thing. So to the exhausted mother the self returns, not reinforced but drained, the juice of belief squeezed out, minus the old hard pits of conviction. And in the conscious retasting and recapturing of identity—for there will be headier wines to sip, and fancier duds, and mother will be hungrily dining out, vainly dressing up for the occasion of the rest of her life—does she always remember? We were not formerly alive; we were most alive then when we were things, not selves, when the thing-without-a-self opened wide the mouth of its bliss with the tongues of pain to speak life out loud. If you are a woman and a mother, it may be that you have forgotten that. But as for me, the cold tower, the animal rite, the barbaric loneliness of the rock I delivered the newborn flesh to, my unique susceptibility: I have never forgotten my loss in the gain of birth.

How I
Made It

I do not decline to be the poet of wickedness also.
                              —WHITMAN

My passion for money has earth-rending and tangled roots—that is *all* the government lawyers were ever able to demonstrate—but there is nothing treasonable about that. Poets have desired more. Dante desired paradise.

For half a year or more after I gave her away, the memory of her birth remained a heavy imprint in my flesh as if someone had stepped on me there and the softness had hardened into the ineradicable solidity of remembrance instead of pain—a pain locked into the tissues. She passed gradually out of mind . . . adopted . . . somebody else's . . . somewhere else . . . only Satori knew where. Her name, her adoptive parents—the knowledge had been kept from me for my own sake. I had gone along with the idea. If I could have forgotten utterly —absolutely—that I'd had a baby, that my body had borne another, I'd have done so. I longed to live in the spirit. If I could have cut away the growth to which I was still attached, and lived sexless, jointless, stomachless, rumpless, headless, legless, hairless, and faceless, I'd have cut my own flesh adrift and followed my ghost. It was a terrible mood of course, and wrongheaded; back to the body was the route to salvation—for me as for everyone else.

At the time, however, I chose abstraction. And within six months I had singled out the single most interesting abstraction the mind of man has ever been able to invent. Money.

For as I recovered, I became aware that I had already made two great journeys. From girlhood through manhood to motherhood; and from human to animal kind and back: more complete in myself, more experienced, I was sure, than any other member of my generation. My double sex had made me whole. A whole person. I had the sense of a special power in my experience.

But how could I swing it, how could I make myself big and stand up, pregnant with dignity, vibrant with power? To succeed, I had to "sell myself"—and I was dismally aware of the two meanings of that phrase. Yet slowly after I got back to the States, I accepted the conditions of power.

Action and money. Probably if I'd known quite how hard the going would get, I'd have settled for versifying. Thankfully, I was innocent, and I simply took on my own shoulders the responsibilities of achieving a certain greatness. Was I afraid that hard lowly grubby work would drive out the poetic impulse? Nonsense. I remembered that Masefield had cleaned spittoons as a porter in a saloon before he became the poet laureate. Was I worried that a career of moneymaking would turn me from my newly acquired enthusiasm for archaeology?

Hardly. I recalled that Schliemann had begun as a poor clerk and built the topless towers of an international commercial empire before he unearthed their very roots—and his—in fabulous Troy. Wasn't I anxious that my money would weigh on my spirit? Not on your life. For I remembered what Father used to tell Sandy, that the great Ty Cobb had worn lead on his shoes until just before the game. The realization of my myth demanded sacrifice. The age demanded money.

The debasement of silver and gold. Money is love spelled backward, and I turned to moneymaking. I accepted the common condition. It was to be a long time before I could spell love forward.

But the confession that follows, I'm afraid, will alienate and embarrass everyone of normal reticence and reasonable modesty. I do not pretend to be normal. Let me say it bluntly. After my experience at the tower, I wanted to possess everyone. I wanted to possess men and women—not sexually—God knows, I'd had enough of that—but in some other way, every single one of them. The experience I gained at the Sardinian tower carried over directly into the field of American commerce. Somehow I had to have them, someday I had to have them. And if all of them were too many—for despite my appetite I understood as well as you that, for instance, no woman can possess all men —then at least as many of humankind as this stony, tender, driven, cunning, needy woman could manage.

How this came about—how I became the bard of business, a revolutionary seer, a mystic, a scientific prophet, a heretic of love, and in the eyes of the world at last an untouchable dunghill—this is the destiny to which I must now address my recollections.

I returned to the United States an athletic girl with serious eyes —warm blue moons in a sunburned boyish face. I smiled timidly. When I smiled, white teeth glistened like new moonlight against my shadowy tan. My body was slender, high-breasted, erect—direct and graceful in motion, pliant in repose—long in the legs and strong on my feet.

Worried about the effects of childbirth on my figure, I took all sorts of precautions. Pelvic and abdominal exercises, diet, skin care, hormones. Luckily, I showed no stretch marks. Even my nipples, once so pale as to be virtually one continuous tint with my flesh, were only a trifle darker, and when a couple of hairs appeared there, I tweezed them out. That year I was obsessed about details. I was as much concerned with lengthening my fingernails as with tightening my vagina. I worked diligently to keep my nails beautiful, I applied coat after coat of hardener and sat with my drying claws raised to the breeze like a ferocious pianist hoping to gouge the keyboard. My sun-pale hair had begun reaching toward my shoulders again at last. I was careful to keep the ends from splitting. I plucked my eyebrows when they showed the least tendency toward the middle. And though I'd never had much leg hair, I began shaving my calves anyhow. I was thankful that my hands and feet, which had been too small for a boy's, were in the right proportion again. Narcissus forever, and unabashed about it: my entombed manhood adored my living womanhood.

I returned to Cambridge after Sardinia, but I didn't return to school. One look at the old place was enough, one smell of the Yard, one feel of the ivy—God, there was no cactus!—one quick tour of inspection through Bertram Hall, the girls' dorm to which I'd been assigned, and I knew I'd been through too much by now to return— how in hell could I be expected to pick up my books again as a Radcliffe sophomore after Noragugume and Barbagia sos Nidos? A myth at Radcliffe? I needed something savage, more primitive.

New York. In that fallow year there were few jobs for girls. The help-wanted columns for men were always longer. Phallic. And beckoning. But not once did I regret my sexual decision. I spent more money on newspapers and subways than on food. I developed a hatred for the subway. To find a job, I had to force myself down one of those infernal stairways into mother earth (an aversion that seems peculiar to me now after a life so closely bound up with excavation). The old dig on the island, for all its deathy finds, was less sinister than the underground putrescence of the subway system. Those ghastly faces opposite: pale electric-bulb minds in slack metallic bodies. And the daily fascinating morbid encounters. With the white-haired old lady screaming, "Jesus Saves. Get the Hell off This Train." With the knit-brow nitwit sitting with an open satchel full of broken watches and working with a jeweler's glass to his eye while the subway shook and perpetually ruined his work. And the sad middle-aged man who asked me to please come to his office and stand on him.

Prostitution? Why not? To be honest, I gave it some thought. I thought of it not once, but repeatedly. "The mob within the heart" —the phrase is Emily Dickinson's—and after that ritual in Sardinia —well, anyhow, who knows and who cares how a poet earns her living? "This ecstatic Nation"—she wrote—"Seek." The intimate knowledge, possession, manipulation, and gratification of mankind— what better function for a poet, overreaching even Sidney's and Shelley's great claims! Part-time hooker—it seemed to me in my darkest moods that the employment might be suitable, a job intimately fitted to my temperament. I walked up out of my gum-streaked subway stairs, home along my spittle-stained sidewalk to my back apartment, a dank lair whose one amenity was a fireplace (I hung on to that place later, even after the money started pouring in), I slumped on the edge of my bed and took off my heels and stockings and inspected the discolored scar I'd got from walking around town looking for a job . . . and I considered the possibility of prostitution frankly and without prejudice. Too degrading? My God, I was no babe-in-the-wood. How many girls in the whole country had poetic scruples—I mean of those who counted? Of those who had made it, or would make it? Few, one had to imagine. Damn few. I leaned over the edge of my bed, staring at my small lovely unpainted toes, and I wondered. I wondered only about success. I mean genuine success. As a million-dollar whore or a top-paid madam. Why not? I had become a mother, yet had no child —I felt womanly, yet wanted no man. What did I want from this squalid and enormous anthill of a city? Enough to pay for my rent and groceries and leave me time for experiments in poetry. Exactly how these modest strivings were transformed, exploding into wealth and the craving for more wealth, is the burden of my peculiar history: a function of the American libido and my own.

> This ecstatic Nation
> Seek—it is Yourself.

How did you get your start? Like other self-made men, I've heard this question more times than I care to recall and answered it more often than I've been understood.

HELP WANTED
PART TIME
CHICKEN BOY

I saw that cardboard poster in the window of a food market two blocks from where I lived. It wasn't merely the money, badly as I needed that by then. No, it was more. Probably no one who has not lived my life can understand the light of recognition that flared when I saw that sign behind glass and below it, two rows of plucked chickens ready to be barbecued. That these chicks, embodying so many early and intimate memories of my family, could also represent money, that these chicks might actually be spitted and turned and roasted and sold by me for personal gain, was a lucky break I had not dreamed of. The double row of plucked chickens brought back an ancient, half-forgotten mist—infantile, deeply private confusions. I responded to the sight of them . . . well, how shall I say it? . . . amorously, sensuously. A hundred of the nation's unemployed might have taken the job and perhaps ninety-nine out of a hundred would have regarded it as tedium. I looked upon it as Revelation. Fortune. Opportunity. My chance to resolve the primal self.

It didn't matter that the sign asked for a boy. Nothing of the sort has ever stopped me for long. I was the girl for the job: I convinced the manager of this fact within fifteen minutes after I began my ardent jabber. Yes, I told him, all tears and smiles (both at once), I knew all about chicken surgery, severing a chicken into its various fascinating parts, I knew about the Pope's nose, and though I loved all little peckers, I was prepared to roast, rotate, revolve, wrap, and ring them up for sale, I even knew why a chicken crossed the road; sir, that was no chicken, that was my wife. Had he heard of Chicken Little and the sky falling down? He had not? And the Golden Egg? And which came first, the chicken or the egg?

"You want a job?" he said crudely. "You can kiss my ass."

"Once only," I replied, unperturbed, "or once a week?"

He goggled at the clean-cut American blonde who'd said that; then he threw back his hairy head and grunted with laughter. "Never mind, miss, you got a job."

For the first months I lived in an uncommercial dream world. Never were chickens more tenderly spitted, more carefully pierced with the little double prongs of their crucifixion, more painstakingly adjusted on their rack of flames, more perfectly browned to a turn. Every chicken perfectly, perfectly barbecued. We used gas, not electricity. It was my boast to know exactly when to lower the gas and pop out the poultry. I not only learned, I loved my business from the bottom up. I especially loved to feel beforehand the cold smooth glide of the plucked prickly skin against my own when the fowl, yellow and clammy, was about to go in, and I loved to feel the difference, the hot final crackle of it when I'd snap its crispness (pure pleasure) between my fingertips. Through the contact of our skins I felt as though my family, our dinner table, the old net of error and terror had suddenly come to life again—I marveled—and slowly through the sense of touch things came back to me, things unbelievable, even by me, I was like an anthropologist discovering in myself the existence of unlikely, unimaginable lore, legends, myths: yes, I, Millie Niemann, had once when small actually believed that a man was a strutting cock or had a feathered cock or both! that a girl either was chicken or was like a chicken or both! that every grown woman would lay a large white egg once a month through her crack! that a chicken's rear end was its penis! that my father's nose, that all men's noses, had something in common with that fowl penis which to everyone's amusement bore the most remarkable resemblance to my daddy's own, and that my mother loved best of all to chew on his! All this now came back to me vividly, though not all at once—a gradual revelation as I pierced and pronged and roasted and removed my chickens, the recollection of a stunning series of primitive beliefs. But strangest of all there also came to me another frightening sensation. Somewhere along the line I had straightened out all these childish twists of thought and automatically given them up long, long ago, just as each child must do with its inevitable misapprehensions; yet somehow, somewhere—could it be?—I had not really *ever* given them up, no matter how absurd they had come to seem.

My part-time job provided food for thought and reduced prices on chicken. So at the end of the first month I celebrated and invited guests to dinner. I called up Mom and Pop. (They were living out in Roslyn on Long Island now. Pop had managed to advance me a little cash during my jobless days, though his legal practice had been dwindling disastrously.) Since my chicken dinner came preroasted, I went to some trouble preparing a special treat for my folks—the exquisite Sardinian sauce whose recipe Mungianeddu Puddu had given me.

I spent several mornings getting hold of the particular ingredients. At a plant nursery I came across some cactus that looked almost right —not the precise Sardinian variety but a remotely similar strain from Yucatán. And at an herbalist I located without much trouble the tiny grains of paradise, *Aframomum melegueta*. My own market supplied the more common ingredients. I followed Puddu's instructions carefully: I trimmed the skin and spines, I cooked the hearts and heads, I dried the mash in a slow oven. Cactus, lemons, honey, the most sparing use of the paradisaic flavoring—I made it just as he'd told me. But it was New York. And at first the thrill of the old mood was gone. I must admit I had my doubts. That Puddu's sauce could in fact be recreated on my stove, no matter how long or how well I blended and stirred and tasted, almost defied belief. It didn't belong to, it didn't want to enter, the present world of American reality. To my mind those intimate experiences on the island, Satori, Puddu, my child, all of Sardinia from its fierce nuragic splendor to its modern bandit pride, were part of the embalmed past. Irredeemable. Yet I kept on sniffing and testing and stirring with my finger. And once the flavor was exactly right . . . unbidden, redemption came.

It's astonishing how few people, except those who had to start from scratch like me and made a mint, are able to understand. Before I'd finished setting the table for dinner I'd conceived the enterprise that changed my life.

The sauce was a tangy success. They raved. I was so pleased. The lemon flavor dominated, and the rind, grated fine, provided just the right effect. Dad especially couldn't get enough. Good old Dad: if it hadn't been for his wild gusto for my sauce that evening, who knows, I might never have made it. And he was famously rewarded. As my general manager he made his fortune.

"What's it got in it?" Pop asked, wiping his lips with pleasure.

"My blood."

He stared. He laughed uneasily.

Mother said, "At home you never cooked." Her eyes grew large with distant accusations.

That's all. We sat, we ate, we drank, we smoked, we talked, and all that time I kept right on thinking. Until after dinner, while Mother used the bathroom, I took Pop aside. I lowered my voice.

Now it takes someone with vision to recognize even a gem of an idea, and I wasn't sure whether Pop could see far enough ahead. But I told him about the moneymaking vision that had come to me over the stove. He fixed his bloodshot eyes on me. I asked him about the present. I asked for his opinion, the one opinion that was crucial to me, "Pop, is it salable?"

He was evasive. He said in that crackling static tone of his that he could amplify at will like a public-address system, "First you're a girl, Millie. Then you're a boy."

"Pop . . ."

He went right on. "Now you're a grown woman and you want to go into business—"

"—can't you see—"

"—marketing a chicken sauce with your own blood in it—"

"—it's the idea—"

"—you'll drive your mother and me—"

"—is it *salable?*" I repeated impatiently. I wasn't sure of his fore-sight, but I valued his bloodhound nose and tongue.

Hoping he'd calm down, I took one of his cigarettes. He lighted it for me, he took one himself, he puffed, he got up. "Who knows? Maybe it's only penny antes," he ventured at last, softening. "But it tastes like a million, Millie."

Gratified, I sighed. And then, amazing me, Pop in a new mellow mood began rubbing his grizzled cheek on mine.

Mom—when she understood what all the fuss was about—was magnificent. "Chicken sauce? Why not?" she counseled. "You can't marry." She knew nothing of my pregnancy, my child, my sex life. But to her my future always seemed clearer than my past: she felt she could look back at it from the privileged vantage point of hind-sight. "Go for the money. You'll always be single." She put her downy arms around me, closing her palimpsest eyes, and breathed on me through her gold fillings.

That night I sweated it out. Pop had agreed to advance me a little money, when and if needed. And not long afterward Sandy, too, came through generously with the promise of a small loan. My brother was to realize a handsome return on his original investment in me. But did he understand? I look back burdened with understand-ing myself and a number of things embarrass me. An obsession? Sure, but also a labor of love—a disturbed field of erotic force, out of which my pursuit of the abstraction arose as it were of itself. Without know-ing it, I had already begun to consecrate myself to the distribution of my truth—the sacred whore, the hierophant of my own sexual mystery.

Spellbinding to me is the parallel with art. I was destined to spend my early twenties in trade, absorbed in sleazy details. The craft of commerce. As in poetry, I was to discover the heart of the matter later. I was, in fact, like many a man who in the course of a knock-about career at long last comes up with the particular product or service intimately suited to his individual genius. When that mo-ment came, I seemed to acquire effortlessly the genuine touch of Midas. But it wasn't so, not at all. For I had already mastered the tools and perfected the techniques of commerce by practicing on something inconsequential, pointless. As once Demosthenes had held stones in his mouth, as once Willie had honed his tongue on grimy tongue-twisters, so now Millie familiarized herself with chicken sauce. An item that was unlikely, hard to put over, and—from the point of view of the magnate I was to become—trifling. But far ahead of me loomed production methods and price structures, securities and loans, incorporation and equity, patent law and international financing. Where the unified, hard-working will holds steady, wishes are granted and revolutions realized. Not only to poets.

I prepared more of the delicious sauce, and Monday morning I took a jar to work. With presumption, without permission, I began coating my chickens before I barbecued them. It was a risk. I might have lost my job, but I took the risk, fully aware of my responsibilities. If even one customer had complained—but not one did. They came back with praise. In two weeks, chicken sales at our barbecue counter had almost doubled. Without telling anyone, I kept mixing more and more of the sauce as it ran out. I made it at home in the mornings, and brushed it on at the counter; nobody saw, nobody knew. In three weeks, the phenomenon of my chicken sales was noted. A number of customers asked about the sauce. I said nothing about cactus or anything else. I just gave them some in little containers borrowed from the deli counter. In four weeks, still rocketing, my sales were noticed with suspicion. My boss demanded an explanation. I explained. He tasted. It was good; sales were good. But when I asked for permission to sell it in bottles, he walked away.

Already by then my ideas had begun to crystallize. One thing I knew: it was important to take this first step, important for me to get immediate marketing experience with my product and to develop a helpful point-of-sales perspective. "Moe, be a good joe," I wheedled.

I followed him around the aisles. "Before you entered the ranks of management," I reminded him persuasively, "you started life as an apprentice butcher." Naturally I'd studied my boss. He looked back, annoyed. "Drop!" he murmured. I thought his annoyance unreasonable, he was annoyed because I was a blonde who could talk sense. He hadn't the wit to take me seriously. I pleaded, as he strode ahead of me, "Moey, the meat-and-poultry counter was your first love. . . ." His day was a sprint—an efficient manager—if you measure a man's efficiency in terms of speed, impatience, and bullish drive —the man could haggle over pennies with clerks, customers, and salesmen—he took a gambler's interest in the outcome—but a new idea? I don't know how I got him to listen, but I did. He turned. He paused once only, long enough to frown hairily at me. "You want to peddle your laces," he snorted, "in my shoestore?"

I nodded. "Three cents on every bottle I sell."

He laughed. He could hardly have imagined that in a few years

I would buy my way into that chicken counter and operate it for the store on a concession basis—not as a matter of profit, but for pride.

I had a label made up for me at a printer's. I called it SISTER MILLIE'S COCK-O'-THE-WALK CHICKEN SAUCE, and it sold. Not only was there nothing like it, there wasn't another chicken sauce on the market, and so far as I know, there *still* isn't today, except for my own, which sells of course under a different name now. Steak sauces aplenty, fish sauces—but not a chicken sauce in sight..

Certain mornings, certain Sundays, I urged myself on. I stirred up bottles and pots full of Sister Millie's Sauce, I stirred with more ardent, abnormal, generous affection than the average employee will ever understand, I made up more than I could sell at the counter in a week's time . . . and I began to peddle the item.

I worked hard. I got around. My mornings were free. I circled to as many neighborhood stores as I could and I pushed. Sometimes my sales talk got only a laugh, sometimes a half-bored flash of interest. I offered a free jar . . . but they'd say, usually sooner than I wanted, "Listen, miss, stop futzing around, who in hell makes this bomb?" Immediately I'd blush and say, "Me. It's mine." Silence. "Yours, my asshole!" Mine, I'd insist, pointing outside through the store window. Outside they could see my baby carriage.

"That's my little baby," I'd murmur. I used to push the product morning after morning in a big black carriage. Remember Uncle Lemmie and his wheelbarrow? You bet. Family wisdom. At the Salvation Army store I had picked up an old baby carriage, cheap and sturdy: it was instinct, memories, and intuition. Sure I got turned down plenty of times. But how many men could resist my pitch? The unmarried-mother sell. They tried to make me, but they bought. Sometimes I'd remember the strawberry mouth and periwinkle eyes and clustering budding fingers of the infant girl I'd given away, but not often. I was too busy. I started out in the morning with a full carriage, and by noon I sold out. They laughed, but they bought. Well, I admit it wasn't only my system. The low price helped. I sold my sauce at just about cost. Frankly, I wasn't interested in quick profits. I had my eye on the consumer market. So I sold by the large jar for immediate, in-the-store use. What I really wanted was to get my little ones up there on the shelves—soon and in quantity.

Stores that bought, bought again: their chicken volume went up, at almost no cost to the counter. I had to quit my first job to keep up with it. Not everyone liked it of course, but it really was good, not just cheap. (It still is. Try it. I can't name it, but it's the only large-selling sauce on the market that says on the label specifically for chicken. As for my blood, I'll say nothing further: I'm not legally permitted to reveal in exact detail the ingredients and spices we used in those early days since the brand name and all rights were subsequently sold to one of the major food companies.) I came, I sold, I waited. When I heard from the clerks often enough that customers had begun asking whether *they could buy it*, I was ready. I hadn't spun myself out too far. I'd kept the sales area small till then because I knew I'd have to hit the shelves first, then spread. And once a dozen markets had agreed to stock it, I opened wide.

I turned my kitchen, living room, and hallway into a messy factory—pots and kettles, boxes and barrels all over the place, bottles, blenders, labels, gluing machine, cartons. I began to see myself as an up-to-date young Andrew Carnegie, starting from the bottom as he had. My short-term goal was twenty-five good stores. Pop—impressed—offered to help me out with all the intricate problems of my small business—licenses and permits, taxes and general bookkeeping.

Looking back at the way I made my mark on the New York business community, it all seems so very simple now—but I'll tell you this, frankly, the first year or so I had no idea if I was going to make it up off the ground.

I consulted Pop, I consulted the government, I drew up a detailed prospectus. Hat in hand figuratively, but literally with prospectus in purse, I approached almost a dozen banks before I got a nibble. Credit was tight, but that wasn't the worst of it. The problem—the real problem—was my sex.

Oh, they were affable, all right. "My dear Miss Niemann, our credit experience with small businesses—" and so on . . . my age, my personal credit, my signature, all risky. And no one admitted it. No one admitted that their policy was tight-fisted because I was a woman. When I brought it up, of course, they shrugged. But the fact was as obvious as the fly on their trousers. Maybe if I'd been a smart young entrepreneur named Willie with a double-breasted suit instead of breasts—well, sign on the dotted line. But lend Millie money? Lend money to an entrepreneuse?

It was a galling, humiliating experience, that search for credit. I was surrounded by invisible grins of amusement. But it was time for some changes. Does it strike you as odd that someone with a binary sexual system should have arrived at these conclusions? I recommend to you the androgyne's point of view. More experienced than any woman my age could ever hope to be, my young manhood had sharpened the buds of my perception. On both sides I knew what I was feeling. Cuntism . . . that's what I called it . . . though the word is too refined, really, to convey the squamous and ugly scorn with which one of my sexes has been abused since Eve and the serpent. Let me remind you of the sacred credo of Genesis: Pussy was made to be used.

My attorney advised me for Godsake, you dope, to form a limited partnership and try to get at investors through venture-capital firms. But *that* was out. Despite this sort of pressure from Pop, who often mistrusted my methods, I insisted on retaining sole proprietorship. And in the end my policy paid off.

I got what I needed finally from a maverick financier, the now well-known Lisle Cody. He must have thought my enterprise was worth a laugh. I objected to his interest rate, but I signed fast. I remember the moment. I handed him a cigarette. Shaking one loose from the pack, I took the trouble not only to offer him one of my own, but to light it for him before he could object . . . then my own . . . and he handed me a pen, grinning, "Young lady, I like the flame in your eye."

"And the cut of my jaw?"

"And the cut of your clothes."

I caught the expression on his face. I was wearing an elegantly tailored pants suit. I knew what he was thinking and I didn't scruple to tell him. "You're thinking to yourself," I said, "now this is one little gal who's got balls."

He denied it chivalrously, every word. He shook his head and flushed. "Not at all. I was merely admiring your outfit. Very chic, very smart."

"If I was smart," I told him, rolling his ivory-encased blotter over my signature, "I wouldn't buy money at your price."

I'd been learning. After a year of operation I was no longer a complete novice. But it was a piddling sum for what I had in mind. I had to hold all capital requirements to a minimum. And I kept accounts receivable at a minimum. While my orders doubled each month, I kept squeezing the drain on cash. I rented a loft on Hudson Street and had my insurance company handle the financing. I put in office partitions and paid for the job by taking a personal investment directly from the contractor. I arranged for a reliable and incredibly cheap supply of cactus from Yucatán. I rented a used assembly-line system with an option to buy at the end of three years and I purchased a crummy outdated bottling machine. I advertised for a commercial food chemist. I hired a veteran salesman to serve as my sales manager. And I put together a small sales force under his command.

My early financial progress is surprisingly little known. I suppose I have grown resigned to the fact that my reputation now, after prosecution for treason and the unscrupulous publicity of international scandal, will never be the same again. In the public mind my name remains as inextricably tied to sex as the name Paul Getty is to oil, Aristotle Onassis to shipping, or Krupp to munitions. Yet I insist it was never physical sex alone, but the incalculable voltage crackling outward from my coiled physical generator to form an inexhaustible network of the imagination—spinning the inner wheels of my spirit from petty bottle caps of Chicken Sauce to the outermost spheres of Paradise—this energy that drove me across constellations like a falling star scraping up golden sparks. It is not often remembered that my early business career was as innocent of physical sex as a candy store owner's.

How to possess mankind: the game had arisen for me out of pure love, and on the job it was sexless. I ran a tight little business. No nonsense. To establish the ground rules firmly, I fired the first man who invited me out on a date.

That may seem harsh to you, but it was no simple matter for me to run the show. A girl—at first I was nothing more to them than a kid in her early twenties who was certainly damn nervy and probably soft in the head. Blonde hair and a black temper. I insisted on the courtesy due to a woman. A reasonable demand, and I got it. (Outwardly. Inwardly, there wasn't much doubt about their attitude. Cuntism.) In addition, however, I demanded the respect they'd have given a man. Boss man. This I didn't get. I made suggestions and got long crocodile faces of inattention. I told dirty jokes and they were silent. They opened doors for me on my way out to lunch and ignored my instructions when I got back. When the bottling machine broke down, they wouldn't hear of letting me try to fix it. The exclusive league of redblooded males.

Only for a while did I try to seduce work, respect, and loyalty out of them. I exerted my limpest self, my dimpledest charm. Feminine and sly, I tried to make every suggestion on production and sales management appear to develop and arise from the man I was talking to—his idea, not mine. But this was slow. I experimented, shifting to the opposite extreme, and got better, faster results.

I practiced crudeness, sarcasm, and bad manners. I barked and they snapped to it. I bit and they moved. I was Andrew Carnegie played by Edward G. Robinson. And I was out to build my organization.

It amuses me now to think back to that loft on Hudson Street: how small and often inept I was, how big and marvelous I thought I was. By any standard of comparison I was still a shoestring organization when the roof blew off and the sky fell in.

My training with Whitey stood me in good stead now.

A visit. I fished paper cups out of my bottom drawer, a couple of bottles from the top shelf in the big safe. I poured two little cups of Scotch. I handed them across to my two visitors. I poured one for myself and raised my paper cup enthusiastically. "Happy days."

The fat one inspected my office with slow-moving eyes. His tarnished face was a nicked silver dollar.

I followed his incredulous eyes. The woodwork in my floor showed a hole. The paint was three-toned in spots where the two top layers were peeling.

Brundy, the eagle, painstakingly settled his rear feathers over the stuffing in my torn leather sofa. He was a U.S.A. bald eagle with a hooked nose. He held his paper cup on his briefcase on his lap. "Honey, your father fill you in?"

I said placidly, "Uh-hm." The near-yawn, noncommittal.

"Did it strike you right?"

I merely moved my paper cup, a deprecatory gesture. "I told you, the old man represents me."

"You won't talk figures?"

"Figures?"

"The hell," Goad said. The fat one was still standing. He put his fingers on his lips and, leaning over toward my desk, tipped the scales of his scaly lips. "Miss Niemann, what kind of offer, may I ask, would you entertain?"

"I don't entertain offers," I said. Both my cheeks were twitching. Setting my drink down, I stood up, resting my hands on my desk and leaning forward. "You two s.o.b.'s come sucking around my office like this was a cathouse, trying to buy me. What kind of crap is this?"

The reader may be inclined to disbelief. I identified all the way with my company and its progress. But I was absurd only in proportion as my problems were painful. It doesn't take an Einstein to see that American business practice is founded on the genital theory of relativity.

"Calm down, sit down," they both said.

"I'll sit down when I damn well choose," I said. "I'm standing."

"Easy does it." Brundy blew his nose through his hook and grumbled, "Nobody wants to hurt you here, darling, nobody. The news spreads. You struck a little market, you built yourself a little business, it's small, but you got yourself a quantity of respect. And on that you can capitalize. Now I know, and you know, that, the company we represent could grind you into sawdust if they wanted. But they don't want it. To them you're a young lady. You're what, may I ask, say twenty-two?"

The frost-blue, cobalt-blue, sky-blue gaze I gave him didn't stop him. He was shoveling it at me and I knew it.

"Miss N., they ain't just company men, they're men, and that's all there is to it, they sent me down here not to give you a headache but a break." The reader may be deceived by Brundy's approach: I wasn't. I remained restless, brittle, and suspicious. Money was Co-National Food Company's only object—power and size—there was no love wasted on Millie. I listened skeptically as Brundy continued, "So we're taking a little—say, excessive language from you. Plus, we're giving you excessive care. But, cookie, we can't negotiate if you won't give us the relevant facts."

I sat. Facts? I finished my drink. I looked at my watch. "What did you want to say to me, gentlemen? Spit it out."

"Oh God," Brundy moaned. "Can that Cagney stuff, we're here to negotiate."

I remained unimpressed. "Cards on the table."

"Okay, scorpion," Goad acquiesced. He disposed himself on a stool. "Who's Puddu?"

"Puddu?" I stared stupidly. For the first time I was genuinely at a loss.

"Your old man says to us, you go ask Millie. According to him, you claim you can't sell on account of a certain wop by this name."

"You want an introduction?"

"Who is he?" he inquired sarcastically. "Low man in your Mafia?" The fat lids of his eyes came lower over his meaty cheeks. He leveled a blunt accusation. "Your partner?"

Serenity and peace returned to my smile. I reproved Goad, "I'm afraid I couldn't say. Not until I had a chance to talk it over with him. Business ethics," I reminded him cheerfully.

"You have a silent partner and you don't tell your own father," he breathed, "your own attorney?" He was really annoyed. "This isn't politics—" his stomach pulsated—"this is business."

"Sweetheart," I said to him, "it's been a good long time since I worried whenever the competition yells they don't like how I do business."

"Competition!" The pink of his tongue went dry. "Co-National Foods and Sister Millie's Chicken Sauce, these are competitors?" This was too much for him.

As he turned weakly away, Brundy rose from the holes in the sofa. He said, "Be a sweet kid now. We want to help." His face was longer, and he was weary and anxious. "Give us a chance. Mr. Goad here is old enough to be your father, myself I've got a granddaughter almost your age." He placed his avuncular hands grandly on the slopes of my shoulders.

"Kindly take your goddamn paws off me," I requested mildly.

He obliged. "Nobody's picking a fight with you," he lied. "Just the opposite, Miss N. If you weren't a lady—"

"A woman."

"A lady. If you weren't, Co-National is big, you'd come to us, we wouldn't come to you. We're playing the softest angles."

"The little pushover angle?"

"For the love of God," Brundy pleaded.

"I've played with the big boys before. Rough. How big are yours?"

"I'll tell you," Goad mumbled in his gut and he repeated, "I'll tell you. Big. You're better off selling. Soon. It's best that way. For you."

I puckered a smile and raised an eyebrow. I answered softly, "Every punk like you sells out someday."

"Soon," Goad repeated with barely controlled brutality in his voice. "The sooner the better. The big boys are wearing their kid gloves for the kid wonder. But only for a time. If you won't take a reasonable offer from us in a reasonable time . . . you know where you stand."

"Where do I stand?" And the truth came out.

"You'll be turned down by the distributors. No truck will carry you. If you find a truck, no owner and no manager will order you, no store will have room for you on the shelf. Co-National will take care of you."

While he was telling me, I lighted up, and flipped the match in the wastebasket. "That's all?"

"Think it over."

I grinned smoke out. "I'm not for sale."

Brundy closed his nostrils, murmuring, "Oh God."

Goad shrugged his stomach.

And I forced my words to issue from my breast in a chesty voice as deep as theirs. "Good day, gentlemen."

The name of the game I kept on remembering those days whenever the going got rough and the financial stakes high, was King of the Hill. Of all the games I'd played with Sandy and his friends once upon a time when I was a sniffly little tomboy, a tongue-tied nuisance with drooping ribbons in her braids, this one kept coming back to me. How happily I'd have been bloodied, happily scratched and torn limb from limb, if I could have got to the top of the hill. Never. One pushy boy or another was always on top. I was too small, too weak, or else I'd have shoved the king down, seized the golden bough, stood my ground, even witnessed my own ritual murder.

"Sell," Pop said.

"Knock it off."

"Sell," Pop begged.

"Not yet."

"Now," Pop urged. "Now, Millie." He paced the office, small and loud-mouthed. "You stand to lose every goddamn penny. You hear me? I won't stand for that."

"Getting and spending we lay waste our powers?" I suggested.

He brushed Wordsworth aside. "Either you sell or I quit."

"You're fired."

He tried to light a cigarette, but it dropped from his lips, and he had all he could do to hold on to his temper. "Sell."

I laughed. "Supposing I sell," I theorized, picking up his cigarette. I put it between his lips and lighted it for him. "What do I do with their check—go buy myself a few shares in Co-National and all losses are restored and sorrows end?"

"Millie, I don't know *what* you're talking about."

"Shakespeare."

"Screw Shakespeare. You'll be sitting pretty, believe you me."

His echoing phrase, "sitting pretty," summoned up remembrance of things past. "You got an investment suggestion? Maybe the old

General Motors franchise?" It slipped out. The moment I'd said it, I was sorry. It was unnecessary cruelty to remind him of his lack of horse savvy and business success, but I couldn't help remembering. I walked over to the window and looked down. I just stood there. It was early in the day. It was starting to snow. "I'm sorry," I said. The cobblestones in snow looked like lace.

"Forget it. But damn it, face facts, Millie. Just for a change."

"Shut up." I turned on him. "You want me to start over? I put my life's blood into this business." I opened up the window and scraped. I tried to scrape together a little snow for a snowball. It melted in my fingers.

He closed the window and took my frosty hands. Then he touched my cheek—cautiously, not paternally. Anxiously, not affectionately. "Millie, you can only go so far. A good idea. Marketable. I said so. A lucky accident, a break. Now I'm telling you. Sell."

His breath was on me, his touch on my flesh reached farther than he knew.

In business you can go so far, it's true, just so far, and then something extra special is needed, some break, some stratagem, some pertinacity—or all three, a single goddamn lucky strategic pertinacious stroke that will settle your financial affairs for the long haul, the curve that carries you away from the common trough of the wave where the little fish are fighting for food and sweeps you over with the whales and sharks.

I thought hard, not long. My instinct has always been to go right to the top. To hell with Goad and Brundy. The question was, who was on top? I phoned my banker. He phoned his broker. And before the end of that day's business, the bank had phoned back and I had my answer. B. Neill Tieger owned 51 percent of the stock of Co-National Foods.

Let me speak candidly. These are the times that make a woman peculiarly aware of her sex. All evening long at home I considered the best way to approach this B. Neill Tieger, what line to take, what wavelength to come in on. My impulse was to phone. I had his phone number and I kept it in front of me—741-5542. Or I could have written, I had his address—one up in Connecticut and another one on lower Fifth Avenue—but even if I knew his bank balance, his lawyers, and his tax problems, I'd have had no clue to the man. What his personal response to my phoning him at home and appealing to him directly was likely to be, I could guess, and I hesitated. I had a long cord on my phone. Hesitating, I actually carried my phone around with me into the kitchen while cooking, into my bedroom while napping, into the living room after dinner. I sat, pad on lap, telephone on the floor, cigarette in mouth. I was in the habit of scribbling verse in the evening, but I couldn't even write a line that night, I couldn't so much as revise my last night's work, nor could I bring myself to dial the number. All right, never mind, forget it, I thought. There was no conceivable strategy that would work. The direct approach would probably misfire or be shrugged off. To get to him, I'd have to con the man. I'd have to hoodwink him from start to finish. Frankly, I was unfamiliar with the con game. And why bother? Why try any angle at all? They had come around thinking I was an easy mark. Instead, defiance. The finger. That's what they'd get. More than they'd bargained for. I'd blow, bluster, and bluff; I'd diddle, dazzle, and defy. I'd jack the price. Before selling, I'd buy a bigger plant, I'd triple the floor space despite their threats. Before selling, I'd incorporate, I'd offer shares and go public. Before selling, I'd develop and market a second cactus product, a liquor like the *abba ardente* Puddu and the others used to drink, and I'd call it Satori. I'd change my business phone number to a combination that had the sound of gold in it—grandiose, like CH 4-5500. And I'd sell for a rocketing price. I had these, I had half a dozen other practical gestures in mind, ranging from pathetic to suicidal, when I went to take my bath. I took the telephone in with me and set it on a stool. Ideas? Not a one of them would have worked: pure poetry, all of them. But I was close to the crux of fortune.

Now I generally like to run my bath water very hot, but that evening it was so hot I could barely step in. One ankle. I proceeded inch after inch, enjoying in memory the old family story I've alluded to (about how Father's innocent mistake nearly made Mother boil me alive once), sinking lower and enjoying the comfortably mounting pain of the searing water. I got both my ankles and calves in. While waiting to get used to the water, I examined my nipples as usual. Two little hairs there again: I reached across to a shelf and with a pair of tweezers I plucked them out. From an open pack on the same shelf I picked up a cigarette. Lighting up, I inhaled. I thought of Puddu, the tower, of all those men. I bent at the knees. I kneeled, ready to embrace the huge heat of the clear water with my thighs.

And it was then that it came to me, as I was exhaling, in the very instant of slow descent when my testicles, had I still had them dangling between my thighs, would have entered the steaming water and glowed again as once upon a time. The imaginary pleasure of that pain, the hallucinated instant of that tremor, the inward clutching and relief and suddenly I *saw*. I saw this B. Neill Tieger's number now on a dial that was vast and swollen and glowering: 741-5542. But the digits all glared and repulsed, while the letters winked . . . they beckoned to me as a poet . . . and still kneeling, I stared at the swollen dial. Damned if they didn't! All together they spelled "PHA-LLIC!" Well, almost! One letter was wrong. Well, what of it? It was so close I couldn't breathe! The coincidence of a lifetime, chance and inspiration, the two requisites of success. For it was more than coincidence. My superheated bath water coincided with my spectral testes, but to me a vision came, and with the clarity of hallucination I saw this B. Neill Tieger's telephone cord as a long penis: everyone in New York, I saw, had a penis like that, everyone! And I had a vision of the entire population of New York connected by their wiry penises to my phone, a vine of communion and community, of society and prosperity. I kneeled—paralyzed, dwarfed by my inspiration.

It was the talismanic spelling of his number that gave me the courage to call, but it wasn't until morning that I was anywhere near calm enough. I waited till 10 A.M. and phoned from the office. I dialed slowly. I had new, endless visions of tangled electric vines. I waited, listening to the ring. A woman answered. "The Tieger residence," she said. The dignity of her voice!

"Who am I speaking to, please?" I requested.

"The housekeeper."

Immediately, with aplomb I asked for "Mr. T., please."

The response was frigid. "Who shall I say is calling?"

"He'll know who," I said darkly.

The moment I said it I had a feeling I'd made a mistake.

"Just a moment." She returned only to say that Mr. Tieger was not at home. "Would you care to leave a message?"

Someone lifted an extension phone—"Hello?"—a woman's voice —and just as promptly hung up.

I tried to be bold: "I had an appointment with Mr. Tieger."

"Is this—" She put her hand over the phone. Silence. She resumed, "Are you the interviewer from *Art News*?"

I was taken off guard. "What?"

After that it was hopeless. She said, "You had an appointment?"

Lamely, I murmured, "Wrong number. Sorry." And hung up.

I swore at myself. Muffed it. Wiped out. Insufficient care. Hadn't

I always learned the hardest routines by planning and exercise? My tongue-twisters, my jujitsu, my sales technique. All right then, I needed training. I had to go slowly, cautiously. I not only had to get through to this Tieger character, I had to convince him. But first things first. It was early in the morning. I dialed the number again: PH-1-LLIC.

Again a woman answered, but it was not the same woman. A deeper and harsher voice said bluntly, "Who is it?"

His wife? Whoever she was, it seemed wisest to pretend I recognized her voice. "Is that *you?*" I chuckled, trying to sound breathless. "Lucky you answered."

This produced a positively diseased pause. Our conversation resumed on a note of hostility. "Is this you again, Harry, because, Harry, you can just go fuck off, I'm tired of games."

"Scratch one," I assured her coolly. Not infrequently on the phone my warm contralto has been mistaken for a masculine tenor. Lowering my voice still further, I said, "Baby—"

"Drop dead. Who is this?"

"You couldn't guess in a hundred years," I ventured into heavy sarcasm, "now could you? Who's the last person that comes to mind?"

A pause . . . she was either going to hang up or guess . . . half a million bottles of chicken sauce seemed to hang on that—

"Pierce," she said, frightened. "Pierce?"

"I'm coming over."

"You want to come *here?*" She was stunned. "You must be out of your cotton-pickin' mind! I'll meet you at the old place . . . tonight . . . tomorrow night—"

"Don't you move, stay put, I'll be there in twenty minutes—"

"Pierce—" her tone seemed unexpected, dangerous. "Pierce, your voice . . ." she hesitated, suspicious, "you sound—"

"Did you *expect* I'd sound the same," I challenged, "after . . ." I let the phrase dangle, "after . . ."—unfinished.

And I hung up.

Not good enough! Con man? I considered following up my lead, but I'd have to go dressed as a man. I soon gave it up: Millie in drag? Out of the question. (I was a tad less fussy in later years. You compromise in life, who hasn't, who doesn't? Believe you me, I've had my quivering back to the wall. But treason? I'd laugh if it wasn't so cruel.)

I waited for almost two hours before I tried again. At ten to twelve I dialed a third time; I was stubborn. Again a woman's voice. But it was a third voice, this one. Crisp and a trifle irritable—his secretary? "Baron Tieger's wire," she said. "Good morning."

"I'm calling from *The New Yorker* magazine," I explained. Baron? "I wonder if I might speak to Mr. Tieger." Baron Tieger! Really, that was a little too much.

She covered the receiver for consultation in the background. She came on again with, "Who in hell did you say you were?"

"My name is Millicent Niemann. I'm a staff writer for *The New Yorker*—I'm no one whose name you would recognize, I'm afraid— but we've been thinking—that is, the editors have been thinking—of doing a piece on Mr. Tieger. Something brief perhaps for 'The Talk of the Town,' you know? Or if Mr. Tieger will consent and the material seems to warrant it, we may be able to go to a full-length profile."

The phone was covered again. She seemed to cover it every damn time. "You mean you'd like an interview?" I said I'd appreciate any time Mr. Tieger could spare. She consulted, and in the background I heard a single loud word—"Crap!"—her voice. She came on again, more politely. "I'm afraid he may grow weary of this," she explained. "He already has one interview scheduled for next week. With *Art News*. Would the week following that do? He keeps busy, you know." I knew, oh I knew, I was understanding, I was grateful. The phone was covered again. "Or how about this week?" she said on instruction. "Would that suit you?"

"Better still." But it was odd.

More noises. "Can you make it today?"

"Today?" That was pressing it.

"At the museum, at, say, four-thirty?" she pressed me. The museum? The moment was momentous, for me and for lovemaking in America.

"Fine." Four hours to prepare? "Oh, and the address—where is the museum located again?" On this *sang-froid* of mine hung the fate of lopsided love.

The phone grew chill in my hand before she replied curtly, "Central Park West at Seventy-ninth Street." So—the American Museum of Natural History. Was he on the Board of Trustees of the museum? She added, "Ask for Mr. Tieger at the Information Desk, would you be so kind?"

But I needed more information. And not, by God, financial. In the four hours remaining, I chased a taxi through the snow and stamped my way up the white wet steps of the Forty-second Street Library. The reference librarians were a godsend. They started me out with the annual index to *Art News*. We ran several years back before we came across the first Tieger reference. His *name* was Baron Tieger—that is, he wasn't titled nobility, his first name was Baron. And from there on it was not only easy, it was like sliding downhill, a staggering landslide of information. The hunt led on through *Who's Who in America* to *Food for the Nation*, to *Our New Financiers*, to *Investment Capital in America*, to the *Art Collector's Guide to Galleries*, to *This Year in Sculpture*, to *The New York Painters*, to *Plastics in U.S. Industry*, to the *American Museum Annual*, to the *National Geographic*, to *The Wall Street Journal*, and finally to the *Minutes of the New York Zoological Society*.

I skimmed of course. I had no time to spare. I had no personal interest in Tieger's money—the inheritance he had come into, and at first turned down, according to the *Times*, at age thirty-five. My strategy never wavered. How often must I say in my own defense that I was not a hooker? I depended not on physical sex appeal but, like Houdini, on physical ingenuity. I finally did do that piece for *The New Yorker*, too. I sent in an unsolicited manuscript, the editors were pleased with it, and later printed it. When it came out, however, it was unrecognizably revised. The editors were right. The profile I did for them had no room for the obscenity of reality.

How I Made It Big

Left to herself, the serpent now began
To change.

—KEATS

I saw him through a glass darkly. It was one of those museum cases —a huge, decaying, and dusty three-dimensional panorama of prehistoric man—it stood in the center of the dim hall. His eyes were separated from mine by thick double walls of glass. His face was overlaid, encrusted with images reflected from other parts of the hall, the duck-billed platypus in Case B and the Australian treefish in "Nature's Pranks" (G, nearest the archway) and the conjectural reconstruction of the crossopterygian, Tieger's own work. Though later we became unabashedly familiar, there remained between us always that double distorting thickness of glass, troubling us with the entire history of sportive evolution.

Atavistic urges were in the air between us almost from the first. The large central case we were both peering at was a feature exhibit in the Hall of Mammals. Lighted from within to suggest twilight, the case displayed a Neanderthal family. A grotesque hairy sow of a woman, with glazed eyes and yellow teeth, squatted in front of an unpersuasive, heatless fire. She was giving suck with her long leathern dugs to the hope of the world, infant Neanderthal. Just then, the Primal Father strutted low-kneed into the encampment with a bloody fawn for dinner. Father's loins were furred, his hair rusted, his nose flattened. Round his fire and in the shadows of his cave naked dried-out children and wrinkled freeloaders chewed skin or chipped stones or gazed uncomprehendingly through the bewildering glass at us two tourists.

"What's your impression?" Mr. Tieger inquired solemnly, his voice hollow in that hall. Around us other tourists circulated to other exhibits, migrants in time. Footsteps through a tomblike silence.

"Dead," I said. "And gone. And good riddance, if you'll pardon me." It was too far back again, too intimate for my taste. The image of a strutting father and squatting mother carried me back through my own prehistory. Besides, it dragged me even farther down than Sardinian archaeology, farther than Satori had taken me into the baked earth.

"Ah . . . I imagine you don't feel at home with Neanderthal Man?" he intoned.

Was he interviewing *me?* The thought, I admit, flitted across my mind. My vanity? My ineptitude? I hurried into the breach again with, "Mr. Tieger, what is the relation—in a personal sense, as *you* feel it—between your activities as an investor and industrialist, on the one hand, and, on the other hand, your involvement with the museum?"

"Well, I'm sorry to disappoint you, but I'm afraid there's only one hand. My brokers manage to take care of my investments for me. That's that, and I find it a very satisfactory arrangement. Here at the museum is my work." He corrected himself. "My profession."

Careful, Millie. Your slips are showing. He had so far managed to dodge every gentle reference to the moneyed side of his life. I looked nonplused.

Mr. B. Neill Tieger smiled at the working girl through puzzling reflections. "Miss Niemann, when you stop to consider where modern life is heading—the automobile and the can opener, huge factories that pollute the earth and corporate industries that pollute the soul, Madison Avenue, slick magazines, public relations, pornography, the latest fads in art, the new movies . . ." His face slid out from behind the glass case, emerging from all those peripheral reflections. He said slyly, "Nowadays even the loveliness of the female form has to be distorted and advertised before it will sell."

It was one of those recognitions, the flare of conscious sexual desire before my eyes, lighting the nearby world, a meteoric recurrence which I find gratifying when it is directed toward me, and which I have always associated with the emergence of human consciousness into history. My later work in archaeology was directed precisely to this point. Yet in B. Neill Tieger? One would be hard pressed to imagine sexual desire in a creature less manlike, less attractive to me, more physically absurd. Over his two ears, like brushes hanging from his glossy bald pate, were two whisk brooms of dark hair. They sat, as it were, across his eaves. He was thin in the neck, and he was pedantically remote. From time to time he shivered, strung from top to toe with high tension. He had three warts, each one dignified and callous, affixed like royal seals to his forehead, to his lip, to his left eyebrow. His eyes, like the treefish's, were goggly, and his long nose belonged to the distinguished family of the duckbilled platypus. He showed, when he smiled, a cunning mouth twice as toothy as yours or mine. And he wore a red vest. Red, ribbed silk. There was something distinctly and horribly pink about him—a fresh raw pinkness in his mouth, around his nostrils, in his eyes—was it only the redness of his vest reflected there? A harsh pink, the pinkness of lechery.

"But in the more primitive stages of life—" he waved his hand nervously, gesticulating vaguely toward me and the exhibit as if to include us both in some single view—and then he broke off. "An eyesore," he said, "Neanderthal Man, the central exhibit in the Great Hall of Mammals is an eyesore, a scandal. I have been studying the challenges of this exhibit for a long time, Miss Niemann. Boneless dummies. You were correct to call them dead. Dry, lifeless, waxen. Madame Tussaud could have done better."

Reminded by this tirade of my "job" as interviewer, I raised my sharpened red pencil neatly over the stenographer's pad I'd brought along. "Mr. Tieger," I said, poised for scribbling, "what is the name of your profession? What do you call it?"

He paused before replying, one extra second of satiric, churlish disdain which I was later to grow accustomed to; then he said, "Does your editor at *The New Yorker* usually send out young interviewers who are so—ah . . . young . . . charming—" he searched for the right word—"so—ah . . . very pretty . . . and so, in short, ignorant in the field of the interview?"

"I'm sorry," I said with some hauteur. But I was unruffled, I was even amused. I had to smile. We were a very ill-assorted pair. Baron Tieger with his money and his hatred of money's accomplishments (he had a bad case, it seemed to me, of Rousseau's fever, romantic primitivism). And me with my economy of scarcity and my energy for enterprise. "Excuse me."

"A pleasure." He fairly shook with appreciation of my charm and annoyance at my ignorance. "We call it taxidermy." He hissed, he showed all his teeth.

"Taxidermy." I wrote it carefully. "But you were a painter before you were a taxidermist?"

"A sculptor—and a painter—and I exhausted myself, I wasted those years of life, I groaned and labored—for what? To capture the world in art, to represent flesh and spirit. There!" He turned suddenly. "There's my view of the flesh and the spirit!" He pointed to his snouty crossopterygian in the case behind me. "Taxidermic reconstruction is a *history* of the spirit. Turn around! Look! The spirit, not only the flesh—am I right? But the flesh, too, we can even go under the flesh. Dermalene has made taxidermy possible for art. And it's possible because modern plastic taxidermy, Dermalene life reproduction, has *made* it possible. The entire animal kingdom—transformed. A visual art. A fine art. Birds, fishes, reptiles. And humanity. Soon humanity. These aren't just effigies," he gestured. "We're penetrating right through, all the way through the old aesthetic barrier."

When I finished writing this down in longhand, wondering all the while about Co-National Foods, Incorporated, I said professionally, "Then taxidermy for you is an art, a way of traveling, of journeying through space and time, of entering into the skin of creatures other than yourself, and of representing your journeys."

"Good! Precisely." He seemed happier with me now.

"And your art is new—that is, considered as one of the fine arts?"

"Ah well, of course there's a great deal of reverse snobbery in the profession. For instance, one of the finest women sculptors of this century, Malvina Hoffman, is admitted to the old museum tradition only because her work, though it is the purest sculpture, aspires as much to the condition of a scientific record as to the condition of art. But among the great practitioners of the old museum tradition, Covelli is generally ranked foremost, and I'd say de Nouym and Staughton Peabody are outstanding in the nineteenth century, and in this century the greatest acclaim has generally been accorded to Loew Cherniss. I studied with Cherniss."

What was I supposed to say to that? Not a single name I recognized.

He added pompously for my benefit, "The date of my meeting with Cherniss is the most important date in my life. It divides my life in two."

I tried, "Was that before or after you came into your inheritance?"

The pink in his face darkened visibly. "My inheritance interests you?"

"It's a fact, like any other fact. Interesting, of course, why not?"

"It is uninteresting, it is devoid of interest. I inherited this, that, what about it—how could that possibly interest you as much, say, as the fact that I gave up painting and sculpture for taxidermy?"

"But of course you might," I countered, "you *could* have given up painting and sculpture for—well, for money, couldn't you? A million dollars buys a lot of leisure. Or it will buy vast commercial enterprises—" I glanced at my notes—"or, as you say, 'huge factories and corporate industries.' Money will buy money or luxury, and instead—well, look at you. You're a taxidermist. It's—well, I find it distinctly, yes, I confess, interesting, unusual. Taxidermy. A millionaire." I waved my red pencil in little circles. "Why?"

Generously, Tieger smiled, but the smile was still cunning. "Call it an obsession."

I wrote the word down. "What obsesses you about it?"

"Let's say I find it exciting."

"More exciting than money?"

For a moment he goggled at me. "Taxidermy seduced me." Then

he led me by the hand—"Permit me, Miss Niemann"—and took me behind the scenes—up the stairs behind a barrier—into and through the section marked "Exhibit Preparation, Closed to the Public"—we passed directly into his incredible studio. Under giant skylights stood those specimens on which he was currently at work, none of them finished. They looked almost as if they were falling to pieces, crumbling to shreds—but in fact he was running the process backward—he was reversing decay, degeneration, and death—half-created specimens, aeons of zoology summarized and bodied forth. Here there was none of the lifelessness of inanimate objects. Flying reptiles—without wings as yet, but with clammy skin. Air-breathing fish—without lungs as yet, but with irregular flame-colored wet scales. A running eohippus who still lacked his tail, but whose mucous red eyelids and sweat-flecked lips registered terror. Everywhere the floors were daubed and speckled with chemical and plastic stains. Vats of plastic, sheets of plastic, commercial ovens, color charts, texture gradations, and shaping tools. He showed and explained the elaborate colored drawings that had to be made to scale from all sides and angles . . . the method of casting fossil remains . . . the art of stretching a plastic skin . . . the paramount, all-important twisting of the inner wires. He demonstrated. Grasping an armature, he made innards of welded wires flutter for me. Dawn horse—tiny eohippus, extinct father of the modern horse—groped again toward life. And when, following his instructions, I was able to extend the black-tipped, flexible, moth-haired wing of a pterodactyl, I not only understood his excitement, I began to share it.

I assert therefore its authenticity. And I assert nevertheless that he was using the authenticity of his excitement to seduce me. I kept picking up flickering signals of disguised seduction along with every genuine flurry of finger and tongue. But I must say that I failed utterly to anticipate his intentions.

He took me into a second, smaller room. There, more extraordinary than the pterodactyl, and more unsettling, was a shape squatting on a low platform under the skylight. "Peking Man," Tieger remarked, examining his handiwork judiciously. "We are just beginning to perfect the textural possibilities of Dermalene to the point where the facsimile of man himself can be more than a caricature—accurate—totally satisfying, to the touch, let alone the eye."

This creature—Peking Man—hovered before us, a monstrous undulating sculpture of dead-alive substances. His moist skin showed bruises, pimples, calluses. He stooped, but tentatively, as if he were about to rise from his squatting posture, and he balanced there, turning to frown. His nostrils were thick with protruding hairs and those hairs were wet, his ears strained as if, like an animal's, they could move to catch the sound of our approach, and his glistening gelatinous eyes were placed sideways. His elbows were horny, his jackknifed knee was horny, and in the pit where his muscular thighs met his belly his shadowed genitals were horny, too, but they were also steaming and fragile. His organic form seemed shot through with nerves, arteries, capillaries, vertebrae, blade-bones, ligaments, cartilages, membranes, glands; his inner cavities were furnished with body juices, pulpy substances, and rank, odorous secretions. Peking Man exhaled with living immediacy, aware of himself as he stooped, aware (one would swear) of his own voluptuous, reeking flesh.

I shivered. The studio was chilly. The simple knitted wool dress I was wearing left my arms bare. Tieger grasped my upper inner-arm peculiarly—professionally concerned with its precise quality as flesh—and led me by that arm, back through the Hall of Mammals, to the central exhibit of prehistoric man—the diorama of the Neanderthal family—his predecessor's work. "My next, immediate project. I'm going to remodel this entire exhibit in every detail," he announced with insistent pride. "Now you can appreciate what I mean. Taxidermy, sculpture, diorama—these words become meaningless, become increasingly irrelevant to my intentions. Just look at this group—god-awful dummies—the stalking hunter has about as much life in him as a broom handle, the mother has the delicate bloom of a laundry bag, the boy is a piece of crayon. I want to do them over. Life-size. I want to make their thoughts audible. I want to make a spectator worry that they might pick up a stone and throw it at him."

Though by now I knew what he meant, I began to feel he was right to call himself obsessed. To preserve the reassuring sanity of a formal interview, I said aloud as I wrote, "Modern plastic taxidermy, then, seeks for a quality of frozen motion—"

"Not frozen motion. Look at that girl there in the mouth of the cave. *She's* frozen."

One of the naked children was frolicking on her back, half in the shadow of the cave, her child-nipples veiled by a tropical fern. Her legs were drawn up, her knees were parted, and her loins were concealed by the puppy she was playing with. If not a dog, then some other early domesticated animal, and she held the snouty thing athwart her crotch.

Tieger bent over me suddenly, saying, "I want to begin with you.

That is, with her." My pencil hung fire. "Miss Niemann," he piped in a low tone, formally, "I want to make you in Dermalene." I never afterward saw his grin look toothier, more cunning. "Would you model for me?"

I laughed. I chuckled. I didn't even trouble to feign alarm. But I said, "No," firmly . . . tickled to death. I chuckled because of course I was flattered, but also because I should have guessed. The over-excited genius, seduced by his own prowess with Dermalene!

"Modern plastic taxidermy, you would say, then," I deliberately continued, taking notes, "offers us not frozen motion, but something fugitive, seeking as its goal the very transience of reality, the ephemeral arc of life."

He darkened to magenta. "I'm not propositioning you," he intoned morally, self-righteously.

"I might *prefer* a proposition." I glanced up from my pad.

"I'm not offering what you want. I want—"

"—try a professional model—"

"—to possess your flesh visually and tactilely—"

"I beg your pardon?"

"Your flesh, yours. Not just anyone's. It's the tone of the flesh that counts and yours is perfect for that particular girl's. I've been studying your flesh ever since you arrived—"

"But she's only a child," I objected.

"And I want to make that child with your skin." He put his fingers around my arm once again, testing it, and gingerly, scientifically stroked the bare flesh all the way up to my armpit. I had no doubt, from that moment on, that whatever he said, his proposition was not entirely restricted to taxidermy, however modern or plastic, but was assuredly—as he had assured me—tactile and fleshly.

"You have cold fingertips," I said since he had not quit brushing my armpit.

He replied, "You see underneath, where her buttocks are flattened against that shale of rock? I want every spectator in this museum to know that she feels the cold of that rock. Gooseflesh. Right there."

He did not, I'm glad to say, offer to demonstrate further.

Nor did I change my mind. "You could put people in there if what you want is live people."

"I don't want living people at all. That girl in there is Neanderthal, to us she borders on the inhuman."

I developed gooseflesh. Uncomfortably I suspected that he was telling the truth, and that *that* was why he wanted me. Not quite human? . . . Perhaps even my skin showed telltale traces of my anatomy to the expert eye. "I'm sorry," I told him, "I simply couldn't think of it."

Yet I did think of it. He'd given me carte blanche. I wanted to pull the wool over his eyes, and he'd offered to let me pull my wool dress up over my own. Wasn't modeling for him the perfect way to blind him, to gain time while I gained his confidence? Or was I rationalizing an overwhelming urge to strip? Had he outfoxed me? Was I afraid of being exposed as a con man? You understand of course that my double-dealing and the doubleness of my genitals made posing —consider, please, my position in the business community—potentially embarrassing. Tieger after all was not a medical man. And the possibility of exposure for either business fraud or anatomical fraud was unnerving. Dermalene reproduction? The old museum tradition? With that poor sucker's telephone in full view? Legs drawn up? Knees apart? With a master taxidermist?

His request for a model quickly assumed—I blush for my own emotions—the fascination of a struggle between business ethics and poetic justice. More than ever before, I began to sense (just as the reader has all along) that there was something strange about me, and not a little bit bizarre. I was more than a sexual throwback, wasn't I? I was an atavism in other ways, too—yes, and my sexual structures had defied more than categories. The interview with Tieger stuck in my mind. Even as I pushed a man around the office by day and pushed a pencil down a rhyme-scheme by lamplight, I felt there was a mystery in me, ancient and undeciphered and prehuman.

We are accustomed to thinking of the primordial as inferior. Let me point out with a due sense of pride that I had in mind no personal inferiority, but a superior modality in myself, an essence, close to the genuine, powerful, and undifferentiated background of all being. I was certain that my own undifferentiated anatomy was only a sign. I was impressed and puzzled by myself: my moodiness and capability, my loneliness and tremendous energy. Once more I began to feel, as I had felt in Sardinia, that I was extraordinary not only in sex but in some other way, some spiritual way, physically and mystically.

The invitation loomed. Despite the cold, I perspired between my apartment and my office. I found myself unable to concentrate on accounts receivable during the day. Trapped between my invoices and my inner voices, I twisted in my sheets at night. There, against my will, B. Neill Tieger's request dangled temptingly. It was a chance.

Miss Neanderthal. Playmate of the Millennia. Oh yes, I knew it all, how tawdry, how crude. I couldn't escape the intuitive certainty, common not only to hermaphrodites, that my sexual endowment had something to say to the world. My body was my grand poetic opus. I would become the only poet whose work, like that of painters and sculptors, was on permanent display in a museum (Plate X). Thoroughly naked, the time-ripened fruit of my body could now be presented to the museum-going public with the same degree of scientific and artistic precision as had accompanied those photographs of my genitals-in-transition-to-manhood in the AMA *Journal.* Here was a unique chance to correct that early impression of me which, irresponsibly offering my parts for the whole, had misled the entire learned world. Urged by fame and business considerations, caught on the thorns of simple wish and complex anxiety—the wish to be known, the fear of discovery—I hesitated, torn. And when finally I said yes, it was out of vanity, a vanity far simpler, the simplest known.

He had admired my skin.

Yet even at that I held out for two days. Even when I telephoned and accepted, I felt obliged to advance an excuse. By modeling for his diorama, I explained over the phone, I could participate more fully in his work. I proposed, with his permission, to continue our interview in depth. He was gratified, he was charmed. Good—where, I inquired, at the museum? No, at his studio at home. At home? That very evening.

Why? His rush was so blunt that of course I expected seduction. But nothing went as expected.

When I got out of the taxi, snow burned in the air, flickered, and lay molten on the street. Frost-white candleflames smoldered on all the spear-tipped railings surrounding his house. As instructed, I rang his side bell. I rang several times. No one came. Sparks of snow continued to fall. I have rarely been so cold. I kept my finger on the bell. Useless.

My petty rage at least heated my bones. It was the first time I'd ever been stood up. There wasn't a cab in sight. I pushed through the snow to the hot air and gold glow of the lobby of the Fifth Avenue Hotel. Pier glass mirrors showed me my face, large red cheekbones and snow-white eyelashes under my fur hat and I was as mad as the Elf-king, I could have ended Tieger's life. I phoned the familiar number, meditating a blizzard of nastiness; no answer— I let it ring, ring, ring. . . . And glory be! He answered!

He was so apologetic, so profusely weak and undignified about the whole thing that I finally let it go (after all, business was business). He begged me to return and ring again. His excuse was, he'd fallen asleep. While waiting for *me* in his studio, he'd fallen asleep! It was not an excuse that pleased me. But there were considerable stakes involved. "Friend," I warned, "you be at that door."

He was. I'd forgotten how bald he was. How tall, how duck-beaked. He wore summer clothes—slacks and an open shirt. Inside, it was deliciously warm, which I appreciated. Up carpeted stairs I preceded him to his studio on the second floor. It looked less like a foundry than his workshop at the museum. It had more delicate skylights, glass eaves on all four sides; it was smaller, more elaborately furnished. Geared easels, swinging armatures, wheeled platforms, glass cabinets of specimens and tools, drawing tables: but at the sides there were also elegant blue-and-gold couches and chairs. On platforms in the shadowy corners loomed zoological reproductions like those at the museum—sticky, dissolving, ghoulish flesh, one might have been a woman—I asked about her. "The Neanderthal mother," he told me, "but the mold's defective, and I'm not sure I can salvage her." She was covered by a semitransparent tarpaulin, evidently muslin soaked in oil.

I made out the extension telephone at once and smiled to myself at the length of the vine. The working portion of the room was flooded with a light like daylight, warm and brilliant—there were several styles and color-tones of floodlamps strategically placed— but the skylights on all sides remained black of course. The skylights were edged with snow. The night there made me uncomfortable. I didn't like the sense of a central brightness and a surrounding blackness I couldn't penetrate with my eyes. It was too much like standing around a campfire in a tundra clearing. There were even animals.

"What's that?" I asked, unbuttoning my coat. "A seal?"

"The common ancestor of our modern seals and otters. Extinct."

It was finished, quite perfect. "Dermalene?"

He nodded. "More beautiful even than an otter."

He took my coat. I said uneasily, "Do you usually work at night?"

"I work when I can."

"Can you describe your work habits or your method? Do you get up at dawn, for instance?"

"Ah, our interview. My method? Step One. I habitually install myself before the panorama of whatever it is I wish to capture." He installed himself at a small desk covered with sketch pads—apparently graph paper—and motioned to me.

I put one hand to the buttons of my dress. "No screen?"

"Do you mind? I can get you one."

"Strip-tease?"

"I can turn around."

The issue wasn't worth arguing. I shrugged and got out of my dress. But I was hardly out of my slip, I was still in my bra and pants, I had just begun on my stockings, when Tieger was seized with a trembling, a private earthquake, small but noticeable, in the chair where he sat. He put his hand to his heart.

"Are you—"

"I'm fine."

"You're sure?"

He took a deep suck of air and nodded. "Excuse me."

Was he sick? I found his behavior baffling—but if it meant what it seemed to mean, then it was behavior unworthy of an artist, unseemly in a scientist. And to me affronting. Quite superfluously, he picked up a pencil. He fiddled and twiddled with it, training on me a long, deliberate, and frankly interested stare. His stare was embarrassing. But I had come too far to fuss over minor indignities. By an effort of will I managed to still my qualms and bring myself under control. By concentration I managed to pretend—as I continued undressing—that I was alone in an Arctic clearing, alone in the aurora borealis of a lovely night. When I was quite naked, however, this became impossible. He took me by the hand and led me to the bathroom. "Step Two. Please shower off first."

"Taxidermic considerations?"

"Skin texture." He adjusted the water for me.

His was either the sexiest science or the oddest seduction. Both? Well, at least his igloo was tiled. Luxurious. "You're going to stand there and watch me shower?" I inquired, stepping in.

"Not at all. Miss Niemann. I'm. Going. To wash you." He was remarkably short of breath. He took a washcloth and rubbed soap into it diligently.

"You're going to wash me," I repeated.

"Mm. May I. Call. You Millicent?" He rolled up his sleeves. "Hold up your. Arms."

He began by lifting and soaping my arms. "Millie," I said.

"Baron," he said.

Familiarity thus established, he proceeded to soap me and scrub me—"The surface oil," he muttered—carefully, but getting pretty wet himself in the process—and all the while sucking air in nervous gulps. I was breathing with some excitement myself, let me tell you. After that blizzard outside, even the hot rush of water excited me, tingling against the recollection in my skin. And he treated me— I'm glad to say—not quite like a mannequin. The cat's-tongue caress of the washcloth, somewhere between a lick and a tickle, foamed over my shoulders, soaped and sopped across my boobs (with un-necessarily gentle repetition, I thought—how much surface oil did my breasts retain?). Soap purled and purred below, cleaning my tummy, whitening my fuzz, startling my saddle—"Is this standard procedure in modern taxidermy?" I murmured, watching my own body (I confess). But he seemed too absorbed, too intent, to reply. I was pleased to notice a certain reticence or modesty in him on at least one detail. He averted his eyes from my pubic area. As you'll immediately understand, this was reassuring to me—it made a favor-able impression on me at first. I showered the soap off. He handed me a towel. I dried myself. I repeated myself. "Am I to assume the worst, or is this all in the line of duty?"

He poured a transparent oil onto his palm. "You insist on an interview?"

"That's why I came," I lied.

"To investigate my work habits?"

"Of course. I plan to publish everything, every little move, every pass you make."

"Ah, I'd better be careful, hadn't I?" He poured dripping quanti-ties of oil on both my shoulders and began rubbing more oil down my back.

"What's Step Three?" I said.

"A lotion we use for skin casting. It keeps the Dermalene out of the pores."

"Are you going to cast a mold of me?"

"Watch."

At times a woman feels she hardly needs a man to excite her. Her own body is so entrancing it is almost provocative. And yet she needs a catalyst, an excuse—her *agent provocateur*. Rubbing oil

into my skin—a liquid like rosewater-and-glycerine, only heavier—
he worked in an upward direction, diagonally across the grain, so to
speak, paying particular and respectful attention to my breasts. Small-
breasted (though, as I have had occasion to insist, my breasts were
still perfectly turned and high, the nipples still pink after pregnancy
and childbirth), I found his attentions in part flattering, in part officious. I watched as he cupped each of my breasts in turn, rubbing
oil assiduously into the softness at the sides. I asked, I forced myself
to ask, "Which contemporary artists, especially in this country, do
you admire most?" There was really no question at all in my mind.
He was trying to stimulate me—and I was in fact breathless, unable
to listen. He answered my question serenely, and I found myself
unable to retain a word.

"Am I more beautiful than an otter?" I asked, dazzled by my
own shimmer. I tried to resist. I rebuked my own sensations. Hopeless. It was annoyingly clear who had the upper hand. That's what
bothered me. Only that. I'd come to diddle and con him, and here
he was, fondling, conning, and diddling me. An otter!

"Brings out the veins," he said noncommittally. I was ashamed
to acknowledge who held the balance of power, but I looked. The
blue blood-vessels at the side of one breast glowered at us from under
the moist shine of oil. He held up both my breasts gently in his oily
palms; the veins darting through my puffy aureole nipples were more
piercing, more vivid, than I'd ever seen them.

I insisted, "Do you hold certain theories or opinions about the
newest directions in contemporary art?"

At the touch of his oily stub of a finger, my left nipple budded
reflexively, then the right luxuriously. Taxidermy? I thought wildly.
Is this really called taxidermy? I'll have to find out later. But not
now, oh Lord, not yet. His chunky palms and indelicate fingers were
at work below, oiling my calves and rough pink knees, my locked
thighs and garish white belly, my tall tail and short ribs. His hands
swept upward. My veins, shooting across my glinting hipbones and
vanishing sharply into the furze of my groin, had acquired all the
splendor of faïence-blue branches. "Has your professional life," I
stammered, ecstatically, "been satisfying?"

Did he nod? Did he pause? Lightly, again and again, working
from back to front in long upward sweeps, his sliding fingers kept
slipping with miraculous ease and equal pleasure into a couple of
clefts I was trying to keep closed. "Pff!" I went, sucking my breath
like him sharply through my teeth, and then, "Hh-h!" His finger.

"What's the matter?" he said. I'm willing to swear his eyes were elsewhere, but not his finger.

"You hit a nerve," I breathed.

"A sensitive nerve?"

Two fingers, perhaps, were inside me. "A silken nerve," I lied. "Be careful." Though by now I was sure of my womanly anatomy and its womanly excitement, I was dead set against research.

"This feel better?" He began a massage. I could feel myself opening and swelling with lotion and oil of my own when suddenly I caught sight of Tieger—good Lord!—my catalyst—with oil on his cheeks and soap on his beak—soggy-backed, wet-shingled, dog-eared—he was erupting bodily, a seismic disturbance. He rocked. He quaked.

And that was all! No seduction followed. I was baffled, I was appalled, I was furious.

Baron Tieger and I were linked more closely than he knew. We returned, after this shower-massage, to his studio. There the strategic arrangement of lights still banished the darkness outside, but no light could dissipate the night each of us had brought along from the inner darkness. I was so highly oiled that I could see the flare of the floodlamps shift along my glossy breasts as I walked. I was a glow-worm who couldn't turn her lamp off. He led me by the hand to a platform some three feet high. I forced myself to lie down on this uncomfortable counter—a doll on a shelf. My belly, the well-oiled reflector of a floodlamp, glimmered candescent before my eyes like a luminous source. I was not at all surprised that Tieger touched the texture of my skin again, some remnant of tenderness filtering through his fingertips. Still he surveyed me, his eyes grew misty for a second or two. And I began to understand that the financier had indeed made a profession of taxidermy, and further that, however sardonic, lecherous, or even cynical, there was nothing in Tieger of the insultingly impersonal artist or the brutally objective scientist. He turned away with difficulty. I watched with interest. At a table nearby he took a pair of scissors and began cutting a sheet of heavy muslin into rectangles. He dipped these into a low warming tub—a chafing dish filled with liquid Dermalene. While he worked, I tried to hook up Tieger the titan with Tieger the taxidermist, I tried to hook up my salad-oil unreality this evening with my clothed reality in the daily business world. He turned to watch me while his muslin "cooked." Something about the combination of his silence and my nakedness grew slowly embarrassing. I ventured, "You are an interesting example of an artist whose personal wealth enables you to collect—"

"Money again?" After his deliberate, characteristic pause of disdain, then annoyance, "You," he said, "are an exceptionally irritating example of impertinence. And keep your hands away from your body," he snapped. "Don't smear my oil." Then he added, "Monetary value in the art world is founded on the hideous principle of usury. No restorer's work can remove the crust of interest and speculation that makes old canvases ugly."

Quite maliciously, I said, "What percentage of your net worth would you estimate is now invested in works of art, your collection—"

"What do you know about my collection—" he was positively incensed.

I threatened, "Either you let me have an interview or I quit now. Your collection, Impressionist and Post-Impressionist. In this house and in Connecticut."

"You're well informed."

"The public library is well informed. What percentage compared, say, to your investments in securities?"

What in hell was he angry about? Taking up a pair of tongs, he turned to the warming tub behind him. "Affluence, my dear, is perversion. Be advised. It's no use your grubbing for money in this house, or for that matter in this world."

To steal from the rich? He was so wide of the mark, I grew incensed, I lost my head and remarked coldly, tactlessly, "If there's anyone I detest, it's the wealthy type who denies allegiance to his class, a lapsed capitalist, a lapitalist, a man sitting pretty in the lap of luxury who spits in her face."

With his tongs he lifted a patch from the warming tub. The porous square now emerged thickly coated with the grey ooze of soft plastic. He came bearing his heated patch and applied it to me without waiting for it to cool. He stuck it to the top of my thigh, my lap of luxury. "Sadist," I said.

"Normally I wave it, but you inspire me. Hot?"

"Warm."

He switched on a fan. Two fans.

"I'm cold."

"Good. Gooseflesh. It registers better that way. The detail is finer. Lapidary," he muttered. And patch by patch, he proceeded to take the impression of my skin, applying squares and rectangles—

he waved them first—to the soles of my feet and the sides of my breasts, to my calves and ankles, my belly and butt, my back and sides go bare, go bare, my neck, my cheeks, my temples. I looked a patchwork-quilted clown of huge Band-Aids when he got done. And on my squares he stuck gummy identifying labels.

I was still in this bandaged naked condition when a door opened at the dim back of the studio and a girl in a nightgown trailed in under the lights. She was broad, almost square, with family-size mammaries poking away at the transparency of her nightgown. Very young, very slow and soft-footed, her arms had the dull glossiness and her face the full prettiness of a well-kept, well-kempt barnyard animal, with heavy hard nostrils that opened to sniff and unblinking, long-lashed, protruding eyes. She seemed intent on staring me down. She sat down and flared her nostrils and gaped away at me with a meaningfulness that was painful, but entirely unclear. Tieger looked at her, then introduced me to "The mother of all Neanderthals. Recognize her?"

He pointed to the reproduction I'd noticed, the ghoulish figure of a woman under muslin in the corner. "Instead of all these shreds and tatters you've got on, I tried to do her in a single mold, a single large body-mold. She was all but mummified—the process didn't entirely agree with her—it works on animals, they have to be either dead or drugged first and the result is accurate but entirely lifeless. It lacks the expressive fluency of sculpture."

She said not one word. I tried to read her glance.

To her he said suddenly, "Are you satisfied?" And to me he said, "Dickie should be upstairs in bed now, recuperating, but she couldn't resist the chance to come down here for a good look at you."

She hissed.

I blinked.

"Try not to move, please, you'll spoil the set of my plastic." He placed a nervous, cautionary hand on my thigh and another restraining hand on my neck. "Pierce, I'm surprised at you—don't you recognize your wife, Dickie Reilly?"

My body went numb. Almost powerless to budge, I struggled to get up, lifting my head slightly. He hooked a bent hand around the crook of my neck. With the other hand he firmly turned my head back into position. With maddening slyness he dipped the tip of his tongue slowly out over his wet lower lip. "Surely, Pierce," he said sentimentally, "you haven't forgotten your Dickie-bird."

The girl in the nightgown trembled with malice, Tieger leered.

I was defenseless and panicky, an anxiety increased by being un-dressed and looking ugly. My naked flesh was disfigured, patched, and labeled. I exercised what, to this day, the more I think about it, strikes me as astonishing self-control. "Would you turn off the fans?" I requested.

"Gooseflesh?"

I nodded. "How much do you know?"

"Clairvoyant." The fans went off.

Dickie was leaning toward me so far that the fat nipples in her wineskin gourds almost pushed through her gown.

Over Tieger's left eye his wart, inflamed like a carbuncle, twitched. "Leslie was on the upstairs study phone—"

"The extension—"

"Despicable habit—she lifts the receiver for a second and then pretends to hang up, but she just clicks it again and stays on the line—"

"Your wife?"

"Leslie. My secretary. She runs my life. I practically had to sneak you in here tonight." He leered. "Sorry for the delay."

His leer was wintry, satanic. "I had to have Dickie's cooperation," he said. I wondered how they intended to dispose of me. Trembling in every part of my diagrammatic form, I concluded that they in-tended to cut me up according to my labels like butcher's cuts of meat, in marked, manageable chunks and sections, and then dissolve me. . . . Tieger was telling me, "Oh, she didn't guess from listening at first who you were—or weren't. It was only after 'Pierce' called and got everyone upset. Dickie rushed out hysterically and came back in a frenzy and phoned the loony bin to find out who'd let him out— but Pierce was still safely tucked away in Pennsylvania, it seems."

Without warning, Dickie got up. She hesitated, but clearly she could think of nothing to say that was sufficient to express her un-forgiving contempt. Abruptly, she backed off and sidled out of the studio. I saw her again, but except for our first talk on the telephone, the curious fact is, I never heard her speak.

"And then *The New Yorker* phoned. By the way, you will do that article, won't you?"

"Of course."

"Thanks."

"Don't mention it."

"You were very good on the phone—Leslie let me listen—it was only that stupefying question about which museum—"

"I asked for the *address*."

"Strange for *The New Yorker*—Leslie put it all together—she called your magazine to check. Lovely telephone voice you have, rich and seductive, I was most anxious to see you in person."

He began removing his plastic patches one by one. He peeled them off my skin. They ripped away with a rasping noise. "You'd even left us your real name. Leslie knows a lot about Sister Millie's Chicken Sauce by now—your assets, your credit rating—and I know the depth of your navel," he said, ripping the patch from my belly with pleasure. I began to look more like a woman and less like a collision case.

"What's your game?" he inquired bluntly. He smiled. "I imagine it has something to do with Co-National Foods?" He seemed untroubled. "What do you want?"

"I'm trying to crack the staff of *The New Yorker*."

"A very suitable lie," he said.

I wasn't flustered. It was evident that any man who left the management of his securities entirely to his brokers would have not the slightest idea of how the executive officers of great Co-National handled, man-handled, or mangled small firms. Nor any interest at all.

He ran a finger along my pelvic bone. "What are you after?"

At last I was entirely at ease. My nakedness was lovely again, a trifle more pink perhaps, but unblemished. Sitting up, I bent his head forward, playfully I kissed the bald parchment between the two whisk brooms of his hair. The balance of power. Into his ear I whispered, "How much money can I manage to squeeze out of you?"

He reached for my breasts. He never made it. Not that I resisted. But again he began shivering and twisting in the eyeteeth of his hurricane. Overcome, overmanned, with anguish, he desisted.

He muttered something about coming again, his pleasure.

It was clear who had the upper hand.

My life from nine to five remained religious. I served the sun, and so did those millions of others who snarled down into the subways before nine in the morning, how else could one account for the savage fervor and whining obsession with which they entered the earth each morning like ants, mindless in the prostituted primal womb of gold and silver, and then like bees until five, enclosed in their honeycomb cells closer to the sun, labored to secrete honey against the future?

The drive to commerce insures the continuance of life not a whit less than the drive to copulation—whatever the driven copulator thinks he is doing. Commerce is fertility. Every day they worshipped and served the mystery, every day their feet took them along the same path to the archaic ritual, their hands and minds performed gestures and wonders. Like primitives whose language is deficient in conceptual powers of abstraction and combination, they faithfully and reluctantly and fiercely adhered to the rites of antiquity and called it "making it," or "making a pile," or "making a living" (but their maker was served).

I did the same—the only difference was, I knew whom I served: silver and gold, cash and divinity, life and being-in-itself. I didn't merely pursue money, I worshipped it. And if I knew that above the shibboleths of wealth, success, and power hovered the radiance of sun and moon, it was because there were in me tropisms that were prehuman, responses that were still savage.

Unreligiously, as the exigencies of business permitted, I modeled during occasional lunch hours and on Sunday afternoons. After preliminary skin tests Tieger arranged me in the position of the Neanderthal girl in the diorama—on my back with my legs drawn up. I found this pose difficult to maintain without tension. Patiently, Tieger insisted that I get rid of any signs of strain. But I found it incredibly hard to relax in the nude with my thighs opened. Lying there was easy enough; lying there without the tension brought on by my old demon—that was another matter, let me tell you, and nearly insuperable. I found my own bare body, my fresh-fruit girlish figure, more and more attractive. I worried that my masculinity, deeply enfolded and hibernating, retracted and quiescent under my labia, might slowly be aroused and arouse attention. And once that were to happen, I felt I would be letting go a peculiar but essential reserve of selfhood (all barriers down), without which—once Tieger had finished with me—I would be exposed to the meanest, most vulgar observation. My naïve enthusiasm, my sentimental yearning to figure prominently before the museum-going public in the compelling flesh, dwindled day by day. I recognized dishearteningly (and I recognized it by modeling for Tieger and understanding him) that I would be placing my image before the sort of gentleman-observer who imagines that his unobstructed contemplation of nakedness is a form of mastery: that scrutiny is victory. I longed to destroy Tieger's own confidence in his work, his method, his conviction that he saw me. I was called upon to make a sacrifice. Does not each poet have to bring himself to a fineness of self-creation and self-revelation, a potentially anti-social act of exposure which immediately opens him to the petty triumph of the trivial reader and, more dangerously, to the mind of the general run of critics who, when they have seen and compre-hended a man's efforts, feel thereby superior to his struggles? Neces-sary. It was surely necessary. So I bent my heart to the agonizing task of learning the poet's craft.

I opened my legs. Often in distress, I would watch my excitable taxidermist. He worked hunching over a round table at a varying dis-tance of five to ten feet from my square platform. Studying me, he set up an elaborate armature in the posture of my reclining skeleton —life-size—then he built up plastic supports, ligatures, and tendons. His table was mounted on bearings, so that it could be easily rotated around its center, and it had well-lubricated, silent, darting wheels. Suddenly Tieger wheeled to the left of me, around me, to each and every point of the compass—behind my head, port, starboard, off my left ankle, off my right ankle—every major point of the compass but one. Never, not once, did B. Neill Tieger dart his round table between my knees, dead front and center. I found this single omission puzzling—and after a while not so relieving as it had been at first. Originally I had attributed this peculiarity in orientation to his lack of stamina. At each one of his other positions, he was tormented. As he waxed enthusiastic with his eyes and eloquent with his hands, he would suffer in due course the contortions and contractions of his dance—then immediately he'd wheel his table round and take up a new point of view. Baffled, I concluded that he couldn't risk all his aesthetic resources on direct confrontation with my crotch. Until Sandy explained insistently over peach pie one day how wrong I was, no other explanation ever entered my head.

Put merely as a case, phrased clinically (as I tried to phrase it for Sandy's benefit), Tieger had a tendency to immediate, recurrent orgasm in the presence of the female nude: his aesthetic delight was thunder, his erotic response lightning. Decades of psychiatric care had only partially calmed his weathers. I learned in time from Tieger himself (but how could I have included the truth in my *New Yorker* profile?) that these violent seizures of his had been the reason for his abandonment of the fine art of painting—not all that eyewash he'd offered me at the museum. "For a year I restricted myself to land-scapes." He was studying the configuration of my gums or my toe-joints as he said this. "For two more years I did nothing but still lifes," he mused in confidence (and he had good reason to confide in me). "But it was Siberian exile, child, it was Nanook of the North, it froze the handle of my brush and the handle of my genius." He clutched the inseam of his trousers graphically, all five fingers grasping his unruly sexual organ. His true genius, his painterly love, had always been a passion for the flesh—for sea-born, sea-borne Aphrodite emerging from her scalloped shell. But she had been also his pestilence, the curse he couldn't shake—working with the nude, in fact, had nearly exhausted him. Never had he been able to have a go at her dispassionately. Discipline, method, creation—enthusiasm, involvement, energy—every sublime sublimation of libido imaginable in art—he'd tried them all—on psychiatric advice, the most expensive available—and nothing, nothing short of taking leave of Aphrodite altogether, had helped for more than a month at a time. His genius had trapped him. Neither flowers nor trashcans nor the male figure could inspire him; but Aphrodite—the demonic female nude—she electrified him. Even painting her form from memory triggered the reflex of his genius. And when he worked directly from the model, she made his brain burn, his veins expand, his muscles snap. The tungsten of his imagination sizzled white-hot above, until below he fried. Madness had been his working method—and the resulting canvases and sculptures were worthy of his exhaustion. He had banished his former work from his studio now for safety's sake, but I saw his work later at his home and at a retrospective show at the Whitney —lascivious sculpture in bronze and bottle caps—he had moved with the times—paintings that were rutty Cubist nudist and goatish abstract Expressionist. His theoretical attack had varied, but whatever he'd turned his hand to had shimmered with the authority of orgasm. Year by year his canvases had commanded the ink of mounting praise, the clink of mounting prices, and the mounting stink of publicity in the press. Today the millionaire artist was renowned—but the man of course had lived close to collapse.

His incurable weakness for the image of Eve once taken from his side is apt to strike one's funny bone. It tickled mine. And yet the more I got to know him, the greater the degree of bewilderment—approaching awe at times—I felt. It wasn't only the essential gentleness behind his satiric manner or the innocence masked by his clownish features and by his pathetic withdrawal from the modern world. No, I refer to Tieger's weakness. And it is for his weakness that I ask respect.

At first nothing but art would do. Finance? Industry? Not on your life. He'd fought over this ground with his grandfather (his father had died when he was three), the old food Baron once known to the trade as "Red Tieger"—fought the same fight from before the time he was in prep school till the first Baron's death. By the old man's iron will, a trust fund had been placed like fresh-killed carrion in his road. Edible only on condition that he abjure—formally and in perpetuity—the career and practice he had chosen. "Chosen heart and soul," he said to me, gesturing obscenely at the poor fang behind his fly. Invariably, his doctors (half a dozen), while trying to work their more professional psychiatric cures, had counseled him to take his medicine. To take the fortune that would come rolling to him, to take up his position, his legacy, his responsibility. In short, to go into business for his health.

In a moment of great weakness—of utter sexual prostration—nearing forty, Tieger had yielded to temptation.

"My dear Millie, the entailment of the legacy, the terms of the will, don't you think my attorneys could snap them like *that*," he snapped, "now that I've got my fist around Red's loot—but do you think I'd squeeze, do you think I want to break my balls again?" Always in vulgar terms like these he defended his submission to his grandfather, and anyone could tell from the obscene ferocity of his rationalizations that he regarded his entire life as a chain of weaknesses, and especially his submission to the old man. And what shall it profit a man if he gain the whole world and lose his lust?

He'd gone into taxidermy. It was the right profession. But it had started merely as a hobby he desperately needed after he came into his money. And slowly, perhaps inevitably, it had turned into his new life's work, a choice of great perspicacity. Anyone examining his early painting, those haunting canvases, is struck by their animal violence. It is unarguable that Tieger's vision of woman had always been animal—extravagantly, piercingly animal. At her worst she appears menacing and swinish, she has the charm of a rutty, oestral, salacious beast. At best she seems hypnotic and equine, she has the perfection of a yearling mare. I doubt that he had once looked at a woman as if she were fully human. Certainly in my case I had been only his prey. When he got his hands on me, he'd proceeded to skin me, clean me, put an oily dressing on me, and set me up where he could work me over. It took him a while to discover I was no ordinary model.

As for the details of his physical anxieties, I'm sure you'll understand: delicately wired as he was, subject to overloading his circuits and blowing his fuses, he had never been able to consummate normal sexual intercourse. If he so much as approached a woman with passion aforethought, he was finished. I found it poignant that however ugly and unattractive he was to me personally, he had suffered to represent my sex in art, he had given, if I may put it precisely, the suffrage of his life to the sex I'd elected.

It was only recently that he'd begun his dubious new progress. From tailed animals back to tail itself. His latest creature was the buxom Dickie Reilly whom Tieger had employed to mold the huddling figure of the prolific Neanderthal Mother in the diorama, and then unselfishly passed on to Leslie. (But that's another story; to which I'll come.) Saber-toothed Tieger had finally traversed taxonomy. From the missing fish, his hypothetical crossopterygian, to the missing link. The link to mankind. Me.

> I cracked
> an egg, I lunched
> on a pride of sperm,
> the missing link
> to nebulae.

Fondly, fitfully ever since that bestial business in the studio, I've fancied myself as the mysterious break in the chain of evolution: Millie, Early Woman.

Our collision in time and space was mutual. On my back, legs drawn up, head uncomfortable, I lay in ambush for Co-National. I lay staring sideways at his telephone or up at his skylight while he worked away on his idol, his simulacrum of me. Or I'd read a magazine, holding it on my tummy, where it went up and down with my breathing, and all the while I could tell that modeling was a challenge to *me* whose meaning I still hadn't, couldn't, dared not grasp. The struggle to open myself, to reveal my hermaphrodite loveliness, stamen and pistil together in my flower, was ultimately beneficial, as well as sacrificial. I know that now. The degree of my final success can only be measured by the clamors of outrage which the years have brought to my work.

We owe it all to Sandy. "Millie the Kid," big brother kidded me. He grinned, looking round at my office. "Give me a pinch! Tell me I'm dreaming!" He kissed my nose affectionately. I had already been modeling for some time when my brother dropped down unexpectedly from Boston for an interview at one of the major New York hospitals. Finished with medical school now—Sander Niemann, M.D.—he was making inquiries about psychiatric residency programs.

His face was pink with cold. While he peeled himself out of his wet overcoat and muffler, I reached into my lower left-hand drawer (the location of Father's hidden hooch at home) suggesting, "Would you take a pinch of this instead?" And offered Haig & Haig.

He said nothing, gazing idiotically at my leprous walls and floors. I'd rarely seen Sandy at a loss for words. Through the partition came the inescapable heavy whine of my defective bottling machine. I quoted, " 'In dreams begin responsibilities.' Scotch?"

Only one paper cup left in my drawer. I filled it, fished all around in my messy wastebasket to find a used one, flipped the cup out, and wet it. "Here's mud in your eye!"

We drank together to the bad old days. In a couple of seconds my brother confessor found his tongue. "Millie—" he leaned back against my old-fashioned rusted safe—"you're a goddamn liar. Is this really yours? You expect me to believe it?"

"Pretty grubby," I said modestly.

The constant rumble was a musical vibrato to me, and the faint aroma of cactus was my perfume. I'd written to him several times over the past couple of years, but I guess for him seeing was disbelieving. He was still slim, energetic even when relaxed, and as skeptical as ever. His grey eyes were more prominent, they were heavy-lidded and hazy with a kind of pulling force behind them, a perceptible magnetism. It exerted itself on my gaze with a peculiar force like suction.

"Poetry—you've just given that up?" he asked.

"I keep a hand in," I smiled.

He smiled back minimally, confidentially, the smile one gives to a private joke retold. "And no more archaeology. Always it's something new—how do you manage?"

"Simple," I said. "You've got to keep changing to stay alive." I wondered if he understood the nature of change. "If you believe in yourself completely, other people will, too."

His admiration—was that what I was after? Whatever it was, I didn't expect much from Sandy. But a few words would have helped: that I was a goddamn clever and beautiful girl, that he'd missed my Byronic features, that he was bored without me and my antics.

I showed him our continuous blending system, our heating and drying facilities, the whole plant. We were primitive: four assembly lines running the length of the loft. Processed cactus and lemon mash stacked in wooden flats at steps along the line—mixing, filling, cap-ping, packing. I introduced him around—to Arthur, Kipp, little Red; to "Doc" Braith in the back office. I showed him how we had to guide each basket of bottles into position by hand before the big trembling undependable mamma machine would condescend to lift them up to meet her udders. We went over to the big vats near the fire escape and looked at the blank warehouse wall opposite. Sandy said, "You're not in this for keeps, are you?"

I shrugged. "For keeps I don't know—I'm in up to my neck, I'll tell you."

"For the money?"

His question made no sense to me, and I told him so. "No, for peace of mind."

He shook his head, disappointed in me.

"Go to hell," I said.

It was his turn to shrug.

"Listen, do you know what I take home?" I jerked my thumb in the direction of our packing clerk, Arthur. "About two bucks more a week than he does."

"But who—"

"Our salesmen," I cut him short, "and the rest drains down into the business. That machine," I told him, "is the bitch, a real loser. We've got to replace her."

"Her?" His fair hair seemed out of place in the grime of my loft. "Millie, look around you. This is what happens to you when you bridle and restrict your sensual gratifications." I'll take a Bible oath he said something like that—I've probably garbled his words, but they were so outrageous that it hardly matters. He'd invested in my company, but it was evident he hadn't grasped the commercial possibilities I foresaw. Bridle and restrict! He rumbled on about "Pregenital orgasm and substitute pleasures. But the capacities of sex extend to all the five senses and four corners of the body, so that any effort to restrict the full scope of human sexuality to the pleasures of orgasm alone tends to produce the factory and the city, a false economy of quantitative production, based on the illusion of gratification in wealth."

"Lay off," I told him. Not that I disagreed: at any other moment, in fact, these dandy-Sandy reflections would have appealed to me. I was my brother's sister. But right now I really couldn't take much of this gas. Instead, I took him through the wet streets to lunch. I stuffed him with pastrami and pickles. In the overheated restaurant we crunched our rye together. And instead of allowing him to spout, I explained the bind I was in with Co-National Foods.

"Can they do that?" he queried innocently.

The little lunch place was crowded, there were people crawling behind our backs, but I leaned over and filled him in—both the dilemma and my solution—quietly and in detail. There was no one else I'd have trusted with the complete picture.

He blenched. "Millie!"

He didn't get it. All he could wrap his brain around was my method, not the goal.

He blurted, "You're modeling for the principal shareholder in Co-National Foods!"

I was very patient with him.

He blared, "Who also happens to be a taxidermist?"

"An unusual person," I nodded, "so your methods in a case like this have to follow suit, you roll with the punches. Entirely ethical."

"Just one of your millionaire plastic taxidermists."

It took him a while to get over this hump. I don't think he ever caught on to the commercial threat to my company. But when he heard of Baron Tieger's psychosexual sorrows, he sat up and took notice. He blinked and blanked at me.

"You mean not once? Never screwed at all?"

"So he says. Should I believe him?"

"Damned if I know. Most peculiar form of satyriasis I ever heard of. A satyr who can't make a faun, who runs away."

"Not away. He runs in place. Feet jerking, eyes rolling."

"The way you tell it, his seizures might be epileptic."

I'd been modeling for Tieger for several weeks by this time, and I knew what I was talking about. "Maybe I exaggerate, but he's a quivering leaf."

"A wonder he once could paint at all." Sandy, unlike me, had recognized the artist's name and remembered seeing his work. "Very strong, it's true, but nothing pornographic."

"Between fits," I pointed out, "he's an artist."

"How many did you say—"

"Anywhere up to twelve, maybe. Who counts? Some of them would pass for shivers, a kind of nervous tic. He calls it the wind of inspiration blowing through him."

"Fascinating. Absolutely. You say he looks at you, becomes 'inspired'—and poof."

"Poof! But never looks right up here—between the legs. Averts his eyes, avoids the whole area." And I explained to Sandy what I'd observed of Tieger's peculiar inhibition.

"Fascinating." He sat, hands clasped behind his neck and elbows spread wide. "Fascinating."

My brother already sounded like the doctor I'd had in Cambridge.

"Hopeless," I said.

"Not a bit. Not at all hopeless."

"Sandy, I tell you he's had psychiatrists—all kinds—right up to here—and still, look at him."

"Oh that," Sandy delivered himself skeptically. "The trouble with psychiatry—psychotherapy, psychoanalysis, the works—is plain lack of guts. Almost no one has the nerve to take the whole theory seriously."

"Seriously! Come on."

"I mean *literally*. They're afraid to put ideas to work directly—the way, let's say, modern physics puts quantum mechanics to work in direct experimental tests of its sufficiency."

"You lost me, buddy boy," I said, stirring the mustard on my empty plate with the tip of my pickle.

Sandy slid his piece of peach pie in front of him and surgically, with the tines of his fork, slit the tip of the wedge. "Look, you say he very carefully avoids looking at the pubic area, he takes pains to avoid visual contact—why?"

"Why?" I thought a second. "He's saving it for dessert."

Sandy lowered his fork. "Have you read Freud?"

I bit my pickle and shook my head. "But I can guess. Fear of castration."

"Too general. No. Avoidance is avoidance. He averts his eyes. Aversion is aversion. It means just what it says, what it's telling you."

I swallowed. "What?"

"Disgust. He finds the female organ disgusting. He can't bear to look, he prefers not to see."

Pickle and mustard together, I discovered, burn the throat. I swallowed hard, my eyes flushed—wet, hot, wide open. "Shit."

"What's the matter?"

"I have a pain."

"Where?"

I motioned.

"Lower left quadrant?"

"That's not where I pointed."

"Read Freud," Sandy shrugged. "The evidence is impressive." He leaned forward, emphasizing his words with the tip of his fork. "Every little boy finds his own little penis so wonderful, so beautiful, and so immensely valuable, that when he first notices his mother's sex he believes that hidden behind that big bush of hers she, too, conceals a penis—otherwise his mother's sexual organs could have, to his tiny mind, absolutely no value whatever."

"To Freud's mind," I suggested.

I watched his teeth open, close, chew. The pie went down. I watched his Adam's apple bulge. I watched the half-moons of his fingernails reach for his coffee cup, I even watched the way his flexible, strong, never-chapped lips opened and curved to take the lip of the cup. Though I disbelieved every word he was saying, my heart —despite my will—believed—it was still the same. I could refute his toothy absurdities now with my own tongue, but I was trapped, all the same. He had only to open his mouth. "Every little boy tries repeatedly to reassure himself—about his mother, about other women, about little girls—until he is finally forced to conclude, against his most cherished infantile beliefs, that indeed the entire tribe of woman lacks the beautiful, precious organ that he, the little boy, possesses. In severe cases the disillusionment that results may be so extreme that he reacts to the facts not only with shock, but with disgust. The female genitals become suddenly abhorrent to him, repugnant to contemplate. Womanhood may still seem to him appealing, the body of a woman exciting . . . but her sexual organ remains taboo, offensive, unappetizing."

"Unappetizing—must you?" I said.

"The attitude's perverse, Millie, but the resulting conflict in the child—and later in the man, as in Tieger's case—is pathetic. It's a harrowing conflict. The woman often remains for him infinitely desirable, endlessly provocative—and yet sexual consummation remains forever impossible."

"Harrowing," I said. "Are you finished?"

He nodded. While I ate my pie he studied my face oddly, meditatively.

For days this conversation disturbed me. It came at a time when all I really wanted to think about was the office—repeat orders had begun to fall off, it wasn't hard to figure why—and sometimes by three in the afternoon my nerves were as shrill as a ringing telephone: I wanted to forget Tieger, modeling, taxidermy. What had started as a cagey maneuver had ended in my personal entrapment. Could I possibly have remained aloof while modeling for a taxidermist, I ask you, given my checkered past and ping-pong anatomy? But that wasn't the worst of it. It was my brother's new view that burdened me. I thought him wildly wrong. But if Sandy was right, my obligation was clear. I suspected myself of evasiveness. PH-1-LLIC? We pick not merely phone numbers, but consequences. There were too many coincidences for the event to be natural, neutral, free of responsibility. I had called him in response to a vision. Many are called, but few are chosen. We had selected each other, Tieger and I.

Charity is profitable. Not just in my case. The annals of American business are chock-full of similar instances.

Fifty-one percent. Irritably, I put aside *The Wall Street Journal* I'd propped awkwardly on my belly and glanced at the watch I'd placed next to me on the floor of my square platform and said, "Baron, in half an hour I'm leaving." He was twitching unpleasantly—he was now into his fifth or sixth of the afternoon.

So far we had been chaste. We had preserved the aesthetic distance between us. But the decorum of art must transgress, once it recognizes, the thin boundary that separates it from the pornography of life. Readers who are sensitive would do well to skip pages here.

The replica of me no longer looked like an engineering construction. It looked disturbingly alive. I had just seen my maker's fingers descend the spread compasses of my thighs into the trigonometry of the crease between my cheeks. The fleshy work was nearly complete, its plastic skin was as dry—and as moist—as my own.

He bent to look at it. Then he mixed varying dabs of color on a plastic square and, coming over to me, held the testing square against my side to compare its colors with my own. He bent to look at the underside of my leg. He squinted.

I clapped my legs to.

"You've gone white," he said.

I tried breathing naturally. "A pain in the lower left quadrant. Nothing at all. A cramp." For Godsake, I argued with myself, couldn't I undertake a trifling sexual struggle in my rock-bottom birthday suit when all day long I faced bankruptcy in high heels and a fur coat? But I couldn't budge my locked knees.

"Color's almost back," he murmured. "The classic painters would have taken pains to get the exact color of your skin for their cherubim and angels."

"Now, Baron, why," I asked, "would any self-respecting angel of God want to look like a girl in the raw?"

"Take a look," he suggested after a moment's dour hesitation.

I took a two-minute break. I got up and took a complete turn around my Neanderthal twin, regarding my sister self—almost with jealousy. "I'm beautiful," I admitted.

He nodded. "Osteology, Millie." He began going over an exposed seam in her saddle with an electrically warmed shaping tool. "Her beauty is in her bones," he was saying.

"Not skin-deep?"

"Primitive beauty was locked into the joints, and like good hunters, they left us only their bones. See," he paused, "you can even tell from her bones she's a girl—by the way her legs lock into the pelvis."

I stooped. "No, I can't tell. Not that way." Her sexual organs were unmodeled. I backed away from prehistory, my loins shivering a bit, knowing a confused amalgam of disappointment, pride, prurience, and relief. "Look at the relaxed savagery of that girl," I said admiringly. "Baron, you're amazing."

"Back to work. Twenty minutes more."

I resumed my pose, knees akimbo on my glacial rock.

And then for the first time since I'd begun to model, Tieger came round. The construction table on which my replica reclined had wheels; he'd often taken the effigy in a circle, working every side of me. Now he placed it opposite me, facing me directly, in such a way that if I raised my head I could see the savage girl's knees between my own, some six feet away. Tieger was staring at my crotch between a couple of "V"s: between her parted knees and my own.

He wasn't quaking. He showed neither emotion nor motion. His control was clinical, steely. He shaped my genitals with gritty, stoic, mathematical blindness, first modeling them with his fingers, then applying his electrical tool. His eyes weren't averted, yet something in them was. They were glazed over, they were blurred by something behind his eyes—by his pathetically endless love of beauty bare, a heaven full of lust. Insatiable. I watched his curved neck bend to my plastic twat; studying me, he bent to his eternal yoke.

I felt like Leda, and powerful. When I lowered my head, Tieger's domed head loomed exactly above and between my breasts and between my thighs—balloonlike, disembodied. It was unexpected and grim and satisfying, the sight of that bodiless head growing, so to speak, out of my groin—his lascivious charcoal face dying over my own ripening, goldenpink belly and the goldenbrown thrust of my deceitful mons. He would certainly bypass my flesh and penetrate my being—surely he would see and understand the source from which my body had flowered, the poetry of living cells which now made me sweat under his gaze. He saw everything. He saw nothing. And not even for a second did I experience the inward sense of violation I'd been prepared to undergo. Before my eyes, my honeybrown curls shook like a tiny field of wheat, and I laughed out loud. Coolly, icily, amazingly, I finally said, "Notice anything special about mine?"

I held my breath. It was unfair to put him on the spot like that. He had no idea how much depended on his answer. A little touch of vanity, it may have seemed to him. Unanswerable and quite fatuous.

Yet he handled it with truth and some grace. "The trapdoor to paradise," he smiled so that the wart on his lip quivered.

"But even harder for a rich man than a camel."

"*Touché!*" he whispered. Though of course he didn't put a finger on me, the moment constituted, if I may say so, a kind of laying on of hands.

So I made my choice, I made an effort I'd once deemed impossible, scandalous, outside nature, outside art, out of the question. Yet I had once given life to a baby girl . . . somewhere in this world and nameless to me . . . but all my own. And my faith in that birth made today's effort possible. Certain sutures had given way during my labor and childbirth. It was therefore no trick. I'm not trying to boast. But it wasn't easy. I thought of Flaminia. I thought hard of her sun-hot dress on the picnic blanket. I thought harder of the tune-up I'd once given her. And hardest of all I thought of flooring the old accelerator to hot-rod happily down the freeway into her countryside. . . .

It might have worked. Who knows?—but smack in the midst of this unsettling effort, a woman swept into the studio without knocking, without warning, holding a shiny fountain pen in her hand like a small scepter. She gestured at me with her golden pen. "A small formality," she began in curt, creaking tones. "I supPOSE you're Miss Niemann, look, I've had a hell of a day. Sign."

I was startled as much by the sarcasm in her voice as by the intrusion. Tieger, without looking up from his work, proceeded with the delicate molding of my snatch. "Leslie, I don't want her to budge—"

"—sneaking her in. How many times has she been—"

"—countless, numberless, sit down, we'll be through in ten minutes."

"I haven't got ten minutes. Do you realize, do you have any idea, do you care what's going on upstairs? In ten minutes I hope she'll be dead. She's locked herself in the bathroom."

"You look worried, Leslie, positively overheated. Take a break."

"I need a VACAtion. She's flailing around in the bathtub—*your* bathtub—"

"*My* bathtub—"

"—screaming with jealousy and threatening to cut her wrists."

"Charming, but unlikely. In any case, the bathtub is a sensible choice, far better than jumping out of a window."

"Please go over there and have a look before the police do."

Continuing work, he reached behind him for what appeared from my vantage point to be a couple of hair curlers. "Leslie, pick up that phone, will you, and ring my bathroom extension for me, and tell Dickie I *order* her to slash her wrists. At once. Or else kindly have a seat, relax here with us, and prepare yourself for Dickie's demise with a calm mind."

"Nosy historians, phony *New Yorker* writers, compulsive suicides—" She began unfolding papers. "All I need, Baron—"

"A signature. I know. Miss Niemann will sign. But she's a businesswoman, she'll insist on reading the fine print . . . won't you?"

"I do insist."

"You see? But she'll sign. I assure you that unlike our Dickie, young Millie here is a perfectly reasonable, an amiable and unexceptionable person. Sit down and wait. Ten minutes. In the meantime, I can guarantee she won't make a scene."

An echo of Satori's phrase recurred to me: "Only adore the scenery." So I admired Leslie: her nervy chin, her mature, estimating eyes, her attractive energy. But after a few seconds it became clear that, for Leslie anyhow, it was I who was scenery. She didn't sit. She made a circuit of the studio, regarding me from all points. The presence of a woman as completely clothed as she was, studying me, made me much more aware of my own nakedness, she made me feel less like a model, more like an exhibitionist. And what made it worse was, she was peculiarly dressed in a wool challis robe-dress with wide monkish sleeves and a cowled collar—the sash of her robe was a belt of gold coins—all of which gave her the air of Tieger's spiritual and financial adviser rather than his secretary. I studied her quite intently as she circled me—her clipped, mannish, hipless walk. If she'd had long waxed mustachios, probably she'd have tweaked and pulled them at me. "What exactly am I expected to sign?" I queried.

"A release."

"For what?"

"For him."

"*From* what?"

"From everything."

I took this more seriously than anyone could have expected. Nietzsche speaks in *Beyond Good and Evil* of total release, of letting go completely, as in fact an artificial condition, an unnatural state of being. Nothing either in human nature or in any other part of nature, and nothing in any of the arts, he observes, exists without obeying an essential discipline of life-giving, form-giving order. Complete release then, anywhere in nature or art, is not merely undesirable, it is even destructive, a condition of being leading to degeneration or death. Yet how then account for those violent transformations we observe in the cosmos, occasionally in nature but especially in man, explosive swings from one form or order of being to another: those creative transitions often signaled by the apparent breakdown of anything that can be called order, by floundering chaos and unnatural anarchy, by the offensive, the gratuitous, and the perverse?

In barely a moment I'll come to Tieger, but I want to say here that it wrenched my mind and unsettled my nerves, to abandon, even temporarily, the rigorous womanhood I had achieved. I proposed to release not merely Tieger, but temporarily myself, into the sexually male creature I'd once been and battled to be, by disordering myself at the thought of a woman.

The atavistic urges that dimmed the air between us from the beginning now struck me forcibly and I understood our mutual repulsion and attraction. Science and art, big business and small business, millionaire and moocher, heir and con man, Co-National Foods and Sister Millie's Chicken Sauce were in their important ways irrelevancies. I looked at Tieger—sexually helpless and brilliant—and saw that he was my possible throwback. I'd have remained short-circuited like him—crippled, peculiar, impotent—if I hadn't dedicated myself to the life of action and transformation. And with that path of thought, I came to a precipice. Gritty resolve, rocky willfulness. In vain.

In vain I tried to stimulate myself by thinking of his 51 percent control of Co-National. No power, no influence, could help me now. In vain I tried to concentrate again on Flaminia. The moment had passed. In vain did I try to arouse myself by concentrating on Leslie. Indisputably handsome she was, but there was nothing about her that could excite the man in me, neither her money-belt nor her monkish cowl, and certainly not her unblinking notary-public attitude toward my privates. "It's not a bad copy," she was saying to Tieger, finally turning away from me to examine his work, "but could any Neanderthal girl have had a body like hers, with an almost invisible golden down on her coral flanks?"

The feeling in her tone surprised me. I lowered my gaze and looked freely at my own body.

"The theory of imitation," Tieger was saying, squeezing my plastic groin and wrinkling his lips reflectively, "has been much misunderstood. Aristotle's word for it is misleading. Properly speaking, art neither mimics reality nor gives birth to it. Art mates with reality."

Spoken slowly between my thighs, these words captured my desperate attention: tossed off at random by Baron Tieger, they were to become my aesthetic credo. The entire event—the generous, vulnerable state of my mind, the frank exposure of my genitals, the astute critical force flowing from the mature artist-scientist to the apprentice-poet—these forces, that moment, released and bent the twig of my career. I felt my inhibitions dissolving, my dichotomies revolving, my powers growing. I lowered my gaze and looked squarely at my own naked body and saw the fact of its unutterable beauty—shimmering girlbody—there was nothing perceptibly masculine about it—I accepted it wholly. And immediately—without pause—few things have ever seemed so beautiful and intensely provocative—my phallus and my generosity expanded together.

Leslie had retreated to a seat near the phone. Only Tieger saw what was happening. He saw it and studied it and changed color and stiffened. He began to vibrate. He seemed to undergo something more profound than orgasm, it looked more like electric shock therapy. His broad grooved tongue lolled, then curled up toward his red bulb of a nose, and then his facial muscles began to twitch uncontrollably, his features contorted into a series of gargoyle masks, his wrists and arms flapped and jerked, his torso twisted round like a man fleeing without the use of his feet. He collapsed—still writhing—on the floor of the studio.

Leslie had seen nothing of my experiment in poetic mercy. But she saw him spin and fall and heard him gurgling on the floor. She bolted out of her seat.

While dressing, my mind now blank as a camera, I watched her attempts to revive him.

Neither of them paid any further attention to me. My mind stayed open, like a stuck shutter. My limbs wavered, my fingers clicked. With some difficulty I got my galoshes on over my heels and left.

I reached the street by sheer effort of will, walking without tears like a whipped, stubborn child, terrified that she'd done something irreparable. Not to B. Neill Tieger. To myself. I couldn't see straight, I couldn't think straight. I'd released my jack-in-the-box—and was I now the same Millie who'd gone into the studio an hour earlier, was I me, was I he?

I tried hailing a cab along Fifth Avenue but I couldn't even raise my hand. I just stood. After a while a taxi stopped anyhow, the cabbie looked at me quizzically. I got in.

He drove me a block or two straight ahead, asking me twice where I was going. I said nothing. He stopped the cab. We were on the edge of Washington Square Park. He pulled to the curb and turned around to look at me. I opened the door wordlessly and got out. I think he started to yell something and then hesitated, looking at my face. My expression must have stopped him.

I hardly saw him. I walked to the nearest phone booth.

It was self-defense, it was genius. The instant I started to dial the office, the instant I got my finger into the familiar, reassuring little holes of my own business phone number, the world straightened out around me, it came crashing up into firm precision around my blank eyes and I knew again with passion why I'd gone into business in the first place, I suffered and accepted with almost sensual relief the knowledge of who I was and why I'd chosen my life.

I recommend such moments.

Before they even picked up the phone I was myself again.

"Nothing from Peerless?"

Nothing.

"And?"

"Acme."

"In?"

"Out. Strike three."

"Canceled?"

And despite the bad news, which seemed trivial now, I found myself worrying about Tieger: it had been irresponsible to leave him like that, I'd lost my wits, my nerve, my integrity, my head. What

would Sandy have said? Go back . . . yet I was loath to go back
. . . I practically pumped the phone for an excuse. Some urgency,
some emergency that would force me to return to the office. Nothing.
The office was not only quiet. It was dead. Business was dying, as
Co-National had promised.

I hesitated. I walked around the white park. It wasn't very cold,
but I walked holding my fur collar closed, with my hand to my
throat. I walked a long time. I realized what it was that had horrified
me, what had opened and blanked my mind. Not simply the fact of
overexposure. I was too secure in sex, after motherhood, to be shattered in a generous cause, to be exploded personally by a little razzle-
dazzle kindness. No, what had nearly sent me reeling over the cliffs of
my identity had been *how* I'd succeeded. Even in my extremity and
industry, the *how* I should never have permitted. My own exquisite
body had aroused me. My femaleness had aroused the male in me.
And the Prince had awakened to take her. My he adored my she, my
she possessed my he, I was married inside. No wonder I had never
really wanted in the abandoned way, the cave way, the womanly
way, a whole man or a whole marriage—I loved myself, I loved my
Self. I had touched the source of private enterprise. I knew why I
was in business.

A mongrel squatted and stained the snow with pee, making a
yellow circle and hole. A police car cruised slowly by. I stared after
it, my breath misty. I took another breath.

I was accountable. Having asserted my integrity, I couldn't afford
to lose it now. A boy passed, holding a pair of iceskates over his
shoulder. He went by whistling. I remembered, I took a deep breath,
I held it, and headed back.

All in all I could hardly have been gone much more than half an
hour.

I remember the jangling of church bells when I jingled his studio
bell. No answer. Again? Again. I circled round to the front door.
Wide open. Odd. I rang another counterpoint to the church gongs.
I'd never come in through the front door. I waited and peered in.

I think I was even at this juncture of events anxious to see the
collection of paintings I'd read about that first day in the public
library, but I drifted inside hesitantly. I was met by the silence of
surfaces—polished tabletops and old tapestries and marble pillars and
a vast Tieger canvas of three circling nudes. Something was wrong.
In the first parlor I came to, on the table a blue platter lay broken down
the center. Lustreware. Bits of shattered blue flecked the floor. Sudden

anger? Or fear? In the neighboring salon, between two grand pianos, an enormous brocade curtain had been ripped from the windows. I reached the wide curve of the staircase. The wall showed a zigzag of paintings, the carpet a spume of lingerie. Dropped in flight? Thrown? I had no time to study the oils, all by modern masters. I noticed only that Tieger's own paintings hung wildly askew—deliberately whacked out of line. Upstairs in every room, his signed canvases hung at a jaunty tilt. Beds had been overturned and the hall carpet had a curl up the middle like a low loop in a roller coaster.

I heard them, then I saw them. In the library. Under a quilt. Lying on a couple of mattresses jumbled together on the library floor. They were three waves under that quilt, three aquatic forms cresting and billowing over each other. I couldn't discern for a moment as they broke over each other just who was doing which to whom, but the general tide of enjoyment was clear. It was ebbing.

Dickie spotted me first and gave me one of those long vicious stupid gorgeous stares of hers. And suddenly she rose—in terror and revulsion, she wrenched around like a frightened sea cow struggling to rise on its clumsy but determined fins. Keeping the quilt wrapped around her body, she found her feet and jerked through a side door out of the room.

It took Leslie a moment to disentangle herself from Tieger's limbs. She went chasing after Dickie in an unhurried arc of flesh, speeding away like a wet whiteskinned porpoise. (But not, I'm glad to say, without a polite, even grateful, smile at me.)

And Tieger? He came at me breathing weary triumph. I had never heard sex in his voice, such raw exhaustion, such unqualified enthusiasm. Gone was the familiar satiric edge. "It works," he delightedly foamed and boomed, delightedly pointing.

No, it wasn't the pleasantest sight in the world to see him come rolling at me stark naked, with his tool plunging in front of him like a walrus whitened with the salt froth of love. His, Leslie's, and Dickie's. Had my mood been different—less anxious, less personal— it would have been embarrassing. Irrationally, I was angry at him. I turned my back on him.

He caught up with me in the hall. "Of all the fantastic pieces of luck!"

Luck? I was too annoyed to reply. Most undressed men look undressed. Tieger was the only naked man I've ever met who looked badly dressed. He was even less attractive in the flesh than when clothed—a tallish, barrel-bellied, haunchy, slat-chested Don Quixote, rolling his wild eyes and dangling his encrusted sword. "What a wild, stupendous way to get your rocks off," was all he could think, all he could proclaim to the grand empty sweep of the stairs.

I straightened his paintings, one by one, as I descended. He touched my arm. "Hands off," I requested. I suppose I may have been jealous of Leslie and Dickie, but all I actually felt was an utter lack of interest in his success and an overwhelming desire not to be touched.

"You don't understand," he assured me, following me step by step. His weapon thrust, parried, and subsided as we descended. "My utterly fantastic luck," he rattled, "is that you've come back to me just when—let my paintings alone!"

"The artist is talented," I remarked, squaring the edge with the corniced ceiling.

He turned me forcibly around to continue, "Just when I wanted to tell you something. Of course I was shocked. I'm sorry. One only *hears* of these things in the course of one's professional work. One rarely encounters, sees—let me tell you something. No, ask you. Beg you."

It was too funny to laugh. And preposterously clear. "Baron," I chided.

"This isn't a proposition—"

"You've just hopped out of bed and you—"

"I want you to marry me."

"I know," I said and I stared at the idiot. "Idiot!" I told him, and finally, "Child!"

I took a cab back to the office, only slightly wounded, quite able to give directions now, and irritated. I had no trouble at all understanding B. N. Tieger's feelings, I had been through too much of the same myself not to appreciate his sacred male stupidity. He had undergone—late in life, unexpectedly—the most profound sexual initiation of his life, and with mawkish gratitude and white-hot bewilderment and grey awe, he now proposed to marry the mystery herself.

I busied myself with letters. They were on my desk, waiting and ready to be signed when I got back. It must have been some three-quarters of an hour later, I was already into accounts payable, when Baron pushed his way unannounced through my office door. He shoved it closed with the tip of his cane and turned the lock.

He seemed almost to materialize rather than enter: an apparition. His appearance on my home territory bothered me, I remember. I'd got used to thinking of him as belonging to a world apart, another dimension of my being. He was dressed as I'd first seen him, his red vest reflected in the fragile amorous pink of his nostrils and eyes and tongue. Warts and nose, he was the same unsightly sight, the same taxidermical tycoon. But I knew so much more about him now that his intrusion into my business life was shocking.

I moved toward the door to unlock it. He blocked the way. I raised my eyebrows. He said, "I'll be explicit. Listen." When I began to speak, to object, he said, "Quiet down, Millie. Listen to me. Think."

I was thinking of Co-National Foods, but I listened. Fifty-one percent.

"I was upset before. True. Regardless of me," he said, "you must not allow yourself to be disturbed by—Millie, listen to me—by what came over you in my studio. So you got a trifle excited—so what? Perfectly natural."

I lost my breath.

He stood there. He was silkshirted. He needed a shave. He had recovered. He was ugly, he was magnificent.

"Natural?"

"Perfectly. I've seen *girls* get excited lying around like that."

I blushed.

"Don't be childish," he reproved me. His eyes goggled sternly. "Let's call a spade a spade."

"It's not a spade." How could I have mentioned Co-National— their executive officers, their strongarm methods, their harassment of competitors—to their chief shareholder at a time like this? My mind was elsewhere. "It's a miracle."

"Don't talk nonsense. There are no miracles in science. I admit I was a trifle overwrought—any alert naturalist would have been—I was overwhelmed by the discovery. It was an uncommon, prodigious moment, a breakthrough in science. For, Millie, no matter how often one hears of these things in the profession, in the regular course of one's research both in prehistoric taxonomy and in contemporary mammalian species, the fact, when it appears, is phenomenal and its importance is Evolutionary."

Groad and Bundy? Boad and Grundy? "Evolutionary?"

"Mankind as a whole descended, much earlier than the apes, *much* earlier, from an ancient furry quadruped with a tail. This creature in turn, and therefore you, Millie—you, me, and all the higher mammals—all of us derive, still farther aeons back, from some small marsupial—"

"What's a marsupial?"

"Wombats, bandicoots, opossums, etc."

"Duckbills?"

"No." He dismissed this. "And the marsupials derive, through further millennia, from the monotremes."

I became suddenly suspicious. "Did Leslie send you here?"

"Leslie?"

"Yes. Is she worried I'll sue?"

"Leslie's on your side. She thinks you're a wonder."

"I am. I'm a miracle."

He waved this aside with an impatient wrist. "The monotremes derived from the amphibians. And the amphibians in turn from some obscure aquatic creature who possessed both sexes, the male and the female organs, united *within the same individual*. Do I make myself clear?"

"Yes, of course—you're asking me to marry you."

He nodded.

"You want to wed me and master your subject." I was sorry I quipped, he was so serious. I recognized with a heavy, sinking admission that I had never imagined that any man who actually and fully knew what I was made of, sugar 'n' spice and everything nice, worms and snails and puppy-dogs' tails, would in his right mind want me as his wife. Was Baron, in fact—I took the trouble to ask him— "Are you in your right mind?"

"Lucid," he responded. "Millie, listen again. You're neither a miracle nor a monster. In your genes, evolution has been recapitulated —at a higher level, accelerated, prophetic, and more precious."

Neither woman nor androgyne has ever been more deftly, more flatteringly wooed. I blushed to my eyes, I fished for clichés. "Baron, this is so scientific."

"It's God's truth."

"And Darwin's?"

"And mine!"

Tieger, Tieger, burning bright. To propose, he dropped to his knees and lowered his bald scalp.

"Get up," I said. "Don't be preposterous. Get up."

In vain. He kneeled. He lifted my skirt and my slip out of the way and comfortably pressed his mouth to the crotchety V of my panties. Between one kiss and the next, speaking to my groin, he said —always with the same delicate, reverent formality, "You're a human archive. You're a document in the passionate struggle of man to raise himself above the beast."

This method of proposing to a girl unnerved me. The groaning hum of the bottling machine disturbed me. At least the door was locked. "Baron!" He furled my underpants to half-mast. He caressed with his breath. He grazed on my mount of Venus. I swear it freely: it was a joy to see how changed he was! And nearly beyond belief! No aversion! He approached my complex flowering vulva without a trace of loathing, with not an instant's distaste or disinclination. It was gratifying and remarkable. For me it was a pleasure far from simple. I had never believed it possible, it had never even entered my head that my pluperfect genitals, once known, could be desired. I had never imagined such harmonies, hadn't dreamed that my baroque sexual organ could inspire in a man who knew the range of the instrument such towering crescendos of devotion and delight.

Yet Baron was treading on very treacherous ground. If, as every reader knows, there had been the smallest trace of homosexuality, any suspicious caress in Baron's ardor for my flesh or anything peculiar in my flesh's response to him, that moment would have been his—and our—last moment.

There was no such indecency. Tieger had been granted a revelation. His lust was unsullied. His mind was pure. His stubble on my fur was exhilarating. His smile on my pout drove me to paralyzed ecstasy. My labia were lavishly sensitive. It's invidious to compare, but I'm inclined to think that my bivalve structure has somehow made the rich raw fullblooded fabric of nerve endings all along my lips more sensitive than those of others—almost unendurably alive, compelling. I was now no longer foolishly worried about a knock at the door, I was only staggered by the cunning simplicity of Baron's reiterated overtures for my hand in marriage. In an aeon, longer than the time it takes to tell you, touched to the slow quick, I opened to his tender insistence—as perfectly, perfectly female as any woman ever touched there by the smile of a man—as normal as apple pie and ice cream. I was all I could ever have hoped to be, had anyone cared before to let me hope. To me his tongue was more convincing than both speech and silence, and it was greater than silence.

It may therefore surprise you to learn that my Baron did indeed continue to speak. He had bent me down over my broken leather couch. He spoke to my groin as I lay feverishly enslaved and dumbfounded, holding the dome of his head in the calipers of my fingers. And what he said made all the difference between rapture and an affair, between passion and alliance. "To me," he said, "you are the most treasured record of humanity. And beyond humanity, farther and deeper into the ocean, marshes, and very ooze of existence, a clue to the primaeval, archaic mysteries, the long impenetrable linkage with bottomless strata, with trillions of years of cellular will, energy, and life, from the beginning."

I listened. I listened with an ear not of this flesh. I shuddered and believed. It was what I had always thought, imagined, and been confident was true. Listening to his words, my soul thickened to a ponderous and fiery glory and my skin took wings, sluggish scaly reptilian wings, and wheeled in long wide drugged circles.

How I Betrayed Love

If I had to suffer thus for my sister's sake,
I would rather not have any sister.
—WOLFRAM VON ESCHENBACH

Can I ask you to understand, can you possibly understand, my deeply fixed sensation that my unique womb had been the microcosm of all creation, the source of the universal process by which love, beings, and, beyond both of these, reality itself had been generated? My oracular mouth.

Marriage? For days my disembodied body shook and my down-to-earth mind, liberated, took flight with the flesh and followed it upward . . . I had never experienced the thing before . . . what for me till now had been only a barbarous Latinism in love became a barbaric devotion. Cunnilingus: I had transcended my fears and inhibitions. I wanted such transcendence frequently, and what's more, I wanted it for others. Couldn't transcendence be shared, distributed, encouraged, promulgated?

That profound kiss, the first of its kind for me, my womanly awakening to genital freedom, was my liberation. We had helped each other, Baron and I. But marriage? I hesitated. I wasn't the kind of girl who goes tumbling into wedlock on account of a kiss. For weeks, for months, Baron's tongue electrified and praised me, his glorification pursued me like a magnet. And after each flight all my scattered cells and traceries of nerves swung round in another direction, downward. Humming and shimmering with delight, my vulva began thinking for itself. Reflecting, gathering all my energy to itself, it inspired me with a renewed awareness of my mission. I sensed what I might be able to do for women as well as men. Mankind. I looked at my role in the widest perspective. Androgyne, I was the link with evolution, backward and forward.

But wedding bells? Almost all my life I had experienced, as every woman has, the despotic desire of men. The woman in me had never had much trouble seeing through the unquestionable sincerity of that avowed love for our bodies and even our minds that suffuses the tricky relations between the sexes and disguises from most men themselves just where they stand, in the bottomless quicksand of their own needs. Baron's very eccentricity and mania served as an arrow pointing to the center and I saw the core of the problem. Underneath Everyman's coddling contempt for Everywoman, behind the unconscious belittling of women and the conscious obsession with the female body just around every corner of American life, beneath job discrimination, beneath the child-rearing argument for subjugation, beneath the daily and insufferable condescension, beneath all the seductive and insulting advertising, beneath cubbyhole male smut and hubbyhole female slavery, lurked aversion.

Baron had been cured. No case too hopeless. But other minds and bodies remained in bondage. If only my own unified genitals could be brought into focus everywhere, the fetters might fall away and unravel. For the fetters that enslaved mankind were not simply in society, in the economy, in the family . . . but within consciousness and in the body. I saw all this even then. . . .

As for becoming Baron's wife—well, I felt more than compassion, I confess, but every time I considered his reiterated offer of marriage I had the uncomfortable sensation that our destinies had better not be joined: I had apprehensions about his domesticity, about his financial lead on me, about children and relations, about differences in age, temperament, background, and opinion. Yet already he took my decision for granted.

"To the nuptial rites," Baron toasted. "Here's looking at you."

He guzzled it.

To speak frankly, I yearned like any weak-kneed woman for the security he could provide. Not only for passion, ecstasy, and homage. For lifelong security. But something crucial in me made me beware. I could brook no limitation of the total self I possessed.

Sandy once said to me a long time after, "You know, I'm beginning to understand what finally happened between you and Baron and why it *had* to happen. Why you had to turn him down. Millie, you're Little Orphan Annie gradually becoming Daddy Warbucks. You enter the world of business from the bottom, you slowly master its processes and forms of growth, and all the while you're secretly examining yourself. You evolve. You build, transform, mobilize . . . and all these activities, your factories and passionate ads and fleets of trucks, are love affairs. No wonder you have no space in your intimate life for a man."

It wasn't easy, making Baron understand. I remember that we were lying on the floor in the coils of our saurian love again, two fire-breathing dragons in a cooling heaven, when I made it clear to him that my answer was no and would be so irrevocably. I asked him to forgive me.

He said simply, "I feel I owe you my life."

We uncoiled, we disengaged. My little apartment: with its old-fashioned bathtub on four legs and its long telephone cord.

"Millie, if there's anything I can do for you, now or ever—"

"Anything?"

"Anything," he said, and he meant it.

"Money?"

He reddened—this transcendental titan. This perversion of wealth. He blushed at the frank clink of coins in my voice.

But let me say at once that his generosity measured up to his gratitude. With Co-National I had of course no further trouble. Baron called off the dogs—more exactly, he instructed Leslie to. As always she managed his commercial communications. And his gratitude increased. Though I took no money, I did have a millionaire backer now. Rooting for me, Tieger set up a staggering line of credit for me, and I grew, I developed. Larger payrolls and more complicated inventory procedure, market potentials and sales trends, personnel management and board meetings, wholesaler policy and retail contacts, sales quotas and tax problems.

Nevertheless, there were a couple of things I had yet to develop. Utter callousness. And sufficient steadiness of nerve. In the long run, I learned, the difference between a prospering little enterprise and big business turned out to depend on shamelessness. I had not yet acquired the necessary coarseness. The fact is that facing the country, as one day I felt compelled to do, was infinitely more gross than curing Baron. The years that followed soon brought in their train the further enrichment I needed.

Though my life changed radically in this period, I didn't forget about poetry. I couldn't. Obsessions are obsessions, and I had made a commitment. Moonlighting before and after work, rising at dawn often or laboring into the night, I tried to keep in poetic trim. It was only natural that business occupied more of my available time, poetry less. But though I spent many hours—as the world measures time—in trade, yet I lived more intensely in the minutes reserved for art.

My efforts as always were pragmatic. With a fixed will I set to work to learn the *craft* of poetry. I read diligently—early Greek poetry in translation and much modern verse. Not only in English. I turned naturally to the new Italian poets, whose work I could now read in the original; this was the time when the art of Saba, Quasimodo, and Ungaretti was just becoming well known in this country, and the magic of Eugenio Montale. It is my own opinion that the particular sequence, Dante-Leopardi-Montale, that painful music of the head's dreadful landscape, was and has remained the most important influence on the evolution of my work. I don't want to quibble, but a well-known critic's by-now famous attempt to link my technique to that of the astounding Pablo Neruda is somewhat forced (for one thing, I read Spanish with great difficulty) and merely reflects on that critic's lack of familiarity with the modern Italian tradition. I have met Neruda, and I admire his poetry, but I have not been influenced by him.

In any case I read passionately everything I could lay my hands on, all kinds of books. And I wrote constantly, on the theory that if I were going to learn the poet's craft, I should practice as one practices the piano. So I played scales, as it were. That is, I literally trained myself to write poetry with both left and right hands at once (not necessarily at the same instant but always going forward with two different poems, left and right), and I wrote these copious quantities of verse with the *advance* intention of throwing all of it into the wastebasket. Later, I often advised young poets to practice this method of apprenticeship to their trade, but it is difficult. No other poet of my acquaintance has ever written expressly for the wastebasket. As for myself, like every other poet I know, I cannot help falling in love with my work, I appreciate the very cusps and curves that come out of my pen, I worship the length of the lines I have divided, my breath goes at the white neatness of the page and the fierce arrogance of the poem's shape against it, and frankly, not even the greatest lines of Wyatt or Dickinson have ever tongued my soul quite so blissfully as each of the poorest verses I've ever retched out of my own throat. Yet such was my capacity for discipline at that time, so strong then my wish to make the beauty of lingo as common to my lips as a piece of toast, that I bent my will to compose for char and ashes.

I used to cheat of course. I'd save things on one pretext or another, to show to someone or to keep track of my progress, and when I caught myself in this deception, I'd force myself to burn my entire weekly output of work in the fireplace, emptying not only the basket but the flowerpots and fruitbowl and even searching under my pillow, and all the while I'd stand moaning and writhing in front of the flare with the smell of my own flesh in my nostrils.

I think this explanation should dispel the nonsense and quell once for all the vulgar laughter which has annoyed me through the years apropos the subtitle of my first book of poems. Ultimately, I simply couldn't stand the ritual ordeal. I did at last compromise by snatching certain pages from the flames. But those I held back were never, I insist, selected for their excellence. Quite the contrary. *All* the extant work of that period in New York was collected in *Snatches,* my first book of verse, and to my knowledge nothing other than what appears there escaped the weekly conflagrations.

In the same year I went public, *Snatches: For the Left Hand*

Alone was published privately. (By B. Tieger in a limited edition of nine hundred and ninety-nine signed and numbered copies.) This was an attractively printed and handsomely bound volume of some eighty pages, embellished with a dust-jacket design somewhat too explicit for my taste (Plate XI), but contributed by Baron as a personal tribute to me. When at last I held a copy in my hands, my expectations were sweaty. A couple of hundred copies were sent directly to various business acquaintances and cocktail-party friends: I'd been meeting throngs of people through Tieger. At the same time, sales through limited distribution limped. The months went by and my book met with no attention—hardly a purr of acclaim, not one satisfying bark of denunciation.

I gave that failure a good deal of thought. Wasn't it likely that the demands of business had interfered with the demands of art? The possibility, I admit, troubled me, but I remained undeterred. For just as I wanted to put myself down on paper in images and lines that created me visibly, so I wanted in every way and by every deed to objectify myself. History, not art alone, had to embody my spirit. I was resolved to give form in a life—in my own person and not merely in my poems—to the conflict and fullness of my aspirations. Seeking fullness, I took care to nourish the twig Satori had once bent for me. I joined the Metropolitan Chapter of the New York State Archaeological Association and the Archaeological Institute of America.

Indeed, in this period of crowded activity, I began to take part in New York's professional life, attending conferences and lectures, volunteering for committee work. Despite the pressures of business, my time was my own to dispose as I saw fit. Under Baron's direction, at first I think only half seriously, I studied a bit of osteology and taxonomy. Restlessly, I sat in on occasional seminars on physical anthropology given at the Archaeological Association's headquarters in Manhattan, and two or three times in Rochester. Several summers, while Pop took care of all phases of processing and distribution for me, I dug up prehistoric mounds and caves in the South and Southwest: small field trips for members, organized by the State Association. These were amateur digs, but I worked hard at them and I learned a lot. Though I turned up nothing of major scientific consequence, somewhere within me there stirred again the slumbering conviction that I was destined to probe one of the world's grand archaeological secrets. It was my personal bailiwick, I felt: the connections between early industry and early art.

The historical emergence of both, chronologically close together, had something to do (I sensed intuitively) with joy, power, and control; with sex consciously abstracted from the body; and with the manipulation not only of the surrounding world, but of the chthonic world of religious and magical forces. As yet, however, I was laboring in the dark and whistling for a clue. I had no evidence.

In the thick of business I found time during the course of the years for other things. Did my life as a businesswoman oppose—not just practically but psychologically oppose—my life in science and in art? Of course. So much the better, so much the fuller, so much more me. A coin with three sides? Paradoxically, each change in my activities registered the sides of a rapidly spinning coin, the superimposed faces of my perfect spinning self.

Except for an occasional passion for digging, however, my commitment to science remained subordinate. A vestige of the past. I'll have more to say about archaeology and me later. Here let me record only a happy coincidence. Once, returning to the office from the Southwest and a stimulating three-month stint of excavation as Assistant Site Supervisor, I found in a little stack of private mail a letter from the past. I thought immediately of the Commander: no return address, just a Cambridge postmark. I remember studying that envelope, wary of it. Satori? I tore it open. Flaminia!

There was no way for me to have known then. A visit? I wrote back at once and told her to drop in and say hello any time she was in New York. I answered cordially. But I did not write to her first and suggest a meeting, as the government claims. She got in touch. And she came on her own.

The harassment I've endured over Flaminia . . . it wasn't till many years later, when I was singled out for prosecution, that I came to see all my entanglements clearly. At the time virtually no one in or out of government had even heard of the Stony Brook Project. (The idiocy of that name! It was located not in Stony Brook but halfway between Brookhaven, with which it was affiliated, and the city.) When she came to New York, all security arrangements were so tight that Flaminia herself, whose appointment was at a high level, had an incomplete notion of the significance of the new research.

No doubt the hush-hush effort made to keep the project's aim under wraps was futile from the start. Given the normal channels of communication and progress in the scientific community, there was no justification later for watchdog committees to go beating their breasts for shame and the bushes for spies, every dog baying treason and sniffing around me for "leaks." The sophisticated laser satellite system that emerged from the elaborate Long Island facilities is hardly secret any longer, though still partly classified: I feel no compunctions now in speaking openly wherever I can.

That solid-state handshake—how well I remembered it! I returned it with feeling and force. I was just as completely, powerfully Woman now as she was, and I filled her in on the last few years, Sister Millie's Cock-o'-the-Walk and the saga of Baron Tieger.

Telling me about her latest work, Flaminia was enthusiastic. She murmured rapidly on about lasers and masers, microwaves and macrowaves, emission and transmission. The new project was to include experts in optics, astronomy, electronics, metallurgy, physics, aeronautics . . . half a dozen other sciences. "Sounds to me like government work," I said. (A month later I realized I was right: the FBI came to make a routine check into my background.)

"About this we don't speak together," she warned me, and then smiled. "But this my appointment is a quite high honor. Or perhaps only they wish a woman."

Nonsense! I'd always known she was brainy; now she was illustrious. I told her.

"Me? No, for sure," she protested modestly. "Illustrious? Is my group in Cambridge. Last year we have been lucky. For two years in the running. Physics, Millie, nowdays is in groups."

I couldn't help smiling at her wave theory of English. She was still magnetically serious and vibrantly bosomy and quivering with uncountable quanta of personal energy.

"So what's your gang in Cambridge been up to?" I asked.

"Slitting the photon," she explained. She drew waves in space with her finger. "Accelerated faster than light, which was by theory before now impossible, the photon becomes subdivisible. Incredible! But by now we solved theoretically this problem, which permits that for multiple focus we shall be able by resonance to stimulate probably laser overload."

Her incomprehensible physics was impressive, as always. Flaminia herself however seemed less imposing to me. Perhaps because I was older now, she seemed younger—and even more attractive than I'd remembered—she looked lighter and smaller and so *definite.* Everything about her was well delineated. Her vigorous mouth was a graph, with diagrammatic eyebrows. One animated finger wrote light waves in mid-air for me, dotting her photons.

"The Commander," I asked with tenderness, "how is he?"

"The same. Never will he differ." She smiled neutrally, but she shook her dark thermionic hair and shifted her wide photovoltaic eyes.

Oh yes, she still saw him occasionally, she volunteered, but she'd moved out. Years ago. Living by herself now, entirely on her own. I sensed how much she implied by *that*. How out of touch we had all drifted . . . I'd continued to imagine the two of them trapped together in that house in Cambridge, forever muttering Italian imprecations at each other in the night.

"You must tell to me about our Sandy," she said, but without tenderness. Was that "our" ironic?

"Always different. Never the same Sandy two years in a row. He's a Freudian Jungian now." But that wasn't fair. While I'd been mounting the ladder of success, my brother had been throwing down peculiar roots—in my own opinion, an outgrowth of his encounter with Haidu long ago. I believe he'd already begun those explorations into occult states of being and non-being that were to lead him away from both Freud and Jung, and from everyone else I can think of.

"*Plus ça change*," she exclaimed deep in her throat, with deep hostility.

Then surprising me further, she put her thumb and index finger to my jaw to hold it steady and looked me right in the eyes for a long time. With her one-two jab, her rabbit-punch bluntness I'd all but forgotten, she announced, "Millie, forgive, but you *absolutely* I have much trouble to recognize."

I picked up a cigarette nervously. I knew of course what she meant, and it made me uncomfortable to hear her refer to it at all. There had been a time when, in another living room with Flaminia, I'd worn cuffless trousers and a red knitted tie. Now I was wearing a severe high-necked antique Russian blouse. I wanted that cigarette.

She made an effort. I watched her lips, her full red compassionate lips, grow thin, pallid; but she couldn't repress the grand smile that emerged, the crest of a long wave of feeling. "This way you are so more beautiful."

All the photographs taken of me during those years agree that I was. Just as she said. (See Plate XII.) More mature. My sparkle and lines no longer those of a rough jewel. But a single subtle scratch of time on the facet of my forehead had been disturbing me recently. Fond as I was, and am, of compliment, I changed the subject. "Are you going to live out on the Island? You know, you could easily stay here," I offered.

"No, I must find a place for myself. I haven't still decided to live there at Long Island or here on Manhattan. Which do you think to advise?"

"Manhattan," I said. "If you like, you can stay with me till you find a place of your own." I'd moved by now into an apartment overlooking the park, new quarters that were comfortable, in fact elegant. "Loads of room. Stay as long as you like."

I meant it. She embraced me. It was decided. It was perfect. No husband, but a friend. For ten minutes, as we went on talking, I was gloriously happy. I planned a gala welcoming dinner for her—for Baron—for Sandy—and she stopped me. No. Not Sandy, she told me.

"Why not?"

"I would rather please not to see your brother."

"But that's—"

She hushed me. "He was long ago."

I took her by both shoulders. "I won't press you, but I want you two to see each other again. What does it matter that it was long ago? You have everything in common. Still."

"Why, Millie, do you not then go to see Satori?" she pointed out.

"To Cambridge? That's a couple of hundred miles from here," I objected.

"Oh!" she mocked me gaily, caustically. "Yet have you and he in common more, much more. Recently he received in a letter a picture of Mavi."

"Who?" Did I guess?

"Mavidda. Your child."

Mavidda? Mavi? I balked. I drew a long breath.

Let me say in the first place that this remark had been introduced with such unnatural casualness, in a tone so peculiarly pointed, I couldn't believe it was accidental. It was, I felt, intended to wound. In that instant I recalled how bitterly she'd once resented Satori's attentions to me. Like everyone else except the man concerned, Flaminia had accepted the version the Commander and I had tacitly allowed everyone to believe: that he was "the father." But father and mother stood together in that very room—in me—together and divided. Dislodged by the past, my present mind split like a stone, and the womanly half of me sank away, and rested in the mud of distracting pains. The dig . . . the tower . . . my child . . . only rarely in the last years had I thought of her. In fact, heard for the first time, the name Mavidda struck me as alien beyond belief. My guilt-edged insecurities clamored and threatened, something was attacking me—I felt it distinctly—attacking me on all sides, but especially from underneath. "I wanted not to know," I said with effort. "Anything." But I recollected every damn thing.

I saw her features relent—"Millie, I regret"—and a moment later I saw her hurt pride about Satori and me relent, too. Her aggressive gaiety disappeared, her vivacious social grace gave way at once to something lots closer to love: friendship. She exclaimed, "What horrible, stupid thing of me to say!"

"Just forget about it."

"Again you must forgive. I was worrying."

"What about?"

She wouldn't say. I didn't ask. I didn't ask a thing. Her eyes grew wet. She kissed me. Plain and simple. And my civil servant down below revolted. Trapped by oaths of loyalty, the serpent in my grass moved, the tip sparked, my coiled thoughts uncoiled. Mother-love and tenderness welling up together in me became an ache. Shocked, moving away, I said, "There's only one thing I want to know—"

"I hide nothing."

But I denied everything. I put out my cigarette. "What's laser?" I demanded instead.

"Coherent light," she replied.

Breach of security. Here, as I read my seismographic wavering, the accusation of treachery must first be leveled. Never mind what the Department of Justice alleges; the defendant knows best. An accelerated beginning. A non-linear reunion that was more highly charged with old loyalties than either of us had imagined. Incoherent light: a current of new friendship superimposed on the old millivoltage.

And believe me, from this first brief interview with my old contact, I knew. Oh yes, I hadn't the slightest doubt. With Flaminia as with no one else, my double sex was a security risk.

But I'm not used to backing down.

Flaminia moved in with me. And stayed. Of course it wasn't merely the apartment situation in New York, perennially bad as it was, that made her stay on. For a while she looked for a place of her own. Listlessly, I imagine: preoccupied with her latest work, she didn't put much effort into apartment-hunting. And we enjoyed living together. I pressed her to forget about leaving.

It struck me, sure it did, that I had rejected a husband and taken a friend. But I was peculiarly aware of the problem. All my new acquaintances (intentionally, I don't list them here—many of them I've forgotten), all of them lacked for me the special resonance I sensed in Flaminia's presence. While our friendship remained placid on the surface, I couldn't look at her without recalling my child.

In physical need as a young student once, in a calculating spirit of passion, I had slept with a brainy physicist. In incalculable consequence I had conceived. We were mother and father living together —though which was which and who was who I often didn't dare think—without offspring, without intimacy. And the pointless, confused longing I now experienced was compounded by, and confounded with, a sense of disloyalty.

To my own deliberate ambitions. Remorse for having given away my child for adoption—Mavi, the name so remote—went against all common sense and against my better judgment. Irrationally, I resented Flaminia for inducing in me a variety of unacceptable feelings, all of them foolish. And irrationally, for the sake of friendship itself, I found myself becoming unduly cautious in speaking to her, even about her work.

She had plunged at once into her new research and soon had reasons of her own for caution. Of this I had no inkling.

We were reserved with each other. Over the months, I took to reading Petrarch, and Dante again, *e delli altri miei miglior*. But we seldom spoke Italian together. Friends . . . understandably in an atmosphere of constraint. Not friction. It was all so marvelously amiable. Happy to be moderately close, reluctant to draw closer, we kept different hours, followed our private pursuits at home, and saw our friends separately.

When I spoke to Baron about my reawakened feelings, his response was frivolous. Offensive. And Baronial. "What you need, Millie, is a more pragmatic attitude toward sex." His teeth in his champagne glass were suddenly vast, wolfish. He made me feel like Little Red Riding Hood, I admit, when he went on to suggest, "What you and she need is a middleman."

Through the crowded art gallery he maneuvered. He showed me a splotchy canvas that had already caught his trained eye. Three lovers, love in triplicate. He offered himself.

The opening was noisy. We were standing in a wind of breezy people. I wasn't sure what the storm in the gallery was all about, but I hung on to my champagne glass. I thought about my duck-billed snail-loving Baron between Flaminia and me, I thought of Dickie, Leslie, and Baron too, and I said quietly, "If you mean by pragmatism an abandoning of ideals . . ."

"Pragmatism can be an ideal."

"Or a cynical excuse for personal tastes."

He smiled, the carbuncular wart over his eye rising. "What's your ideal?" His teeth flowed and undulated in his glass. "Natural healthy love? Nature itself is both healthy and sick. The pathetic endeavor to exclude the pathological from love is characteristically human—our species' hopeless fling at emotional hygiene."

Elbowing someone in the ribs with aplomb, he bent . . . elegant and dour . . . to remove something from the sole of his shoe, spilling his glass on my purse as he showed me a tack. "If I love this tack lying on the floor, that's love. The rest is circumstance. Accept yourself, Millie, accept your sexual circumstances."

"With that criterion," I pointed out, "you could love a mound of dung."

"I could, I could!"

He was an ordeal. But nothing of this sort could serve to change my feelings.

Flaminia and I needed of course to come to an understanding. We could not forever continue to gloss over our situation. Yet neither of us wished to name the thing. Purgatory: *perchè non servammo umana legge.* Recognition of our thickening feelings by words alone was pointless and worse. Vulgar. Dispiriting. What each of us wanted was this tacit collusion of ours in denying the whole matter.

But all the while I felt a steady pressure, a compulsion to ask one more question. What else did she know about my child?

Breathing audibly, she read a physics journal and sipped her coffee. At breakfast, whenever we happened to have breakfast together, both of us usually pretended to be too near sleep to say very much. But on page 24 of *The New York Times* one blessed breakfast I came across an article about the island I'd nearly forgotten. It went something like this.

SECESSIONISTS BATTLE
POLICE IN SARDINIA

NUORO—The Sardinian regional government yesterday threw all available police forces into battle against shepherds who invaded the provincial capital of Nuoro from outlying areas, wrecking banks and smashing cars. It was the fiercest street fighting since the sympathy riots last year after the seizure of the government's central radio station here by armed secessionists demanding immediate independence from Italy.

Angry mobs sometimes numbering more than a thousand fought running street battles with police as they protested rumors of police torture and the sentencing of two captured rebel leaders by a tribunal in Rome yesterday. The Italian government has officially and explicitly denied persistent rumors of torture by the police to obtain from captured prisoners information on the growing guerrilla movement.

Sticks, bricks, gasoline bombs, and scores of tear gas canisters flew through the air around the Banco Nazionale d'Italia, flames engulfed one government building, and police eventually opened fire on snipers, as the fighting raged through the afternoon and into the evening.

In Rome it was reported that the national government was sending additional police reinforcements to the island to assist the regional government in controlling the rioting. Heavy police patrols were reported on duty in Rome as well, particularly around the central law courts where the two rebel leaders were sentenced. Although it is generally believed that the Sardinian revolt is not a politically left-wing movement but an unaffiliated secessionist uprising, previous demonstrations on the island have received the vociferous and sometimes violent support of leftist groups on the mainland.

Yesterday Antiocheddu Fenusiccu and Franzischeddu Turudda were sentenced to life imprisonment. (Italy has abolished the death penalty.) They were accused of treason, incitement to treason, assassination, incitement to murder, arson, and other offenses.

On Monday the national government, adopting a compromise suggested by the Sardinian Minister of the Interior, enacted legislation to make the vast uninhabited center of the island known as the Barbagia into a "national park." This is the rugged area in which several hundred guerrillas are said to be operating unchecked. Government spokesmen refer to these armed groups as "bandits." The new law reverses a previous act of last May that established the mountainous region as a site for testing small nuclear weapons. This was the so-called "insult of May" that converted many pro-Italian Sardinians into irate secessionists. Monday's action was expected to have a cooling effect on outraged Sardinian tempers. But by nightfall yesterday, in Nuoro and elsewhere, 70 persons had been arrested on the island in the violent protests at the sentencing of the two guerrilla leaders.

I passed the paper across and pointed. I stirred my coffee. I lighted a cigarette.

"Tell me one thing," I said when she had finished the article. "About this adoption business Satori arranged—who are they?" In my mind's eye I envisioned an elderly Sardinian couple: wealthy, stealthy, and wise.

She stared at me over her napkin.

"That isn't what I want to know," I corrected myself. "All I want to know is, is she still in Sardinia?"

She answered me with all seriousness and importance: "Do you wish toast?"

I quoted my Dante: "*E a dir di Sardigna le lingue lor non si sentono stanche.*" Their tongues never tire of talking about Sardinia. Not sure I had it right at first, I got up from the table, found the passage in my marked-up copy, and showed it to her.

"Coffee?"

She poured.

Was it, after all, only a coincidence of our eyes? For the remainder of that breakfast, Flaminia's eyes and mine kept meeting in space. But too often. With great heat. Crossing and crisscrossing. Accelerating and orbiting. A lowered thrust of a chin. Wide eggwhite sleepless eyes—eyes saying something and denying it, eyes contradicting themselves. While beneath a façade of mascara, her cheeks flushed rosewindows of deception and self-assurance.

She went back to diagrams and equations in her journal. She took a cigarette and struck a match. When she looked away, her profile depressed and exalted me. Anxious to escape this particular suction, I left, glad to be able to engross myself for the day in the challenge of business.

From that morning, every motion she made bespoke more than possession of data, more than information undisclosed.

A coincidence of eyes? First I ignored it. Then I wondered about it. Then I denied it. Then I smiled at it. Then I pardoned it. I mocked it. I feared it. Accident? What accident?

At first my place had seemed so large, big rooms and a lot of them, I'd generally had no idea whether Flaminia was home, especially since she kept her bedroom door closed. But I began to know. It wasn't just that she began leaving me love notes scattered all over the house— her theoretical computations—delicate graph paper with weird reptilian notation crawling side by side with centipede symbols. She would pass the open door of my bedroom when I happened to be chatting with Baron on the phone . . . she'd hear the sound of the ice when I was mixing myself a drink after work, and let me know she'd have one too . . . slide unexpectedly round corners in the hall, appear under the dining room archway with a cigarette, snuggle with pencil and pad into the cushion at the far end of my double-length sofa, playing classical records on the stereo console . . .

$$P_r = \frac{P_t\ (A_rA_t)}{\lambda^2 L^2}$$

I knew she was lonely in her field of force and in need of polarity, I knew she found me electromagnetic, I knew her half-life had been reached and that she was unstable . . . and that she would never say a word about it.

And my own attraction to Flaminia? Here I lay myself wide open to criticism. A woman with a woman? Listen, if only I could have looked forward to something so uncomplicated! No, it was poetic licentiousness. My priapic womb. I saw the potential renewal of our love as the regeneration of my voice in art, my polyphonic sensibility.

What is the bond between the lines one pens and the life one endures? Surely it is indissoluble. It galls me to note how often my poems have received praises and my life mockery. My life is an impure gorgeous multiple poem, a long, soiled, highly worked strategy determined by the same primitive and unconscious strivings that inter-fuse my purest passages of verse. The sexual vortex that led me back to Flaminia led me to compose the celebrated "Elegy to Serpent Light." My unholy mind suffering through time led me to sing hymns to

Fucked-out quasars crucified by space.

Why my visions of physics as sordid passion and business as erotic child's play should have brought down on my head such heaps of insults and insinuating criticism is beyond me! Had I composed verses about thorns and roses, these, one supposes with revulsion, would have passed muster. Let me take this chance to point out that it is rash— and libelous—to assume that images of profit spring from profiteer-ing. Or that behind my symbols of radiation theory lie the clues to treason. To say nothing of other nervy charges like lewdness, fanati-cism, and obscurantism.

It was just at this time that I began the plan of the long anagogical poem, *The Physical Comedy*, which was to occupy me intermittently for the next twelve years. Much of the legal confusion surrounding the intepretation of that much-analyzed work will be cleared away at once if one realizes that the laser-maser and quasar-pulsar sequences, the sport of light and darkness, and the explosion of sun and moon all refer to sexual encounters. While they constitute a poet's rendering of physics, still, Planck's Constant, the Eightfold Way, Negative Particles, Antimatter, and so on are allusions to specific people and to physical and mystical experiences. The rough draft of the plan of the work took me only a month, but I was unable to bring the poem to completion for more than a decade. Over the years I came to learn how much more I needed than an antiphonal voice.

Love, surely, and despair besides. For that matter, to sound the depths of art not even genius and technique will serve, not even love and hate will do—the peaks require a steady balance over the short drop to death. For our sexuality alone is immortal, beyond us and outmastering us, crucial to an existence in which we are only its appendages. The germ plasm of our sex cells lives on, literally immortal, from body to body forever. Only "we" die. And who are "we," these bodies? And who is it that lives on forever? Are our minds so important, our personalities, all that uniqueness fostered by the central nervous system and ending in the brain? The female praying mantis eats off the head of the male so that he will be able—able!—to copulate with her. Our own brains and minds, alas, are equally irrelevant to the reality beyond our reality, to the continuity of our biological existence.

"Does it ever seem to you," I remember musing aloud to Sandy once as, watching for traffic, we crossed at the corner, "that there's a peculiar wind blowing slantwise across your life and trying to change your direction?"

We dodged a bike-wagon delivering groceries. Instead of answering directly, he played the analyst, probably unwittingly. "Do you mean a current of wind independent of *you*, of your self?"

"It's as if I'm standing on a slope," I tried to explain by changing the image. "There's a constant pull like gravity. It's almost impersonal—" A scrawny kid of six or seven ran full tilt into me and fell. He picked himself up, pinched my bottom, and ran screaming down the street. "See?"

Sandy only laughed, but even here I sensed there was a certain logic: the pinch of reality. Now I'd often thought that my own career—the life I forged—was in every way self-created: my inner powers at work like a persistent blacksmith on a recalcitrant but malleable reality. Not until the news and recollection of Mavi had it come over me that my life might be taking on a shape that evaded my control, that I myself might be the iron in the fire.

"Then who controls the fire, Millie?"

We stepped out into the traffic, hailing a cab. It stopped for us. We got in, and I merely said, "Is love an uncontrollable fire? Because our old friend's still in love with you."

"What?" Hilarious, he punched my arm. "Did she tell you that?"

"No, of course not."

He gave the driver the name of the restaurant. Settling back in the seat, I went on:

"She never speaks to me about you, but I've got a hunch that's what's up."

He said, "You know, that wouldn't surprise me. She's always loved ghosts. She positively prefers them—that spook in Italy—Satori's son —you remember?"

I remembered. Ghostly lovers. Me, too. And in the cab I told him what I'd wanted to tell him for some time. "Should I ask her to leave?"

"Leave?" His lips, still mobile and pointy, curled. "I don't suppose it ever occurred to you that you invited trouble."

"I invited Flaminia. She's a friend."

Again his flexible lips grew unsteady. "For Godsake, Millie," he laughed. His laughter cheered me. "In the first place, what's happening between you two doesn't strike me as serious."

"And in the second place?" I didn't agree in the first place.

"In the second place, it's the same error you've been making all your life, thinking that all of life is divided into male and female. If you stopped playing by those rules, it wouldn't matter to you whether she leaves or stays."

"Divided?" I was offended. "Division isn't the rule. I've always denied that!"

He went right on talking over my voice. "Separation and reunion, division and oneness. No one's arguing the point. But of all divisions, Millie, sex is the *simplest*. Don't you see that the apparent division provides a convenient deception? The hard border to cross is one where life is neither male nor female, but Self and Being."

Self and what? I didn't want to hear, I didn't trouble to inquire. At the moment our interests were too far apart for me to appreciate this taxi talk, as I was later to call it. If I remember the month correctly, I was then at work on an essay of mine called "Poetry and the Theory of Currency" (see *The Poetic Itch*)—an argument about modern poetry in which I made perhaps too much of the metaphor of words as coins, of the need to find vocabularies that were legal tender, of poetry as the mint of diction, of the inflation of rhetoric, of soft and hard currency in style and thought, of poems not worth the paper they were printed on, of amateur poetic forgeries, of international fluctuation, and of notes-of-hand by poets on the golden treasury, notes that one day become payable and due.

I paid too little attention to Sandy.

Those records she played by the hour! Music, she said, relaxed her and helped her to think. The brash author of one extended, speculative study of our case (in *Espionage, U.S.A.*) suggests darkly that Flaminia brought some of her secret work home, that she innocently but irresponsibly left classified documents lying around the apartment, and that I assiduously went about gathering up whatever she threw down. Well, I confess. Her penciled jottings were everywhere, I did gather them up, and irritably threw them into the wastebasket. I found myself deliberately wandering into the living room on the pretext of cleaning up the usual crumpled pages of litter, but actually to catch sight of her well-turned back and arms and the natural quick way she had of pulling records from their jackets and dropping them onto the spindle. I remember coming to a halt, stock-still, smack in the middle of that big room. I rubbed out my cigarette. I reached down, took off my heels, curled my stockinged toes into the carpeting, puzzled, motionless, perspiring. I adjusted my skirt. I saw that a button had come off my blouse. Music. Vivaldi. *La Primavera*. Spring. I went to a mirror, fixed my hair in it, and left the room.

I blew it up out of all proportion. Except my own. By night the bellows of my imagination burned my lyric thoughts to a white ash of exhaustion, by day the ashes turned black with a desire to burn again. Alone, I invoked Flaminia's insistent flushing, her acquiescent silence, our intimate driving lesson, the collision that had catalyzed Mavi. I knotted the tiniest memories together into a lash and lashed myself. Why was I hesitating? Moral scruples? In my case? Nonsense.

I believed in my desire. Completely. What I wanted to avoid at all costs was a very real threat to me: masculinization. Not again. No, thanks. No more Willie. Nor did I wish a homosexual development. What I was aiming at was no such easy matter. Lesbianism? Too simple. No. What I wanted would always be a chimera in my verse if I could not realize it in my loins.

My inner polarity unpolarized. The abolition of my twoness. The shimmering fusion of my contraries.

However, living one's myth is hazardous. Even in the welter of the daily problems of management, I could see which way my wind was blowing. I negotiated and signed a union agreement for a cost-of-living adjustment. I worked out the terms of a new contract with National Leasing Corporation for automated processing equipment. I approved the small corps of girls Pop had hired, I watched their backs, their smiles, their knees, their glances my way, and I began to have daydreams of playing the fox in my own hencoop. I didn't budge. Not an eyelash. I found myself, instead, indulging in imaginary conversations with the goodlooking new office manager Pop had hired while I was away.

"Sal, how many girls you got under you, you think, would be interested?"

"In what?"

"In—"

"What's that?" she shrieked.

"Quiet, you'll—"

"What the fuck have you got, get that damn thing away, Miss Niemann, what's going on, *stop*, do you hear me, *stop!*"

"Lost your composure?" I gloated.

"What is it?"

"Don't you know, you little hypocrite?"

"Where'd you get it?"

"From my brother," I confessed.

"It's HUGE."

"It's average," I whispered modestly.

No, poetic myth is one thing. Incorporated in one's life it is another. More wrenching and apt to be gross. Mickey Mouse prurience. Raunchy seduction. I was no yahoo. I had to get a grip on myself. But above all—forward, not backward. Progress. But how?

Flaminia made the first move.

"Yes?"

"Millie, you're not busy?"

"Sure I'm busy. What's up?" I was tense, not friendly.

"It may be that I can use an advice." She came in smoking.

I'd furnished one room at home as a spare office. Busy in there, I was speaking into a dictaphone, trying to organize last summer's jumble of exact measurements and speculative notes made during our amateur excavation of North American mounds. None of it was fresh in my mind. I'd let my notes lie fallow and was hoping at last to work them up in some form suitable for publication in the Institute's own records. (I've learned since to distrust delay: my advice to beginners in archaeology is, set to work on your monograph or report immediately. A time lag is inadvisable.)

Flaminia sat. She said nothing. She appeared to be studying critically my office decor, my long lamps and short cabinets, my wide desk and narrow chair. She fidgeted, made herself comfortable, looked up, looked away, then inspected her cigarette severely, turning it in her fingers like an antique brooch.

I handed her an ashtray.

"Thanks," she said, letting out smoke. "You see," she began, "I think you know already what I'm going now to say you. Millie, I am having many troubles with my work."

I can't tell you what a loop this threw me for!

"I must to talk to someone," she said in a high-pitched voice— someone like me, she added, a friend who wasn't concerned, not even remotely, with the project: with physics, with ordnance, with government, with the moon.

The moon? I've never been unconcerned with the moon. She began slowly.

I took a cigarette myself and forgot to light it. The chair under me began to sweat. The moon, *my* moon, earth's lunatic fringe, our moon of scrambled-egg menstrual cycles and milkshake tides, of incoherent light and poetry. My feelings blurred, hovering between horror and laughter while she told me about lunacy. She shouldn't have been telling me anything. But she certainly didn't provide exact details, no specifics that could have comforted a spy. She was a woman in distress, a scientist in a quandary, she talked ethics, not mathematics, she revealed to me not her computations but her conscience.

The broad outlines of the strategic program developed in the Stony Brook Project are by now in the public domain and common knowledge: the clandestine construction of a "sun-pumping" station for solar radiation just under the surface of the moon, in conjunction with a fleet of satellites capable of laser reflection and multifocus.

Sun and moon. Brother and sister. Reality and art. Scorch and glow. Love divine and love human. Now a matter of light and death. I gave not a thought to technical data, not even to the staggering scope of the project. It was neither science nor poetry, neither psychology nor technology, that affected me that evening, it was another kind of information altogether. I don't think anyone, not Sandy, not Baron, no one before Flaminia, had given me a single lesson in simple morality . . . the subjective knowledge of a soul in a state of scare, a profound illustration of the workings of moral inhibition. I think I was more spellbound by witnessing that process than aghast at the power of light.

But that power unsteadied me. Our eyes met.

"I am making many theoretical progresses," she said. "And technically is interesting."

"Power corrupts," I reminded her, "and coherent light will corrupt absolutely." If I remember right, I advised her to have as little to do with Big Government as possible. "Flaminia, listen to me. Listen hard. Work for yourself," I advised. "Not the government. Set up on your own."

She merely smiled at my innocence. "Where I was before in Cambridge, too, and everywhere in the work of modern science, including in the pure research, enters government. The money, Millie, is necessary."

"Willpower and guts is what's necessary. Make up your mind and get out."

"Besides, personally I am not an anarchist—"

"I'm talking about self-determination. Get the government off the back of business, cut the leash it has on science, get physics especially on its own hind legs—"

"Millie—"

"—it's immoral, coherent light is immoral!"

"I am not considering myself a very moral person."

She was right. Abruptly, I could not help thinking of her sexual morals—a wayward thought. But then, I'd expected she'd come to consult me about something else. I reflected involuntarily on her relations with Satori and his son in Italy, with Sandy and me in Cambridge.

There was a peculiar pause, an extended silence of knitted brows and shadowed thoughts on both our parts while I lighted my cigarette at last. It's true that noises of some great confrontation between the major powers, prophecies of final holocaust, were pretty much always in the air. One took them seriously, and yet not. Tin cans. We had tied our arguments to the tails of the smaller nations of the world. So they ran. But one couldn't live in constant panic at all this clatter of metal, and I didn't. Was light quieter? I wondered. More moral? I asked her.

"I have no morals," she reiterated. "Only reason."

"Is that all?"

"I have feelings," she was willing to admit.

"Then get out."

"But you see, dear Millie, nothing is so clear. For mankind, from each point of view, this one is preferable. Light is selective always. In war the thermonuclear explosions should threaten extinction of all creatures living, as you know well, through radioactive fallout which may bring everywhere contamination of the air envelope, land and sea. On the contrary, however, this laser does not do. This one is more effective, more fast, more accurate, more total, but, above everything, does not contaminate. This contaminates nothing. This destroys only."

I was relieved. Puffing, smiling almost insolently, I obliged her to reconsider what she'd said.

Her hands parted in a sad shrug, and she brought them together under her bosom.

Her life (and mine, as a Senate investigating committee later contumaciously insisted) was made suspect by her indecision. I had neither the right nor the experience to advise her then; nor to this day do I presume to judge her. But the facts are, she continued with the project for another year and a half before bowing out gracefully into plainclothes physics again. Surely it is shrill and pathetic for me to be obliged to observe that there's no evidence that I suborned her, not even circumstantial. Nothing in these circumstances suggests that I "induced her to cooperate with the project" while remaining my "confidante" by keeping her "under the continuous influence of a perverse desire."

We talked. Heart to heart. That's all. I did not "surreptitiously record on the dictaphone," as one senile Senator insinuated several times during my testimony, a "full description of the Stony Brook Project." Nor did I later type it all up for "transmission." The pressure of months of silence drained gradually from Flaminia's manner of constraint. Relief showed in her loosening brows and spoke in her deepening voice. Though no decision was reached—nor, I think, wanted for the moment—she was grateful for the chance to speak freely. She told me so and kissed me before going to bed, plain and simple. Her wholehearted quiver of gratitude made me quiver, too. She hugged me, a really loving hug.

The apartment grew smaller, the walls contracted slowly, caving in around us. Mingled desire and reluctance pervaded my study after she left, a perfumed metallic vapor, the odor of broken geraniums. I felt unsettled, dismayed, and unable to continue my work. An old dizziness—not sex, but the faltering of identity—the confusion of selfhood each time I had flipped the lid of my jack-in-the-box came back to me. The contest in the cockpit of my love. I couldn't help recalling that whenever I'd had the foolishness to fool around with my polymorphous biology my mind had gone temporarily blank or burned with doubts. Failure of will? Failure of nerve? You can bet your sweet life it wasn't fear of dissoluteness. It was fear of dissolution. My identity was at stake. Would my existence remain coherent? Was existence less flexible than poetry? If so, how puny! How uninteresting and scruffy!

Archaeology in any event was out. I put aside all thought of field notes and dictation. I considered my nails, I went to get my nail polish and hardener, and then I remembered: on and off for days I'd been sewing on a dress. With discipline I went back to that. But it was hard to concentrate on sewing.

Deterrence through delayed annihilation. Why not build such a station on the earth? Where did one draw the line between love for one's country and fondness for life? Between love of friends and loyalty to oneself? Maybe the north-south dispersion of American mounds could be diagrammed like the north-south dispersion of the Beaker culture. Man the Toolmaker. Flaminia, my old flame, my heat. Did her light threaten Mavi? No doubt it was on account of the time factor in case of attack. Who on earth and where were her folks? Radiance. That blue light in her eyes. And illumination. Satori would know. But never tell. And how can radiance be evil?—it offends the mind. Man the Wise Guy. All science, all technology, because he was born single-minded with an opposable thumb. But Man the Poet because he was born all thumbs with an opposable mind.

Flaminia came to my assistance, she helped me let out my crooked hem and get it even again all around, holding the skirt down, squeezing the bulb on the hem stand, turning me round in front of the wardrobe mirror. And I asked her only the first of questions. "Just one more thing. The name. Mavi. I—"

She sneezed with the powder. She sniffed disapproval. "Are impossible," she said. "I have made one mistake. Indiscreet. When you are going to forget?"

I looked down. It fit. My life. Periwinkle blue eyes she'd had. But something else there. An inlet. A flat stillness. Lagoon eyes, perhaps they'd changed by now. Silted over. "Do they know about me? Do they know I'm American?"

She walked out on me.

Why wouldn't she answer? I had lots to learn. I had lots to forget.

If I wanted to wear the dress in the morning, I'd have to iron it. No, I gave up the idea of ironing. Not tonight. Resewing the hem alone would take me fifteen minutes more. Huck Finn in drag. I've never been too handy with a needle.

She came and stood over me, throwing a shadow where I was working. "Do you think now you could have time to manage for me this, too?"

In her nightgown there were two rips in the seam, both slight, under her armpit and over her hip.

"Take it off and I'll do it right away," I suggested.

"Do it on me."

I did it on her. It hardly took more than a couple of minutes once I could get her to stop brushing her hair. "If you keep that up, I'm going to stick you," I said. When she sat down and stopped moving, I noticed that the stitches along the two rips weren't frayed, weren't pulled. They'd been cut sharp. My razor blade was not where I had put it down either. I noticed.

"Thanks," Flaminia said, and went off to bed.

I took a couple of pins from my lips. My mouth was smoldering. She had been the source of both my manhood and my motherhood, and I felt I was heading for chaos again. Nevertheless, for poetry's sake, with long slow stitches like spondaic meter, I finished my hem and got ready for the calculated risks of Light Amplification Stimulating the Emission of Radiation.

"Congratulation," Flaminia said in her bedroom when I showed her the unironed, but otherwise finished dress, modeling it for her. I laughed and admired the straight hem and my slender calves in the mirror. Then I put my cigarette out, turned her light out, and got out of my dress, and didn't leave. I said goodnight and after a minute or two I turned down the edge of Flaminia's covers. I said, "Room for one more?"

She didn't speak. It seemed to me she might have been crying. "Are you crying?" I asked. She didn't answer.

"Who took the baby? Tell me." She didn't answer.

I got in. From head to toe, from toe to head, I was alive to her. She fidgeted to keep me away. She said in an utterly neutral and innocent tone of voice, "I use in Italy to sleep with, in the one bed, my sister and my girl cousin, this bed was small, this bed was smaller than this, Millie, my God, we could never stop from laughing, very crazy, and when I fall to sleep, she or that other one did always pinch me."

She wasn't crying. I said, "It *is* pretty crazy."

"This?—is wild—is fantastic. You are so near in likeness to Sandy. Besides, technically will be interesting."

We both laughed, but not much. I put my hands over her breasts and sighed.

She consoled me. "They are more smaller, yours, but they are also more up than am I, more higher."

Of Greek Tiresias, whose sex was changed by order of the gods, the gods themselves are said to have asked: in the act of coitus, who experiences the more sublime pleasure, man or woman? From time to time along comes someone who asks me the same question. Man or woman? Neither. I do. Only someone whose very being physically incorporates both male and female can know in the passion of culmination at the same moment the suffocating heights and crushing depths.

That night I discovered that when I made love with a woman— not all at once, by the way; we pecked and patted and sipped and savored, we envied and appreciated each other, and fell asleep doped with excitement, and woke up more and more grumpy a dozen times before morning until—well, how shall I put it? Flaminia, I'm afraid, got left out. With her hot definite woman's mouth against mine and her slowly undulating legs freeing her nightgown, my glow and gladness located themselves painfully in both my raw-nerved womanhood and kindling manhood. Pain—the word does not do justice to the glittering impact. Helpless, I oscillated with a gradually single vibration. I grew hard inside myself and thronged like a crowd inside my space, I surrounded myself, I bathed myself with electric seas, I filled myself, received myself, and took myself. I writhed, I exulted— something cataclysmic, something still profoundly swelling—it was all inside me and I was overpowered, dumbfounded, panicked—something would burst (my cervix? my glans? my perineum?). And with all my being suddenly focusing and towering into an oracular and triumphant spume of radiance, I attained all by myself that glory of terror and possession that normally can only be shared by two human beings, a living sacrifice and the one who cuts out her heart.

That night I shrieked and gasped aloud with more than mere physical pain. Next morning when I got out of bed, there on a nearby chair in the 6 A.M. stillness my attractive dress mocked me: *lusus naturae*. Natural sport? Unnatural monster enriched with sex? My barbed-wire abhorrence of no-man's land returned. I had always proposed to avoid becoming a hooting bleating walking talking Believe-

It-Or-Not circus sideshow curio and freak. Willy-nilly, mother of Mavi.

When I left the room, I thought she was still asleep, but something of the same thought, my motherhood, must have been on her mind. She put in her appearance when I had my dress looped over the end of the ironing board. Without seeing her, I stood heavily waiting, touching my fingers to the iron. Then I saw her. She was standing perfectly still between the double arches of the kitchen, eying me.

I tried to say, "Good morning," or "Did you sleep," but no words came out.

She was not only as decisively immobile as a statue, she was drawn to her full height, statuesque. Arms folded, head rigid, with staring tablespoon eyes like the busts of Caesars. Aging Caesars. The whitewashed shell of her face was about as full of expression, yet unmistakably dangerous, as a lobster's claw.

I backed away instinctively, I edged cautiously to the far end of the ironing board.

Her tablespoon eyes moved, stirring up from the bottom of her face a sediment of feelings . . . fear, hate, and derision.

I was amazed and scared. I lifted the iron, testing it.

She raised her voice like a pistol. "Put down *that!*" She lowered her tone: "Down." Her tone was gunmetal. She cocked the barrel at me contemptuously. "Worried?"

"No."

"Liar." She took aim.

"Look—"

"Shut up. Mavi," she fired, "is with my first lover, she is with Satori's son."

My eyes blinked. She sailed into the room, her hips curved like a hull.

"His son!" I flinched.

I can still feel the tightening at the back of my neck.

She came before the wind, gliding to me, and embraced me vastly, an oceanic hug. "With Carlo," she confided tenderly.

How I
Made
Love

Si suol pur dir che foco scaccia foco.
—GASPARA STAMPA

It's often said that fire drives out fire.

The most awesome manifestation of human helplessness is not our helplessness before death, fate, nature, and accident, but before the suction of our own minds. This is the whirlpool whose power I speak of in *Pissoirs of the Heart*, the second voice in my so-called "Theban Duet." This is the awful eddying gulf at whose periphery we work, think, plan, eat, and love. We dogpaddle or do the crawl round the great circumference—and though we make trivial splashes, we are persuaded by our sensations of sweep and velocity that we have vitality and significance. It is not merely that we do not choose to succumb to the swirling vortex. We do not even admit that it is there, that we swim in defiance, that we are being gradually spun in and down toward the dark slow-moving suck. We cannot admit any of this because we are remotely aware that we are being whirled toward emptiness, toward a terrifying stillness, a hole in our lives about which we know nothing.

So many blind alleys. I came to associate the little dead-end waterways of Venice with my own. Off the beaten path, leading outward from the principal network of channels, were these dead-ends, dozens of them, tiny canals that simply ended, blocked by the *fondamento* (whose English cognate troubled me) as they hit up against a last embankment, vain blind impassable vaginas of the grand whore Venice. So many men in her uncomplaining canals, plying their trade with the long pole, thoughtlessly slipping the sleek, black, deadly-proud images of the phallus they here call gondolas up her Grand Canal in numbers that staggered and enthralled me.

Later I demanded that Carlo tell me straight out whether the gondoliers didn't themselves sense the tumescent grandeur of their craft. He touched my flirtatious lips and reassured me, "No." He had some right to be believed, but I couldn't be persuaded. Hadn't he already taught me those Venetian slang words for the long gondola oar—a whole string of dialect, including not only *ladle* and *leg* but also *pizzle* and *horn*? "For Godsake, Carlo, don't be a prude," I argued. "They must get a charge out of pizzle and come up with little gags about the horn. Come on."

He was adamant. "No."

"Yes—"

"No." He shook his sun-polished cheeks. "About these things they do not think. Never."

"Never-ever?"

"Never."

But he was so polite it wasn't always wise to trust him. He was gallant, therefore dishonest. For example, I remember how years and years later at my trial he swore under oath, committing perjury for my sake, that he had never had "sexual relations" with the defendant. "No." Grey-haired, still sun-polished: the nerve of the man. I rose to protest, causing one of those daily sensations the press loved to feature, while they ignored the heart of the case.

Dry government lawyers, snickering, and the snickering jaded judge enjoyed my insistence that Carlo and I were absolutely splendid lovers and nothing more. Deriding my sworn testimony as a tissue of poetic license, lampooning our lovemaking as physiological nonsense, they had already solicited the opinions of pompous medical authorities in a vicious effort to discredit and a vain effort to embarrass me.

The marshals had to restrain me. With order restored, the United States Prosecuting Attorney reiterated blankly, without a question mark, to his star witness, "You never had such relations with the defendant at any time."

In the fluorescence of the courtroom, Carlo's cloudy eyes brushed my harsh old temples soothingly. "Never-ever." Always the gentleman.

Back there with Carlo long ago in the blind glory of Venice I guaranteed him, "Well, let me tell you," and I was sure of myself, "us tourists don't miss a thing"—the shimmering symbolic sexual ceremony of the gondoliers; those lean bare-throated tight-trousered men nimbly balancing on the rear deck as they rowed.

"Us tourists!" he mocked. "*Dunque,* I will speak for the gondoliers and you for the tourists, Miss Niemann. If you think you are the usual tourist."

I said hotly in the bottom of our gondola, "I'm the most unusual tourist you ever went down on."

I taught him that—the phrase, I mean—although from his U.S. Embassy days his grasp of gritty U.S. slang was extensive.

"Miss Niemann, you're a regular nutcase," he exploded with laughter over my breasts and belly, a tireless Venetian guide on an all-day tour, licking me eagerly here and there for good measure after all our lovemaking, sinking his tongue thirstily into my mossy pubic dike and Palazzo Labia.

It was normal romance for Millie at last. I needed it! Beatific humdrum love.

I intended only a couple of weeks abroad. A vacation from despair. I can still remember holding Flaminia in my shaking arms and considering where I could go now—how far from myself. Where could I get away, where leave myself behind? There was no place on earth where I would not immediately devour myself. I'd felt as trapped and condemned as Augustine, who said it first. But I also remember a vision of freedom, an elusive overdeveloped Technicolor promise: an earlier morning, my nameless creature. Nuoro: the doctor is taking my pulse, Satori is taking my child. Mavi: with her two empty blue-lagoon eyes agape my way. Speak: her astonishingly red newborn lips begin to come open—will she speak?—and suddenly one blue-veined infant arm begins to stretch gracefully out toward me, all her crinkled fingers curling . . . a gesture of benediction.

Recoiling from fatherhood, with Flaminia at my throat, I understood that I had to see Mavi again, at least once in my life. For that blessing.

"If I know Carlo, he'll never allow it," had been Flaminia's final word.

Mainly to disturb Mavi as little as possible, but also to overcome whatever objections her family might have to a visit from her first mother, I veiled my visit in half-truths. I knew I had no legal right to see my child—I had given up all rights when I signed the papers—but I had created her myself, her father-mother, and had a biological birthright that transcended law. Nevertheless, I could see that if I wrote to her adoptive father for permission to visit . . . and if the answer were to be no . . . there would then be no way out, except unpleasantness, except despair, it would be too late for strategies. I therefore proceeded with circumspection, I went abroad virtually incognito.

Taking the address Flaminia had given me (and Satori, we both knew, would not have given me even that), I wrote to Carlo in polite Italian, saying nothing to indicate that I knew his father, absolutely nothing about Mavi, and practically nothing about myself. I was, I wrote, a New York friend of Flaminia's who would soon be passing through Venice on vacation, for a brief stay there of perhaps a week. Flaminia, I noted, had advised me that her warmly remembered friend might very well be far too busy these days to see me, but for my part I would certainly welcome an opportunity to meet an Italian family. FAMILY was writ large. He need not reply, I would look him up.

And dissolute, in need of Mavi's benediction, I did.

· · ·

On arrival I had my bags sent to my hotel without me. Carrying only my attaché case, I went directly by motor launch to his home address. I had no trouble getting there. The moment I arrived in Venice I'd been surrounded by men, hotel representatives, porters, gondoliers, speedboat-cabbies. One buffoon in a striped shirt and sunglasses pressed his attentions on me in such droll squeals of English, "This pretty for me, this one I take, where are your bigs, where are you sleep?" that I couldn't resist. I smiled and availed myself of his help. His luxurious glances my way were standard Italian. The much-vexed-complex-sex-reflex . . . but he had a boat and was quick about it. He roared and spumed me there in no time. I desired ardently not to see Venice. I hadn't come for a tourist trot.

A waterlogged hotel on an end-stopped canal. I'd expected not merely a house; I'd assumed a modest Venetian palace. Handing me up safely onto the landing, the launch driver offered to help me with my leather case. "I'll carry that," I said and tipped him. He flourished his eyebrows under his sunglasses. "Very many thinks," said he, "I think you very many thinks." And off he foamed.

A dead hotel. Inside were cubbyholes for mail and a board of keys hanging in neat rows, but no desk clerk, no one. No bell to ring. I called. No answer. Inside, a small restaurant, tables not set. On the walls, oil paintings. Beyond the restaurant, a garden. I went out into the greenery and called. Trellises, vines, little trees, tables, chairs, no answer, no one. I took the stairs to the first floor—rooms, doors closed—I called, knocked, descended, hurried outside, stood at the margin of the blind canal. I checked the address. Correct. What now? The oily canal was lifeless except for a mangy cat sitting in a flat scow. Leave a note? Find a gondola?

Inside, out of the heat, I decided to wait, someone would be coming along, I studied the paintings, I admired the garden again—so green in the glare—trellises—and—of course—in the corner, half-hidden under the foliage, the figure of a man I hadn't observed before. The desk clerk. More or less in uniform, asleep on a bench there in the shade, his head toward me. Against the wall his bare feet were hooked under an ancient black vine and kept him from falling off his bench. His many-buttoned hotel jacket with its insignia of crossed keys, slung over him as a light blanket with the sleeves trailing, had by now slipped down his chest: his chest breathed a dreamless rhythm.

I shook an empty jacket sleeve. He moaned and opened his eyes, took a breath looking straight into my face, and decided for sleep. I got him to sit up. He nodded, mouth open, eyes sagging off-center, stupefied by sleep, or plain stupid. No telling which. I said, "Does someone by the name of Satori live here, a certain Signor Carlo Satori?"

I encountered on his face the most utterly vacant expression I have ever seen. He appeared to be in his late thirties and not at all badlooking, but when he made the Italian gesture for *Sorry*, his arm swung like an orangoutang's tail, he yawned, his lips turned gradually outward like the anus of a horse about to pout the path with manure, he groaned, "No, no, no, no, no one by that name," and shut his eyes so tight that his lashes retreated like ants vanishing into anthills. He opened them in a flash of inspiration. "You want a room?"

I left him sitting on his bench.

He caught up with me outside. No one else in sight. Yes, not quite out of sight, someone. Bent low beside the rim of the canal where a bridge crossed a corner, an old woman in a long black shawl crouched, urinating into the canal.

I showed him Carlo's business address and asked directions.

I sent my name in through the receptionist. The Real Estate Agency of the Costa Smeralda was located in a suite of rooms on the ground floor of one of the big luxury hotels on the Lido. Before leaving New York, I'd checked carefully into the company. It was worldwide, but the Lido office was reportedly, from the sales viewpoint, one of its most desirable locations. Into it poured a year-round influx of selected clients—those most likely to covet a sliver of Sardinia, the well-heeled owners of the deep-keeled yachts. The Aga Khan's Consortium, the international group who were developing the seascape along Sardinia's northern reaches, had begun polishing their costly emerald, the Costa Smeralda. The venture was ambitious, all right, financially brilliant. It made sense to me. The change in Carlo Satori's career didn't. From selling the U.S.A. to selling real estate. I supposed he'd moved for the money. Should I have sensed something fishy?

Years ago the Commander had told me that his son, then a Sardinian lawyer and petty politician, had taken a position with the American Embassy in Rome. More exactly, as I know now, he had served as USIA consultant in the economics and politics of Italy, particularly of his native Sardinia. I had no idea of course that while on the U.S. Embassy staff he had, in fact, been in the pay of the Soviets, reporting to the Resident Director of the KGB. Nor did I know that he had defected voluntarily, communicating his former role to the CIA, thus becoming a "turned" or double agent. Not until years later when I was hailed into a Federal court did I guess that when Carlo went back to politics, he was "sent in"—that is, ordered to infiltrate the radical left—whether by the CIA or the KGB, I still haven't a clue. Loudly resigning (on the surface) in protest over the American position on the Sardinian insurrection, he had re-entered regional politics, drifting always to the left, and become a political wheel in a pro-Independence Party by the time of his temporary exile. Among other figures considered politically dangerous, during the state of emergency declared in the most recent Sardinian crisis, he had been exiled from the island. Forbidden legal access to Sardinia, he was in Venice on "business" when I met him.

Not only *didn't* I know that he was an undercover agent, I *couldn't* have known—as I stressed at my trial. Our country's Cressida I may be, but I've never pandered to the enemy's lust; nor did I fly to Carlo in the night like an invisible worm to peddle Flaminia's lunar secrets. The evidence is everywhere. I had enough lust for two. I had my own millimeter secrets—none of my country's goddamn business. I had compelling personal reasons for looking him up.

To more than one impartial observer the CIA's refusal to open its records at the trial and be frank in court has suggested they're not absolutely sure to this day who Carlo Satori was actually working for in those complicated years: whether he was or was not finally a triple agent, twice-turned—a double double agent—or even thrice-turned— a double double double agent. Now the Justice Department's flattering accusation that I *knew* when I flew to Venice that Flaminia's former boyfriend's latest position was the latest cover to conceal his intelligence activities for both sides—this is an ass-backward hindsight which conveniently credits me with more intelligence than the Central Intelligence Agency had at the time! It was news to me, but according to my prune-faced prosecutor, Carlo had by then already maneuvered himself into an underground anti-Soviet revolutionary party in Italy, the Maoist PPP, which was hoarsely supporting the Independence Movement on Sardinia. Who knows?—in his impartial style, Carlo may have been all along reporting to the Red Chinese as well as to the Soviets and the Americans. Dear Carlo! Passionate perjuror! Listen, I ought to add promptly for the sake of the record that no one has ever accused the Consortium or its Agenzia Immobiliare della Costa Smeralda of being a front organization, no matter how worldwide the Agency's scope and network, no matter how politically and financially secretive the international set that frequents the Sardinian resort coast. The company was genuine. Carlo had suc-

ceeded in planting himself there as a convenient base for political organizing on the mainland.

The receptionist evidently recognized my name: she had instructions to show me into his office. This turned out to be an inner two-
room suite. He would be back in a few minutes, I was informed. I
waited—absorbed by extraordinary photographs set above the desks
and couches—all around the walls ran rock-sheltered, powder-white
beaches, the uninhabited northern shore of Sardinia I'd never seen.
Natural harbors surmounted by modern, yet curiously Moorish architecture: hotels. The designs for new villas, a series of still further developments along the coast—

"I've kept you waiting!" he boomed . . . the power of his voice
came at me from behind. The modulations I heard disconcerted me,
they were so like his father's. But more about that big voice of his in
a moment. I turned: the resemblance to his father was subtle. Carlo's
face was humorous, a diverting tangle of courtesy and pride and cruel
good looks, a face of egoism made philanthropic by friendliness, the
remote curl of arrogance redeemed by his savage cheerfulness. Broad
at the base, pointed at the cheeks, his face was mobile and more than
that, manipulative; all his features insisted at once on my most cheerful
response, and in the mobility of his stocky body gliding toward me
glided the exhilaration of life itself. He was close to forty-five then,
with a muscular vigor plainly announced under his light suit, stated
in the crisp heaviness of his forward-leaning walk toward me and the
power-driven precision of his hand. He took my hand in both of his
with deliberately controlled force. "Miss Niemann—grand pleasure.
When did you arrive?"

"I just got in."

"And you've been waiting here?" he shouted again and flourished a
wrist at his office suite, "here? With all Venice out there?"

I never got used to Carlo's vocal excess—that chesty pedal tone.
He seemed to mean what he said and yet, too loud, he seemed to be
standing far away behind himself, unabashedly indifferent to what he
said. Engaged with the world, but personally lighthearted, he was a
man whose solemnity was fizzy. "Nobody has the right," he rep-
rimanded me fiercely and jauntily, "to look at pictures of Sardinia
during her first hour in Venice."

"I've enjoyed waiting. They're exquisite photographs."

"How do you say that—'coals in Newcastle'? Selling the sea in
Venice. How *is* my Flaminia?" He paused, perhaps to reconsider his

"my." He followed this up a bit mournfully, I thought, with, "My old friend."

"Flaminia's well. She's becoming important. She's a brilliant woman."

"She was a brilliant girl."

"She's up to here."

"In?"

"Work. And you?"

"In Venice no one is overworked."

That was *all* we said about Flaminia's work. No use pointing it out. If Carlo's office had been bugged, if a tape recording of this conversation were still available, I have little doubt the FBI and the Attorney General would be able to find in these remarks insidious evidence of disloyalty. We continued to speak of Flaminia of course, but not of her work.

"You're staying a week?"

"About that."

"At the Gritti Palace?"

"You know?" I was surprised. In my letter I had given him the date of my arrival, not the name of my hotel.

"Of course. One investigates. Curiosity is sometimes a duty." He looked at me with two curiously different eyes, one business eye, so to speak, and one eye appraising something else.

That trick of the eyes was impressive. He seemed able to work one eye independently of the other—and let me add, I don't like people who can see around me. "You investigated my hotel?"

"Well, let's say I was expecting a different sort of person."

"Different?"

He shrugged. "Less well-to-do." He smiled, and from his glance I knew what was coming next. From his eyes any woman would have known. "Ma Lei è una poema!" Flattery—but the courtliness of it! No one had ever called me a poem before . . . few compliments have ever startled me more. He laughed with pleasure. He looked me over double. "Ma che poema! I'm grateful to our mutual friend."

No compliment could have been more splendid—more arousing. Caught off guard, I murmured, "She speaks of you fondly."

"Ah, then you know the worst. What does she say?"

"Not enough."

He waved that away. "But you're here on business!"

He was so loud! I looked surprised again, and for a second I worried: *did* he know? Disguising his alertness, Carlo pointed tranquilly to the leather attaché case I had rested on his desk.

"No, only a few documents. Unimportant papers." In leaving New York, I'd taken along some unfinished business. (Later I realized that he never really did ask me about my business—as he would have asked a man—in fact he wanted not to know.) "I'm on vacation."

"And never been to Venice—are you free this evening?"

This was more than an invitation, it was an implication: his dual-control eyes and the sparkling timbre of his voice made it a shade too eager. "Tomorrow maybe," I scrupled. "During the day if that's possible."

"Of course, why not, Venice by day," he agreed merrily. "Art? architecture? history? beaches? restaurants? What shall it be? In one week—everything?"

"Daily life," I demurred, "watery life, the life of the tiny islands, the life of Venetian families—how *do* people live in Venice? I'd love to find out."

"*Porca miseria!* The Italian family! You've been to Italy before!" he chuckled.

I made bold to suggest, "Perhaps I might visit your family?" When he made no reply to this, I even went so far as to add, "I have the address. Would it be difficult to find?"

"I'd be delighted," he countered expertly, "to show you around during the afternoons." Was this eagerness—again—or evasion? "And evenings," he smiled healthily, pointedly. There was no mistaking it.

I switched my ground. "I'd like to meet your wife," I said, just as pointedly, though it ill suited me to play puritan.

"My wife!" he remarked, feigning vigorous disbelief.

"I believe Flaminia said you were married," I observed dryly. "A family man."

"Not any more!"

Liar? The queasy feeling he was openly lying to me came over me. I smiled uneasily. "You're not going to tell me you're divorced, are you?"

"Divorced," he reiterated with irony, expecting to be disbelieved. I didn't believe him. "Are your wife and child here in Venice?"

"Child?" he said. "I have no children."

Baffled, irritated by this game (but it was no game!), I saw nothing for it but to come to the point. "I came to Venice to inquire about a child."

"Ah well, of course I guessed *that* . . . but not . . ." It came over him suddenly. "*My* child? Where—*where* did you get that idea?"

"From Flaminia," I said, and hoping to pin him down at last, I added, "You enclosed a photograph in a letter to your father."

"That's true." Was he laughing at me? His synoptic eyes, taking it all in, slowly stifled his humor. He said, "I'm sorry to smile." But he seemed on the verge of it again. "All I did was prepare the papers." I stepped away from him. "The adoption papers," he continued. "Years ago in Cagliari my old man asked me to handle the legal aspects of an adoption. The photo—" he laughed—"the adoptive father sent me a snapshot last year, I sent it on to my old man. . . ." He was choking with amusement. "Your name was familiar . . . please, next time you write, a little less deception—" he was snorting with laughter now—"I suppose you have no notion how suspicious your letter made me. . . ."

I do not take kindly to criticism, to laughter, to accusations of deception. "My wish was to protect—" but I couldn't go on . . . the muscles in his face had suddenly begun to sag unnaturally.

They hung loose. He yawned, he swung his arm like an orangoutang's tail, he turned his lips out like a horse's ass—the hotel clerk! —and groaned, "No, no, no, no one by that name," and shut his eyes: ants into anthills.

Then ever more raucous with howls of laughter, he practically stunned me by shouting across the room at me, "Where are you bigs, where are you sleep? I think you many many thinks."

I stalked out of that office. I was hot with mind-sapping pride. I had never felt so toyed with and put down—the motor launch driver, too—I was furious! Coarse clowning!

I had no knowledge then of Carlo's taste for comedy. Even when I got to know him well, I must say I continued to think his low talent for foolery assorted ill with his political agility and subtle grasp of situations. But both were held together by his inborn lightness and acquired disdain for most forms of sentiment, by what Castiglione once called *sprezzatura* and *disinvoltura*.

I walked out on him, attaché case in hand. I stalked through the hotel lobby, down through terraces and walks. He followed me. Intolerable!

My feet hated him. I crossed a mall, blank white-hot sun. I saw nothing, neither water nor earth. He followed.

I walked alone through a void of sunglare, nothing but searing light, my thoughts sweaty, my feet gradually nonplused.

He said, "I can, of course, help you out."

Pacing beside me, he said after another long while, "If you wish, I can write to the child's family."

"If it doesn't trouble you."

"Trouble *me?*" he replied quickly.

It was a strain to be civil. "Whoever she is, her mother is a woman, she'll understand. Where are they?"

He avoided that. "Yes, unquestionably she will understand, and be absolutely opposed. But in the long run her wishes really do not matter. Other things do."

"What?"

"Political issues," he said incomprehensibly.

We turned left, right, left. We crossed a promenade, we crossed a square, we crossed a shadow. I imagined that for the remainder of my stay in Venice I would be sightless with outrage and despair. My objectless love had taken away my wits and now derided me—what daughter, what child? I understood that without an object to love, love is not only absurd, it's abject. I've learned since that it's also treacherous.

He looked at me seriously, sidewise dark pupils. Yet there was something else there—a wily hankering—a blink of the eyelashes that could mean only one thing. My own eyes were sticky, but they were ready to open and see.

"One thing . . ." I began.

"Yes?"

"My daughter—"

A subtle, precise jerk of his chin in my direction. He said, without emphasis, "Your daughter?" He was looking right at me now. He continued quite softly, yet each word masking, I felt, a certain discipline in his thoughts, "Miss Niemann, pardon my frankness. I'm sure you must have considered whether it isn't a sentimental mistake to confuse the act of giving birth with motherhood."

To say I was unsteadied by his bluntness would be to understate it. I wobbled like a toy gyroscope at the view of other people's water under my bridge, my heels too long and memory too spiked, years vacant and unfillable.

Betraying my country? By the time the sun came down that afternoon I think I already knew what I was doing. Betraying Mavi. Walking alone, I kept my eyes on children more or less her age running in Piazza San Marco, scattering pigeons up into the sunset. Loopholes in

my story, inconsistencies in my testimony? There were loopholes in
the colonnades in which the pigeons roosted. There were inconsistencies in me. The child I'd dedicated to the gods of the earth: she'd
brought us together in Venice, the city wedded to the sea. Flaminia's
old lover . . . I think I already knew without astonishment that he,
and not Mavi, would restore my wavering sex, intense womanliness,
and overwhelming certitude. The pigeons circled, turbulent over the
colonnades. I watched their flights from the head of the square, I
watched some more from Florian's, and I walked. I spent the evening
alone.

But I was followed, I'm sure of it, trailed. By whom? By the flower
vendor? When I turned to look at him, he offered me a violet—a man
as thin as an exclamation mark, as cherry-lipped as a boy, the pathetic
wild features of a mime who smiles, and he was gone. By the old crone
in a black shawl? No, but I was kept in view, I was never lost sight
of. Persistent as pigeons, everywhere in Venice, men circled and
came after me whenever I so much as moved, stiffening their necks
and lowering their gaze, a gurgle of vowels in their throats and their
quills bristling in their pants.

In retrospect I saw. Maybe there was nothing I could not have
seen at the time if I'd looked deeper into the slow-moving canals of
my own responses. But just in case you're confused, let me reassure
you: this personal history of mine is no spy thriller. It's my sacred
mystery, the chiller of my pubic puzzle, mine and yours.

My singularity. And his. My duplicity. And his.

And that leather attaché case? Poor pickings there. Documents?
Formulas, trajectories, mission, timetables? If Carlo did, without my
consent, explore the dull contents of my attaché case, there's no
doubt his intimate explorations with my consent were more rewarding.
Top-secret? Close surveillance? Crossing my path, two Napoleonic
gendarmes paced the square in step, glistening with sashes, buttons,
capes, cockade hats, and swords like trailing plumage.

Above their heads, leaning toward me, the Campanile moved. Expanding balloonlike, the golden cathedral wavered.

He let me in. The manipulative humorous smile again. "A little unfinished business," he said in English. "No, don't go, they'll never finish.
If you wait right here and make yourself good and visible, very annoyingly visible, they'll hurry up and . . . skoot?—how do you say?
—skedaddle?" He left me alone and returned at once to the other end
of his double suite.

A conference of several clients of the Consortium and their lawyers and perhaps an architect or two—so I first thought—a real estate
group conversing in Sardinian under glossy enlargements of a lovely
villa and a cape of land. It did not immediately strike me as strange
that they were speaking *Sardo*, which is not a provincial dialect of
Italian but a distinct island language. It was a tongue I'd had great
trouble learning to comprehend during my stay there. Occasionally
I could make out words and sentences, mostly Carlo's resonant boom
and the querulous objections of a snappish old man who talked more
than anyone else. The others kept their voices low; indeed they
glanced at me with an uncertainty verging on protest, and I saw
that Carlo had to reassure them.

It's hard for me to separate what I now understand about that
meeting from my chaotic observations of it at the time. I paid not a
great deal of attention, I can't recall the exact number of men in the
office, or their features, but I do retain an impression of nervous dis-
agreement, centering apparently on the wording of a long document
they had in their hands—they all had copies—and which I now realize
must have been the "Letter of Unity," the pact of the United Independence Front which the guerrillas themselves, alone of the Independence groups, later refused to sign. ". . . but the name is *not* unimportant," I picked up. Carlo was coolly broadcasting something to
the effect that (I put down here, as if it were a single remark of his,
what I had to piece together phrase by phrase) "of all the legitimate
representative groups, of all the economic sectors and parties, with
all our evidently conflicting interests, the Partito Sardo d'Azione is
the only available *historic* structure, broadly based, the only one on
which we can build an effective organization, it already exists, it can
serve as the historic nucleus for the coalition—" and every once in a
while his voice would lilt to sudden irony— "or would you prefer
to build a coalition out of thin air and our disagreements . . . ?" That
was the substance, or close to it, but mainly I had to rely on tones, not
words, and his tone was remarkably buoyant for affairs so weighty.
Even his irony conveyed less his skepticism and satire than his sprightly
assurance and princely *sprezzatura*, his pleasant unconcern—his fundamental astonishing indifference to these negotiations, to a pact, to politics, to the gentlemen in his office this morning, perhaps to life. They
were rephrasing certain sections and subsections, they had reservations
about certain covenants and secret clauses, but what I heard was how
persuasive indifference can be. They might make a gesture, Carlo's

voice seemed to tell them, a binding political decision that would complete themselves. Not that he cared. It would be for themselves.

My attention drifted gradually. . . . In the light of my subsequent political engagement and sometimes daredevil commitment, it may disconcert the reader to be made an unwilling, unsubpoenaed witness now to the wandering state of my mind. But you can bet your sweet life that even subsequently, no matter how feisty, how selfless, how politically dramatic I became, I did not, I do not, I will never, repudiate the subterranean unity of sexual love and social conscience, nor the endless pact, with all its bitter concessions, between art and society.

There was a piece of sculpture I hadn't noticed last time, right by the window where I was standing: a torso of pale wood, rough yet very highly polished. Carlo's face had the look, almost the grain, of that wood. All at once the long silent pain of Flaminia's love for him came to mind; without warning, the bewildering night in which I had conceived my child came back to me. The old dizziness returned, the wobble in the knees, and between my legs the tender moisture infiltrated the nerve-ends of my sex. Watching Carlo and so remembering the Commander, and Flaminia, and Mavi, and Sandy, I knew again the haunting pleasure. I knew that for me the first and last ecstasy would always remain the chains of love. *Inrupta tenet copula:* the progression and order of sexual love, the gladness of couplings, the triumph of impossible, undeniable unions. I touched the statue. Happily I ran my fingers over the blond glossy body of the wooden boy—shoulders, ribs, belly—leaving for a few instants, like the track of a snail, a faint track of light against the grain, an involuntary message on the polished surface where the perspiration in my susceptible fingertips had passed and paused and rested. Immediately Carlo looked up. Had he seen? Standing at the edge of the little cluster of men, idly absorbed in the play of their conversation, he turned his head. I saw his eyes. I blushed. How impossible I was! Still a child. For no reason, flustered, I began taking off the thin beige jacket I had on over my blouse. The insignificant motion relieved me somewhat.

Magnificently, subtly, he acknowledged that he had noticed. He came over and handed me a note. *"Due minuti"*—two minutes. I'd have waited an hour if he'd asked.

They were still bargaining, I suppose, over a codicil, a slippery phrase, over a name—haggling as if at an auction, they had taken it upon themselves now to decide the price at which the pact of unity would be knocked down, the old man insisting that the price of political compromise must be less; a younger man claiming, however, that an appropriate price, while less than the asking price, was surely higher than *his* suggestion; a hitherto quiet fellow, apparently an associate of Carlo's, speaking up suddenly and agreeing that the advantages of a pact *deserved* to command at least such a price . . . and so on. Carlo took no part in the details of bargaining. He looked at his watch.

"Yes," he reassured them ingeniously, vivaciously, "all parties stand to lose. No party, no group, is guaranteed success. Only the success of the coalition is guaranteed. But after all, there's no need to make up your minds right now," he said. "It's an imposing document, but it will be here tomorrow."

The knot of compromisers drew more tightly together and their insane bargaining became more heated. I stared at Carlo. That surely had been a ruse—especially his crudely looking at his watch—were they blind to tactics, to pressure, no matter how coolheaded? But it was not a strategy, not a maneuver to close a "sale"; a few seconds later I discovered that Carlo had meant what he said. Still, for the moment I thought I'd caught him in a deceit. While their bickering eddied, Carlo walked arrogantly away and came by and said to me in English: "You recognize the old man?"

"No. Should I?"

He mentioned a name later to be world-famous, a figure in Italian socialist circles whose identity it would be reckless to divulge here. "Can you follow any of this—this heroic contest? Don't worry, even we can't."

"He seems stubborn."

"Stubborn? No, today he must find fault with our manifesto in order to revise it so that in the future he can tell the world that he authored it."

I hadn't given the old man much heed, and I didn't do so now. I was shaking. Although Carlo had approached me with a casual remark, my pulses were telling me other tales and the heat had come back into my cheeks because I could sense that he was not in the slightest bit interested in whether I recognized the noted gentleman or in whether I'd followed the discussion. He was standing close. I wondered how I could maneuver *him* . . . a ruse as clever as his . . . he said, "Are you on my side?" (His side!) I took advantage of my genuine ignorance and pretended to show the confusion of a girl who knows she *ought* to be interested in politics but isn't. I shook my head vaguely and, holding my arms tight around my breasts, bit my lips very slightly in half-amused embarrassment. It was almost artless, and I think maybe convincing. I had the upper hand, the pride of the moment. "Are you all making secret deals?"

"Secret?" he laughed. He called back over his shoulder shamelessly to the others, "I would prefer you not to make up your minds in a hurry, I would rather have you think about it, I'd like you to be sure, really I'd prefer it that way. Think about it. Go back and think."

I was sure that this pitch was brilliantly designed—so honest was his voice, so forthright and convinced his assurance—to force their hand and obtain their signatures. But no. Over their objections, he practically drove them out; inoffensively, with charm—he would not talk about substantive changes—a gentle and insistent friend. Yes, they must certainly hold another meeting—as soon as they had consulted with their own organizations—tomorrow, absolutely, whenever they liked, yes, yes. When they were out the door, he came back to me, pulling down his vest and dusting his trousers as a man does who has been disarrayed in an unimportant tussle. He had beautiful hands—they were browned, with a rough pattern of veins like the bark of certain trees in the Italian *campagna* whose name I don't know, and very pale nails, and sprouting fingers that looked fine and flexible. He offered me a cigarette from a silver case I'd caught a glimpse of yesterday; when I refused, he put the case away and did not smoke. And suddenly his face lighted—not a smile, it was a relaxation of lines and muscles. "Can you come for the entire afternoon?"

"Where to?" On the phone I'd accepted only an invitation to lunch.

"Does it matter?"

"It might."

"Are you worried?"

"No. Not at all. Delightfully amused."

"Sometimes it is even more delightful to be worried."

He *did* amuse me, I wasn't worried, I was shaking in the loins. Half-eaten already. But I felt like the tiny garden shrew who in the tearing desperation of her hunger throws herself ferociously against a creature of the woods larger, more assured, and normally more violent than herself. Instincts rushed out, and into the darkness and vacuum reeled a vision of myself as shrew, tearing chest, ripping throat, my minuscule teeth slashing where he was least protected and my claws like diamonds hidden in the reluctant warmth of his belly, propelled into this cyclonic meat-loving frenzy on a blur of heart-beats. He had removed his tie, baring his throat. I stared, fixed and hanging there in my imagination. His neck was sunburned and thick and it beat when he said: "I will make this delightful."

Was he going to seize me right there? He was taking off his jacket. I had no idea. I waited and hung there, hung on. His polarized eyes were still distant, they were *still* distant, off somewhere in that indifferent fizzy haze of theirs. For no sufficient cause I could comprehend, suddenly a murky grey leaden hatred poured down into me. Again, unreasonably, I hated him. I said coolly, "This whole island that's up for grabs, I've become mighty curious, tell me, does the Consortium know that here in these plush offices of theirs you do more than sell their attractive real estate?"

His two panoramic, periscopic eyes adjusted. "I do much more," he said, which was no answer at all. "I'm interested in saving the island from bloodshed."

Slightly piqued at this deft evasiveness, I proceeded to annoy him by telling him pleasantly and smoothly that I was interested in the advantages of acquiring a small coastline property in the Mediterranean. "I'm interested in European investments," I added sensibly.

He put his jacket down idly on the desk. Muscular in his vest, he turned away from me. "Later," he said. For a second I caught a glimpse of the bunched whiteness of his shirt between the back of his vest and the back of his belt as he disappeared unhurrying into the hotel lobby through a side door.

I waited. I would not at first admit my displeasure. I looked at the wooden torso. But instantly it bored me. My mouth was burning, that very special, familiar sensation of flame. I looked at Carlo's jacket and thought of going through his pockets. Instead, I took a little waxed match from the cardboard matchbox that was lying on his desk. I lighted it and watched the flame, then put my fingers to my mouth and snuffed the match delicately with my saliva-moistened fingertips as Sandy had taught me to do long ago. Outside, Carlo's shouts. It was silent inside. I could smell the wind from the sea. I might after all resist him. Quite possible. I thought of it only to enjoy the shock it would cause him. Inside I laughed. I was mildly insulted. There was a combustible mixture like crude oil on rags, comedy and desire, the cheap ease of my success and the costly insult to my person which I perceived keenly. I'd asked to discuss real estate. Dropped. It wasn't merely that my financial worth had been discarded. *I* had been dropped. He was at home in political finagling, I was at home in commercial finagling. A lukewarm half-hour of distance, just half an hour's worth of any sort of homespun serious financial dickering, was important to me. Instincts had collided too quickly. It was true I was half responsible: I'd drawn my own hot damp line on the cool glaze of his statue. But to me that made his oversight no less offensive.

He returned through another door, calling a few words back over his shoulder at his receptionist, and announcing to me, "It's all set. We have a gondola." But I was determined now on a course that was more than coy, it was my mastery in the unmastered situation, rapidly developing between us, that I wanted to salvage from the start, and I said:

"I've got a couple of things to take care of this afternoon." That was strictly true. "I have an appointment to phone New York—" this was a suicidal remark since I was dying to ride in a gondola. But I wouldn't have taken it back for my life.

"Yes? Fine. What time?"

"Five."

"I'll get you back."

He locked up.

It was a worn-out, wet-bellied, splintery thing. Tail curled in disdain, black teeth in its beak, steady in the water. I was unsteady. At the landing near the Municipal Casino he helped me in and I missed my footing. The glare on the water turned cross-grained, the quais on all sides of us were shoved by the tremors of a minor sea-quake, one great window of the Casino abruptly burned itself up in the sun the way a frame of film burns and peels into orange light, then into sheer white. I shifted sideways on the seat, recovering, and saw Carlo, laughing as he turned the long Venetian oar. He stood up behind me on the rear platform and bent toward me slightly in his shirtsleeves and vest, the tight line of his body slanting easily at me in the same even motion I'd already watched from the shore. I touched the gunwale—I touched it appreciatively, though the black wood was rough and broken in places, though the cushioned seats were not thick velvet and purple silk but a tough dark fabric, often torn and resewn. "Is it yours?"

"Mine and a few friends. We share it." An arc brought us swinging into an alley of water. The gondola slid down a termite's maze of tiny canals, where old unused steps of green algae vanished under the waterline, blocked above by unused wooden doors. The buildings on either side were very close, a tight squeeze, a low bridge under which our two curling ends of gondola drifted, a sweeping turn, and we were out on open water.

I didn't say anything for a while.

Everything moved gradually away from us. Lunch? I asked him about that. We were out in the lagoon. "In America," I said, "we call this kidnapping."

"In Italy it is called *pranzo*. It is called kidnapping only after lunch."

"And if the victim has no appetite for lunch?" I said, "or in a rare case, for her kidnapper?"

"Appetite will come, don't worry, it's a long way, and in any case, *I* will be hungry." Egoism close to ugliness. He smiled rapaciously.

So. He wore his vest while rowing. How ludicrous! The oar pivoted on a curved wooden rest that rose like a snake to hold it: in response the gondola lifted gently high, hung, and let drop again with a dipping surge. Forward and back he swayed on the balls of his feet. I watched his relaxed hands press his full weight on the long pole that made a parabola of ripples in the chop of the lagoon. "I want to be hungry myself," I decided. "Let me try."

He shook his head. Still smiling.

"Let me row."

Still smiling. Was that not even worth an answer?

So, so, so. There were just certain things. Evidently a girl simply didn't stand herself up there on that stern deck and take a long pole between her hands and rock her gondola forward . . . well, for the moment, it was about as well—I had no desire to tip us over into the lagoon. I decided not to fight the temptation, the candied privilege I had fought in a sense *always*, all life long, the heart-sweetening head-fattening rule of never being allowed to row your own gondola . . . never-ever . . . I trailed my fingers in the cool water. I supposed I could try to become what he evidently thought I was already—simply a goodlooking girl, an utterly cliché blonde. Why not? The rewards were obvious. I gazed up at his tight hips clasped more tightly by his black trousers each time he seemed to step forward against the height of the oar, and I could sense his muscles bunch in his thighs and calves, I watched the rhythmic release as the top of the oar was turned and drawn back. I said, "Would you do something banal for me?"

"What?"

"Sing me a song." To be clear, I added, "A love song."

"But that's not possible in Venice—to sing of love to an American girl while rowing the gondola—not with a straight face."

"Then break your face for me, and sing anyway." If I had a certain limited power as a girl, by God, I thought, I was going to use it. I was going to get my reward.

"Well, I will sing you a very trite song, miss," he laughed, "but short, for it is important to save one's breath. It is a long way to Alberoni."

It was quiet in the gulf. Large ships were visible at a distance and an occasional gondola passed slowly at cross-angles. Sometimes there was the far sound of a motor, sometimes the vicious yelping of gulls right overhead. The cupolas and domes of Venice drew farther away, obscured by the haze, which had lifted from the city but clung in patches to the surrounding water and now accumulated with distance, blocking a clear vision. I hummed, trying to get the tune and the words. Elbows leaning into the oar, Carlo sang into the rocking silence. It was something like:

> *Vieni,*
> *C'è 'na strada nel bosco.*
> *Il suo nome conosco.*
> *Vuoi conoscerlo tu?*
>
> *Vieni,*
> *È il nido del cuore,*
> *Dove nasce l'amore,*
> *E non muore mai più.*

Each time he finished, it was quiet. He sang it softly, then over and over at my request, until I got it; and though I don't have all the words correctly now, I've never altogether forgotten them or the necessary sound they made in the gulf. He stopped. Only the gulls.

Sophisticated military weapons and technological developments! I had no idea how dangerous he was.

A trifle dizzy, I lay down in the bottom, and there I became aware of the nibbling noises the long liplike waves made against the sides of the craft. I pressed my ear hard against a wooden strut, and promptly the nibbling became chewing and spitting and smacking sounds. The hungriness of the sea's small teeth.

"What's down there?" Carlo asked, seeing me with my neck bent to listen.

I beckoned to him. "Come here." He lifted the oar into the gondola, dripping, and laid it down. I pulled him, intending to put his ear where mine had been, but his torso against my hands changed that. I had him in my hands now, literally, and I pulled his head close. When he smiled, I slid my hand along his sun-hot vest to his open collar. His flesh was as hot and silky as his vest. When he kissed me, I rubbed the little hairs behind his neck.

It was very hot and still out there. We were rocking. Everything was rocking. I tried to take not only his tongue but even his lips into my lips and then, half-drifting into a self-willed trance, I imagined myself the sea, my nibbling teeth the swirl of the tiny chopping waves. Carlo's tongue, slowly moving and pulling, became the oar: searching just beneath my surface, proving that there *were* fathoms unentered. Very quietly I began to make my faint humming cry, but here it seemed deadened, distant, underwater. I was salt, he was shell, his coral hands were half a fathom into the slow drift of my thighs. I surfaced. Following my currents up again to the air, I began to open his fly for him—to show I wouldn't mind if the hungry mollusc came out of its shell to dine or swim in me—but Carlo sat up.

He pulled me up with him and kissed me briefly under the throat. Then he took up the damn oar. I stared, bewildered, and on the verge of formless rage. He went back to the stern deck. I considered tipping us over. Yet his manner seemed so friendly—and his movements so absurd: with the big oar sweeping sideways to turn us again in the right direction, and with the bulge in his partly unbuttoned fly following its own direction as he turned his chest into the stroke, he looked as if he had four or five arms. Anyhow, what was that big smile of his all about, athletic and gleaming and fond and uninvolved? He said nothing.

But I was not going to be put out; I *would* not be annoyed. I lay right down again on my back, adjusting my skirt and swinging my knees in time to a waltz in my head, and soon I said out loud into the ear of the blue-blue sky, "Too fast for you, these American girls?"

Still he didn't answer. Just that broad smile of pleasure.

I did not know it yet, but sex with Carlo was to be a wholly different experience, before, during, and afterward. Close to dying, yet unlike death; like watching one's own escaping breath and blood become one of the deepfreeze beauties of space so far from this planet of organic warmth that one would have chosen the marvel over life.

We reached at last the great breakwater that fingers the sea far out to the east and guards the deep channel at Alberoni. Rocks, battered boulders, chunks of cement. Sunken and vanishing vaguely into the depths, they were soft green, waving their sea lettuce. Above the surface they poked out orange, pink, and yellow. As we approached, a rat scrambled for shelter, down into the rocks.

"Mussels for lunch," Carlo announced. "With luck, oysters." He had his clothes off—only a loincloth bathing suit—slipped on a pair of fins and one glove, left hand only—slapped the water with his chest —the gondola rocked—and shaking spray from his hair, he caught the gunwale with one hand. "The knife," he said. "And the bag. And the mask."

Lurching in the water, he fitted the mask. "There's some bread under the seat if you get hungry," he said. "And a bag of lemons."

"What's the glove for?" I asked, handing him everything he'd asked for.

"Oysters. They're harder to find, but we're going to be lucky."

I watched him going under. Down. Slapping and swishing with his fins to get down.

Gone. Down.

Climbing out, I hopped over the clutter of giant strewn rocks until I saw him break the surface near the breakwater's edge. I called but he didn't hear. He was under again. Down. Gone. Deep.

I warmed myself on the rocks in the sun. Off in the distance there were fishing boats plying the channel. Suddenly close up, practically underneath me, there was Carlo working several yards down. Beneath the clear water, in another world, he broke clumps of shellfish from the rocks like bunches of grapes from the vine and liquidly squeezed them into the bag at his waist. The water, blue with unaccountable gold lights in it, threw him around underneath me. It hurled him against the rocks sideways. A sudden tow shook him as he held on there with one hand, the hair on his legs snaking in the wash like little whips.

National security! Counterintelligence!

Lying there out on the rocks, I worried about my own internal security arrangements. With Carlo. And I had misgivings about my loyalty, not only to Mavi but to everyone—to Flaminia, to his father, even to Baron, and of course to Sandy—so many furtive alliances. Curiosity, he'd said. Sometimes a duty. There was no telling . . . might not Flaminia have written to him long ago about the Commander and myself, recounting his father's belated passion for a wide-lashed slender yellow-headed student, a little finny flounder named Millicent Niemann? It filled me with uneasy pride to remember the source of the swimmer now gathering oysters for me beneath the surface, the root and seed of the diver who seemed so consummately sure of himself and self-contained; it made me tremble and smile to think I knew that root so well, the Commander's crinkled organ of generation.

For me, the links between us on every side were poetry, like the canals of Venice, short, filthy, lyrical. It would be like drowning gladly. An ancient network of relations beckoned me into its familiar waters. A beautiful maze of will and fate—my will, my fate—called me down into it. I longed for the plunge—a little scared, it was true, but without guilt or shame—a skinnydipping child as always, diving always one more time please, gladly naked amidst small boys and girls all gigglingly naked together, falling happily into the ripples they (and she!) have already made (oh together!)—not concentric merely, but ripples that have by now spread and raced and returned upon each other, crossing, weaving, interlacing like filigree, as complex as needlepoint, a hypnotic bedazzlement of light and shadow, of glare from the sky and obscure instincts in the water, of brilliant innocence, twilight sex, and the dark fear of drowning.

So that when at last we took each other, after oysters and lemon, lying low in a hollow of the sea wall, caressing on hard cold rocks, for an instant, for two, for three, I was gorgeously appeased . . . while he kissed me, while I held him . . . and then I saw the tail of the rat. Only the tail this time. It undulated. Flicked out of sight. Vanished into the breakwater's jumble of rocks. I undulated, too, a shudder, and his hand came down along my backbone, urging every vertebra. For a long time. The sides of my breasts. Each in turn. He praised. My lips. With his. While only the backs of his knuckles slid down my belly. So that when at last, kissing me there at the edges of my sex, he broke through the surface, without warning the entire sea wall on which we were lying came apart, flooding over and breaking beneath us as the weight of the stones and cement blocks sank into the mud below.

Shocked, I struggled to rise, but the sea, hypnotic and impersonal, had already engulfed me, and fighting, coming, shivering, I was lifted out of my mind, choked, plunging through bubbles, I clutched him, he grasped me, I couldn't breathe and I tore his back with my fingernails, I dug them into him, his wet back swam with me hot and smooth, but no breath! no breath! I panicked, I fought to swim up, he held me down, gave me his breath to breathe, and coerced me toward the sun-filtering depths where seaweed caught at us, I grabbed him viciously

Something lacerated me in a private place, part of him was part of me, the lance tip alone throbbing and forcing entrance into my squirming body as I slid over his, bucking, a creature of land

Not like this, not drowning, it was not too late, I could still see the shimmering waterline above us, the blindness below, he was swimming inside me and all around me, and then his mouth became my lungs again, and it was too late, giving up all hope of air and sky and life and sun I chose this underwater thrusting propulsion down into my

Nothing

I fought nothing

I fought nothingness

Until in that compressed blackness and emptiness a medusa pulsed behind his head, luminous, on and off, pulsating slowly, as slowly the ancient head of a giant tortoise emerged from deepsea night to stare, and I screamed without breath, while dolphins raced by, arching playing twisting racing lurching smiling the serene intense uncaught unutterable smiles of lovers playing twisting converging separating

After them we raced

Our lungs burst

And nothing can suffice to tell you the heat, the height, the bursting violet velocity we overtook them with and took each other with as we swept out of the sea upward through air into the bright sun, the end of the rainbow, or how we potted its gold, flaunting our colors, or how the sea wall rose again, leaving us each a throne to sit on, each in each other, still.

I welcomed this treachery. It came for me. I'd traveled three thousand miles for her . . . and knew I'd given her up. Faithlessness. Mavi . . . my will-o'-the-wisp, my maculate conception: I needed him. Breaking the surface, currents of floating sewage-guilt caught up with me at odd hours of the tourist day. But in the main I confess they were easy undertows. My remorse, my bad faith, my loss—these were in no way equal to the pounds-per-square-inch pressures of my fathomless joys below with Carlo.

I recognized how low I'd committed myself. I implored him not to write to Flaminia, and certainly not to write on my behalf to Mavi's parents, not to mention them to me again. It was now out of the question for me to leave him. Not in this tumultuous flow, not at this seditious, crushing depth. In my most depressed moments later on I sometimes thought he, too, knew what he was doing—depriving me of

Mavi, of my desire to see her at all, by forcing upon me something I needed more, his love.

Within days I'd moved out of the Gritti and into his hotel, into his room. No argument could make him consider the reverse direction. The change had nothing to recommend it except Carlo; the neighborhood round about was dreary, the place itself was cold. But the moment I got inside his hotel room, I nearly ran amuck with happiness. With every tourist attraction excluded, absolutely denied by a speckled floor, spotty ceiling, and four plain walls, I was at home.

Had I really come to Venice feeling two-sexed? too male? extraordinary? I could no longer bother to remember. Carlo transfigured me. Into the essential commonplace. The bliss of our mutual banality! Politics? Spies? Fooey! I could feel myself growing normal like a weed. Hallowed and normal. My toes dug in, my scalp shivered like a tuning fork, I was vainglorious woman and submissive girl, indiscreet and immodest, impure and in love. With his tongue at my ear and his penis touching my uterus, I felt circular and completed. Singleness had come to me when I most needed it. And quiet. And rest. The smooth hairlessness of his chest was my pillow even by day when he was not around. On it, as it breathed someplace else in space, my curly mind rested.

I examined my happy face in the mirror endlessly. Was that a new scratch of time in the glow of my forehead? Was I glowing with fever? Was I windburned? I examined each feature, each limb, each patch of skin. Was I too soft here, too tight there? When he was with me in our bulb-lighted room, I loved the moving pool of shadow under his collarbone; I adored the changing angles of his elbows. The harsh regard of his nose, the counterpoint of his baroque eyes. Day by day in the listless intensity of that room he lay lazily on his back and made me do things for him I had never dreamed of doing for a fellow American—like massage the tendons of his neck and shoulders or pick up his mail and iron his shirts or flutter my Valentine, his heart-shaped balls, with a stream of air from my lips when the day was hot.

Blind in the city of sights. Aeons ago, I've been assured, before the human brain evolved, there were only tiny bulbs of nerves bunched at the top of the spinal cord in the most primitive creatures: flashing centers of sex and smell. Like a water rat, I lived in my primordial brain. I saw little of the grandeur of Venice and less that touched me. For me there were water rats everywhere, casually at home under the landings, for me there were rotten orange peels and vegetable scraps and dead cats floating in the Giudecca. Nevertheless these details for me were sweet. For the first time in years I found myself without one thought for my responsibilities, for forging ahead, for the future. Time had slowed down, and was nearly still. I hadn't the faintest desire to write a thing, neither poem nor letter. I cabled, but rarely. Hardly anything touched my mind but the present instant—the pulpy peel as it slowly turned in the embracing water. Didn't the flow of time, too, I thought, really imply something motionless against which time was moving? I felt sure that we could normally only experience the flow because some part of us rested in, or desired to rest in, a timeless stability. In dreamless sleep each night with Carlo I seemed to enter that realm of absolute rest. And in sunlight, too, it lurked not far away. More prosaically, I felt that for my especial benefit Carlo had come along and somehow managed to tear down Manhattan—an island which for all practical purposes no longer existed—and he had instead built up around me all these smelly little islands he called Venice.

The churches reeking with incense, the fumigated palaces, and the stinking sinking rest of the show, *Cà* this and *Cà* that, the Doge's pink follies and his golden lollies, San Marco's millions of pigeons and spires —that whole show, the greatest on earth. I was the admiring type. But I wasn't born every minute. This city whose beauty begins with sluggish water and crumbling embankments terminates on high, as everyone knows, with pigeon shit on her domes; this city whose lyrical canals by common sense and consent are sewers, to herself has never denied her undersides.

In the public eye, magnificence. I noticed it. But if you catted it along the side alleys, the stagnant troughs to nowhere special, you noticed the reverse. And I'm afraid I loved the reverse in that private stay. Walls fallen in, mold where the building lines used to meet the waterline, backwater bridges with broken slats and rails, human feces and the odor of urine under bridges. But there was worse: unlovable quarters, cavelike tenements, and venomous sweatshops. Through a back door, half open to let in some air, I discovered a herd of shepherd girls from the mountain provinces sitting in rows down long lines of brown-papered tables. They looked maybe sixteen years old. They were assembling little glass animals for the tourist trade, so far as I could see and it was hard to see: the glass beads were extremely tiny and the light in which the kids were working was extremely dim. All the ground-floor windows on the street side had been covered with brown paper to keep the tourists from seeing into the shop.

The state of the nation. If you looked close. If you weren't too overawed by palaces to see the patches in Venetian pants. There *was* grandiloquence—overhead, and economic chicanery in the same high places, and tourist money underfoot in the piazza. How much longer would the nation hold together? How much longer would bigger patches and more thread do the trick? It was half a century since Mussolini had come along and offered to make the hopelessly rotten cloth whole again.

All this was noticeable . . . thinkable . . . obvious . . . but I admit I noticed it mainly because Venice happened to suit my soiled and gorgeous mood. Venice touched my divisions. The fraying core of the Millie-fleshed ego. I felt (*very* frankly) that the strong smell of deteriorating biological waste carried out to sea by the flow of her canals matched the familiar, terribly pleasant sniff in the dark of my radical medical comical tragical cynical cloacal honey-haired cunt.

Traitor and traveling salesman of my country's dishonorable intentions. Indiscreet associations and leaks in security. Poor judgment . . . or worse . . . conspiracy . . . the race for space . . . laser satellites . . . secrets of state.

Dull sublunary lovers. We rarely talked about the world outside the confines of our bodies, let alone about the jockeying for power, East and West, or the social and political shambles all over Italy. In the Italian press there were accounts of turmoil on Sardinia—another political kidnapping, a wave of arrests, a renewed terrorist campaign for complete independence from Italy and for immediate recognition of the island's sovereignty. I noticed them. But I mainly read American newspapers, hoping to keep abreast of the U.S. market and economic conditions at home, and these papers hardly knew the island existed. The *Times*, however, did occasionally print a dispatch from Sardinia, and one of these had me flabbergasted. I couldn't believe my eyes. Puddu? Mungianeddu Puddu? To this day I've treasured that clipping. Excited, I insisted that Carlo read it at once. And on this piece of news, I did indeed question him.

SARDINIAN NATIONALISTS SEIZE OFFENSIVE

CAGLIARI (AP)—Bandit-torn central Sardinia is in the grip of fear again in its darkest week of ransom kidnappings and political insurgency this year.

In a rising wave of violent secessionist protest since last weekend two model villages under construction by the mainland government were seized and burned. A prominent government official and with him the son of a wealthy Cagliari businessman were kidnapped.

Another well-known industrialist reached home, worn-out and bearded, after his family paid kidnappers a bargained-down ransom of $16,000.

The new crime wave was the defiant reaction of Sardinian guerrilla bands to the latest crackdown by 4,000 national police and army troops ordered into the island by the government in Rome to stamp out violent political agitation. Resort to banditry represents only the extremist faction of several separatist groups working to gain independence from Italy. Terrorist tactics have been repudiated and condemned by moderate groups.

The outlawed rebels, made up of impoverished islanders and escaped prisoners, are reputed to be led by a young shepherd less flamboyant but more systematic than the dashing Giuliano of Sicily. The picturesque Sicilian bandit is still vivid in the minds of Italians. The already legendary new bandit chief of Sardinia, Mungianeddu Puddu, is hardly older than Giuliano was at the height of his youthful career. He is described by those who manage to catch a glimpse of him as shorter than Giuliano, less handsome and less romantic a figure, but more ingenious as a tactician.

In addition to political kidnappings, his guerrilla tactics have so far included hit-and-run seizure of government offices, doles of ransom money during mayoralty elections in an effort to replace old-style terrorist activities, and allegedly blasphemous masses at isolated towers in the countryside.

This week's events brought the number of ransom abductions in Sardinia since January to seven. Two shepherds apparently suspected of having informed police have been slain.

Most ransoms were paid in whittled-down deals. Most of the kidnap victims reach home safely. But police are rarely given valid clues to work with.

It is an illustration of the old proverb: The sheep in Sardinia have no ears. Local people claim not to have heard anything, seen anything, or know anything.

I was astounded, skeptical, thunderstruck—there had been hardly a trace of anything like this in him, at least so far as I remembered that intense solemn lad—though I had to admit that in me there hadn't been much trace of the business magnate either. But more upsetting to me than Puddu, parties, secession, or any of these bewildering developments on the island I'd lost touch with was something else. I couldn't help being concerned for Mavi's safety. Featureless as she was for me, I worried.

There's no need to conceal the fact that the article hit me personally, not politically. I was more than curious. But I was turned inside out and topsy-turvy by what I got from Carlo when I asked. A fond grunt at first, an elusive distracting kiss on the forehead until I persisted, "It's the idea of kidnapping—"

"I know, but—"

"You *don't* know. It's for Mavi I'm—"

"Mavi!" Laughing, he put down my copy of the *Times* and picked up his own paper. "You think she might be kidnapped?" he chuckled.

"For all I know she's the adopted daughter of a wealthy landlord who—"

"Mavi is in no danger." He asserted this flatly.

"Promise me," I said.

"Promise you?" He turned a page. But he didn't go on reading. He stared at me. Then unexpectedly, he thrust the evening paper away, under our bed. "She won't be kidnapped. And I'll tell you why—provided you first promise *me* something. That you won't try to find her."

I gave my word.

He squinted at me before beginning. "When my old man asked me to take care of the adoption, he came to me suggesting someone who . . ." he paused and continued as soon as I'd stopped trembling, "well, frankly there were a couple of questions in my mind, but he was getting married—and to a woman with money, besides—a childless widow in Nuoro, twice-widowed, in fact, and three times married, very unusual in Sardinia. Her first husband was from somewhere around Bosa, I think she said. From him she had only a bit of money. From the second, the Nuoro one, she got a genuine inheritance when *he* died. I imagine she married her third for his manhood—and discovered instead that she'd married a wolf. Though I hear she's something of a she-wolf herself. Anyhow, tough-minded and hungry for husbands. Her third one, the Sardinian he-wolf, the one my father suggested, he managed to get hold of her money, as much as he could, and promptly plunked it down for the Independence fight, and when the kidnappings started, and the bombings, it wasn't safe any longer in Sardinia for the wife of Mungianeddu, she packed up with the child—"

"Puddu?" I screamed.

"Mungianeddu Puddu."

I clutched Carlo. Mavi *wasn't* with a stranger! I sobbed. I was beside myself with happiness. "Where—"

"Mother and child are on the Balearic Islands, in hiding. Quite safe. When the trouble's over, they'll come back to Sardinia."

"Where in the Balearics—"

"That's enough. It's all you need to know. What more do you want? Beautiful child. Did you see her picture—the one I sent to my old man? Last year his wife must have sent Mungianeddu snapshots of the child. We had some business. Actually it was something of a fight, a quarrel—he sent me by courier finally a picture of Mavi as a token—a sign of his memory and respect."

It *was* enough. And it was nothing at all. And indeed he wisely refrained from telling me anything further about Mavi. About Puddu, however, I was at last able to satisfy my curiosity. I admitted I was baffled about him. "When I left him, this Puddu was hardly more than a violent kind of grown-up kid, but—"

"Have you forgotten Sardinia?" he laughed. "The young are desperate."

"But why Puddu? At the top? How did he get there?"

Carlo shrugged and squinted. "Because most of the others have been killed. He has some brains, he has guts, he has luck, he was persistent, and he means business. He has also turned out to be something of a military genius, at least in the mountains. And he's crazy."

"Mad?"

"Wrong. Insanely wrong, pathetically wrong. The bloodshed could have been avoided and independence achieved in ten years, twenty years, by constitutional and legal means. And with Italian economic support. Now he can't win and all we can hope to do is hope—hope to save him, hope to stop the killing and . . . look, even if he took control of the island, even if this young lunatic won, which is impossible, the island could never survive without the support of a major economic power—Italy, France, the U.S.A., you can pick one yourself—what does our poor Sardinia have, a few chocolate factories, a few coal mines, some sugar and salt, fish in the sea—an entire people would wither of starvation—the economic factors alone—but why are we talking? They will gun him down."

There was more to it. I had to wring the facts out of him. Puddu's halo, as Carlo put it dryly, his rising popularity and authority among Sardinians who formed the base of the secession movement, had originally been founded on the number of times he had eluded and escaped from the police even when seriously wounded. His violence and ingenuity had been respected, his luck had been considered a sign of special grace. But he had risen to a height of undisputed pre-eminence during a coup of sorts. The Sardinian Independence Movement, though decades and even centuries old, was now, in fact, widely dated from the day Mungianeddu Puddu, the adored outlaw, this hotheaded shepherd of little consequence, had with his small guerrilla force, in a carefully planned operation, surrounded and seized the main radio station in Nuoro. The guerrillas had held off a police siege for almost three days while Puddu himself and Surba, the prewar jurist and architect of the Secession who had once been a member of the government, took turns constantly broadcasting their appeal for all Sardinians to join them in the just cause of a revolutionary war against continental Italy and against Italy's puppet government on the island. And then, astonishingly, they had evaporated! dissolved and escaped! The miracle of escape, which seemed unaccountable at the time, had been effected by means of a series of tunnels, previously constructed, which led through the basements of nearby buildings. In civilian garb, quietly, the guerrilla forces had managed to penetrate out through a ferocious cordon and find shelter once more in the mountains—to the proud acclaim of encouraged Sards.

But I recall that when he had finished telling me this, Carlo repeated mournfully, "But one day they will gun him down," a phrase which did little to calm my anxieties in any direction, least of all for Mavi.

As to any danger Carlo himself was in, he said not a word. As for the open maneuvering in the Italian parliament and the semi-covert preparations which the Partito Sardo d'Azione, his umbrella organization for a veritable shower of underground political groups, was making for a direct appeal to the United Nations Assembly on behalf of Sardinia; as to the irremediable factionalism and rivalry—which was murderous, I now realize—among and within the various splinter parties of the Sardinian secession . . . all these matters remained off limits to me. I was his woman. He kept everything spectacularly to himself.

Certain indications there were, certain portentous suppressions and frightening encounters.

Some of them still make me blink at my credulousness, my addle-pated inattention: Carlo was rowing, plying the single oar and leaning into his strokes. We were returning from the old ghetto. Sitting at his feet, loving the sun, I watched a motor-driven craft ahead of us pull out purposefully from the side of the canal. It was a barge, fat and heavily freighted. On board, sealed in a cargo net, was a single vast crate marked with what seemed to be Arabic lettering along one side. It caught my attention because I wasn't sure that that looming netted crate could pass under the small bridge ahead. But the barge captain, cutting his motor, slowly drifted into our path, making straight for the bridge. Three others on the deck of the barge stood watching us impassively but closely. Carlo swung us out with the big oar in a swift smooth loop around the slowing barge. From dead ahead, visible now from under the bridge and bearing down at us slowly from the other direction, came an empty garbage scow. The man on the oncoming scow waved ferociously, the freighted barge backed water and veered unexpectedly toward us, toward the center of the bridge. Carlo, shouting obscenities, scooped me up. Holding me with his left arm he caught the net that bound the crate and climbed. Below us, our gondola split, the fragile claw of a crab, crunched. The two big boats had rammed, splintering it. My mind went white. Carlo was still screaming obscene dialect, bellowing at the men in the barge (who kept coming at us) while, at the same time, swinging me up and securing his feet firmly, he caught hold of the lower rim of the bridge as the entire barge—crate and all—passed beneath it and away from us.

Below, the canal's watery light, purpled and pinked by oil from the barge, shook and hurt my eyes. We dangled there for a minute. Passers-by, leaning over the bridge with sudden faces, hauled us up.

A simple accident? I innocently supposed so. During my brief sojourn in Venice I never even saw, let alone solved, the jigsaw puzzle. The labyrinth within me was enough to cope with. In the maze I'd entered, I kept stumbling over all the jagged pieces without picking them up. Carlo soothed me expertly afterward. It was no joking matter, he admitted, it was serious, but he would *say* nothing serious about any part of the episode, nothing that made sense to me. I observed that he made no attempt to prosecute anyone, to recover any damages, or to describe the incident to the police. It's obvious to me now that he wanted to keep the police out of it. But when I questioned him at the time, fuming over his inaction, he put me to shame with his treasure-chest laughter.

Days later I thought of a love-offering. The idea of buying him a gondola excited me, as you can imagine. I strolled down to the landing where I'd seen dozens of them. They were moored out there in the water among tall thin sticks. It was twilight. Fairy-tale lanterns with elfin hats and lattice windows had been lighted. The gondoliers, dressed in somber black and white, a crowd of gondoliers, they sat smoking and chatting all down the stone stairs. I interrupted the first one I came to and told him what I wanted.

He sneered. Openly, without rising, he sneered! His face grew more heavily tanned, his features worked to a sudden eddy. Enigmatic. What misunderstanding had I blundered into? I repeated myself ingenuously. Removing his hat, he clapped it sharply against the calloused palm of his left hand. He put it back on his head. But his arms flew up. Not a word. Insulted dignity? He got up and walked away.

Before I could retreat, half-a-dozen others surrounded me. I was the lucky American. Guilty with money. One of them quoted a price, outrageously high. He hissed it. Another hissed a price still higher, "for a gondola complete with furnishings." And then the entire crowd tied into a knot around me. Silent. The two who had quoted me prices jeered and walked away.

The knot tightened, the situation felt menacing, the eyes eying me were venomous. I tried to back out. Someone made the customary obscene gesture with his arm and someone else broke into tinny jeering abuse. I swung to confront whoever—and caught a glimpse, instead, up there at the top of the stairs, of the thin man with violets, the sad cherry-lipped face of the flower seller I'd seen my first night in Venice. He was making a couple of short inconspicuous movements with his palm close to his waist.

The crowd opened. Little by little the knot came loose around me. One of the gondoliers spat. The glob slapped the quai. They moved in twos and threes away from me.

I remembered later having seen my rescuer, if that's what he was, daily, everywhere in Venice. Carlo could tell me nothing about him. But Carlo was informative, if less than comforting, about the rest of the business. "They have a strong union."

"The gondoliers?" I was taking off his shoes. "A *union?*"

"Very radical."

"Very sullen!"

"Communist."

I tried to take that in: Red gondoliers in black and white for me was oxymoron double-talk.

I must have looked perturbed, bewildered. The smile he gave me, compressed and lovely, was the most charming of all those smiles I can remember. It came to a peak, it rippled before it died. His nose did something, a sneeze that never came. He offered me his socks. "It wasn't personal."

I rubbed his feet and gently pulled his toes.

In a few days he had his own gondola. This one, too, belonged to "friends," he said. I never met them. I never asked to. And so much for the government's preposterous allegations that I was actually the owner of the gondola he used. One of the more amusing charges leveled against me in the pretrial committee investigations by Congress was that I personally transported the so-called "gondola papers" to a "dead-drop," to a hidden cache, a hole in the ruined walls of the Franciscan monastery on the lonely isle of San Francesco del Deserto . . . from which unlikely spot the secret documents I "supplied" then made their way into eager enemy hands! Drivel. Witchful thinking and mass-ass hysteria.

An espionage rendezvous?

We *did* go to San Francesco del Deserto, an exhausting haul it was, too, across the lagoon (how Carlo sweated in that unseasonable weather!).

And ten days later he vanished. Just like that. *"Ci ho da fare."* I've got some things to take care of, he said; the phrase provoked memories in my sleepless head all night. And next morning he was gone. I have reason to believe he went to Trieste, I'm not sure. I made an effort to trace him but he had covered his tracks. He disappeared, leaving me alone in his hotel room, leaving me no messages, but leaving me a legacy, my varicose memories and the bloodshot eyes of love. And for my poetry in due course more than that: a legacy of engagement with the divisive issues of my time.

But I suppose I ought to comment further on the absurdity of the prosecution's version of the San Francesco expedition.

We made love. In those towering reeds. In that brackish channel. Throughout the hot night. And for once that night I came to dread the secret weapon concealed in me. I set down here, as wholly as I can, the facts one cannot even hope to convey in court. (But see my "Aubade.") Far from the monastery, hidden in our gondola, we committed miracles.

Nothing moved or rocked. Hardly flowing under our gondola, the waters of the inlet were stagnant, soundless. Over us invisible clouds went up like a tent, snuffing stars like candles, censoring heaven by blacking it out.

But I'll tell you what the prosecution failed to find out. Catching up my pliant legs in the carpeted bed of the gondola, he drew them back until both my knees were at my shoulders and jackknifed, clowning, we played territory and mumbletypeg, we played spheres of influence and diplomatic exchanges, we played till my throne was velvet. And he held me in chivalric embrace, slaking his demon thirst in my cup. I offered him lees, I offered him dregs, I offered him the tipsy tip of my womb. He just rested there, drinking in harder, swilling in deeper, each time a little deeper, I struggled to break loose, each time a little farther, the edge of this world was coming, until with a pang of unworldly desire we left this world, leaped off the edge, fell beyond it, and helplessly he let me draw my legs down around my grail revealed to him and I found him as he came falling through my starless vacuum horror, pressing and squeezing and extracting the shimmering pulp of northern lights, the hair of comets.

I stirred. I woke. Disoriented in overarching darkness, I found him mapping me again with one hand, my shoulder and ribs and breast and throat while I kissed his teeth and one remaining flare at the end of his love lighted the night between my thighs.

And later, in utter blackness toward dawn, he interrogated me. Never had his fingers spoken like that. Responding, I answered questions silently, I answered back, an intent conversation between two breasts and a hand and five fingers. But all this speech turned to mere left-handed compliment set to music when his musical right hand went down, paying absolutely no attention to what the other three above were still talking about, and strummed me softly, a most delicate pick, now pizzicato, now legato, playing in my instrument, fiddling with my bass, harping on my viol, and keeping me enthralled until, unwitting, he found my pedal point, the resounding octave stop in my miniature organ, so that at the glide of those gifted fingers, often repeated, softly repeated, I began to swell, a prey to rousing choruses along a double keyboard, dissonant chords of song and dance where everywhere under his deft touch he held me bewitched at the dead center of my attention, unwittingly unfurling my staff of life for me in the yeasty moistness, uncurling me tenderly while I danced for him, rocking with his flute making moan in me.

Now I was all, some last objection overruled. I was all and he was there and nothing could be far enough, long enough, deep enough, high enough, splendid enough, green enough, blue enough, easy enough, terrible enough, expressive enough as his fingers spoke, musical enough as his pick plucked, graceful enough as my whole being danced my happiness around his whirling Maypole, and then to our spellbound amazement we *were* enough, deep, far, long, high, splendid, green, blue.

Easy.

And terrible.

We recovered.

We slept.

We lay sleeping. We lay wakeful on the carpeted floor of the gondola.

The shocked sound of a match striking. Glare. Blackness. His voice.

"What was it like," he mused, "when you made love with my old man? I've always been curious."

We lay exhausted in each other's limbs. "Your father?" I breathed profoundly, a dazzling intake, a fiery gasp of air. I wasn't exactly astonished that he knew, I was relieved. I was grossly eased from the topmost layers of my fair skin to my slimiest innermost organs. No, I didn't murmur bitter secrets, prurient truths into his ear, I took his whole honey ear into my mouth and rolled my tongue around its hive. I told him nothing at all.

"The sins of the fathers," I admitted, however.

I burned to tell him more. I was still more relieved when after a bit he muttered, apparently amused, "And with Flaminia?"

"You keep well informed."

Behind his cigarette he smiled an indulgent smile I could recognize from a couple of lines and he seemed to wink. "I've recently resumed contact with certain well-informed agents in New York."

I imagine I laughed. Out there in the reeds of San Francesco del Deserto, at the bottom of our gondola, it seemed a pleasantry, I saw nothing more in it than that. "You believe in keeping tabs on your friends."

"For picking up tabs, old friends are best."

"Your Flaminia?"

"Your Flaminia." He caressed my frank thighs. "You two! Of all people," he laughed goodnaturedly. "I don't understand."

The prose of love is redhot on the tongue. Instead of speaking, I took his hand and guided it into my singular duplicity.

Subversion . . . squalid subversion . . . the menace that admits of no deterrent. Toward dawn I conspired against myself. Guilty beyond a reasonable doubt. I was guilty of subverting the miraculous by insisting on sexual truth, the whole truth and nothing but the truth.

It registered slowly. One independent eye appeared to revolve in its socket and center on me. Then both his devious eyes came to a single point of delighted light. He sat up in the carpeted well, the bed of our gondola.

He was hilarious, he was raucous, he was thunderstruck, and I couldn't understand a word at first. Swamped with laughter, he rebuked me, "But why didn't you tell me!" I was one source of information he'd never penetrated. "Can you get it out?"

"Out?"

"Out. Up. I'd prefer it that way."

Light broke under heavy clouds over the eastern horizon. A slender cleft there showed like a bloodshot eye. Instantly the whole lagoon was flecked with shifting colors, varicose veins of light running away from us.

I've always had a hard time with the dialectic of my nature. Love of God is unison, but the hair's-breadth light of ecstasy refracted through my poems as through prisms, the simple sounds of desire I made into fugues of version, inversion, diversion, perversion, conversion, all this radiance and invention comes from having binaural ears and, like Carlo, binocular eyes, a long division and a gorgeous multiplication.

Many years later, when I came to realize Carlo's double-dealing in full, was I offended? Hardly. The poet, too, is a double agent who assumes a cover identity. He lingers, he wanders, he sucks up information, he communicates by subtle cipher with the central intelligence agency in our head. The successful poet is never unmasked. He is the one who keeps passing information to us while at the same time he exposes our secrets. The poems he writes, convincing messages from the enemy, bring us unbearable data, a code within a code.

How I Came to Fight

*Noi del nemico a far l'alta vendetta
ancor de' sogni le radiose cime
tenteremo ribelli.*

—SATTA

To take high vengeance against the enemy
we'll still attempt the radiant peaks of dreams,
we rebels.

I was put ashore on the west coast of Sardinia in a warm moonless darkness just before dawn. I came in on a hired fishing boat. The captain cut the engine near the beach and we drifted in. Noiselessly, I dropped over the side and walked in through a shallow wash of water and pebbles. I waded up out of the foam.

Aphrodite, her private beachhead. Foreigners had been forbidden to enter Sardinia. I rolled down my cuffs, put on and laced up my boots. I was wearing old trousers, a beat-up jacket, a shepherd's cap. Taut in my neck, backbone, every muscle, I stared up at the only height nearby, wondering if my landing could have been observed from up above. The shape was familiar: *Cazzi del Diavolo* or Devil's Pricks, as the shepherd call these characteristic erections that rise along the western coast. This black slab was a vague silhouette thrust against the star-clouded blackness of the sky. When the fishing boat, which had brought me over from Corsica, put out again, I turned, facing the invisible sea. Carrying a canvas bag full of equipment, walking backward, I slogged heels-foremost up the dry part of the beach till I gained the hard ground near the road. Reverse-walking in sand is awkward, but the precaution was necessary. My first wet prints would soon vanish in the incoming tide. If any investigation were to follow, it would appear from the direction of my remaining tracks that someone had shuffled down to the sea and apparently vanished.

On the road I waited for a lift. What arrived—slowly, out of impenetrable distance with an intensifying roar that scared the starch out of me, a roar that kept coming and coming long after the vehicle itself, as I judged it, should have appeared—turned out to be merely a farm tractor. By then I was so nervous I didn't even hail it. I was quivering and suspicious—what was a farm tractor doing lumbering along the shore at this hour of blackness? I didn't hail it, I didn't hide. I stood in the lights, stupidly holding my bag, paralyzed. It stopped.

I squeezed up alongside two men . . . farmers? They were heavily bundled in jackets like mine, plus scarves and caps. My own cap hid my hair, I looked suitably masculine, I offered cigars, which were refused. We rumbled clamorously onward, broadcasting, as I felt, my presence to an entire landscape. Farmers? The worst possibility, the one I couldn't get out of my head, was that I'd already been intercepted, that they'd been waiting for me, that they were carrying me into a trap. Even in the tightest precautions there are loopholes: I saw them all. The Corsican captain had notified the French police before I'd set out, the French had at once informed the Italians, and

I'd been picked up within minutes after landing. In a tractor? I was too tense to think clearly. But my suspicions hardened—we rolled into a roadblock.

My heart raced on ahead of the tractor, pounding as we droned toward two wooden barriers, set one behind another, closing the road. There was an armored vehicle on one side, and near the road a small white house with barred windows. We crawled to a stop so slowly, with the azure hint of dawn still so tentative, the grey mountains so close, I had plenty of chance to make a jump and run for it. But it was my first experience of this kind and I sat frozen, aghast. A sleepy soldier lazed over to us. A corporal. Heavy overcoat. Long heavy-eyed shag face. An ox with a submachine gun.

Another soldier was asleep in the car. The corporal, who had yawned his way over, leaned his weapon routinely against the tractor and asked for identity cards. Bleary-eyed, bullock-eyed, he looked at the tractor driver's papers, but he hardly glanced at the other man's. So feigning nonchalance, I merely troubled to show him I had a card and shoved it back into my pocket. In Corsica when I'd learned at virtually the last moment of the new regulation restricting foreign nationals to mainland Italy, I'd got hold of a phony Italian I.D. card. The document was not very convincing, but it was the best I could get. It was improperly stamped: the part of the seal over the photo of me didn't match up with the part adjoining it. "Documents, please," he said again, yawning.

This time I opened the folded card briefly in front of his nose, then pocketed it once more.

"Get down," he said. I got down as if I had palsy. "Documents!"

"I'm looking for work," I explained. "I'm from Trieste." This was utterly improbable. But my card said I was from Trieste.

He took the card I offered him, seized the canvas bag from my hand, looked dubiously at the bag, and opened the little folded card first.

The two in the tractor yelled—they were in a hurry—the corporal yelled back at them. Under his flashlight he studied my forged document at his leisure. He could see nothing wrong with it! He handed it to me. "There is no work in Sardinia," he said.

I took my bag from him gently, but he didn't let go. I asked him to give it back, he replied he wished to examine it, I pulled it away from him, protesting that my documents were in order and therefore he had no right to open my bag, the two in the tractor yelled again—they would leave without me—I climbed back in, the corporal cursed, raised his snouty submachine gun at us, the driver shrugged and made a wry comment to his friend, he set the machine in gear, the corporal ran in front of us, we moved sluggishly forward toward him, the corporal's fat gun wavered. We throbbed off past him into the morning. I had my bag on my lap. I was panicky, I was paralyzed with relief. Sardinia was guarded, but not well.

When I am asked, why did you join Puddu? I reply, to possess him, to make him mine. No one believes this.

For me the grammar of moral passion is copulative. New constructions of the conscience unshackle the poem, a discovered syntax of moral delight frees each soaring line from the little pursuit of its own happiness. For a poet, the genitive is plural possession . . . well, let me speak for myself alone and no man else: I'll have less need for apologies if my case is accusative. My mood was the feminine imperative of a singular man, a lover neglected in the conditional past and in the tense active present craved.

The economic, social, and political injustices inflicted on Sardinia are less well known to us than similar miseries in, say, Sicily or the south of Italy. But though markedly different in detail, the sufferings of human beings perpetuated by callous and mindless systems of oppression all over the world bear a gross family resemblance to each other, a remarkable blood kinship, and will not require rehearsal here. For let me speak truth shamefully. About grinding conditions, though I cared a little, I did not care sufficiently to have acted. About political and social inhumanity, though I care because I'm human, I'm afraid I did not care sufficiently to have chosen. I cared only that I did not care. But about that I did care. I cared enough to propel myself to action by fooling myself, by acting out of self-deception and for the wrong motives . . . for reasons that were unworthy, despicable, but in the end deeply effective.

First desire. Then commitment. First courage. Then outrage.

The paradox will be recognized. I had to act first, before I had the will to act . . . before I was persuaded . . . before I could convince even myself that my impulse was genuine. My impulse was not genuine. Which is precisely why I wished to possess Puddu, to make Puddu part of me, or myself part of him.

I had come across Carlo's doubleness with surprise. Be it noted that I chose to support Puddu in his struggle, rather than Carlo, or rather not what I mistakenly thought Carlo's position was. Not only because Puddu's fight was cleaner, starker, and more to my aesthetic taste: epic. No. In looking up Carlo I'd wanted to overtake the past again: Mavi. In seeking Puddu I wished to create myself: my life.

My expedition to join Puddu, then, was something other than I supposed at the time. Years afterward I came to see that it was a gesture of supreme vanity. First, only half-aware of the forces that were drawing me, I singled out the father of my child. I fixed upon Puddu because I felt he would convey perfect possession, unchallengeable self-possession without any further concern for my child. Second, I wanted Puddu because he had already attained that stature of violent and desperate magnanimity—a greatheartedness from which, for all my efforts as a businesswoman, I seemed to be excluded, perhaps on *account* of those too prudent efforts. Out of my heroic egoism, I chose his heroism.

Puddu is dead now and lost to me again. And yet as with joy I turn the soiled pages of my mind I am convinced that nothing dies in the great cycle of a poet's procreation. All my poems, like all my lovers, like all the ova in a woman or all the eggs in a chicken, were already on the page when I was born, an inconceivable number, of which I managed to fertilize only several thousand in a lifetime of art. The others lie fixed, one beneath another, in all their variant readings, a palimpsest for yet unborn poets who, inspired, will hit upon my final texts.

So, too, will Puddu be theirs, not mine. So different from me he was that though I could touch, smell, and look at him, I could hardly see him. But they will see him. They will decipher his moan of murderous affection better than these corrupt pages of mine can translate it. He will rise from the caves of Gennargentu where his cry was muzzled by death, and they will hear and see him as he was in life. Ugly, with his ugly melancholy smile and his cynical careful rat's eyes, nervous and dry and dying of old age in the blossom of early manhood, a lover of mankind who could not kiss because his teeth were in the way. A bullet, he entered men's hearts for an instant, a fraction of a century, that they might die and so not perish. Mungianeddu they now called him affectionately, a name in the man's own image of fondness: a name which had to be mouthed to be spoken at all, and then either swallowed with a grimace of disbelief or expelled proudly and malevolently between the gums with his deadly hatred for oppression. He was the friend only of those who knew they had already been cut down, slaughtered with all those around them, even while they were still standing and could smell no blood. He asked them to hate more than they already hated, he demanded that they love less than they were able to love, he left his godforsaken wife and my daughter, his mother-forsaken daughter, he abandoned my lamb and slew a hundred rams and assembled his flock of wolves and in the end, torn apart, racked, he died for nothing, for hope, which is less than nothing, which is only the hope that hope will not die, which is everything.

After Carlo it was not easy to commit myself to anyone. Each time after the death of love, which does not die either, the easiest thing is to go endlessly into suspicion. The most useful thing is to swing profoundly into hate. My labor of hate for Puddu's sake was not authentic; in the nature of things it could never have been. What was for him and them a war of the greatest complexity was for me a dishonest adventure, unreal, no matter how painful it seemed to me at the time. Nevertheless, it was honest in this sense: it was a line I had to cross. Though taken in self-delusion and bad faith, it was a necessary step before I could learn to handle with something approaching authentic valor and responsibility the entanglements of slavery in the mind at home, that skein of complications and realities for *me*.

I am ready to admit that clarity of motive should not be a necessary condition of intelligent choice. By misconstruing our real motives, we often reach a point further along the path we *would* go then we could have reached by struggling to attain a reasonable degree of clarity beforehand. Yet looking back after all these years, from the perspective of my later poetic wars to end the social diseases of the sexual-technological world, illnesses which fester primarily in consciousness itself and from there continuously reinfect the procreative economic structure, illnesses whose symptoms must therefore be treated simultaneously in the reproductive and phenomenological conditions of our rotten existence—from this perspective, my decision to make common cause with Puddu must appear astonishingly simple-minded. I am too ready to judge it harshly myself. An act that seemed to me then a shouldering of my neglected responsibility now appears to me irresponsible. Unrealistic. Perhaps worse. Romantic, histrionic, and frivolous. And worst of all, fundamentally lacking in integrity.

For example, I gave insufficient thought to my own interest in money, stake in capitalism, and commitment to business. Not, of course, that I was unaware of these matters, nor even that I was unaware of the plain opposition between the poverty of Sardinia and my comparative personal wealth. On the contrary, I saw the contradictions, and saw my decision as an effort to resolve them, even to expiate them, a kind of service to the social revolution which I particularly, as a businesswoman, owed . . . and would render. I failed to see, however, that the contradictions were not between me and something outside me; that the contradictions were within me; that I had already been thoroughly conditioned by the divisions of our postindustrial postcoital post-Depression society. At that time I was unable to see that for me the most effective battle (for one is never passive, one can and does retaliate, as Sartre has pointed out, with conditions of one's own choosing) was to fight not in Sardinia, but at home, and with the weapons I knew best, poetry and business, against the syphilitic deterioration of sexual consciousness.

None of this was clear until I had taken the true "false" step. For me in those weeks and months an immediate choice on the Sardinian question seemed imperative . . . and self-evident. One side was right, the other side was wrong. One side had endured centuries of deprivation and duress; the other side had remained indifferent to this unchanging detail of the social order. One side, convinced that suffering and indignity were no longer tolerable, had staked its guts on revolution; the other side had determined to disembowel the revolt. One side fought with hidden means and open desire; the other fought with open power and hidden greed. It was *possible* to choose. It was impossible *not* to choose. Choice was a general human privilege, one that imparted a kind of dignity. And for me the choice was personal . . . a family matter. In joining Puddu, I was rejoining myself. In defending Puddu, in supporting his claims and interests, I felt I was defending and supporting Mavi in the best possible way. Far better to expend my womanhood in her father's defense than to try to hallow it with her blessing.

In this, the century of choices, it is amusing and comforting to reflect that, however difficult our own decisions may be, the century following ours will ask for decisions immensely more difficult. For it is certain that the dislocation of power everywhere in the world, and from whichever quarter, will bring in its train choices of conscience more harrowing, more binding, more impossible, than any we can now imagine. As structures of consciousness grow more complex, as the material structures surrounding human life grow more unwieldy, conditions of choice will grow more desperate.

Should I have returned, when I left Venice, to corporate management? Should I have attended lectures at the New York State Archaeological Association, as in point of fact I did do later on when I finally got back to New York? Should I have joined their editorial staff and helped edit their journal, select their monographs, and chair their meetings; should I have lived alone, paid my respects to Baron, and had long lunches with Flaminia; should I have picked my way after lunch through the rotting neighborhoods of New York's West Side, including the one I had once lived and worked in, and seen how much after all it was like the sweatshops and crumble and garbage I'd seen in Venice, and still have been quite unmoved, for surely neither of the two blights could have touched me? Or should I have remained waiting in Venice with Carlo's ghostly presence between my thighs and his bass voice still in my skull, should I have waited there to endure the atrophy of love, indefinitely hoping for his return as I grew more sophisticated politically, month by month, diligently following in several domestic and foreign journals all the news and editorial views of the Sardinian situation—

. . . If the present regional government can bring the island out of its economic stalemate, it may be able to rout the hard-core separatists for good. All loyal Sardinians should be encouraged by the renewed confidence their victory has inspired not only here in Italy but in all the NATO countries. Sardinia's unique cultural heritage, treasured by Italians, need not be sacrificed. But separation is utter folly. . . .

. . . Now the Sardinian left has for some time been divided into several competing factions, each showing a dangerous adherence to Moscow, Peking, or Havana. Alone among hard-core Secessionist groups, however, the Movement for Sardinian Independence (MSI), the guerrilla faction, is the only element that, remaining stubbornly Sardinian in its refusal of any recognition or alignment from abroad, continues to appeal broadly to the notoriously island-centered populace. It is true that the Independence Movement is again credited with most of the recent terrorist action, from kidnappings and shoot-outs to derailment and industrial sabotage. But even its opponents must be impressed by a style so cocky that, until the second State of Emergency, its members were by night delivering regular news releases to local newspapers, in order to take credit for each new act of violence. There can be little sympathy in Italy, but there must be realistic respect for the rebels' abilities. The guerrillas, whether moved by justifiable loathing for the social injustices of today or by centuries of stored-up and now irrational resentment against continental domination, should be recognized by the government of Italy as an effective, if not legal, expression of Sardinian opinion. . . .

. . . The chief of the Sardinian guerrilla movement yesterday accused the United States of triggering the renewed Sardinian crisis. He warned that any U.S. intervention on the "pretext of safeguarding the integrity of the NATO missile base" would turn the island into another Vietnam.

Mungianeddu Puddu, head of MSI, the guerrilla group that virtually controls the Sardinian hinterland, refused to say whether his movement contemplated action against the missile base. "We shall liberate Sardinia," the young guerrilla leader said.

He did not elaborate. . . .

—should I have read all this and not felt overcome with compassion and exhilaration? Should I *not* have felt that I was responsible (and you, but let that pass), I myself, because I desired to act and could not act, though Mungianeddu Puddu had been my friend and more, wrong or right? Should I have loved forever on the sidelines? Or should I have gone on to challenge myself, as I had always done, by possession and transmutation?

All over Italy developments had long been chaotic, but in Sardinia they had become brutal. The Barbagia—the region of rugged mountains in the province of Nuoro—was now entirely held by rebel forces. Regular troops of the Italian army, augmented by *carabinieri* in the villages, by mobile police units in the countryside, and even for one desperate month by a division of the crack *bersaglieri*, had so far failed to flush the insurgents out of the mountains. Interestingly, the *bersaglieri* had had to be relieved of duty. They had been returned to the mainland on the pretext that new outbreaks of pro-Austrian terrorist activities in northern Italy demanded their presence there, but actually to avoid wholesale disaffection and the highly unpleasant possibility of mutiny among the troops, for many of the *bersaglieri* had political sympathies with the Nuorese guerrilla fighters. The Barbagia itself, with its serried gorges and towering escarpments, was a natural fortress. Direct military engagement with the rebels had turned out to be difficult to establish. I myself soon observed how easy it was for a line of guerrilla troops to vanish instantly at the first cracking sound of a jet plane, simply by slipping under the pitted boulders, overhanging crags, and fantastically sculptured rocks. Combined operations of ground troops, airborne troops, helicopters, and jet bombers had moved into the region in massive assaults, only to encounter no resistance. No guerrillas, only the local high-scurrying *muffloni*, wild sheep observing them from still higher peaks with glazed animal cunning in their unwinking eyes. The rebels had slinked into the villages (it was said) or into the cliffs. The villages in any case were theirs. After each army assault, rebel action continued to mount: arson, kidnappings, extensive demolition. Another group of captured rebel leaders had been tried and incarcerated for life, new reports of torture leaked out, but remained unconfirmed. And the military situation had devolved into a long-term holding operation, a war of attrition. To seal off the Barbagia, Italian government troops now held the major towns, especially Nuoro, and ringed the coast-line, though not, as I had discovered, very efficiently.

The men in the tractor remained uncommunicative. They dropped me where I asked. I realized now how important it would be to stay off the roads and consulted the detailed maps I'd brought. I took my bearings.

Heading for the interior on foot, I felt for the first hour like a silly Miss Stanley in search of Livingstone. "Mungianeddu, I presume." With the straps I'd brought I had converted my bag to a knapsack. Had the corporal put his hand inside, he would have found among other things my miniature camera and tape recorder, first-aid kit and light canteen, four concussion grenades, automatic pistol, several dozen rounds of ammunition, and my poetry notebook. I had every-thing—rations, maps, compass, pocket edition of Byron, sunscreen lotion, insect repellent—and I cut across gradually rising country in gradually rising spirits. By nine in the morning I was sweating pro-fusely. But I was full of pep and ebullient confidence. I had to cross a couple of roads near the coast. They were empty. I struck out northwest until I spotted the riverbed of Su Flumineddu.

Most of the day I followed the river. The Flumineddu flows in an irregular arc at the base of a humpy, virtually impassable ridge of mountains. The ridge curves toward the center of the island. By fol-lowing the river's course upstream, my ascent was slow, always in-ward toward the high wilderness of the Barbagia. It was midafternoon when I reached the pass.

I left the river and clambered up, using my hands. I was a four-footed ant in a gorge of white boulders. Remnants of a landslide, jumbled, these piled rocks were peculiarly square, like a child's build-ing blocks, but enormous, and exhausting. By the time I reached the top, where the pass gives way to an extensive plateau, I was dizzy with fatigue.

The soil up on top was eroded. Folds of dust. I'd seen soil erosion before in Sardinia, to the north of the Locoe and once near Noragugume, but nothing like this. It was all kinky ravines here. To get through a terrain as contorted as this, I had to walk a crooked line, narrow, with sudden gulleys on both sides. Every few yards the crust of earth gave way underfoot and turned to powder. As the late light changed colors, I had the feeling I was walking the fibrous folds and sensitive convolutions of a gigantic brain, my eyes blinked at a landscape of cerebral tissue, I walked a tightrope, the sun burned into the horizon, evening blackened the gulches, I slipped—an entire ridge slipped with me—I slid, clawing a powdery ravine for maybe a dozen feet, that's all.

Only a dozen feet. It was above me on all sides, I pulled and clawed and dug footholds and inched up . . . and down I slid in puffs of crumbling dust. I wasn't in a hole, I wasn't trapped in a pit. I could run both ways along my tumble-down ravines, which cheerfully met other ravines, embracing and twining in every crooked direction, but I was always at the bottom.

I kicked my way along till it was fully dark. I wasn't despondent, I was angry. I ate, studied my maps by flashlight, and lay down hopefully. It was warm. At sunup I planned to follow the corrugations all day if necessary till I found a way up and out.

In the morning I pursued a single compass direction through the zigzag. An endless basement of mazes. I picked my way carefully, but whatever rut I singled out would behave unpredictably, twisting, doubling back on itself and veering off again.

As the sun rose, the trenches overheated. I wound through heated coils. I stumbled, losing my cap. At some point I fell, got my face, hair, mouth full of the chalklike dust. The earth was furrows, wrinkled, curving, intersecting, downstairs, no way up. The dust on my lips, the dustless confident sun. I tried over and over again to persuade those tantalizing slopes, slowly crawling a few feet and slithering down. Puffs of hot irritating dust went up my nose.

By nightfall I was closer to the center of the Barbagia—I had everything I needed—but which way up and out?

The day following that was worse. The water in my canteen, which I'd been carefully rationing, was nearly gone. Constantly thirsty, I could only moisten my lips. If I walked, the sun followed me on a leash. Sitting still was tantamount to waiting on top of a funeral pyre. If I ran, the sun played games, zapping me like a metal ball down pinball alleys of glare, bouncing me off the walls.

The heat rose in the morning. I tore off my jacket. The air was heavy. It was compressed. I was under pressure, trudging through

sealed tunnels, down at the bottom of roiling liquid air that was running now all over my body and down my sopping clothes. I took off
my shirt and ran bare-breasted. I rolled in the dust. I slowed down
and walked. When I walked, the sun circled me slowly, searching me
out, focused on me. Someone was reading me with a magnifying glass.
I bolted up a long powdery wall and discovered I was sliding down
instead, rolling and tumbling to a lower level still. A sub-sub-basement.
Deeper corrugations and wrinkles of this flaming brain. Mad to break
loose, I stripped, I took off my peel, my pants, my underwear, rubbed
sun lotion all over me, and jumped along, footloose. Free. Bounding
off. I scattered everything. For a while that felt ecstatic. Then
my soles burned. I ran back for my shoes and couldn't find them.
I trotted on, baby-naked, loose-limbed, hot-headed. My brewery
breasts sweated beer. My knockabout shanks rocked like a horse, I
was riding myself. My out-of-pocket elbows crawled up a landslide,
my stewed bottom skidded. I careened. Dust. Backsliding, sidewind-
ing, elbowbending, nose, pores, teeth, tongue, lips. Dust. Lower. A
sunken cavity. Hotter.

Words and faces came to me at last not from my own frying
brains, but from the thirsty crinkled brain underneath me. The CIA
simmered. Below, in my gigantic earth-brain, I opened twisted negotiations with Mungianeddu. He and I had a splendid bargaining conference, a dream with all the trappings of labyrinthine reality. I spoke
to him at length of the strategic missile site, of NATO, of U.S. intentions and limitations, of the coveted Maddalena naval base. He was
wary. He was unrealistic. I was displeased with him. "The economic
factors," I argued.

"We have coal. Cork. Sugar. Fishing. Salt. Chocolates—"

"But, my friend—" I expostulated, throwing up my hands.

He smiled, showing all his teeth, many of them rotting. "Your
friend! I am offered friendship." An angry grin. To his lieutenant:
"Make a note of that. She offers us friendship."

Unperturbed, CIA in my nightmare, I smiled patiently, Ameri-
canly, procedurally. I brought him back to business and down to
brass tacks. "I didn't come over here empty-handed."

He extended his hands slightly. "Americans are open-handed in
surprising ways." He opened the fingers of one hand, showing the
palm. "They offer friendship." He opened the other hand. "They
offer aid." He looked at me. Slowly he closed his fingers. "If we refuse, they are disappointed." Two fists remained.

I was sympathetic but hardheaded. "You need—"

"We need nothing," he said. "We will win *because* we need nothing. We are shepherds, for us this is normal life, guerrilla life, out here in the harsh sun, out here in the middle of nowhere."

"And weapons?"

He shrugged. "Everyone needs weapons."

"If the arms come from us, then the kidnappings will have to stop," I objected. "The terror must stop. Public opinion in my country—"

"We must do what we can. Sardinia has been enslaved too long. It is now too late in the history of nations for Sardinia to remain polite. Italy tells us that we are a region of herself, but in fact we are her colony, an oppressed colonial people, under the rule of a corrupt puppet government, under the thumb of an army of occupation. We know this clearly because we have suffered not one but many invasions from the earliest times to now—Carthage, Rome, Spain, the Arabs, the French, and now Italy—but always we have lost one master only to be yoked to another. Italy is the present, the very last, the United States must not be the next, do you understand my meaning? You speak tenderly, like a father, of the missile base in the south, you dream comforting maternal dreams of a new naval base in the north near La Maddalena. But we will never invite a new invader!"

All this while, stiff and unmoved, he held his two fists outstretched. I allowed myself a bit of boldness. I reached out and opened his left fist. I pointed to his palm—empty, calloused, and steady. "What would you like in there? Tanks?"

"Tanks," he said, examining his palm, "are visible. We would be destroyed. Do you know how many people there are in Sardinia?"

"One-and-a-half million."

He nodded. "Do you know how many of them believe in the freedom of Sardinia?"

I didn't know. "One-fifth?"

"One-and-a-half million," he said, "but do you know how many *true* believers there are in the freedom of Sardinia?"

I thought I might venture a conservative estimate, but I had no chance.

"Less," he said before I had spoken. "The number of true believers is equal to the number of rifles I can furnish."

The guard in the doorway spoke up unexpectedly, or rather shouted at me, "For every rifle, two of us!"

"Rifles," Mungianeddu repeated. "The Colt AR-15."

"We can't supply American weapons," I explained impatiently.

He motioned with his chin. The guard disappeared into the shadow, came back, and placed a rifle across Mungianeddu's open palm. "We already have one," he observed. "Mine." He didn't exactly smile, but his mustache appeared to get longer and wider. "When fired, it hits with very high speed. Interesting. It seems to explode whoever gets in the way."

"American arms are out of the question," I repeated politely, realistically. "We want to leave no traces of any deal. But we might be able to supply the German T-223. In limited quantity." I moved to open the fingers of his other hand. He kept it shut. Clenched. "What would you like in this hand?"

He didn't let me pry it open. He didn't answer. He kept his right fist clenched and his eyes steady. "And ammunition?" he said. "What about ammunition?"

"Sufficient ammunition," I nodded, "of course."

"Then," he said, opening his fist, "in this hand, friendship." I clasped it and was nudged by a foot. Foot nudged me repeatedly. It turned out to be a boot. Didn't know I'd been sleeping, didn't even remember lying down. I yawned and stretched. Boot kicked me. I sat up sharply.

Slung over his back was a rifle. He wore the shepherd's costume. Peaked cap. Scarf, heavy jacket, pants tucked into his boots. The scarf was wound across his mouth. In this heat! I was overjoyed to see him . . . them. Above him, up on the ridge, were two others. Their scarves, too, covered their mouths. Expressionless. Wordlessly peering down at me. From their eyes I saw that I was naked. Eyes eying me over their scarves. Gun muzzles eying me over their shoulders.

Not a word. Lying on their bellies, they lowered a rope and hauled me up. Below me, their friend watched steadily, indecently, as I climbed.

At the time it never occurred to me that I had been under very steady surveillance since I had entered the pass, watched mistrustfully from one of the nuragic lookout towers high on the slopes of Gennargentu. What had saved me was ripping off my male clothes.

They were hungry. They'd come down fast. Who knows how many months they'd been up there, isolated in the mountains without a woman? Only in retrospect did I consider that factor.

Deprived of my weapons, cash, and documents, gracefully equipped with my bare self only, I was no doubt at a disadvantage. In thinking back over my close call and subsequent arrival at the guerrilla camp, I am again and again astonished at how I was treated. My nakedness was covered at once. I was given something to put over me—a woolly sheepskin jacket—too hot, but at least it reached my thighs—I was given water, a cap to keep the sun out of my eyes, a ride on a donkey. Of course I was also treated as a prisoner, my hands were roped behind my back, but the best part of it was, I wasn't forced to walk. And when you not only remember how long these men had been deprived of women, but recall how brutal the Sardinian attitude toward sex can be, realize how far we were from the nearest town or army unit, and imagine how simple it would have been for them to have taken me by lousy lust right there in the dust, the forbearance and discipline of these three men seem remarkable. Only half-rational still, hardly able to speak, I regarded their gentleness as miraculous.

My captor, however, was human. He rode behind me, spurning the reins from time to time. As though for sheer luck, every now and again he would rub my breasts bobbing under my jacket as his surefooted donkey slogged and lurched clumsily along the ridges.

They took me not to their lookout station, but to headquarters. We passed gradually through a canyon and up into the boulder-strewn mountains. Intercepted by sentries along the route, we were soon escorted and surrounded by eight or nine befuddled armed men. We clipclopped into a rubbly clearing some thirty yards distant from a Bronze Age tower. I grew apprehensive when another dozen men appeared, shouting hearty, grim approval of my sweating beauty.

"*Lampu mi falet!*"

"*Tittas!*"

"*Regalu de Deus!*"

My savior and captor quickly got off. He slid backward off his small donkey and came toward me . . . to untie my wrists? . . . no, to take back his *mastruca* jacket. Idiot! He'd decided I would no longer need it. I protested vigorously.

He desisted—fortunately—for by now the megalithic foundations of the immense tower had begun oozing men. Dozens of armed guerrillas came trickling down through invisible gaps between prehistoric stones. They didn't pour or spill out. They seeped, sauntering over at their own honey speed. There I was, a ludicrous sacrificial golden-headed sun-virgin trussed up on a donkey, with shuddering udders and sweat-anointed loins looking askance through an opened jacket . . . and these warriors didn't push or hurry. No people are more callous when it comes to women, more dignified and tough-minded, and in their own way chivalrous. They offered to help me dismount.

There were well over a hundred of them now solemnly milling around me. Though I trusted them individually, I didn't trust this undisciplined crowded situation, I was alarmed by their numbers, by so many moody booted smelly leatherskinned gun-handling men. My hands tied in back, I tried hard to get myself down off that donkey.

"Let me alone!"

"Allow us to help you!"

They were too gallant to let a lady manage all by herself, they offered me two hundred arms. I remonstrated frantically, that I'd come to join them, that I was all for Sardinian Independence, that they had no right to treat me as a sexual toy, that I was an American citizen, etc. . . . No use. They were determined to assist me. Now it is remarkable how long it can take a hundred determined men to remove one pretty, foreign, naked, and protesting girl from a small donkey. Politeness here overreached itself. Discipline crumbled. I found myself at the center of an unruly obsession to help move me up, off, left, right, forward, backward, down, around: a thousand awkward fussy fingers.

There's no telling how far out of hand things might have slipped. But at the height of this demonic courtesy, a frigid disturbance seemed to gel the crowd, crackling icily inward. Suddenly I was vertical again, my two legs came together, I discovered I was standing shakily, unsupported, my own two feet on the ground, unsquired. Men parted around me; I found myself face to face with a figure of immediate authority: short, but absolutely ferocious. This scowling devil . . . I didn't recognize him.

I should have. He hadn't changed much: he had the contemptuous eyes of a fanatic, he was scarred at the chin and forehead, he was heavier, more lined, a rigidly tensed muscle of a man, more and less than a man. The ironically patient voice and scornful mouth of a zealot sure of his time and biding it. Puddu of course, but I was too dizzy and short of breath to know him. He knew me, at least! Dear terrible Puddu, who had delivered me once in childbirth and now again delivered me.

He spoke only a few words, charged but quiet, moving his thick neck bluntly from right to left as he reminded each one of them crisply of the American girl who had acted as "one of us." He recalled to their minds the gravid foreigner, he spoke eloquently of the young mother interrogated by the police immediately after childbirth, who had said—what? About the ritual at the tower, she had said—

he reminded them—not a word. She had seen nothing, she knew nothing.

I knew *him* now, I recognized him with a ripple of shock, and grasped what his eloquence was about. To the Sardinian, silence when confronted by the police is a statement of kinship, an act of blood brotherhood, and in a foreigner, probably something that can best be described as a personal affiliation with the terrain and its inhabitants, with the geography and history of a rocky people. Like and unlike the parallel *omertà* in Sicily, the silence of hard Sardinia has been a reductive, abrasive rebellion throughout her subjugation, covertly nationalist in mood, and defiantly independent in fact. I did not know then that word had also spread about other matters as well: it was immediately understood by every man whom Puddu addressed, it had been widely reported ever since the event, that the heroine-celebrant-mother of the tower was also something more than a woman. As Satori had written me once in a letter the year after I left the island, I had achieved in my absence something of the status of a myth.

Good God! Unbound, I was now regarded with as much superstitious reverence as before I'd been manhandled with gallantry. My sheepskin was touched for luck and kissed for grace as I made my way, following Puddu, through the once turbulent, still sex-starved troops, who accorded me the respect of total silence. A couple of grumpy old men who hadn't been able to get near me before slyly lifted the hem of my *mastruca* to dip their fingers in for blessing as I went by. But after being tested like ripe fruit, what a pleasure to be treated like holy water! At that moment I was helter-skelter with happiness. I had come to put my body on the line as a fighter; I could hardly have anticipated that in due course of time I was also to be venerated—by all those troops serving in the Barbagia—as the Liberation's sacred whore.

Puddu left me in the care of a man considerably his senior, white-haired and evidently a high-ranking guerrilla officer, Surba was his name, who led me into the tower. (This was Neneddu Surba, the greatly beloved former attorney who now drafted all the political strategy, the propaganda and proclamations of the MSI.) We entered at the side, under a typical nuragic lintel construction. We were in semidarkness, he helped me over great protruding stones as we ascended the corkscrew passage. He took me to my "room"—this was not much more than a niche, a cramped stone recess. Damp straw on the floor. Windowless, but with some light dusting through the chinks. Surba's wrinkled smile, his swollen lips pressed in a confident arc, his soldierly salute, gave me courage. I got something to drink, something to eat, something to wear.

I'd made it.

And then I slept, unmolested and unheeding, for twenty-two hours.

When I appeared outside dressed in boots, heavy pants, shirt, and cap, the men cheered. I was taken at once to confer with Puddu.

He sat on an outcropping of stone that had been a wall millennia ago, talking energetically in the midst of a group of his lieutenants, some even younger than he. "So," he said as I came up, and I was taken aback by a note in his voice that wasn't a shepherd's bantering, by an unkind mockery, "tell me, what are you now, a Doctor of Archaeology? Are you planning to dig up another buried city for us? More of our past?"

"I'm planning," I replied with military formality, "to build the future and help create history."

He shook his head caustically. He snorted. He laughed indulgently and said to the others, "I know better than you who she is, she's the first American tourist to visit the new Sardinia!"

"Tourist!" I disputed this hotly, even (I'm afraid) insolently.

He consulted with the other officers in sudden Sardinian, which I couldn't understand. I observed him closely. Clean-shaven, but with a mossy mustache, harsh cheeks stained reddish-brown like cork-tree bark, wind-lined, sun-hardened, he was somehow organic with the terrain and yet, for all that, unnaturally tense in his oversized hands, every movement rapid-fire. To Surba he swung, and then to me, and challenged in Italian. "The truth! Out with it! Did you come to give the world an entertaining, exclusive, personal interview?" He jumped up from the wall. "With me? With us?" He gestured at his men.

"I came to fight!"

Everyone laughed goodnaturedly. A couple of them lighted up those nearly black, crooked, familiar little cigars—*fica*—puffing with amusement in my direction.

"Fight?" Puddu too chuckled, unimpressed. "Do you know what you can do for us?" His heavily arched brows signed this as out-and-out lechery.

"How many men do you have?" I asked.

"One thousand, one hundred and twelve," he replied promptly. "In the mountains. As of yesterday."

"And one woman," I replied firmly. "As of today."

I knew my men. Mungianeddu's lieutenants jumped up to congratulate and appreciate me. They clapped me on the back and shoulders and elsewhere. I had my first chance to look them over. Besides Neneddu Surba, there were Trumentu, Pipiè, Diddinu, Totoi; sinewy, intrepid men whom I got to know in due course, though then naturally I didn't know their names. They were badly in need of shaves and roughly dressed in army fatigues and brown sheepskin jackets. (Gone was the antique Sardinian costume I'd grown used to seeing years ago, the black stocking-caps and white balloon trousers, gone with the advent of the present day.) The besieged, beleaguered rebels. I'd never before seen a group of hemmed-in officers. Hungry? Exhausted? Chopfallen? These men, in fact all of Mungianeddu's troops, to my surprise looked well fed, ticking with energy, chuckling and sanguine. It wasn't only food.

I guess Puddu had begun studying my stalwart stance. For some time he'd been moving around me in circles with a sinuous muscular heaviness that suggested a jawful of fangs beneath his mustache, beneath his humor. When he moved like that, though shorter than the other men, he looked deadlier.

He surprised me by putting his hands on my shoulders with weight. He stood blocking my view of everyone and everything else, examining my eyes. Was he thinking of Mavi? Neither of us, I knew, would say anything about her. I could not help detecting the old unpleasant odor, ashamed as I was even to notice that I noticed it, Puddu's memorable powerful body odor that was animal and vegetable both. I frowned. I had perspired freely for days myself. This was something else. Was I mistaken? At an angle of the tower's embankment nearby, I'd glimpsed on my way over a couple of monstrous wild boars—recently killed, they'd been strung up—and though I didn't shift my frown from his scowl, not for anything now would I have done so, my nostrils reeled, I thought of the boars and thought the redolent stench was theirs. But no, my first impression had been accurate. I breathed him. We breathed together. Puddu breathed, I breathed, we breathed in unison, I breathed his breath, my nostrils wide. All of a sudden he turned away and said, "She will fight."

I confess the smell of the man still weighs on me. I came in time to associate it not only with the odor of terrorism, kidnappings, bomb-throwings, and knife-stickings, but with the man's saintliness as well, his unwashed odor of sanctity in the service of an oppressed people. Then, however, it only distracted me, and I frankly despised myself for being American, hygienic, snout-hearted, and at bottom insensitive.

He led me, followed by the rest, directly to those two mammoth bristly boars dangling from ropes. He shouted something. Someone immediately tossed him a long butcher's knife.

Puzzled, I watched him cut through heavy fat and muscle. He worked expertly, careful-careless with the reddening knife, slitting the abdomen to an exact point. Out toppled the massy pink-grey-blue organs. He caught them adroitly. The metallic odor of warm pig blood was in my nostrils now. Calmly, he whacked off the whole liver of the boar and brought it to me. He sliced off one end, steaming raw liver, chewed it and swallowed it.

My turn.

I downed my wedge.

How I
Came
To Trial

I dream'd that Greece might still be free.
                    —BYRON

The touching respect I received from the guerrillas never let up. They were loath at first to let me get into the fighting. A woman guerrilla? In this respect they were backward, pigheaded, chauvinistic, intolerable. Had I been unalloyed woman, I'd never have made it. My epic genitals, however, commanded a certain veneration.

From their behavior toward me, sexual and otherwise, I can only judge that they saw me as I saw myself, a woman alloyed with the metal of a man. Magnetic, animal woman. Within a few short months, I had the nerve to compose poems in Sardinian, a tongue I barely knew, and quickly, to my grand astonishment, I became a new rallying figure for the Secession, the idol of the guerrilla troops, their heavenly mistress, albeit chaste as yet, the embodiment of the liberation in female form, flame, and force, somewhere between their Helen and their Homer, their Maud Gonne and their William Butler Yeats, their François Villon and their Joan of Arc. They honored me and made the most of me.

Their attraction to me was paradoxical. Partly, it was awe before the mystery. They'd been told, they were incredulous, yet they believed. My female pudenda bore the male addendum. I was a prodigy of nature. But most of them had never known an American girl before and amused me by attributing my masculine womanhood to national differences. In part they put the whole thing down, blondeness and boldness, breasts and balls, to my being American. Whatever the basis of their awe, I soon won something better, their wholehearted admiration—respect for my free and vigorous bearing, my womanly self-confidence, my will to make common cause with them.

I was taken in hand frequently, with a kind fellow-feeling that extended to training maneuvers and battle positions. For long days, interminably, I was shown only how to service weapons, not even how to fire them—how to take apart, clean, and reassemble rifles and machine guns, usually with someone's flattering attention to my muscled arms, hidden breasts, and small hands. I wore men's clothes of course, but there was no denying I was softer than a man. Soon they were showing me how to shoot, adjusting my stance, holding my arms steady, squeezing me as I squeezed the trigger. They showed me how to take aim from behind a boulder, how to spread both my semidivine legs wide for maximum stability, how to sight over the vertiginous drop of a crag, how to fall—just so—flat on my special belly, how to keep the tempting line of my body safe behind a small rock while firing: I got more tips than I needed in perfect bottom alignment, comfortable breast arrangement, and fine crotchety adjustments. To illustrate the most effective positions, often they lay down on top of me. I couldn't blame them. Their help was not disinterested, sure. But it was generous, and once in battle, with a thoughtful care I'll never forget, Mungianeddu Puddu himself covered me at the height of intense gunfire.

But we were rarely alone together. When we did meet, I felt as though right through our skins a communication began taking place between us, but a communication without content, a tangible eerie communion of our flesh based on Mavidda. A couple of times when I brought up the subject of Carlo Satori he seemed uneasy. And finally I confessed that I knew what had happened to my daughter. It cleared the air. We each recognized the logic that obliged us not to make a habit of speaking of her. Nevertheless, once, not long after I arrived, he surprised me by saying into my ear, "These days I remember why my daughter is so comely." Then unexpectedly he burst into a white-hot sun of a grin, as resplendent in him as I felt suddenly dark and hurt and tender.

Though he didn't ask me to cook or sew, it took a long while before he would let me see action. I had all I could do just getting used to the painfully rugged, physically difficult conditions of guerrilla life, an existence these men had been used to always as shepherds. Toughening-up "maneuvers" for me for a couple of months consisted mainly in accompanying our couriers (Trumentu was in charge of this phase, and he had a highly developed courier system), serving as a scout high up out of the way during daylight infiltration, and trudging through the jagged sole-wrenching wilderness from base to base. Every division moved, Mungianeddu believed in moving us around to keep us safe and to confuse the enemy by putting in frequent appearances where our men were least expected. Remembering the American Revolution for independence, I was hopeful. Hadn't General Braddock been vanquished by equally small forces of American guerrillas employing similar tactics? On these dreadful mountain expeditions, by the way, I often managed to pick up prehistoric shards, flakes of flint, and worked cores. I had to throw them away of course, I wanted no extra ounces of weight, but they served to recall the scientific life with Satori not far from this very region. I vowed again to return one day if I could to a peaceful free Sardinia to fulfill my girlish vow of casting a clear light on the origins of civilization and becoming someday (how far away it seemed then!) an archaeologist in my own right. Some of the hidden caves we passed, and some we camped in, were quite spectacular. In them, the obsidian pieces I came across simply by scratching through the top-soil were now and then beautifully chipped, perfect little blades. When washed, they looked strikingly like phalluses cut from precious stone. In the end, weight notwithstanding, I succumbed. I brought a couple back to the States to show Satori.

By day and most often by night, in bands of five men, no more, we stumped over jagged terrain, weighted down with guns and ammunition. I seemed to grow feeble, not stronger. Tears of self-pitying exhaustion, which no one saw, escaped my eyes right on the line of march. I drank my tears because I was tormented by thirst, too. Occasionally we were spotted by reconnaissance planes and I perversely found these planes a relief. At least the endless pushing had to stop. The monotony of fatigue was broken. On a number of daylight deployments we were strafed by machine guns from helicopters and planes, large and small, and several times pounded with bombs. The ferocious slashing impact and gut-grabbing boom scared me absolutely miserable, I confess, even though the bombing was ineffectual: we kept always to the thick of rock-sheltered cover, we were only a handful, a scattered, invisible target. It was lots easier, I noticed, for one of our well-concealed marksmen to hit a bee-mad, bumbling, spitting plane than for those lightning-fast insects to connect with one of us.

Puddu had very little time for me. I saw him intermittently when his missions crossed mine or when I was called to take part in maneuvers under his direct command.

His policy, he once told me—and military policy was his, not Surba's—was to discredit the government. He made absurd their claim of a "blockade" in the Barbagia, not by getting out of it (his guerrillas could not yet survive outside the natural protection it provided) nor by challenging the enemy in even a limited engagement (which he could not afford) but by piercing the periphery of the net nightly, at will. He therefore kept up an astonishing rhythm of onslaughts against highways and railways—curves, overpasses, bridges, embankments—hoping to demoralize the reluctant Italian boys, the continental troops hemming him in, and in any case to show his fellow Sardinians everywhere that his, Mungianeddu's, own strength was undiminished. His strategy, which he nicknamed "Mosquito," was to move as many men as he could as soon as darkness fell, in units of five men, five to ten kilometers apart. These Mosquito units, tremendously mobile, obtained from Separatist supporters in the villages volumes of information nightly about the constantly shifting disposition of government troops and vehicles and potential targets. These were often daringly assaulted.

But I think what probably galled Rome and Cagliari even more than his military audacity and invulnerability was another form of audacity—Surba's doing. That year, Puddu began to issue "laws"— in effect proclamations and decrees. First, barely a month from the time I arrived, he proclaimed the *de facto* existence of a new nation, the sovereign nation of Sardinia, and declared his army of volunteers to be the temporary trustee for the future national government. In the latter's name, he then "abolished" the existing regional government, "passed" land distribution laws, and "decreed" a moratorium on the villagers' debts. Though their practical effect was nil, the propaganda value of these measures was enormous. They were gestures without force, but they were convincing to the villagers. In a number of villages, elections were gradually held during the year and officials appointed, forming a local infrastructure of government —clandestine, rudimentary, but with representatives appointed and ready for the forthcoming revolutionary assembly. Surba was looking forward to an actual gathering, the secret convocation of a constituent assembly somewhere in the mountains by the following year, to institute an extra-legal underground state.

To accomplish this and invest it with credibility, the pace of armed maneuvers had to be kept up persuasively. In effect Mungia-neddu was trying to tie up and occupy the entire countryside after nightfall. It was on one of these night treks in fact that I underwent my first trial by firearms. It occurred by accident, outside a village at an *azienda*. We were surprised by a handful of government soldiers. They were as surprised as we were, probably because they'd been stealing from the farmers. We ran into them as we rounded the corner of an isolated farm building. The fighting was instantaneous and for several minutes intense, I was frightened completely sick and senseless, it was dark, everyone collided, running and swearing and screaming, and the invisible guns going off were inches away. I felt, rather than saw, a shadow raise a shadowy rifle from a pale half-open doorway, into which he must have been about to flee, and I ran toward this shadow insanely, pressing the trigger of my automatic rifle without taking aim, trying instead to get the end of my rifle as close to his darkness as possible, I was trying to stick him with a sword, hysterical, all my training gone. But I shattered him. I don't know how he missed me, maybe because I was running. Running so fast that as his shadow fell I ran right into him, supporting him as he went down, that solid limp uniform. He seemed to bow, he seemed to kneel, he seemed to hand me his rifle as he went down. But he was dead.

We regrouped afterward, back the way we'd come. Now at each rustle in the surrounding countryside every man in our "star," our customary formation for precaution, dove for the rocks and vanished from sight. It wasn't till we were well away from the farm that I felt a thing, and knew my fingers were drenched. The feel of that sagging soggy uniform lingered on my fingertips, the very texture of death for me. Was that sweat? Or blood? It was much too dark to tell. Liquid fear is what it was, the sorrow, satisfaction, and terror of a few moments ago had come oozing out underneath my fingernails, my underarms, my eyes, my lips, my groin, my heavy lucky feet. Were his feet, less quick than mine, pursuing me? Turning, I reassured myself. Yet circling away from those farm buildings as in a slow nightmare-after-death, I had the distinct feeling that somewhere back there we had killed each other, and that somewhere he, too, was still moving on, in the other direction.

Turudda had been injured in the left arm, perhaps by the same shot that had failed to hit me, and he confirmed the fact that I'd taken my first enemy soldier. I wasn't congratulated, we swept round the village and continued without comment, but I discovered in succeeding days that I'd become a kind of heroine-mascot-idol, all in one. Puddu, at Surba's suggestion, made me a corporal. And I was nicknamed "hazel nut." *Nuzòla*—the little nut.

The men looked forward to my presence in any action—as though it assured them of some sort of special blessing—always surrounding, protecting, and praising me. I took part in a number of strategic assaults, but one of them especially, an attack on a mountain sentry station, will interest readers familiar with my later archaeological career. Puddu had determined to eliminate the post by burning it to the ground with gasoline. But because it was so well defended, we couldn't get close enough, and he resorted instead to undermining it with a tunnel. I took no small part in the digging operations: I held lanterns, emptied baskets of dirt on the double, and helped maneuver timbers into place. Telephone lines had been cut as the attack began and the station's radio actually stolen half an hour before the attack by an old man. Working under Puddu's instructions, he had delivered a supply of wood. He'd put the transmitter into a sack and walked away with it! Still, there was no telling when regular reinforcements might arrive, and the tunnel was dug with all possible speed. Our men kept up sporadic fire, meanwhile concealing all evidence of digging, starting the tunnel shaft from behind a hastily erected barricade. Fortunately, the soil was easy to dig, there were two men with pickaxes digging side by side in a tunnel six feet high, they were amazingly quick about it, each pair relieved in rapid shifts, while shovel men and basket men emptied the dirt out at a run.

When it was done, Puddu delivered a message to the besieged station, sending it with one of the prisoners who had been captured in the first rush on the area. This pathetic devil was forced to walk toward the station, shaking with horrible fear that his own troops would shoot him by mistake as he approached, or that we would get him in the back for spite. The message he bore revealed to the besieged (and the prisoner's own observations confirmed) that their post had been tunneled under; that they were standing on dynamite; that the men inside had five minutes to surrender or be sent heavenward. They surrendered. We took everything we wanted rapidly from the post, including two mortars, two tripod machine guns, and dozens of automatic arms. Puddu then released the prisoners as always —we could not keep prisoners, and would not kill them—admonishing them as always to persuade their buddies that our cause was as just as our men were merciful (an amazing technique which reduced the army and police will-to-combat enormously, making no friends, maybe, but hordes of lukewarm enemies who surrendered easily and themselves kept the enemy troops in a constant state of demoralization). Minutes later, Puddu allowed me the honor of setting off the dynamite charge to destroy the empty station. And the blast went off some twenty yards to the left, leaving the station intact!

Highways and railways were cut nightly. Assigned to a sabotage unit, I soon got to be fairly expert in the simple art of setting charges. We took the main roads and connecting roads, severing bridges and toppling embankments, and railroad service in Sardinia became not service but a joke. I don't wish to give a boastful impression of derring-do, but there's one explosion of talent, one daring exploit I can't refrain from relating: in the very midst of all these activities I managed to do what I needed to do to survive. Yes, I managed to write poems.

Poetry in these frayed, bloody times? I must be careful not to paint a misleading picture of my guerrilla experience. Readers may very well be avid to hear more about my combat record. These memoirs, however, are not a simple account of the outward bravado that leads to history, they are a circle around the interior dread that leads to art. Would it upset you to hear that the bloodiest of ambushes did not frighten my spirit half so much as the good poems I brought off, sometimes two or three a week, composed at times on the teetering seesaw of survival? One by one they fell into place, a cycle of revolutionary sonnets whose subject is actually the history of revolution and change in poetry from Hesiod and Heraclitus to García Lorca and Allen Ginsberg. This virtuoso sequence, in which, sounding the call for revolution, I imitated in modern tonalities the mood of each poetic innovator, working entirely from memory, later earned me my first major recognition when the sequence was published upon my return to New York. In fact, as these pages should make plain, the two shivering impacts that transmuted my poetry from brass to gold and beat the plowshare of technique into the sword of art were two great departures from the self, the journey of love and the journey of courage.

Trivial by comparison, but enormously helpful too, were the Sardinian combats in poetry out in the field. The ancient art of the poetry tournament: this taxing tradition is still very much alive on Sardinia. Oral epics, long ballads and satires, and improvised verse challenges. It was considered a sport. Contests between rival would-be poets and between accomplished masters formed a frequent entertainment. The men were used to them at home, they told me, after the *ballutundu* on feast days, and they loved the sport loudly. They clung to the ponderous stones of the nuraghe, a setting genuinely romantic, while below in the clearing, surrounded by the rest of their audience, two or more poet-contestants would stand, flinging rhymed couplets at each other, challenges, sharp questions, innuendoes, even insults, to which reply would come in equally mordant and often elegant put-downs. Saverio Balloreddu, a quondam lawyer and now a captain in our forces, was a master at this game—his style a good-humored homespun, covering a rhetorical dagger of wit. When he improvised, he had the men laughing with him, verse by verse. They hushed with respect when he recited memorized verses (of his own making of course), sometimes, it seemed, by the hour. They were listening to stanzas about themselves—individual men and particular battles—the long poem on the fight for Secession which he was apparently always composing in his head while on active duty. When I mentioned to Balloreddu that I, too—well, you can imagine. He had me up there with him at once, and we had it out. I foundered, I tried, I blushed. Often I didn't even get all the details of what he was saying about me that made the men choke with gargoyle laughter. Yet if I managed to reply with a couplet, however lame, however *italiano* instead of *sardo*, the men responded with enthusiasm. I was expected to cut a poor figure in their language: but how they appreciated it if I made the attempt! The point was not how well or how ill I composed my lines; the wonder was that I could do it at all. They were so amazed that by the end I was voted the winner (one of the only times Balloreddu ever lost!).

I competed often after that. And I learned to invent lines I was sure I could handle, about simple personal things for which I knew simple personal words—about my own fears and the panic of my thoughts under fire, about being dead and causing death, about blisters and tears and Mungianeddu Puddu. I always improvised, every word. Though I never stopped making mistakes in *sardo*, I developed fluency, confidence, and a sense of dramatic phrasing. Later on, the games I played in English verse with audiences all over Europe and America, my spontaneous improvisations on a theme suggested by the audience, for which my poetry recitations quickly became renowned, were nearly child's play for me. They had their start in these boisterous relaxations from the strains of armed conflict.

The prosaic conflict, the dangers of the daily fight: I tell you, what saved me again and again, the blessed thing that kept my nerves cool even when my thoughts panicked, was that I really did care about something else other than Sardinian Independence and our military victory. I cared about art, even about solitude, and certainly about being physically, sensually alive in those primitive cliffs, as alive as the bees and the big black ants. I cared intensely that I was being carried living and whole on the bosom of Gennargentu (only later did I penetrate beneath).

Once, flushed with the gladness of life, I went up to Puddu and demanded that he tell me something. "Does she know I exist?" The question momentarily confused him—"Mavidda," I said—but I could phrase it no better.

"That you exist?" He scraped the mud off his boots, hesitating. He looked distressed. "She knows she was born of an American woman and that I delivered her. She knows she was adopted." He took off his soggy jacket. "Her mother told her."

"I'm grateful. I'm grateful to your wife."

"She told Mavi to punish her," he added.

That, at the time, I couldn't grasp. Almost, but not quite. He would say nothing more. I let it pass. Still, the news that we knew of each other's existence now in some way, any way, overpowered and pleasured me. In a way I was fighting for my child's sake.

I lived and fought and worked with Mungianeddu's men for fourteen months. During that time my body grew tough, stringy, and almost neuter, or so it seemed to me. Yet, as I have suggested, my life as a guerrilla fighter did not remain altogether sexless. I had brought along certain resources not otherwise available in the Barbagia, and despite toughness, despite superstition, despite taboo, my body was month by month invested with an intensifying sexual magic. Gradually I found myself surrounded by a cult of adoration. I did not take any of this personally. But the way in which I was sought out and importuned was moving. It wasn't just the *fica* they smoked in my presence. In a spirit of supplication numbers of the men began bringing me dead songbirds, scarab beetles, rings of twisted thorn, and tiny vermilion snakes. Others presented me lovingly with intricately carved staves, gourds full of medlars, baskets of prickly pears, and small lozenge-shaped loaves, still warm and baked with a slit in the crust to represent the female sex. I accepted all these graciously, as a demigoddess should. But of course I was pressed to accept more than tokens of reverence. The gift of men's bodies. I was pretty imperious about it at first. I had come, I insisted over and over again, to fight. Yet the nerve-racking dangers to which we were all mutually exposed were inherently arousing. And sometimes the particular daring of this or that heroic fighter was irresistible. When he approached me—when I felt in all good conscience that I could reward him—with a certain ceremony and a certain passion I did. Was I at the same time appeasing my own anxieties? I'm sure of it. But these reckless favors of mine, which were in part spontaneously granted for particular hardship, risk, or courage in combat, were soon noised about despite my efforts to keep them clandestine—and they came to be considered an honor. The man a hero. Jealousy for my dispensation spread.

Everyone contributed what he could, of course, and I had more to give than sex. I made myself useful to the Independence forces in other ways as well, in each case tapping talents within my special competence. For example, the information our Independence fighters were receiving almost nightly from informants in the villages—how many troops, how heavily armed, which units, where stationed, where heading, and the like—had never been fully utilized. To be efficiently exploited, all of this data had to be on tap. Here my business training

stood me in good stead. One of my first contributions to Mungianeddu's rebel army was to set up a file-card system, replacing the
older system in which his lieutenants had attempted to keep everything in their heads. Any businessman knows how unsound the latter
method is. All data received were typed up at once on a battered but
beloved portable which previously had served only to issue communi-
qués. All hard information, including data on our own men and
units, movements and resources, was filed and cross-filed. The use-
fulness of this system to Mungianeddu, whose "staff headquarters"
remained constantly on the move, cannot be exaggerated.

My experience in archaeology was not wasted. On large military
maps obtained through our partisans in Cagliari, I plotted the coordinates of all nuragic towers . . . their relation to each other, to
government fortifications, to sympathetic localities. I have previously
mentioned how I then came to see with a jolt that these prehistoric
fortresses were dispersed along geodetic elevation lines in such a
fashion that line-of-sight communication could once have been maintained (allowing for the missing upper stories) from one fort to the
next in numerous lines or chains across the island. With this realization to guide us, Mungianeddu's men were now able to scout vast
mountainous areas where there *should* have been towers, and actually
come up with them!—crumbling, overgrown, but still usable megalithic mounds—a series of hinterland discoveries which provided
Mungianeddu with unparalleled resources (because unknown to the
enemy) for ammunition storage, emergency retreats, heliograph signal
systems, and winter headquarters. In one of these he even had a printing press installed later.

For all these services, I was elevated to the rank of lieutenant.
Some of the men, unused to obeying a woman, showed a certain
resentment, especially under conditions of combat (and this may
have been one of the reasons Puddu finally encouraged me to leave).
However, whenever I could be freed of other responsibilities, I continued to see action until, in one fray, I was wounded and put out
of commission.

I captured a machine gun. I don't mean I cleaned out a gunners'
nest. But I took the weapon itself during an unusual day's work.
Orgosolo, one of the most desperate villages in guerrilla territory, the
most friendly to Mungianeddu Puddu and most hostile to the mainland army's invading forces, had had troops billeted in it. This Mungianeddu regarded as a deliberate challenge, one to be met with a
swift demonstration: demonstrating that villages close to the heart of

the Barbagia and the heart of his people were ours, not theirs. He therefore sent Diddinu in to sweep the place clean. Sweeping is not too far from what the operation looked like. Some three dozen men, no more, all from Orgosolo, started by surrounding this village whose every house, stable, alley, and cranny they knew intimately, and then converged from the hillsides in twos and threes down every street with tommy guns, grenades, and guts (we lost four men), ferociously slaughtering every government soldier who didn't surrender (halfhearted fighters, most of them did) during this death-dealing evening *passeggiata*, a macabre parade against great odds right to the center of town and out again.

The gun I took was mounted on the back of a truck. I'd been stationed as usual outside the melee, with the men not from Orgosolo, a demolition group guarding one end of the only road out of town. The truck, fleeing at full speed through the twilight with half a dozen soldiers on the back, raced toward us. Our mines failed to explode. I threw a lucky grenade. I got the wheels, which swerved, toppling the truck. As the enemy troops tumbled out of the truck apparently unharmed and raced for cover, I fell with my whole sprawling length across the overturned gun. A couple of incredible pains pierced my legs. In an outburst of indignation, very moral, I righted the machine gun and began spraying everything in sight, walls, men, stone fences. It's fortunate my aim was wild—I'd been hurt by two bullets—or some of our own men might have been cut down, so frenzied was I with mindless pain and stupefied with appalling, impotent fury at the outrage to my flesh.

Despite my crazied aim I did wound a few of the enemy and received, from Mungianeddu himself, the credit for taking the machine gun. Indeed, the glory! "You have more prick than I thought," he said, "but try to stay alive." I was given the rank of captain! Lines of worshipful admirers gathered outside the tower where I lay, and it was only then that the thought of what I'd done, of how close a thing it had been, scared me. It was to be closer.

The developing danger was infection. I'd been wounded (of all places) in my scarred heel—the upside-down Achilles' heel I'd had ever since infancy when my mother had once accidentally dipped me heel-first into boiling hot water and I'd screamed in time. The bullet there had emerged, but another one had embedded itself in the calf of my other leg, just below the knee. Luckily, all bones were intact except for a little piece of the heel. A small operation to remove the deeply lodged bullet was performed without anaesthesia, without drugs; there were no medications in the mountains. Afterward I was sick, my eyes grew huge, they burned, my leg alternately glowed and seemed frostbitten, and my insides grew weak. It was feared I might have contracted typhus, but whatever it was, I recuperated slowly, recovering (I felt) from the power of knowing I had to.

I was out of action. But I was put to work. Captain Niemann did chores which smacked of woman's work: cook's helper, washerwoman, water carrier, nurse, and seamstress. However, since Sardinian shepherds are accustomed to doing all of this for themselves, I couldn't take it amiss. Captain Niemann performed all these duties at a time when she could barely walk; I was weak from lack of food because I couldn't keep food down. In my leisure hours as soon as I could get about better I began scratching around under the openings of the many caves in our vicinity, and with a trained eye I unearthed numerous microliths chipped—accidentally?—with that same odd and splendid phallic elongation. Was I seeing things? At the time I could only speculate in vain as to their origin and significance.

But the one thing I remember best about my convalescence was the miracle of the return of my appetite. That and the extraordinary feast we held to celebrate the Third Anniversary of the Independence Movement—the celebration of the seizure of the Nuoro radio network and the subsequent three days of Puddu's appeal, openly broadcast, for open rebellion.

Marvelous things we ate in the Barbagia. Roast rabbit, succulent with baby doe stuffing. Mouflon braised with grapes. Guinea hen surmounted with broiled wild artichokes. I helped prepare dinner. Early that morning we dug a substantial pit in the earth outside a small unused tower. We cleared the base of our pit neatly, spread it with laurel branches and myrtle leaves, and cooked therein one roast for us all: we jammed a suckling pig inside a gutted sheep inside a gutted calf. The pig wore the sheep like a coat, the sheep slept in the calf like a tent. Pig-in-sheep-in-calf was buried upright in the pit, packed round with stones and soil, dinner cooked invisibly and without a scent, though a fire burned above it for the better part of a day. Exquisite meats. That was the day I also learned to make *sanguinaccio* —how to wash the shit out of interminable yards of hog gut, how to pour pails of hog blood, without a funnel, into tied-off ten-foot lengths of intestine, how to swing a ten-foot hoop of these blood-and-guts onto a couple of sticks, how to keep twirling these soggy mushy sausage balloons round and round, on the sticks, cooking blood evenly over a campfire. Every once in a while, I'm afraid, my hoop of *sanguinaccio* fell into the fire and had to be picked up out of the coals, dusted off, and replaced for me on the long sticks before I could go on twirling.

When I succeeded at last, someone brought me a gourd. With the spicy *sanguinaccio* now, everyone was drinking. I had a sip. *Abba ardente*. It danced all the way to my stomach.

During dinner, as it grew dark, I tried to talk to Mungianeddu. It was hopeless. He loved to eat, he would not talk. Each time I wandered over, he waved me away. Once I protested. He put a gourd of the ethereal liquor in my hand. I told him no, thanks.

Wiping the grease from his mustache, he pressed the gourd into my hands, a trifle arrogant, a trifle sly.

I told him again no, I'd already drunk more than I could. . . .

He regarded me with an expression first pained, then offended. "That was not an invitation," he said. "Drink."

Liquor must have loosened in me the resistance I'd always felt when it came to talking about my wealth. I talked freely.

Couldn't I help, I suggested to him, couldn't I fight with more than my two arms and legs? I had resources. Money, connections. It wasn't necessary, it occurred to me in my cups and I conveyed to him in his, for foolhardy people like me to go flinging themselves across the road to sprawl over enemy machine guns. Weapons could be purchased. I'd pay.

Of course I was prompted by my still vivid fright; my cash generosity was the overflow of something less worthy. From the first I might have offered to help finance the Secession. Instead, I'd demanded heroism of myself—and kept my money quiet. I felt less heroic now. I was ashamed.

But Puddu was astounded, he was interested, he patted my wound, he stared at my wealthy face. Getting a large arms shipment into the Barbagia from abroad looked next to impossible to him: not impossible, however. Pensive, he offered me a *pastori* cheroot. (He didn't take one himself. I realized that since I'd arrived, I had never observed him smoking one of these. Self-denial.) "We'll talk of it in the morning," he said, drinking while I smoked. *Fica*—a lovely delicate glow flowered through my skin. Slowly.

Surba wandered by, clearly drunk. Puddu pulled him over and mentioned the scheme to him. Irrationally, Surba looked annoyed. My offer seemed to turn him against me. He smiled at me almost tauntingly, swaying, gourd in hand, with a peculiar silvery impact

of physical and moral uprightness. "Do you know," he said chal-
lengingly, "why we are fighting?"

"To relieve poverty—"

"In this wretched island?" he interrupted. "We are fighting to
change lives, not incomes. To give the impoverished, who are joining us, and all those who don't, not wealth but dignity. Every month
we hold out here in the mountains is a revelation—the knowledge
that they can accomplish miracles. That's what the fighting and the
dying are about, and that's what our elections and assembly next
year will be for. To create Sardinian confidence, and from confidence power, and from power dignity."

Though drunk, he was as expressive as always. I was interested,
and questioned him further: what economic, legal, and governmental
changes would he make. . . .

He spat and drank again and handed me his gourd and said,
"When you get back to your country, go ask the black man." And
he left.

Puddu and I were alone for a few seconds. I took advantage of it
and, mentioning his faraway, already twice-widowed wife, asked him
to tell me what she was like. "She must miss you terribly."

Nodding, he said boisterously, "*Come una capra che si gratta la
fica con le corna.*" Like a she-goat that scratches her cunt with her
horns. Then he waved that aside, brushing the droplets from his
mustache and saying with sudden confusing depths of tenderness,
"You know what she told me when I saw her last? When I was
leaving? She said, 'Remember, please, our house is also your house.'"

"Your wife said—?" But no, not his wife.

At the thought of his wife saying *that* to him, he detonated into
crashes of amiable laughter and put his arm on my shoulder to steady
me and said fondly, mimicking Mavi's voice, "Remember, Papa,
please, our house is also your house." The contours of Puddu's face
altered with his voice. I heard Mavi's tones and saw her eyes. Mine.
And I wondered why he hadn't taken and kept her there in the
mountains with him . . . though I saw how impossible that would
have been.

He went on, "A very quiet child. But I think she thinks that
this unknown American mother of hers and I once—well, she believes—" his nostalgic gloom returned abruptly, then broke against
laughter—"that she is our child, yours and mine! But that I am stubborn! And will never admit this, not even to my own daughter, even

though she knows, because I must hide everything on pain of death."

In the dead fullness of night, still glowing, I heard footsteps in the passage. The noises ceased. I positively strained to sleep. Back to sleep. The noises—feet shuffling in straw—began again. Rustling sounds through the chinks in the ancient stones . . . the next chamber . . . it was as if we were sharing the same few inches of straw. Off came his boots. I heard his belt buckle swing against stone, I heard straw crackle and crunch as it yielded to his weight. I heard him turn.

Then I smelled him. Through the crevices in those stone walls wafted his intense greeting, tweaking my nose, settling in with me. At first it was sharp but vague.

Then as the acrid sourness accumulated it grew intimate, pushy, thickening round me, filling the night with its outrageously demanding claim on my attention. Sleep? I was being bullied by whiffs. I turned over. Sleep? In that rank darkness there were no walls, there were no chinks, there was only a smelly frankness in a black void. We were in one bed of straw, the tendrils of scent from his close flesh were my covers, they warmed and caressed my flesh heavily, callously. He leaned on me. I wanted him to move over or else to get up out of the straw.

But there he was, immovably there, I could hear him breathing, not snoring, already he was asleep, fleshily asleep in our pitchblack hot stench of a straw bed.

And I was taut, awake. Soon I began to discern his separate odors, through the wall I could distinguish fluctuations and particulars. I could smell his armpits, I could smell his groin, I could make out the back of his neck and—perfectly clearly now—his scalp. Yes, it was his scalp, that heavy musk. I went over his body, scent by scent, the grain of his cheeks, the shag of his chest, the tendonous inside of his elbows, the hair around his belly button, the rope-veined backs of his knees, his rancid, crusty toes. I knew him. I have never known anyone so intimately and at a distance, so long and so superficially, so slowly, wholly, and part by part.

There was nothing left of separation between us, no further revulsion or familiarity, no carnal or spiritual knowledge ahead. What barrier still remained to be crossed? None. There was none. Never having loved, we were old lovers.

In the morning, together, we set to work compiling a list of the most urgently needed items.

Not only weapons. What we agreed to attempt was a small printing press; medical supplies and drugs; clothing and blankets; two-way radios; binoculars and telescopes; detonators, fuse cord, and time pencils; and of course rifles (those I finally managed to purchase were in fact the German T-223 I had envisioned in the eroded waste!) and machine guns (German light machine guns with bipod mountings—the M1919A6).

We were enthusiastic. But the logistics of international purchase and transportation proved complicated. Puddu, to my horror, chagrin, and suspicion, suggested I return to attend to the shipment myself. He wanted me to go! Had I disappointed him last night by not coming to him? But on the subject of love he remained close-mouthed.

Not so Surba. A high-level conference was convened. I was invited to attend. Mungianeddu, Trumentu, Iste, and Neneddu Surba were present. I was startled to hear myself reproved. There had been, Surba noted, a good deal of resentful murmuring among the troops, especially in certain quarters, with regard to my private life. (He did not divulge from which quarters the resentment came; later I was to learn that Totoi was behind it.) Was my private life, I objected, to become a matter of policy? Surba nodded. I was still more startled to hear what he proposed. Did he think it took outstanding valor to sleep with me? I asked satirically. Under his flamelike white eyebrows came eyes saddened by long subtlety, and beneath the furrows in his cheeks a marked power of persuasiveness in the very absence of his smile. My intimate relations with the troops, he insisted calmly, would have to be formalized. Hitherto I had selected my men. From now on I was to be given only to those officially designated as heroes.

Should I have felt honored? Surba seemed to think so. I wasn't so sure. But I must admit that whatever my preliminary doubts, it seemed only natural and pleasant to me that the ceremony as Surba designed it now came to include all sorts of ritual objects. (Yes, a couple of the details at first struck me as altogether absurd. But years and years afterward I was startled to learn about the great goddess Nut, whose representation on sarcophagi shows her as taking into her arms the dead man, the hero of this life who returns to her for shelter and second life. And remembering my strange arrival in the guerrilla encampment, I was enthralled to discover that Nut's frequent baring of her night-dark womb and full-moon breasts . . . of the entire galaxy of her naked body . . . was counted by her worshippers as a divine epiphany. Even the killing, destruction, and sacrifice which surrounded her image were understood to be a transition necessary for the luminous birth of the new day.) In any event, our ceremonial encounters took place at sundown inside a small nuragic tower. A wide ring of fire had been lighted inside, shaped like a boat rather than a circle. It was a low fire, not very difficult to leap through or over, and in the middle of this boat of flames I waited.

Outside my fire and well beyond its reach, somber tapestries had been secured, hung on cords all around the inner chamber. At the entrance to the tower the floor had been strewn with cut grass, on which a water jar had been placed. Entering the nuraghe, the hero was first required to sip from the jar, then parting the tapestries, cross through the fire and bring it to me. Before I sipped, I had to recite: "This is an evening of great mystery. Let not the eye see it, nor the mind know it, for it is to be hidden."

In the midst of the fire boat rested a thick round stone with a circular hole in the center. By a rope of vines running from my left ankle to the heavy stone, I was attached to the hole. Each time, immediately beforehand, I was obliged to don a skirt made of broad cactus blades from which the spines on the inner side alone had been removed. I had dabbed the coagulated black blood of a goat behind my ears, my elbows, and my heels. For a while outside someone would play the three-piped *launedda*, a reedy flute-high wail over a sonorous bass, monotonously repeated and repeated, and then silence, firewood snapping all around us, and pulsing crickets, and our close breathing while together we smoked one of those twisted cigars. *Fica*.

Sacred prostitution? For the decorated man that night I removed the luciferous halo surrounding my person at most other times. But I never kidded myself. I was faintly phosphorescent. The man was solemn enough—awkward, inclined to make melancholy jokes, inclined to forget the whole thing, and yet in a very fever to be loved. Often he was a good friend and hesitant to approach my ambiguity, but in every case nevertheless ravenous for the form of love, for the womanly body he had seen, heard, and knew I possessed.

Yet how much reassurance some of them needed! Sometimes I thought nothing would be enough, nothing would do. Of course every once in a while someone would come at me like a ram and force me, rapacious and quick. But generally it was the reverse, we were oppressed by solemnity; the time dragged. Often patiently and quietly I had to hold a man and talk to him for a long time inside that boat of flames before the stimulus of *fica* and his courage took effect.

Ultimately it was he who had to reassure himself. He unbuttoned my rough shirt and felt how my breasts stretched to be free, two living beings. Still hesitating, for a while he made love to a nipple, then he stroked my waist, carefully making his way under my cactus skirt, descending cautiously along my sacred abdomen until I was absolutely struggling to be touched. Our love became frantic. Often he sat on that rock to hold me better, to envelop and absorb me better, to drink my womanliness. Forbidden to remove my cactus, dodging my thorns, he worshipped my belly, he squeezed between my thighs, he took a grip on my ungraspable ecstasy. And presently invaded my holiness, igniting me to my farthest walls, muttering wild incantations as my spines tore him, and me out of my head and body as well, our lovemaking an unholy image of fiery beatitude as he suffered and I clasped him, as he adored me and I blessed him, knowing that he had altogether forgotten both pain and pleasure, both sacredness and whorishness by now, as he rolled to get more divinely into me if humanly possible, and all heaven aside, we ascended together.

It was during this period of recuperation and sanctity that I tried over and over again to communicate with Baron Tieger in New York through couriers. One message actually got through to him. Yet it became disastrously apparent to me, isolated in the Barbagia, that if anything were to be accomplished, I'd have to do it myself, and I was fiercely unwilling to leave. Leave? I refused. Never was I officially ordered to leave. I was consulted and I objected. Mungianeddu, I think and hope, understood. Nevertheless, he told me angrily that I would leave as soon as my convalescence permitted me to travel. But as a matter of fact, I considerably outstayed my convalescence—redoubling my efforts to make myself enormously useful on the spot, right where I was.

The ticklish, horrifying circumstances of my departure are worth reporting in some detail. Before I do so, let me say that though I left the movement, I continued to aid it, I did carry out my promises. Even now it would be less than expedient to disclose the sources and channels of that shipment. Let it suffice to say that I was willing to expend a large part of my capital and dig into my credit; that to preserve my anonymity, Baron Tieger had my power-of-attorney; that the pharmaceuticals were American and the arms West German;

that payment was arranged through Swiss banking interests; and finally that the entire shipment, assembled in Luxembourg, was deviously routed by air freight to North Africa and thence by sea to Sardinia. The transaction, from preliminary financing to arrival of material, took months. But all that was much later.

My real Achilles' heel—my vagina—the sheath with a sword. When the news somehow got round that I was a rich American, and when it was reported that I was going to leave, a festering resentment surfaced among the men, hidden suppurations of dangerous feeling erupted all around me. It is very difficult for me to be sure of all the sources of this mood of ill will. I was a woman; I'd been promoted too fast. My sexual favors, though ritualized, were now openly desired. And the feelings of veneration that had surrounded me since my arrival had gradually turned to jealousy. It was nastily said that I had had a remarkable affinity for men who (because they were brave and often reckless, let me interject) had subsequently been killed in battle or taken in ambush. Was I Bad Luck? To make matters worse, when it so happened that my departure was announced on the very day we received news of a grisly ambush near Oliena, where Diddinu and several of our veteran fighters were surprised and totally wiped out, an irrational suspicion fell on me.

The suspicion was no less than that the provocative American was an *agent provocateur*, that the ambiguous rich American was an agent of the CIA! Totoi brought this charge, speaking hotheadedly for an undisclosed number of men. And though the top leadership at no time showed any distrust of me, Mungianeddu felt it would be safest for me if he acceded to Totoi's demand for an open inquiry. Privately, Puddu warned me that he was acceding for my sake, that what he was unable to control, if I were to try to leave without facing my accusers openly, no matter how preposterous their charges might seem to *me*, was vendetta.

I was appalled. The ingratitude, the illogic, seemed gross! CIA agent! But I thought of my dream, my own unconscious maze of possibilities. In this century of duplicity I might have been. And I came round to understanding that the guerrillas were at least entitled to doubt and error. Nevertheless, I felt pretty depressed and bitter; I could hardly help resenting their suspicions.

(By juridical irony later on in the States, one of the phoniest positions taken by the prosecution during my trumped-up treason trial was that by service in a foreign army I had forfeited my right to U.S. citizenship. Let me tell you, my earlier ordeal by jury in

Sardinia helped me to comprehend my treason trial at home better. When at last I came to judgment in the ritual solemnity of an American courtroom, the prototype was behind me and I could see exactly what was happening. Behind the charges, in both cases, lurked outraged and ill-concealed sexual feelings: I was implicitly reviled for the poetic ambiguities of my life.)

But at the time of my trial in Sardinia, the charges struck me as ludicrous. I never allowed myself to feel I was in danger.

In such a situation, however, the upshot was unpredictable and Mungianeddu must have known it. Indelicate, absolute, and primitive feelings were involved. A crude "trial" was held out in the open, on a bushy hillside beside the same small tower that had served as my sanctuary. There was no evidence worthy of the name, but there were dark words, gloomy stares, flashes of ferocity, and speeches of considerable length and passion in which my death wasn't merely demanded—once or twice it was described. I responded with scathing logic myself, which convinced no one. Far from assuaging feelings, my scorn seemed only to inflame animosity. But Mungianeddu spoke for me, a moving declaration that summarized my womanly and manly contributions to the revolutionary movement and put my accusers eloquently to shame . . . to silence. It grew late, it grew quiet. I guessed from his reluctance to bring matters to a close that Puddu was worried by the silence, still worried about vendetta. He demanded an oath, the most primitive and absolute. He ordered the camp butcher to bring over two of the captured mountain mouflon, a ram and a ewe.

The ewe was slaughtered before our eyes and her vagina cut out with precise strokes of the butcher's knife. I will not describe my reactions to this, they were indescribable, I'm going to be brief. The ewe's vagina was passed through the crowd from man to man, each man (and most of them were shepherds) either licking or kissing it. Meanwhile the ram, a hoary wild beast with great arching horns, was summarily slaughtered, and his testicles and penis lopped off. Following Mungianeddu's orders, I retired alone to the tower and managed there to do as instructed. I inserted as much as I could of the ram's bloody penis into my own vagina. It was messy . . . awful. When I reappeared, I was fully dressed, holding the thing inside me. The ewe's vagina now slowly reached the front of the crowd again. It was handed to me. While several men held a blanket around me, I withdrew the ram's penis from my own vagina and, kissing it, inserted it through the ewe's.

Now vagina and penis were held to my lips and I was obliged to take an oath: that I had never been a traitor to the Sardinian revolution, that I would never betray it in the future if I left, and that I was not now, nor had ever been, a CIA agent. This I swore on organs of generation.

Then, bound together, vagina, penis, and testicles were slowly cooked.

They were soon passed around from hand to hand through the crowd. Each man took a tiny bite, swearing that he trusted me, that he would abide by the decision, and that he would seek no act of vengeance against me. The dreadful organs circulated past me several times, making the rounds; I had my share.

Thus did Mungianeddu protect me against physical harm. I was nevertheless wounded, lacerated somewhere, and I underwent a gathering revulsion, calcifying blisters of the mind.

How I
Distributed
My Flame

Consider Sexual Organisation, and hide thee in the dust.
—BLAKE

I come now to Fica, to that great controversial enterprise I was destined to launch. The note I appended to the lyric poem, "I Fuck, Therefore I Am," which appeared in my *Sublunary Lovers*, sheds searching light on my commercial intentions. The note reads:

> My poetics: the four-letter word as proto-poem. The poet as ghostly lover. For feeling and obscenity are opposed only as Self and Skin, & my poetry mediates these. Through the transfiguration of the dirty word as the conventional tool of language into the same word as play, the word becomes a fulcrum outside the world to move the world, the focus of a burning glass to burn the world.

As I saw my task with marketing Fica, it was not to debase my archetypal womb, but to restore the energy of a primitive reality to a public which had involuntarily lost touch with its own sources of sensual force.

The Italian liner, powered by tugboats, had slid ponderously through the Narrows and Harbor of New York. I had stood at the railings, reminded inevitably by the slosh of water that Manhattan, too, was an island of rock as infertile as my Sardinia. Its windows glared—no welcome there. Its barren skyscrapers were my towers. We slid toward the thousand soggy fingernails that were its docks. The Statue of Liberty went limp before my gaze. The metal city turned to rust. The sun clotted the horizon with blood, and the helpless moon rose and shrank like a dynamited lump of cement.

To bring the whole island and the entire country round to accepting my phallic womb was a vast undertaking. But when I returned to the old world of business . . . with new cunning and callousness . . . I was ready. My personal and poetic resources were at last equal to the task.

I took care of that shipment of arms and supplies for Puddu. And I sent him funds from time to time through banks in Switzerland and Luxembourg. Yet I continued to feel pretty grim about my trial. For Carlo, too, I would suffer at times. Unexpectedly. The havoc of nostalgia in the body. But for Sardinia I lived always with love fouled, thwarted, and dispersed.

I saw Baron again of course. Frequently. He was company, he entertained me. Sometimes I tried to persuade myself that what I felt for him might one day turn to love. But this was illusion. A spell of despondency. The nation was experiencing an economic recession. I was in a void myself, all around me the old existence. Emptiness was anguish. The release for me was poetry—

That if you want the house to stay
You've got to

—and I determined to lick my own Slump single-handed. Aesthetics and economics.

The appearance of *Towers in a Landscape* met with a heady mixture of literary astonishment and political execration. The volume soon attained a considerable notoriety. I found myself on the threshold of my first period of artistic recognition. Baiting the hooks of inspiration in the shallows of New York, I set to work to create a poetry permeated by unabashed erotic obsession . . . the earliest drafts of *Sublunary Lovers* . . . and the rush of visionary energy that ensued staggered me. It overflowed from the poems . . .

. . . into action . . . into the commercial deployment of my myth. . . .

I told Baron Tieger about it. I told him about the means—Fica—and I told him about my goal—just as in my poetry—daimonic possession.

To possess the country and the world at large. For my double-decker genitals were both totem and taboo. They had a curative power. But it was too private. I had to have millions. I wanted to amplify the sexual imagination of vast populations. I longed to absorb and envelop mankind. To confront and awaken, infuse and restore, conquer and quicken. And I told him how.

He was befuddled at first. "All this with a cactus cigarette?"

"Tobacco mixed with cactus."

"Called Fica—?"

"In Italian, cunt." In myself I was too small to take on every man and woman in the country. But I could peddle my abstract cunt to multitudes.

The artist in Tieger slowly grasped it: "Symbolic obsession . . ." The heir to millions, however, looked worried: "Does it do the trick . . . this particular cactus?"

"Have faith," I told him. "Every man's got a little of the poet in him."

Dick Urey was known disrespectfully to his colleagues on Madison Avenue by a nickname. The oversized bald hill of his scalp was translucent, milky, and shot through with veins like chalcedony. Under this brainy dome he held his eyes still. Buck Rogers' "Dr. Huer," all right. We talked.

A preliminary shipment of the cactus, the genuine Sardinian variety, had already arrived. It was still in the testing stages: in the hands of phytochemists and pharmacologists. For months I had been consulting with industrial engineers on the design of automated processing equipment.

He listened. Only gradually did his penetrating stare—the hypnotic force of those somnolent, bulging, slightly bluish and bloodgrained eyes—make itself felt. I handed him a sample of the pack I had already had made up for me. The design was still tentative: a fuming cigarette held lovingly between two vertical lips.

Huer turned the pack over and around skeptically. "What the hell is it—Fica—Italian?"

I went into the brand name in some detail: its meaning and derivation.

He shook his head decisively. "Forget it."

I don't forget easily. "Back in Sardinia—"

"We're not in Sardinia."

"What's in a name?" I tested him.

"Everything."

The right man. "Exactly. The thrust of the product in your hand is a poetic strategy applied to business." I elucidated: "A physical erotic response is never enough. It always has to be phenomenological."

His skull rippled. Wrinkles spread down his scalp into his eyebrows. "Listen, it won't be so phenomenal when you get thrust in jail for making phony claims about a peculiar erotic stimulus you can't prove."

"I've considered the risks," I insisted, "and I say I don't have to prove it. I'm counting on what the consumer adds to his cigarette. Imagination. Sure, we may have to put ourselves out on a legal limb—"

"We?"

"But if we do," I persisted, "we can promote not only a smoke but a cause."

"Which is?"

"The sensual revitalization of this country."

He blinked.

At forty-seven Richard H. Urey headed up one of the fastest-growing drug ad agencies, rapidly expanding now into liquor, automotive, and industrial PR. No one was better qualified for the job I had in mind. Later Dr. Huer would help elect two state governors and mastermind the successful nomination of a U.S. presidential candidate. But already he was not the sort of executive you asked to come see you. I had gone to see him. "That's all you had in mind?" he inquired caustically.

He was a fleshy man. But on account of his bone head I found myself peculiarly aware of the way his vertebral column came leaning over his desk at me.

"I'll be frank. For me, Fica is poetry."

Puzzled, he demanded, "Look, Miss Niemann, why don't you at least change the name to a moneymaker . . . something like . . . well, like Arouse . . . or Heaven . . . or just plain Fun?"

I shook my head. For me the reality of the name was paramount. Puddu's word for it. (And Sandy's. And Haidu's. And Whitey's.) "Fica," I said. "That's its name."

"Well," he shrugged, "I suppose we could always tell them it rhymes with Topeka."

"Eureka."

And leaning back, I laced my fingers behind my head.

"Topeka," he insisted. He opened the pack and pulled one out. "What about those pharmacological tests?"

I reassured him. "Two private research labs and my own chemist. They all agree." I handed him the most interesting of the lab reports I'd received, and at the same time I summarized out loud for him their general findings. "No one's been able to isolate any chemical capable of inducing the peculiar effect the cactus ingredient seems to produce." I hesitated. "Of course, not in everyone."

"A complete shuck?" he insinuated. But he seemed relieved. "If it's only a psychological effect, we ought to be able to promote it. Are you sure it's all in the mind?" he demanded, amused.

"In the body," I maintained. "The smoke rings of sex in the mind penetrate to the skin. Psychogenic. You'd be surprised. It works even on some of the biochemists who can't locate the chemical."

He read the report over rapidly. I was interested to observe, below the fixity of his eyes, a sly grin over which he apparently had less control than over his other features. It came and went as he read:

> I theorize I must have got some on my hands earlier and thus accidentally ingested an undetermined small residue of the concentrate with dinner. Peculiar symptoms, 11:05 P.M. Sensation of heat at back of nose, pleasant, soon spreading down through chest. Undressed for bed, but remained wandering through the house, noting with emotion of pleasure contact of different temperatures of cool and warm air on

surface of skin. Toes especially sensitive. Textures of carpet, linoleum, wood, tiles. Went to bed about 1:03 A.M. Personal note: Wife complained. Struck me as funny. I was rubbing myself all over her, and when she complained, I began laughing out loud, continuing to rub myself against her from head to toe, for 30 to 40 minutes, penis fully erect, but no apparent impulse toward consummation, just distinct, highly pleasurable tingling all over surface of skin. Difficult to describe. Actual erection appeared relatively unimportant because unusually strong sensations of satisfaction were running all over me elsewhere. Wife kept complaining. I kept laughing. No intercourse. Fell asleep.

No aftereffects next day. Must determine relative speeds of ingestion and inhalation.

Urey smiled. An extra-long mouth, I felt, with thoughts to match. Sensual? Perhaps. But most exciting—and I found him immediately exciting because I sensed in my *own* bones that we were going to make money together—was his skull, imposingly brainy and lustrous. I had to restrain myself from kissing the blarneystone of his skull for luck. The sexual excitement of making money: with your permission, that is how I see it . . . and I see no conflict between that excitement and the more philosophic basis of my commitment to Fica. In the creation of wealth *ex nihilo* there is something paralyzingly erotic, a lover perpetually held at arm's length.

I warmed to my subject. "Now as I see it, the most effective kind of publicity on this would center on . . . may I?"

"Go ahead." He looked me over, sizing me up. "I'd be interested in hearing," he said, but his chapped lips were pursed now, ironic. He hadn't committed himself to anything. Yet his help would make a difference to me, it was important to convince him. "Okay, the kind of cigarette ads I had in mind would visually suggest or show the mouth as an archetypal Vulva always holding in loving embrace a glowing Phallus—"

Grimacing and muttering, he cut me short. "Look, there's already too much fuss about tom, dick, and twat in—"

"Granted. Everywhere. But it's never right up front where it's respectable and respected. That's the trouble and that's why there's so much emphasis on it. I want to raise the world by lowering people's attention."

"I think you're actually serious," he said. He looked uneasy. "Are you?"

"I am," I said. "I'm serious. Why not?" I reached across his desk for the pack and shook a couple out. "Care for a match?"

"Hell no."

"It's got an interesting taste."

"Taste has nothing to do with it."

I sighed and rose. I took one myself and lighted it. I'd tested them again recently, several times. With Baron and by myself. And I knew perfectly well that after half an hour's chain smoking, I could easily imagine myself a creature of nothing but erogenous zones all over—to my full height—cunnilingus without release. With one difference. No matter how sensitized my body grew, my head remained lucid.

I went to look out his window at the madness of the Mad Avenue below. One of us was wrong. How was I to persuade him? I turned and tried again. A few facts. "The base is the local island cactus, *Carnegiea spinosa nuorensis*, carefully processed. It's smooth and cool. Different from tobacco, but better. And when mixed with to-bacco—well, try it. It's unusual."

He took one and examined it. "I assume the bouquet is gratifying." He struck a match, lighting up dubiously. "But what market did you have in mind? To capture the marijuana market you'd have to first get this cactus placebo of yours declared illegal—and then we face the FBI. Besides, if it's any sort of drug or narcotic, it'll be outlawed anyway in a few months by the FDA. And if it's all hocus-pocus, we'll be stomped on for false advertising by the FTC. An interesting flavor—" he exhaled—"but the nation isn't ready for this. Miss Nie-mann, you're young, you're inexperienced."

Inexperienced, was I! "America is changing. And it's *because* I'm younger than you that I know that all it takes is a little love and a little gall and we'll conquer the country, coast to coast."

"A little gall," he repeated. "You listen to me." He tilted his scalp and fixed me with his protuberant eyes. "Love I don't know. But in the advertising world, all gall is divided into three parts. Anxiety, lust, and lies. In polite circles here, these three are referred to as creating new needs, conveying sex appeal, and establishing an image. The trouble is, you're starting with the oldest need of all, the product's name has no sex appeal, and unless you change the design of the pack you're going to be handicapped by the world's most impossible im-age."

You see? Typical. At least he was honest. "Exactly right. And I'm here to change all that. To shift the balance."

"The balance of what?"

"Of cock and cunt. There's been too much yin and not enough

yang." He knew the world, he knew advertising and the three galls, but he ought to have known them better. I told him so. The Great American Erection had all along been the nation's principal archetype, and not only in advertising. Big, great—the Washington Monument, the Brooklyn Bridge, Giant Sequoia Trees, oil wells and launching pads, the thundering train and hurtling automobile, the great frontier of spurs and firearms, the new space age of jets and rockets. Why had our Manifest Destiny always been expansion? Had he ever thought of the elongated shape of the island of Manhattan? Maybe he ought to look closely at a map. Couldn't he see the link between the commercial ascendancy of New York and the enormous thrust of its buildings? Up.

Up was by now a compulsion in the architecture of affluence. Those great erections in the city, in one of which we now stood and sat and argued, had always maintained the meaning of New York's potency at the deepest levels of the nation's mind—psychologically, mythically, poignantly. It was the same in advertising. But the national mind was changing, and *would* change whether or not he came along. I knew. As a teenager I'd once worried myself sick about Only A Silly Little Millimeter Longer. I'd grown up discouraged about it's Not How Long You Make It, It's How You Make It Long. Never again.

Exerting myself to convince this hypocrite, I discovered that my whole mind and body were trembling. How had *he* interpreted those menacing ads, I asked, the ones exclaiming It's What's Up Front That Counts? And what exactly did he think they really meant by Longer Than Kings . . . Come Up, Up, All The Way Up . . . and (I pounded the desk) The Biggest Should Do More? It wasn't just cigarettes. Coke, I cried. Why had Coke swept the country? "Mr. Urey, public relations has a symbolic responsibility—"

"Creative advertising?" He perked up.

"Poetic advertising. Perhaps poets *were* once the unacknowledged legislators of Mankind. If so," I flattered him deliberately, "their power has passed to Madison Avenue. If we play it right, our publicity campaign can *transcend* sexual prurience. I want to reach out, through business and beyond business, to minds and bodies. Are you interested?"

He put on a pair of heavy glasses. Behind his lenses his twinkling pupils played along with me. "I'm interested. But one question, Miss Niemann. Do we conduct this campaign of yours for the sake of money or for love?"

Under his blue gaze he produced one of those slowly spreading, eerily suggestive smiles. And I knew he was feeling it. I murmured, "Don't you sense anything special?"

He crushed out the cigarette first. Then he reached out for me, touching me. "You."

"Don't be a ninny," I advised him, "and please don't take me for one." My business practice has always been chaste.

He withdrew slightly to consider me and contemplate his burnt-out cigarette. "You know—" he put the tip of one finger on the tip of his nose—" we might just get away with this. The question is—" he ran his fingers erotically to and fro, up and down, along the bridge of his nose—"the question is, how."

For readers of *Fortune* and *Esquire* who may have chanced on the spate of articles concerning my spectacular manipulations, some of the details that follow may be repetitious, but let me outline my efforts briefly. I hired experts of every description—the excess personnel of the vast industry I was challenging—veterans of tobacco buying, production, and distribution. Wherever possible, I kept my administrative and managerial slots female. There was a time early on in the new game when I considered employing only women. But I quickly saw that this would be tantamount to dodging my problem, the insoluble problem to which I was still committed: how to possess mankind. I bent over backward, however, where it came to men: assembling the right top-level management. It was hard enough to find women with first-rate tobacco experience . . . but you won't believe how hard it was to pick up the right men. I'm talking about men who had the capacity to work under a woman; I'm talking about unemployed executives as well as men who already commanded six-figure salaries in the tobacco industry and came to me for more. For a price—and the price was right—most of them said, and probably believed, they'd have no trouble taking orders from me. But I knew better; I had to have a team I could depend on. Sizing them up beforehand was at best a hunchy process. But I devised a variety of tests. My favorite—I loved to raise this question—was to ask them if they'd mind calling me "sir." The correct answer was: "Yes, ma'am."

I found myself engaged in two enterprises at once, the poetry of business and the business of poetry.

"You," I called to the foreman as I passed by with my visiting Baron, "tell 'em I said to lay rubber mats. I don't want these dollies running through here without mats."

"Mats yet," he said truculently.

It was all new to me—but not really strange—building a new business from scratch was a familiar feeling. But the job was enormous. I had arranged by now for the importation of Sardinian cactus on a stand-by basis. Once I had worked out satisfactory guarantees on cultivation and supply, I tied it all up. The terms we had settled on were advantageous to both sides. And I expected my efforts would give the economy of Sardinia a much-needed shot in the arm. Much easier on this side: the quality and supply of American tobacco on the open market I left to veteran buyers. Despite obstacles placed in my way by a skeptical but wary competition, I was close to completing negotiations for a warehouse-and-plant complex in Virginia, additional warehouse facilities in Jersey, and sales-representation space in Manhattan. For immediate use I had bought out a large processing plant in Long Island City—the old Parke-Dant Company. And I was having it remodeled to get ready for the rush I anticipated. Work crews were gutting the whole ground floor for me and redecorating.

Off-white for the bricks and beams. The old wooden uprights were seriously flawed by long spectacular cracks. But the I-beam bracings on top were solid. Cross-beaming in the ceiling made it feasible to recess the lights and air-conditioning out of the way of the sprinkler systems. This time I was going to have myself a decent office: carpet and all.

We picked our way, Tieger and I, stepping between painters' ladders and thick electric cables. His enthusiasm for Fica was nearly equal to mine. More rewarding to me than marriage, our renewed alliance was constant again, argumentative, and entertaining. But I was determined to go beyond him, to reach out for the sex of millions. I showed him around the remodeled plant and offices. "This is going to be Accounting. In here. And over there, on the other side of that fire door, a new access to the warehouse, right up close to the truck landings, outside, remember? Where you saw the freight elevator? Ah! Humble paperclips." I bent to pick one of these ubiquitous little items out of a full carton and showed it to him: "This *is* poetry!"

He shook his head, his hands thrust into the pockets of his ribbed pants, unwilling to touch the clip I held out, his red vest buttoned down tight, his carbuncular features cocked at a sad skeptical angle. "You're heading for corruption, Millie. Better stick to sonnets."

"Horse manure," I laughed. "A crock of it."

My office. Incomplete, but already furnished with what I needed.

I handed him the Cumulative Supplement to Milgrim's *Trade Secrets*, when the phone pealed on my desk. I took the call on one of the jump numbers.

"Pretty good," I said. "Having a hard time catching up with you. No, I was calling in regard to—hold it." I covered the receiver. "Baron, could you pass that over?" I pointed. "No, that one, behind you, *Corporation Code*. The red one—over there." With the manual in hand, I got back on the phone. "So what was the proposal they come up with? . . .

"Uh-huh. Okay fine . . .

"Yeah okay fine, but tell them we got to absolutely protect him from additional expenses or—" I winked at Baron.

"Maybe so," I continued. "But I gave them six minutes to decide, and that's the way it stands. We handle it on that basis or not at all."

"What were we talking about?" I said, hanging up.

"Paperclips," Baron muttered, "as spiritual hardware."

After my return from Sardinia, somehow or other he got the impression from all this bustle and hustle that in effect I was abandoning art in favor of business. "Whoever told you that?" I shouldn't have been irritated or surprised, I suppose, but I was. I had to explain to him the tricky relations between poetry and power, always different, always there. "Look at the different frustrations of Dante and Milton —or of Raleigh, Pope, and Shelley, say—or think of the various frustrations of Wallace Stevens, Robert Lowell, Yeats in the Irish parliament. . . ." Though financially he was cooperative, he remained skeptical of my ideas. He even questioned my integrity:

"Business for art's sake?"

I told him, "That isn't as funny as you think. Where *are* the sources of poetic consciousness? In the clouds? In meadows and skylarks? In thin air, 'pinnacled dim in the intense inane'? The sources of poetry are all around you, in the economic realities of the times. Marx was a grouch, but he was dead right about that. And in our time, in this country, I mean business. Poems are private contracts holding the fabric of society together, and if poets and their poetry are becoming unimportant to this nation it's because the whole poetic shebang has lost touch with the lust for greenbacks and the sexual joy of free enterprise."

My hair was now very short. I kept it cropped close (Plate XV)—a bit mannequinish, a bit mannish, but certainly an appealing hair-do with a curl of fuzz over the ears. Don't know what they thought of me, though I can guess, the gawky crowds of passing citizenry, and my tactless fellow diners in the restaurants I frequented. After dinner I generally smoked one of my own private stock of hand-rolled, almost black, Special Reserve cactus cigars, which helped remind me of the ritual at the tower. Night after night their glory filled me . . . slowly . . . completely. I didn't smoke them only for the effect, but for that memory. Sometimes hilarity, I suspect, ran hidden from table to table when after dinner I lit up my evening smoke. Well, I let them laugh. I stuck to the rough tree-branch feel of it in my mouth.

It may seem to you I'd grown terribly masculine. Will you credit my sincerity if I insist that I was still womanly? I beg you to understand that in a sense I'd simply returned to the mind-splitting polarity of my personality—a public man with a private womb—returned however not to manhood but to womanhood with new insight and energy and a deepened understanding of its Siamese-twin implications. I saw that I wanted—no, needed, *had* to be—myself, fully *me* —not manly, not womanly, but both at once. The conflict existed not only in me but in society at large, and it was essential to achieve both.

Poetry was thus crucial to me. To characterize poetry as my feminine activity runs counter to tradition: the great poets have been men. Precisely. They have been obliged to find by cunning what women possess organically: a womb. Poetry is parturition—not couvade, not a ritual. The procreator, mating by a finesse of strategy with his own womb, labors involuntarily until the birth, when the poem literally cries out. So it is precisely women who need not resort to verse. Except in a rare case. Sappho's, for example, and my own.

The cigars in any event were only a small part of something in me that was wider. I saw it gradually: my manicured left hand, so to speak, gradually became aware of what my cigar-holding right hand was up to when it flicked cactus ash into my coffee cup. Not for others, not for an audience, had I become a fantastic figure. For me: I was on display before the appreciative amazement of my own imagination—an exceptionally solid base for creating poetry. First, I felt, I had to achieve sureness, a prophetic stance, in order to be able to create an absolutely certain poetry, that persuasive articulation which issues only from a voice that is self-dramatic (not self-dramatizing). Second, the self of my voice in poetry had to establish foundations elsewhere and not in the poem. For nourishment at the roots, for exfoliation at the heights, the poetic self needed saturation.

So I smoked my twisted cigars, I basked in the pall of my smoke, I scratched the back and the top of my head while thinking, I spread my elbows behind my neck like elephant ears while listening, and I shook hands from the shoulder. I was deliberately heading for discordance, the greatest endurable inner incompatibility: an unacceptable tension of existence out of which would leap sparks of poetry, a serrated lightning that would close the gap between the poles. I have embraced filth, depravity, vulgarity, heroism, power, money— the rest of it. To my admirers and detractors alike the rough outlines of my career are familiar. What has seldom been sufficiently appreciated, however, is the literary strategy behind it.

Public relations and publicity I left to Dr. Huer. But I participated in all major strategy huddles on the kind of copy we planned to run. The important trick, among others Urey explained to me, would be to create copy that made absolutely no sexual claims whatever—and nevertheless to come up with unmistakably sexual copy: ads that made the aphrodisiac point plenty clear.

Working together, we soon hit on our answer. Copy? Why not? Copycat. We did, and it worked like a charm. Parody . . . satire . . . our ad strategy was like guerrilla strategy all over again, making menacing use of the other fellow's movements . . . so that he hurt himself . . . so that he helped you on your way.

Our sheer effrontery, as it turned out, captured the imagination of the consumer. Our ads were intentionally undistinguished, our slogans remarkably familiar:

It Leaves You Both Breathless

How did we dare? We were sued at once. Urey kicked off our copycat campaign by running full-color spreads in all the major slicks and I followed through by distributing a million cigarettes in free samples.

Our layouts featured lovers—their lovemaking a bit more explicit than usual, it's true. And our slogans remained all too familiar:

Tastes Like A Cigarette
Works Like A Miracle

Copyright suits multiplied. But I had already retained a distinguished firm of attorneys to represent me. And I wasn't worried. Not a bit.

A Mile?
I'd Walk Farther
For Fica

The brand name caught on slowly. Sure, it was a sore spot.* But I was optimistic. The invention of the wheel, the computer, the printing press, television, gunpowder, bronze, the sail, the steam engine— each of these had had incalculable and prodigious effects. How could anyone calculate the impact of my product? Would doctors call it dangerous? Would lawmakers hold it illegal? Would public opinion brand it immoral?

For a while there none of us were sure. Some weeks we were clearly in business, riding a crest. Some weeks it looked black as hell and red as bankruptcy. Day by day I swung like a crazy weather vane from an east of cold despair to a west of clear happiness. At night I would take the elevators to the top of the Empire State Building and, remembering everything, regretting nothing, look down over Manhattan, the infertile cement island I was fighting to overwhelm, overwhelmed myself by the dazzle and blur through which truckloads of newspapers and magazines sped to deliver my message to my people, and I would cry because my island was so beautiful, so ugly, and because I was small, and it was perhaps too vast to conquer—hopeless? A lunatic ambition? And I would run, I'd shoot down and out and hail a cab and weep for happiness. It was exhausting. I had weeks of grinding pessimism and terrible dryness, I lived with the certainty of failure, and then again I would spring back into the most exuberant confidence and wild good cheer.

On the job, however, I was indomitable. At the plant my bossy manner was invariable because it had to be. I had learned discipline. I'd ripened. The old friction I'd experienced was gone. I had acquired

---

* I'm perfectly well aware that a certain eminent critic has conducted a search for sore spots in my art in order to correlate them with my advertising and pin the blame (how convenient!) there. This line of critical argument is beneath contempt. Nevertheless, one must admit it shows a certain wonderful disregard for intelligence, as well as a wonderfully funny "disregard for those years of intimacy" he chooses to allude to, by which I assume he means, on my part, a tolerant, if cold, respect. But I will not stoop here to defend my sore spots against his fondness. I will only point out, with all due friendship, that one ought to know something about commerce and advertising before one writes about them. About poetry I add with all due hilarity that one cannot expect quite so much. I will limit myself to this brief rejoinder: The "ineffable *frisson*" which he is kind enough to experience in my scribbling has no other source than the esoteric presence of archetypes; these are embedded in the matrix of my poems, not merely in their imagery. But the correlation with advertising will escape him; one knows. I therefore append: Advertising is the soul of commerce as poetry is the soul of literature. Both the Body of Commerce and the Body of Literature decay whenever they betray their mythological wellsprings. Indeed, if I may go further, American advertising is the nation's living religion.

I hope I will be understood when I insist that poetry and advertising are not equal.

a confidence in more than my stamina: I now had a womanly self-certainty that turns men into self-hypnotizing subjects. Radiating personal assurance, I'd glare with sly friendliness at my warehouse hands lined up before me. "All right, you slobs, simmer down. Take a seat. I'll make this snappy. All I want is three things, just three. Fidelity to the firm, pride in the product, and no cheek to the little chick on top." This always brought the laugh I wanted, it established the current of humor that ran the show. Deep good-humored male laughter from down in the chest, horse laughs, bull grunts, tomcat chuckles. Whenever I entered the male maelstrom, it warmed the cockles of my heart to see so many pairs of pants taking orders from a skirt. They were men who had some feeling for the product, too, and earned their F.I.C.A. wages. I was now well on my way to appreciating the relation between financial power and sexual megalomania. For it wasn't a matter of mere money—nor even of simple sexual dominion—but of their crucial relation: manipulation itself.

Manipulation and gratification. A phrase of Blake's kept running through my head—"the lineaments of gratified desire." Fica, as my opponents saw it (I quote a well-known, nationally syndicated columnist), was "a wholesale attack on the whorishness of American commerce and culture." But let me put it my way. "To be effective, change in this country is going to have to be erotic and total, physical and mystical, spiritual and bodily," I replied in response to a needling question on a television talk show. "Total change. And my own contribution, both as poet and entrepreneur, can best be made along those lines . . . given my particular talents, my own conscience and insights. As for my so-called 'obscene and illegal' ad campaign, I'll say this. The mass media would like to swallow us, all of us. In fact, you and I, we're living in the whale's stomach right now, alive, but not well, like the sick ulcerous whale itself. The only solution is to turn Leviathan absolutely inside out—copycat—the massive and subversive use of the big belly—to reverse its destiny and our own."

But I was too belligerent. Looking back objectively, it seems evident to me that in no other decade could I have been given the same reception, not merely warm but grateful. Marijuana had paved the way. Some smokers felt the peculiar "low" right away; others didn't. But rumors of the sensational stimulus began to pass at a furious pace by word of mouth, and even some of those who felt nothing often kept trying and sometimes succeeded—whether by force of poetic imagination or of chemical stimuli, I must still legally be careful not to argue. In any event, the product's ingredients were clearly marked on the pack: my cigarettes contained absolutely no substance prohibited by law. (Nevertheless, you'd be surprised how many people thought they had to smoke in secret.)

My impact was soon . . . well, no need to boast. The cigarette industry was in the long throes of nicotine poisoning. Death was on the consumer's mind; love was in his eye. Anyone who had happened to come along as I did, offering a fully legal smoke with a vastly lower nicotine and tar content, together with the promise of another experience of bodily love, stood to make money. For tens of millions of Americans I was the answer. While marijuana appealed to certain segments of the population only, what I produced *everybody* wanted. I not only broke the cigarette habit for millions. In time I transformed the specter of lung cancer into the spirit of lovemaking.

In so doing let me point out that I transformed more than something physically cancerous; I cured a disease of the spirit. For following the full revelation of the hazards of cigarette smoking, what was it that had caused millions and millions of men and women to continue to choose the near-certainty of death? The only answer can be: the contact with death itself. The torch in the mouth was not merely an ingrained habit, but a mortal danger—an excitement consciously or unconsciously *willed*. If we consider the glow at the tip of the tongue and the smoke inhaled with one's breath, we recall at once the dual property of fire. Lifegiver on the one hand—nurturing warmth and natural energy . . . and on the other hand, the power of total destruction—char and waste. The *control* of death while warm with life? Surely the cigarette smoker's most profound satisfaction must always have arisen from the inspiration of life and death. The breath of fire itself, into the lungs: mortality, that close. The medical revelations of the death-dealing properties of tobacco, as I see it, had enhanced its original, fundamental appeal.

But the choice I offered was not the rejection of death in favor of health—an impossible choice, historically and psychologically. I offered a much simpler turn. A much more compelling turn. From death to sex.

Helps Build Strong Bodies One Way

Our publicity gradually grew more venturesome. But we had to step forward gingerly. We watched the general public's reaction to our increasingly graphic advertising, sounding them out frequently through consumer polls and through careful analysis of sales distribution and volume. Yet there was remarkably little need for caution, and no question about one fact. We were widely appreciated. At last Dick Urey took my advice.

We altered the pack design to my original bold conception, and in one way or another our ads began to suggest the lighted cigarette as a tiny phallus. An incandescent erection held in a mouth whose two lips were vertical.

It's The Only Way To Fly

That was a half-truth, no doubt. It wasn't the only way.

Behind Every Smile

We continued to state nothing. We implied everything.

Don't You Wish Everybody Did?

That was the whole truth, unvarnished.

Testimonial letters began pouring in. From old people rejuvenated, inhaling sex and full of new beans. From middle-aged couples who thanked me, body and soul, for contributing to the richness of their union. From young people anxious to join my staff or grow their own. Obscene letters, too, paper missiles charged with violence and filth. Not all responses to Fica were heartwarming, I admit. I remember one party Urey took me to. Body painting, black lights, strobe lights, a foghorn sounding from the music room, several TV sets with signs reading *Destroy Me* and hammers conveniently attached, nude bathing in the heated pool, and everyone smoking with pleasure. My cactus. Situated in an alcove near the foot of the stairs, rising from a decorated porcelain tub, towered a single cactus plant, multiphallic and succulent, potted as an object of veneration apparently, like a Hindu stupa. I was something of a celebrity that night, I suppose. And I was glad to recognize friends, people I'd met through Baron mostly. Calder Cunningham had come, the precocious Newt Rutherford, Gideon Lang was there, too, with his beautiful wife Casey, though at that time nobody had heard of the Langs, however celebrated and opprobrious the Lang group has since become on the international scene, a woman named Jerri Czerny (now director of the Unisex Center I funded), and the brilliant Japanese film maker Kimosabe. I had a long amusing chat in Italian with his sophisticated Japanese wife, who knew no English but had lived for years in Rome, and I had a satisfying exchange in English with her husband on the vexed subject of the influence of cinematic techniques on modern poetry and vice versa. But never mind all that. One image only sticks in my head. I passed a bedroom door. The door was open, and indeed everything imaginable in that room was wide open. There were four couples. Sprawled separately. Four couples rutting, and all alike.

Four pairs of female knees were drawn up into the air, four pairs of female thighs were spread apart, four "V"s, four churning widespread female buttocks surmounted by four pairs of testicles, rising and falling. Four voracious vulvas cupping four kinetic cocks. Four small oil wells being worked by the rotating diesel action and thrust of four long shafts. The shafts rose high out of the oil-bearing cups only to descend again, rise again, sink again. While some went up, others went down. While some plunged in, others plunged out. Up and down, in and out, over and over. Never a sound. Never a change. Never an irregular beat in these unstoppable machines of ideal lust, until the paroxysm.

Urey congratulated me on this scene as he stood there with me . . . sure, there was the smoke of cactus in the air . . . but one is entitled to doubt that my product had anything whatever to do with drilling. Fica can't be credited with all things sexual in this country. It certainly didn't lead to dildos in the drugstore, but they were there, all right, and so were artificial vaginas. Response to my product, I have always insisted, varied not only with susceptibility, but with the individual imagination and its immediate context. The context must be considered. Always. I remember one delightful analysis of the cactus trend in *Newsweek*, which reported that on account of the "no smoking" signs in the subways, many New Yorkers had taken to smoking beforehand, on the way to the subway twice a day, in order to enjoy the contact of bodies during the crowded rush hour. Certain general effects of course one must acknowledge. In fact, our private research organization confirmed that sensory response to smoking Fica in most cases dominated all direct libidinal response. The so-called "honeymoon aura" of love rose uppermost in lovers' minds. Less screwing, more wooing.

I projected production figures to keep pace with the trend. By now in books and magazines, on screen and stage, latitudes and attitudes had been so broadly established that, try as I did, I hardly felt revolutionary. Even in consumer ads sex was not exactly new. But no one before me had made a determined effort to find the limits of the nation's tolerance for Eros.

There were none. A warning from snooping Federal agents . . . an advisory interim opinion from the Food and Drug Administration . . . a clear threat spelled out in an excise-tax inquiry about my cactus import from the Alcohol and Tobacco Tax Division in Washington . . . there was no doubt our ads were making or had caused . . . what, an impression? . . . a sensation? . . . shock? In this country? Not much. Let me assure you, not much. The nation was ready for it, I'd said, and I was right.

Not everyone in the nation, of course. I was summoned to a House hearing on drug abuse—my first appearance before a Congressional investigating committee in Washington but not my last—and accused of everything under the moon, from profiteering to the corruption of youth.*

But there was nothing illegal in my operation. The poetic imagination was not in the Federal jurisdiction. The FDA (abetted vigorously by the AMA) had searched in vain for my "drug." What drug? The purest poetry, my Fica aroused smokers by a delicate process of friction with their own needs.

The government's hands were tied, and I remained unhampered. "The Sexual Explosion," *Life* called it. And though the term was a misnomer,† it stuck.

* REPRESENTATIVE CREEK: Do you realize that the youth of this nation . . .

REPRESENTATIVE GRAHAM: This is getting us nowhere. You used the word "genitalization" before, Miss Niemann. You said, let's see. I think you said, "It's the genitalization of this civilization—"

MYSELF: That's out of context. What I intended was—

REPRESENTATIVE CREEK: The syphilization—

REPRESENTATIVE GRAHAM: Will you please let me finish questioning the witness?

REPRESENTATIVE CREEK: I will not stand by while the newspapers of this nation tolerate—

REPRESENTATIVE GRAHAM: Miss Niemann, in fact don't your ads allude, in however disguised a fashion, to an actual physical stimulant, based on absolutely no scientific evidence?

MYSELF: Eros is a state of mind.

† A more conservative and more accurate term is given in White and Garfunkel —"sexual de-alienation": "People began looking about for someone to rub up against, day and night. In the process of this change from specific intense attachments to diffuse fondness, the range of possible objects of love became broader. The distinction between men and animals showed a tendency to blur, as did the distinction between man and woman, anything warm, furry, or smooth tending to become an object of affection to habitual users. Kissing with the whole body became the rule, both in casual greetings as well as kisses of passion. However, subjects frequently spoke of obtaining as much sensual satisfaction from their own clothes as from their mates. In fashions and styles we have already noted the trend to looser garments, to permit and enhance the pleasures of contact; silk and silklike synthetics rose in popularity among men as well as women. Clothes with holes in them, to permit the free passage of air, became popular, and offices were frequently heated to temperatures five degrees or more above previous norms. Many large firms and factories installed floor-level fans to enhance the workday. Most important of all, the previously clear distinction between the isolated moments when one was

There were civil lawsuits of course, respecting my unconventional ads; there was further interference from the Federal Trade Commission. My attorneys fought all cases, grouping them from court to higher court.* Injunctions were issued and contested before the bench. Subpoenas were served, evaded, answered, and filed. My familiar, much-anthologized sonnet, "Pyrrhic Victory," was composed during a half-hour recess in court while my hard head ached for a movie. I was riding a commercial and cultural crest—but maybe it was the strain of court appearances. Or maybe it was the impersonal scale, the vacuum of big business, after my breezy affair long ago with Chicken Sauce. Whatever it was, something was wrong, I had begun having an unaccountable feeling . . . that I was suffering, undergoing one long-continued catastrophe even as I moved forward of my own free and busy will toward the power and happiness I'd longed for. Journal entries in the notebook I kept during that New York period show my sundered mind. To quote only one:

> The Poet must wage poetry. Give battle on their own grounds: success. The plains of the nation. You knew what you were getting into, you can't back down and head for Parnassus when the going gets rough. Or rather, yes you can, but what does that say for the poet's spunk? I fell upon the paperclips of life and bled.

The sultriness that had descended on the city hung in his waiting room. I went to the curtained alcove to have a look out the clinic

---

making love and the general time when one was not making love broke down. The phase of decision, the conscious option at some point in time either to make love or not to make love, this awareness seemed absent in our subjects' minds."

Of course this analysis was made years and years later. But in all modesty, I think there can be little doubt that the mood of the nation was changing anyway. Moving my way. Perhaps I did contribute—personally, I'm sure of it—but as I grow older I grow more and more convinced that sexual generosity and freedom in love and genital equality were on their way . . . with me or without me. And today the road ahead beckons reassuringly. I did what I could. In any event, it pleases me to note that in their standard work on psychosexual change, White and Garfunkel credit Fica, along with the Pill, as one of the major instruments of the revolution in contemporary attitudes toward the body.

* I am glad to say that in the end the Supreme Court of the land, after years of costly legal argument, sensibly upheld my view. The Court ruled that although the element of parody in all my advertisements had made a profit for my company, the content of the ads did evidently constitute satire—social criticism, not infringement of copyright—and further that the alleged public obscenity of my campaign had had redeeming social importance. Citing Walt Whitman, the Chief Justice eloquently clarified the majority opinion of the Court by distinguishing between licentious enterprise and free enterprise. Walking that fine line, I continued to confront the country with my redeeming awareness.

windows. I pulled the drapes to one side, and stopped. The crunch and sprinkling of heavy objects breaking in Sandy's office stopped me . . . a splatter of destruction followed by a groan that came from someone's guts . . . and right after that came a yelp of pure fear tearing its way up and dying into registers only a dog can hear.

Don't know if I should have broken in on the privacy of a psychiatric consultation. But I did. I was into that office in no time. I pushed open the door, I rushed in.

Sandy was leaning at a menacing angle . . . half-crouching . . . knees bent and parted . . . arms loosely dangling like a gorilla's. His eyes were fixed on his patient, a woman of perhaps a little over thirty —my age, I remember thinking. She was huddled into a corner alongside the air conditioner, and from the looks of it, Sandy had just attacked her. The terrified patient was protecting her mouth and her groin, one with each arm. She looked positively green, an armadillo, with horny scabrous skin. Between the desk and the bookcase, a floor lamp had fallen. The reflector had shattered.

Neither of them moved an inch. Sandy was in his shirtsleeves, cuffs rolled. I could see the girl's lizard eyes fixed desperately on Sandy's and it occurred to me that my brother might have mesmerized her. After several seconds Sandy's hand, the one nearest the door, flicked impatiently at me several times, abruptly.

I backed out through the doorway. I closed the door.

My body was afraid, shot through with questions, tingling. I gave it up. I trailed to the windows once more and opened them. The muted raucous throb of traffic came wafting in. This was the first time I'd ever actually seen him at work, and I couldn't make sense of what I'd stumbled on.

Five minutes after he'd shooed me out of his office with a flick of his hand, he let me back in and I greeted him. But I wasn't exactly overjoyed to see him. "What was that all about?"

To me he looked as if he'd been out of the sun too long—pallid, with faint charcoal shadows about his eyes, and a concentration that was almost a squint. He was very serious. He didn't reply. He picked up the floor lamp and settled it in its place. With the toe of his shoe he brushed a few shards of glass into a corner.

"I'm hungry," he said when cleanup was over. I had spoken to him briefly on the phone yesterday. He suggested, "How about dinner? I want to hear all about it."

I couldn't get that woman out of my head. "Don't I get to look around first?"

"No. Forget that. This isn't a zoo." Hungry? He was angry. It was hard to say at what. My interruption?

I was more than a little annoyed myself. I persisted, "Why don't you take me up to visit the wards? I've never seen the inside of a mental hospital."

He closed his eyes, tired. He sat at the desk, began scribbling in a folder, and said as he wrote, "I really don't like to bring visitors through the wards, Millie. Anyway, nothing to see, you'll just see a lot of men or women sitting around looking bored, staring at the walls or sleeping on the floor."

"Like animals?"

"Like people." He paused, gave me a quizzical squint, then went on writing. "The dormitory bedrooms are kept locked during the day. They have to camp out on the dayroom floor or in the halls. They curl up there out of sheer boredom. You would, too, any sane person would, there's no way out. What we need are wards without doors, and someday that's what we'll have." He closed the folder. "Right now the system," he shrugged, "makes animals of us all."

"Just answer me this," I blurted finally. "What in God's name were you doing to that poor thing with the green gills?"

"Come here, Millie," he said. Putting his arm around my shoulder, he thrust his chin out at me. "Go on. Take a poke at my jaw for old times' sake. Or, kid, lay off, and let's go get a bite to eat."

There's a virile amiability I find irresistible, in Sandy or anyone else.

He put on his jacket.

Out the back way past flitting nurses and orderlies. Through medical stations and waiting rooms. Clean barren fluorescence gave way to dusty twilight out of doors.

We had dinner, a pleasant dinner . . . but where was the witty beast in him I remembered? The driving, illogical animal. I missed the furred creature. It wasn't till afterward that I felt like telling him much . . . my restlessness with business . . . the riddle I'd been avoiding . . . the theory that gripped me. He listened to everything with his characteristic assurance of brief intense penetration. "Your myth," he summed up.

I offered him a stubby cigar. It was still early. Smoking, we walked to his place. "I'm not indispensable to Fica."

"The hermaphrodisiac cigarette," he quipped. We reached his

door. He punched the elevator button. "But are you serious about archaeology?"

"Is sex serious?"

We rode up together. "It's beyond that."

And just before the elevator door opened, he turned and permitted himself to say, "Bless your heart, Millie! Tools!" His lips curled, and taking out his keys, he unlocked his door. I rubbed out my cigar.

Inside, he turned on the kitchen light. "Would you like another cup of coffee?"

"I'd rather have tea," I said. "I'll make it. Let me. I'd like to."

Into the sink he tapped ash from the cigar I'd given him and pointed to the cupboard. "Tea's up there."

I put the kettle on and found him lying on the couch, face down. His jacket, tie, and shoes were in a pile on the floor, his cigar in an ashtray. "Tired?" I asked.

He grunted. "Crick in the back."

I sat down next to him and massaged the sweated place between his shoulder blades with the heel of my palm. He was narrower than Carlo. Sensitive after my smoke, I glowed. It felt good to touch my brother's shirt. But I hadn't forgotten. I'd avoided it all during dinner, but after a while now I brought it up. "Was I imagining something this afternoon, or were you actually attacking that patient in your office?"

"That miserable bitch?"

"Sandy, answer me."

"Yes, I attacked her."

"Why."

"Because she's scared."

I gasped. "You attacked her because she's scared of you?"

"Of me, of everyone and everything. Of life. I got her to scream, too. Finally."

"That's good?"

"It's damn good."

"That scream was vile."

"Vile, my eye." He rolled over suddenly on the couch. "She saw the real world and she screamed bloody murder. That's vile? For her that's communication. She actually saw what was happening to her for a change."

"That's professional treatment?"

"Rape therapy."

The kettle whistled a warning.

I got up and made the tea.

So far as I know, this was his first use of the term, and he used it casually. Our conversation will naturally be of wide interest in view of my brother's later celebrated analytic work, and especially in the light of the maxim now associated with his controversial career: "The mind is the body."

Sander was then at that delicate and important point in his professional career where he had begun to branch off into the mazes of knowledge and down tunnels of the psyche. With his intellectual grounding previously established in nuclear physics and by this time in psychoanalysis, with his daily life solidly based in medicine and psychiatry, he now felt driven to synthesize physics, metaphysics, and the occult into a system of his own.

I brought in the tea. He had moved to the window seat. I poured. We clinked our spoons. We drank. And I told him in greater detail about my hypotheses and uncertainties.

"What do you think?" I asked. "Should I chuck it?"

"Chuck one or the other," he said. "If you're sick of riding, get off."

"It's only a gamble," I pointed out. I'd already talked to Satori about it—but I'll get to him in a moment. "A hunch. Nobody's been able to solve it."

"If anyone can, you can. Do you know anything about the anthropological background of your own heredity or about the esoteric meaning of the double sex?"

"Sandy, I haven't had time—"

"Of all people, you should take the time." And in the next few minutes I discovered that during these years, while I'd been living in the world of action, my brother had been meditating on me . . . all these years! "Do you realize, Millie, that not only for centuries but for millennia, as far back as anyone can trace it, the union of two sexes in a single being has meant not only sexual richness, but the final union of undifferentiated matter toward which the world itself is moving? Do you know—you ought to know—that a two-sexed being was once upon a time considered a heavenly figure, a kind of emblem of divine unity, and also at times a suspicious and even abhorrent underworld figure, reminding everyone of some aboriginal darkness?"

"This is the twentieth centur—"

He interrupted me, "Chaos, Millie. The primal Chaos from which the world emerged . . . as well as the blessed unity to which it returns. The earliest gods, the ones way back before Zeus, were the ones represented as being two-sexed . . . of course . . . they had everything . . . and I mean all over Africa, America, Central Europe, the Middle East, Polynesia, Melanesia, Australia, and Indonesia. In Borneo human hermaphrodites, because they spanned male and female, were also thought to span Heaven and Earth, and they were seen as intermediary between men and gods. And in the farthest, most ancient Chaldean version we have, the creatures of this world were not only half animal and half human, but half male, half female. And remember the Bible? 'Male and female created He them'? The old Talmudic thinkers decided that what this passage really meant was not Adam and *then* Eve. Not on your life. But that *all* human beings originally were two-sexed. And the importance of this androgyne concept runs all the way from Jewish mysticism, Arab esoterism, and Christian gnosticism to medieval alchemy."

I was not only fascinated. I was delighted. "That's right. That's exactly right. This is the twentieth century and I've been trying to bring all of that back into everyone's consciousness."

Saying nothing, he went to his bookshelves and brought back a much-thumbed volume whose crusty spine was cracked. The *Corpus Hermeticum*, so the spine said. I passed him a Fica and lighted it for him. While I settled back, enjoying my own, he opened the book to a placemark and, standing, read aloud to me:

" 'You say then that God possesses both sexes, O Trismegistus?' " He looked up, still exhaling smoke, then continued:

" 'Yes, Asclepius, and not only God, but all living beings, and even vegetables.' "

"Vegetables?" I laughed.

"Millie, don't you see? Even if you forget about the Philosopher's Stone . . . the *prima materies* . . . the alchemical Adam *philosophicus* and their *Mercurius philosophorum* . . . and the Rebis—all of them bisexual, all represented as hermaphroditic—still, the important idea here isn't really sexual, it's the conception of ultimate Power as a synthesis of all potentialities, a procreative Power, hence in every way bisexual. It's the thought of cosmic regeneration and plenitude as the abolition of our dualities, tensions, and contraries—the vision of some final transformation of the qualified Self, the Self of our own limiting everyday situations, into the total and unlimited form of perfect Being. From Chaos through Self to Being."

He shut the book thoughtfully and finished, "And as far as I can see, Fica has been only the *reductio ad absurdum* of your potential power. And everyone else's."

I was both angered and moved. Profoundly. But I understood him . . . my divided feelings came together slowly . . . and I got up and kissed him. It was more than I intended. My tongue panicked. A silence of birds. My silence throbbed on his lips like the necks of birds. Our nests touched. The spell. Snapped. Broken. A stillness of beaks.

He stared. He stepped away. He opened his encyclopedic mouth, he took a few breaths, and you know what he did? He turned suddenly and slapped me.

I felt like the green-gilled lizard in his office.

Controlled . . . earnest . . . witty . . . gallant to the last, he said with the vacuum of our love still hanging in his eyes like lights far away, "I apologize, Millie."

How I
Lost
My Life

Thanne hadde erthe of erthe erthe ynogh.
—ANON.

One of the last things I had got round to after my return from Sardinia was going to see the Commander. Cambridge. Harvard. Satori. A crowd of reminiscences had knocked at his door. Me once idly buzzing, tiny in the sunny world. A few changes now. Professor emeritus: in the Museum of Man his lair was one flight lower down, yet much the same—oversized books, typed monographs, maps strewn open across tables and shelves, cigarette butts thrown in every crevice of his cage, his light thick with tobacco smoke. And the beast in the man: yellow hair whiter, encrusted features, splotchy skin, fat in the abdomen, thin in the chest and everywhere else. A lion drying up.

We talked at great length of Carlo and Flaminia. I was hardly candid with him, I was the soul of discretion. But he came to his own jumpy conclusions, I'm afraid. Carefully he brushed invisible specks off the knee of his trousers. There was white granite on the knuckles of his hands when he did that. "Is there nothing ever out of the question with you, Millie?" My eyes rose, my eyes fixed themselves on his sour old Adam's apple.

"I know how you feel," I said.

"You know nothing of how I feel." He scratched his nose and ear, he fingered the bifocals dangling on a black cord from his neck, he polished the lenses on his shirt cuffs, he shoved them on and squinted at me. "You sadden me, Millie."

A red second-hand crawled up the left side of an electric clock. "You're getting old," he said, and I didn't feel like laughing.

The signs of my coming middle age—like the stratification creases of a deposit—had begun to show in my skin, three detectable time-lines in my forehead and a couple of windswept crinkles below in the future desert of my neck. But the genuine Sahara was still a long ways off. The second-hand crawled all the way down the right side and crept partway up the left side.

We talked on about Sardinia and Secession, about Fica and archaeology, everything under the sun. He seemed happier when I showed him the prehistoric flint and obsidian pieces I'd gleaned not many miles from his old stamping grounds. He admired them. He examined them closely to see if he could determine which blade-tool "industry" or tradition they might belong to. For my pleasure, while he went about this, he brought in from the museum a number of chipped stone implements and microliths from the Dordogne, along with a couple of blades from the Urals. With all these lined up alongside my own, I could not fail to observe again the phallic shape of the blades, each with its delicately tapered glans, each with its veiny shaft. Some even had a flange resembling the human foreskin. To my eye, the microliths were especially interesting since some of them appeared to be defaced replicas of the male organ . . . that is, if one looked at them with even a droplet of imagination. Seeing them all together like that, my own Sardinian collection suddenly took on a new significance for me.

When I mentioned my reactions, Satori laughed, putting down his magnifier.

He wouldn't take my hypothesis seriously. "Look." I showed him what I meant by lining up my pretty collection directly beneath his classically perfect samples. "Couldn't the crude blades I picked up represent a transitional stage?"

"Between what and what?" he scoffed.

I sketched in my theory rapidly. "Between religious art and technology. Between statuettes of the erect phallus—that is, religious erotic art—and the discovery, the realization, that similar forms could be adapted for use: man's earliest invention of tools."

"Hooray." Ironically, he clapped me on the back. "From the tool to the Tool. Millie's Law. Stick to business and gun-running," he advised.

The lust for greenbacks . . . you know, even a poet, who is widely presumed to be in perennial need of cash, is allowed that unholy desire. But what is the link, people are always asking me, between your life in art and your life in archaeology? This has always struck me as a peculiar, if not downright silly, question. From Chaucer to Stevens, from Marlowe to Pound, from von Eschenbach to Yeats, from Snorri Sturluson to Shakespeare, from Dante to Milton, from Virgil to Goethe, it is always the same. The poet's being, to say nothing of his art, is founded on his relation to present power and his penetration of the historical past. In my own case compelling, intimate reasons of anatomy led me to go further back, deeper into the past, than any poet before me. I'm fond of seeing connections between the depth of the dig and the profundity of the poem, between strata of soil and levels of meaning, between cultural diffusion and literary influence, between skeletal remains and symbolic structures. But these are matters for the critic. Enough to say that my life has been an endless dig. Money and love, poetry and archaeology. All my efforts have been one: to uncover. To probe. To penetrate my father's idle remark to me: "You never know what's underneath." Under the ground, under a pair of pants, under the layers of time, under the folds and slits of flesh, at the bottom of my mind and yours and God's.

For archaeology is surely not the reconstruction of mere outward forms, and not the study of the past merely. Archaeology is an exploration of the present inwardness of man: self-revelation. This is not to deny its scientific foundation or objective value. In the sciences of man, subjective essence (provided it be essential) is objective truth. What man has been, man is. What all men have experienced, each man recapitulates. What each man is, I am. These three points are circular and may be read backward. They form the three-pointed spur that goaded my research: self-discovery at all points. At the bottom of time, I am convinced, lie all the sufficient clues to my present and future. The extraordinary nature of time, its unique one-directional flow—the only irreversible dimension, the only irreversible flow—holds the secret of the energy of Being. On this fulcrum science and religion converge. And in their convergence archaeology digs down to a profundity greater than itself.

So at archaeology seminars I mulled over those little blades, if blades they were. I pored over the literature on the subject—to no avail. Nothing and no one was helpful. A couple of months' digging out near the Oglala Sioux reservation proved utterly fruitless. How was I to proceed? Please remember that erotic worship during the Ice Age was until recently a novel idea in the field of prehistory, yet to be substantiated. Given the dead weight of scientific opinion then current, together with ingrown sexual prejudice, my burden of proof was far from simple. What I found, of course, and where I found it all, became one of the classic sites in modern archaeology.

But it was difficult to let go of the past. For how many years, I asked myself, would I continue to be too engrossed in art to consider science seriously? I had been writing with an urgency that accelerated during these years, a pump of poetry that worked by night and deprived my eyes of sleep and my heart of desolation. During one fall season my financial career was analyzed in *The Wall Street Journal*, my artistic career was scrutinized in *The New York Review of Books*, and both together were appreciated in *Esquire*. I was booming. Yet hadn't I resolved years ago to quit after I'd made a million? I had gone up, now was the time to dig down. I finally examined all my vested interests in a series of tangled inquiries I entitled *Irrational Numbers*, but it was not until I had finished the very last poem in that volume, composing it in a feverish five days and adding it decisively to the rest when the manuscript was already in the hands of the printer, that suffocated elegiac scream, "My Square Root," that I knew what I had to do.

I now felt certain I could solve the enigma of the rise of human civilization. Like Heinrich Schliemann and Henry Christy before me, each of whom had amassed a fortune and abandoned moneymaking to devote his time and wealth to the past, Schliemann to Troy and Mycenae, Christy to the Stone Age in the Dordogne, I was free now to do as I damn pleased. Perhaps I should say to do as I was damned, to satisfy the daimon that possessed me. For unquestionably I was driven.

The scientific acceptance nowadays of phallic transfer in the rise of technology makes it hard to appreciate how wild and curious the idea seemed when I first propounded it. The notion that there might be an observable sequence from tool adoration to tool function, a hypothesis that gained respectability as the facts began to accumulate, at the outset only made my colleagues stare. After presenting a speculative paper on the subject, I submitted it to the *Proceedings of the New York State Archaeological Association*, where it was rejected for publication by unanimous vote of other members of the board even though I was a member of the journal's editorial board myself. I was irritated, but far from crushed. By persistence in the face of such scientific scorn, had not Schliemann discovered Troy? Of course I didn't have as much of the ready in those days as the unbelievably wealthy Schliemann had in his, but I had more than enough, and more than enough persistence. What about those early promises I'd made to myself? There were expenditures and profits in life that mattered more to me than dollars and cents. Fortunately I was not forever denied the chance to make a signal contribution to man's understanding of himself.

According to my original hypothesis, nothing was more probable than that very early man, regardless of whether he understood the role played by sexual intercourse in procreation, would have venerated the sexual act purely for the godlike sensations it produces throughout the whole organism, the transcendent sense of perfection, exhilaration, and grandeur, of infinite power and well-being. These are plain physiological facts to which all mankind can attest.

I simply theorized further that the origins of civilization had flowed directly from that veneration. I postulated that the invention of tools of chipped obsidian and flint in Paleolithic times—stone knives, stone axes, etc., to which all human progress since can be traced—THE grand technological revolution to which all later ones are subordinate—had *not* been the direct achievement of rational man. Not a step taken by *Homo sapiens*, the daylight breadwinner and engineering utilitarian. I saw the rise of civilization, the transition to a toolmaking culture, as the consequence of the religious impulse to artistic expression. *Homo symbolicus*, irrational, dreaming, libidinal, subliminal, godworshipping, transcendent man. Early man's religious chipped image of his personal tool—hard, long, round, and pointed—led him by a leap of thought (religion → art → technology) to the stone tool in its impersonal sense.

My theory was suggested by the facts we already had, but they were meager. What was needed to confirm it was a sequence of sites establishing by stratification the priority of the stone phallus *in situ* and the development of the stone hand knife in lineal stratified ascent therefrom.

I had already started to make preparations to carry my ideas into action when unexpectedly that year I received a crushing personal blow. Puddu had been captured. I had some hysterical notion, so heavy was the news, that if I got over to Sardinia again I might somehow or other be instrumental in securing his release. This of course was a foolish delusion. Internal factions, it was reported, had betrayed him. The legendary Mungianeddu had been not only taken, but taken alive! And within a couple of weeks, if one could trust the Italian papers, the back of the Liberation Movement for Secession was apparently broken, resistance demoralized and destroyed except for scattered fugitives—the usual spate of bandits in the mountains. Not long afterward, Mungianeddu was sentenced to life imprisonment. I inquired several times about visiting him, but visiting was impossible. There was nothing to be done. Yet I continued to hope something would work out when I got back over there.

I began to slip down to Washington from time to time for consultation with the staff of the Smithsonian. They were most helpful. Generously, unstintingly, they gave me the benefit of their experience. I found them an altogether dedicated group. Indeed, no esteem is too great to lavish on that remarkable institution. Criticism of the Smithsonian, which one hears frequently, is misguided. I say this despite the fact that the senior archaeologist expressed grave doubts about my qualifications and intentions. By his standards I was, after all, an amateur. In the circumstances, his doubts were natural.

Skepticism at the Smithsonian was one thing. But for Satori to tell me to my face, when I consulted him a second time, that I was unfit, to shout at me that I was vain and foolish, this was too much to bear. After all, he knew the depth of my motives and the range of my talents, he knew the size of my ambition and the fertility of my touch. I told him so.

A nose for money, he growled, was not the same as an eye for detecting the intricate ontogeny of civilization.

Ah, but how well I remembered the man's quivering tool of the trade, his divining rod! I laughed in his face. He had become splenetic with age. On and on he hectored me, ranting, "You have no right, no training, no knowledge, no science, nothing. Nothing except money!"

"And love," I pointed out.

"What?"

"Love. Will you help?"

The work proceeded slowly. Satori unquestionably knew more about the archaeology of Sardinia than any other man in America, possibly in the world. He had never been able to resist me. In the end, for love, not science, though he never admitted that once, he came through magnificently, offering detailed counsel and making available to me the resources of Harvard and the Fogg.*

Preparations went forward. My business training would not permit me to overlook a single detail. I took care myself of both "soft" preparation (research) and "hard" preparation (material, contractual

---

* A few words about procedure. Though we knew in a satisfactory way the location and distribution pattern of all Sardinian artifacts, the first problem was to choose the most likely spot to begin excavations. In this I was aided by a hunch about the geological formations in the area I'd fought my way through. In the tests I had made at the Smithsonian (under their direction) and whose results I submitted to Satori, puzzling discrepancies had shown up in my attempts to correlate the relative ages of prenuragic and nuragic fragments: stone implements, bones, figurines, and potsherds. A triangulation of dating measurements obtained respectively by archaeomagnetism, radiocarbon, and thermoluminescence yielded contradictory results. One possible explanation was that the volcanic stone, whose remanent magnetism was unstable, had simply given us an inaccurate index of the magnetic field of the earth. But results obtained by potassium-argon dating of the sparse fossil remains from the same area suggested a much older period. (This conclusion, however, Satori himself stoutly resisted, given the slim evidence, the contradictory dates, and the questionable reliability of the potassium-argon method when applied to fossil materials. Statistical reliability, however, is a function of diffusion errors, decay constants, metamorphic processes, and the amount of radiogenic argon. On all these grounds I was satisfied to accept the test results at face value.) Further, the volcanic stone implements had gradually suggested to me the notion that it might be best to dig farther to the west and higher up, not on the mountain plateau of Satori's own dig, but directly into the slopes abutting that plateau, since these had been thrown up by volcanic action, long extinct, dating from the early Pleistocene.

arrangements, transportation, and so forth). With the advantages of my not inconsiderable wealth, I put together a conservative, highly organized, rather lavishly equipped dig for its size. The staff was small. Me. No reputable archaeologist was willing to join me in this venture. Go it alone? If necessary, I could, and did.

At the eleventh hour I had to make a crucial decision. The possibility of harsh political reprisal, including a prison sentence, if my presence in Sardinia were detected, had not failed to occur to me. So far as I knew, the identity of the onetime goddess-guerrilla was a safe secret still, but other dangerous possibilities could not be discounted. To avoid arousing unnecessary suspicion and incurring both personal risk and risk to the project, I determined to conceal my gender—the very least I could do—scientifically neuter, let me assure you, but outwardly male. Sandy, at my request, got a passport and gave it to me.

I paused in Cagliari only long enough to sign the requisite papers. Since all permissions and arrangements had been worked out in advance by detailed correspondence, my visit to the regional government's offices went off without a hitch. In male garb I felt entirely safe and at ease. It could not have occurred to anyone that the cigar-chewing archaeologist might be that certain unidentified woman who, it had been alleged years back, fought for Secession in the doomed ranks of the MSI.

Though I'd planned to set out from the provincial capital on a Saturday morning, my excitement of Friday night couldn't be stilled or made to wait or urged to sleep. Furnished with the necessary permits and passes, I left Cagliari shortly after midnight. The truck I'd had shipped over ahead of me, with all the gear stowed away, was ready. Driving the truck, I passed villages that were utterly dark—whitewashed one-story houses running desperately through my headlights as if to escape. The roads were deserted, the villages set farther and farther apart. The stain of dawn bleached slowly upward out of the island. I swept along a tortuous ascent into undulant upland plateaus: grey waves beneath inaccessible cliffs. I remember one old lady all in black and toothless, caught in the lights as she stooped, huddling over a charcoal burner just outside her door. And a line of three women marching single file in size places along the edge of the road, each carrying a small forest of brushwood on her head. No hands. Olive orchards flashed by, then trees with branches like mutilated arms, maimed prophets imploring the land.

And lumbering and twisting up the pass between Desulo and Fonni, I could see in the distance at last—looking me over, too, in the first of the light—the peaks of savage Gennargentu.

Broken garlands of violet cloud hung up there, flowers and streamers of cloud, drifting down from the summit. As I drove the heavy vehicle, I had the queer experience of anticipating a gentle bump, a soft landing on the far side of the moon.

In Mamoiada I looked up Urru, Satori's old foreman. When I came upon him he was standing by a wheelbarrow (reminding me —one of those abrupt eerie flashes of memory—of my Uncle Lemmie). A shepherd nowadays, though unemployed, he'd also been a mason in the course of a lifetime and had had some experience in the mines near Iglesias. Finding old Urru turned out to be a stroke of luck. He was a reticent small man, a wrinkled wiry five feet of quivering muscle and stubble, and he knew the back country.

Satori, I told him, had given me his name—I was confident that after all this time Urru could not connect the mature archaeologist in rough male clothes with the pregnant girl of that expedition years ago. He asked about "Professor Satori," and he talked to me freely too about Mungianeddu Puddu and the Liberation Movement. "They've tortured him of course—" Urru was convinced of it— "but he will not die, and whether he lives or dies, it doesn't matter, it will go on, *it* isn't dead. And it has to be finished."

My heart . . . struck suddenly . . . a cracked stone. We both had memories to quell, and unable to explain myself or offer details, I shared silently the burden of his intractable conviction. I summoned up enough stoniness to keep my mind on science.

I knew in a general way where I wanted to go, south of Orgosolo beyond Cucurru e Paza, where in my opinion the karstic limestone formations were most likely to yield cave-sites probably habitable during the Pleistocene. Dozens of small extinct volcanoes in the area, cliffs honeycombed by fissures I had personally inspected, and the heavy concentration of obsidian fragments, all suggested to my mind that a certain narrow canyon was the place to begin hiking about. I spent day after day with Urru, exploring possible sites. These and later observations incidentally enabled me to confirm the presence of a profusion of mineral ores, including antimony, steatite, cassiterite, iron, lead, copper, nickel, tin, and zinc; none of them, however, in sufficient quantity to make it profitable for anyone to undertake extracting them from that inhospitable region. Down and up. We crawled, clung, and climbed through a hideous country of lava fields and dead volcanoes. The carcass of Gennargentu here was pock-marked and harshly wrinkled, littered with jagged boulders. Certain creases in this waste were literally strewn with obsidian flakes—that opaque, sometimes transparent, volcanic glass treasured by prehistoric man for making implements because it could be chipped, and thus shaped and sharpened. What I was finding were merely the chips discarded in the working process. I knew I was on the right track. The trick, however, would be to find the tools themselves with other datable remains, in stratified deposits, in a virgin cave.

The stark ridges nearby were outcroppings of that rusty-looking limestone; higher up this gave way to sheer granite at the ominous, craggy summits of the range. In the early Pleistocene, several hundreds of thousands of years ago, these towering metamorphic formations had been propelled violently upward out of the sea, a thrusting action that had opened holes of every size and description. Urru took me to see cave after cave: I explored them thoughtfully. There were grottoes and grooves and measureless caverns, scratches and slits and pockets and pits, inscrutable chinks and bare ruined choirs, black holes and sleepy hollows. Where to dig?

People have often asked me how I made my choice—a choice which proved so extraordinarily felicitous for science. Here of course we are dealing partly with science, partly with my intuition. Yet even so, a hunch is very far from accident. What often goes by the serene and dippy name of inspiration—sudden brainstorm and break-through—is most likely a logical process, however concealed from the investigator's own mind.

One cave I considered, quite close to the one I finally excavated, had a wide interior and a high-vaulted arch, very roomy inside. Above, from the grooved vault, dangled a reddish stalactite. And from the floor of the cavern, just within the entrance, rose a stalag-mite of iridescent hues, purple, red, and shocking pink. Looking into the cave from several yards away was a little like peering into an inflamed throat. Another grotto, which promised to be a comfortable site and easy to reach, like a nose at the base of a granite face, had two arched openings separated by a limestone obstruction. Another which interested me, but was difficult of access, was perched up near the brink of a cliff where undulant whorls of eroded rock framed a tiny ridged hole that rather resembled an ear. Still another was an aperture situated where two long crests of pinkish karstic limestone ran together like a crotch beneath an overhanging belly of stone. Access was through a vertical cleft, a gash that pitched downward

and led to a cramped lobby. The lobby fortunately continued, although the more profound passage was partially blocked by a ring
of limestone. This elongated cavern had evidently been created by
the trickling and seeping action of springs flowing from within and
above. Outside, the narrow lips of the opening were surrounded by
vines and surmounted by a showy tangle of flowering bush.

I didn't hesitate. My choice was immediate.

With Urru's help I found workmen at Mamoiada. I had to
settle for old men. The young men who were not political prisoners or random fugitives in the hills had been drafted into the
armed forces mainly, and I ended up with a somewhat antiquated
bunch—eager, however, to work. (Unemployment, I discovered,
was still high; money, food, clothing, everything was still scarce.
Even the new cactus market I'd established had provided no flow of
wealth, but only a rivulet trickling down through a dry landscape
of want.) Curiously, Urru, who did the actual hiring, selected only
small men—whether on account of his own height or because he
thought small men would be more adapted for work in cramped
quarters, I never did find out. Trolls: he assembled for me a heavily
muscled group, most of whom had been shepherds in their time,
gnarled, self-sufficient, earth-grey people.

It was a brisk spring morning—the chestnut and cork trees were
just coming into leaf—when we set out together in the truck. As I
approached the site again, the mouth seen from a distance was a dark
slit opened into the pink flank of the mountain and blackened above
by the accumulated soot of ancient flames, campfires under her
overhang. Her overhang caused a stir when we had all clambered
up from the truck to the site. The workmen stood around in silent
bunches, gradually turning red in the face and then looking up. I
said, "What's the matter?"

Urru, explaining for the men, creased his forehead and chuckled,
"She's pregnant."

I studied the pronounced bulge of the rock above. Evidently
they had some compunctions about this site. "Let's get to work," I
suggested in my most practical tones, "she's only a cave."

Taneddu, standing nearby, nodded. Then he touched my belly
significantly.

I should have known. They all knew who I was, of course. But
they accepted me—and more. One does not need, in a daily way, to
question the motives of deity. Perhaps if I'd known in advance, I'd
have given the problem more thought. Not the problem of detection.

They were wizards at that. I mean the problem of being a legendary figure for these men, alone so much with them on Gennargentu, their boss, yet their junior. Old as they were, desire had evidently not forsaken them. After work, night by night as the job progressed, their attentions to me became not cruder, but more courteous and subtle. As they cleared their throats, they made clear their minds.

Predu was a tranquil nut-brown man with a chinless face and a sun-dazzled look in his eyes who sat cracking thick knuckles and nightly pursued me with a narrow stare. Tidu, still rather handsome, had a mildly arrogant countenance, a hint of virile defiance in his swagger, in his leaning turn with loosely held hands and tightly held smile. Boricu was an ugly dawdler, scrofulous and heavily corrugated from the top of his bald scalp to the back of his neck. Jacheddu was a man of sarcastic gestures and volleys of loud lewd laughter. Taneddu was skinny, Pineddu was chunky, and they were both deep thinkers and rare talkers. Bustianeddu was deaf, a moody little man. And Totoneddu was polite, dreadfully determined to be gallant.

First things first. We had to hack away all that bush, a matted hair of vines, brush, and cactus obstructing her lips. In the cold, earliest flush of spring, even her cactus had yielded a delicate flower, a spiny glory. Down it went. She was cleared. In high spirits, all of us, we forced her at once, entering with pick and mattock, working her in and down.

Her short lobby was covered with centuries of dried bat dung. Into this floor I had the men hammer two lines of wooden stakes. Down each line of stakes I stretched a length of cord. The sides of my trench were thus established and digging began in earnest. They broke the ground with a will. So high was her floor level at first that if a man, distracted, quickly raised his head, *clunk!* It happened too often. Only the men's softly cushioned caps protected their noggins from injury.

None of them wore the traditional long black stocking-cap, or the ancient billowing black-and-white costume. Gone from post-Revolution Sardinia, gone for all time, was the majestic pageantry that had accompanied Satori's dig. After hours these men wore frayed modern jackets of corduroy. On the job they wore checked shirts tucked under belts, heavy twill pants tucked into boots. Everyday men, ordinary garb—yet seen from a little distance, at work within the mountain, they had for me that odd look of trolls, bent over, picks in hand.

I dug too whenever I could, despite their frowns. Though I reluctantly accepted the physical impossibility of doing all the dirty work, I kept wishing that somehow I could drive the passage myself. Never before had I so deeply experienced the feeling that the men working under my direction at every inch of the way were extensions of myself, parts of my physical body. It was I who was laboring in there to open her up. *I* was bearing down into her. And stroke by stroke, slowly as I pierced her with intense concentration and care, so thoroughly did I identify with the object of my work that at times I came to feel that the cave was my cave, the opening mine. I was piercing myself. I was digging down into my fissure and entering myself. Inward and downward into me I pressed. The chink of the picks sang through me, ringing against the sides of my intimate places.

Day by day, thrusting forward, through my lobby I drove my shaft, pressing my way foot by foot into my beckoning soil, pushing past my inner labial limestone, until I reached the hymeneal rock, which had to be hacked to bits before I could proceed.

We *all* felt exhilarated. For the workmen, I think, never entirely forgot the extraordinary opening out there in the daylight that had made them blush and stare at first. Aroused, playful, in a ribald mood as they worked, they could hardly contain themselves, and one of them had the wit to ask me if I thought the mountain experienced pleasure.

As I excavated, types of soil kept changing. Underneath the bat dung we found ourselves digging in sandy earth, quite gritty and inhospitable. To my surprise, this gave way to a marvelous moist loam which I took as a good omen, a soil that was soft, rich, and friendly to the touch.

Layer by layer I proceeded. I kept written records of the changing soils, numbered them, and pegged cardboard labels right on the section face: the side of the trench. I divided the men into teams. In each team my pick man now very carefully freed the soil, my shovel man deposited it in buckets, my bucket man made the ascent, and my sieve man, out in the open, had to sort the earth for specimens. There were none.

At night, discouraged by finding nothing so far, and yet excited by the work and by their isolation with me, the men grew more persistent in their courtship. We slept in tents. I had my own, with a cot and sheepskin blankets, quite comfortable. No one ever molested me of course. Whatever they wished or imagined, it was unspoken. The fires were lighted, the dinner cooked, tasty Sardinian fare prepared by the men, in which I shared. We ate it sitting in a circle, listening to the hooting of owls, glad of the warmth of the fire. After dinner they smoked *pastori* and sang. Taneddu and Pineddu were especially good. Deep resonant wavering uncanny music. I felt that they were serenading me without telling me. When they all sang, it made me quiver. And they played Morro: a game—were they choosing for me?—played with the fingers at ferocious speed and screaming intensity, a sport which obsessed them every night and which looked to me as if it would end in a killing. It never did. And always I was surrounded by old men and old arms and queer cunning old eyes that told me what they meant and wanted.

Once Tidu, seconded by Predu, asked me with a lifted eyebrow, wouldn't I wear a dress at dinner time? For safety's sake I stuck assiduously to men's clothes—the roughest and toughest of workpants and workshirts. Only at bedtime in the privacy of my tent and in pitch black did I don a nightgown—to save my sanity, or at least to comfort my femininity.

I had gone down several layers. Not one sign of prehistoric man. His garbage of cracked animal bones, his pots and pans, his arrows or fires. Nothing. I grew a trifle discouraged. Had I made a mistake? It wasn't too late to change. Again I examined other caves nearby. The Cave of the Ear? The Cave of the Throat? No, I was sure. The dig went on.

On and in. From a distance of only a few feet inside my outer lips, I gradually managed to get in thirty-seven feet. In and down. Downward, I sank and gouged and got into my womb a good thirteen feet.

From a generator housed on the truck, cables ran the length and depth of the cave, and floodlights provided adequate visibility.

We quarried and removed a thick ominous layer, a leathery brown grit, resistant and rubbly, mixed with bits of stone. To my anxiety, as I went down the soils grew harder and harder, one by one. We reached an orange-grey crust, a tenacious seal that evidently had no sympathy at all with the idea of excavation. Hacking our way through it was arduous.

But as soon as I had broken away this crust I began unearthing my human past. A pair of obsidian spear points. Each point had a beautifully tanged butt.

Tidu found them. Urru's flaked lips parted in a grin. Predu chuckled. The men crowded over, their heavy brows creasing in apprehension. We were digging up *their* past, too, and they knew it. Not one of us had ever seen anything like those dark delicate spear heads.

And after that first strike, we began turning up things daily. The more we came across, the higher everyone's excitement ran.

The following morning, half an hour before lunch, Tidu found two neolithic axheads. When washed and cleaned these turned out to be weapons of considerable beauty, an opaque glossy obsidian, highly polished to the deep sheen of jade. It was a rare find, and a signal of more to come. That same afternoon Tidu's pick unearthed an obsidian pressure-flaked flat-ax. By now quite jealous, Predu managed triumphantly to turn up a fragment, the elongated haft of a carefully worked flint knife.

From then on all manner of things were poked loose underground. The hardest part was to keep track of it all: we began turning over thousands of flint and obsidian fragments. Mainly these were chips, flakes without much worth, but every find had to be evaluated. My work became difficult, but I was far from complaining. Day by day we came upon precious, even exotic items. Predu pulled out of the ground a translucent macehead. It was triangular. Perforated all over, its head was slightly cracked. We found leaf-shaped obsidian arrows and barbed flint ones. Trapeze-shaped knives. Awls with squared sections. Flint cores. A tiny obsidian amulet in the shape of an ax. Two necklaces of stone beads. Unidentifiable bits of worked quartz. A bone point. A bone spatula or perhaps a hairpin. Another rounded bone pin. And several slender, pointy items that, so far as I could see, must have been nothing other than bone toothpicks!

With these I picked my own teeth at dinner that night, as did my men.

Jacheddu insisted on trying his hand as my pickman one day and was indeed the first to pull out several shards of pottery. These were reddish in color, incoherent fragments from which we could not make out the original form. But Jacheddu, elated at this find, turned out to be careless with the pick. After he had broken several more fragments in finding them, he had to be replaced on the front lines by Tidu once more.

As we worked down into her, both of her walls widened naturally, the quality of her soil changed, and at the same time the apparent level of her bedrock dropped away. We had come to a pit, either man-made or natural. I therefore experimentally widened the area of excavation, doubling the width. This proved to be worthwhile.

I had hardly made my decision, I was still inside the cave taking notes on the new measurements when Urru, standing beside me, snorted heavily. I turned. Tidu stood transfixed, his pick in the ground. With a jolt, I thought he had uncovered a human bone.

It was not. It was animal, and proved on inspection to be the metacarpal bone of the horselike hemippus! My time with Baron Tieger had not been spent in vain. Grandson of eohippus, hemippus was a half-ass. Elated, I brushed the bone free of dirt before anyone could touch it and took a photograph then and there. I need hardly have bothered. The leg of the half-ass hemippus was only the beginning. Next there appeared in the floor of the pit the characteristic hinged jaw of the wart hog! And before we were through digging in this first pit (for it was only the first), we had unearthed the bones of wild boar and wild sheep, dwarf elephants and monkeys, rhinoceros and gazelle, porcupine and crocodile, giraffe and jackal, hare, hyena, hippopotamus, and hartebeest.

Of course I was unable to make all of these identifications at the time. This had to wait until later, when they were shipped to specialists all over the world, including Baron. But I have always been an observant pupil, my hours with Tieger were well spent, and I made fully one-third of the identifications correctly. Evidently climatic conditions on Sardinia had once been favorable to a wide variety of creatures.

One thing troubled me. We did not discover a single weapon, implement, or microlith in this deposit. Nor had any of the bones been broken—which might have been the case had this bewildering profusion of animals fallen, say, into a natural pit or man-made trap —nor were any of their bones cracked open for marrow—which would have been the case had they been killed to be eaten—nor was there a streak of soot anywhere about, the normal evidence of cooking. Evidently then, the pit had served as a place of sacrifice. To please what god, to propitiate what demon, to avert what dire event?

Everything had to be washed and examined and—if retained— labeled, bagged, and entered in the books. A rough table and chair were my office. Here I sat, hands in my big basin, feeling bones, fingering tools, and petting microliths. But I longed to be down in her hole, and I spent every minute I could right there.

Boricu set up a shout. Pineddu and Taneddu relayed it. I ran full speed into the gaping womb with my trowel out. In a little while I had her. A female figurine of carved calcite . . . about four inches in height . . . I brushed her off . . . no, wait . . . male? . . . no, yes . . . hermaphrodite! Was it a spook—an item that by rights simply doesn't belong in the stratum it turns up in—or was it a hoax—had Boricu "planted" it there for me? As to the latter, I was certain: I had to scoop and pry too hard to pull the thing free. No one had planted it. But we were now down several strata, we weren't in Neolithic, we were already in Paleolithic, the Ice Age, and what was an item of carved calcite doing here? The image was rough but lovely. Timeless and enigmatic. It had a luminous yellow patination on its round head and body. A nose, no eyes or mouth. The buttocks were vast, free-form steatopygous; though pock-marked, the mammillary protuberances were gracefully maternal, very much like the breasts of the so-called Venus of Macomer; and there was a female "V" incision notched in the groin, from which cleft boldly poked forth the male member. Altogether puzzling. And to me personally quite unsettling. I'd like to be able to report that I later solved the "spook" question. Unfortunately, it remains to this day one of the unresolved archaeological riddles. But I conjecture that this tiny and archaic hermaphroditic image may in its time have reigned over that sacrificial pit, an implacable underworld figure demanding and receiving blood sacrifice.

And less than a foot away we began to come across tiny fragments of pierced bone which formed, when I assembled them, a necklace of rough-cut "pearls" of ivory, worked from mammoth tusks!

At this stage an unscientific disturbance heightened the tension of my work. Every once in a while I headed into Nuoro to pick up supplies. I'd look at a couple of newspapers and worry. The news from the Continent, from Asia, from the Middle East—it was all increasingly gloomy. War was in the offing, everyone expected it. Yet in the shadowy pelvis of my Gennargentu I was cut off from the world. Just as I wished to be. No radio in the truck. And by sheer luck I was thereby spared the ache of hearing the false reports, which circulated for days: reports of Mungianeddu Puddu's death during a prison break.

What had taken place, I was to learn soon enough, was a complex plan of escape which had been maturing for years, organized by collaborators inside and outside the prison hospital. Puddu had been confined there recently for treatment of an old, worsening, and quite genuine skin ailment. (Not *merely* genuine, let me add. It was finally fatal.) Managed by means of the prison ambulance, the escape route had passed first through the morgue, where a previously prepared corpse had been deposited and concealed. Before the alarm for Puddu was well under way, a fiery high-speed road crash of the missing ambulance had been simulated, containing the well-charred corpse. Although authorities were skeptical that the remains were those of the escaped man, their skepticism had been anticipated: it was ingeniously confirmed for them by an anonymous tip and evidence (all of it phony) that Puddu had fled to Corsica. And the search got off to a patchy, wrong-way start. But rumors of his death persisted, even while he was pursued.

The first news I had of any of this came days after the events. On my way downhill to pick up the magnetometer which I kept locked in the truck, I was met on the path by a boy of about twelve who came running at me—one hand outstretched, his mouth hanging open from the exertion of running—who began delivering his message even before he could breathe. He identified himself as the grandson of Surba.

I understood at once. Where? I asked. The boy told me where. I knew the spot. Cucuttu, up above the Cave of the Ear. I knew the way. I reassured the boy, and without returning to the dig, I took the trail past the lava fields and followed it along the tortuous rim of a tilted slab of a cliff till I came to the notch that led up. It was afternoon when I started, it was sunset when I arrived. And it was earlier, I soon discovered, than Puddu had any reason to expect me.

I scaled a jutting mound of red rock. I didn't shout. No telling what other ears were around. I stood at attention over that baleful height and surveyed the landscape for any sign of my old friend. With the toe of my boot I scratched the discolored limestone at my feet. Stretching from my boots as far as eye could reach rolled a landscape of sinister geological formations: undulating ruddy crags and eroded rocks with the twisted, fanatic forms of heretics burning at the stake. These figures glistened with a patina of mica and stains of bitumen. I rubbed my cigar out on the spiked soles of my boots. I turned westward on my mound to face the setting sun and strained my eyes to see the horizon against the glare. Sunset is a remarkably good hour for archaeological detective work. Shadows cast by a lowering sun may be hints. Did I detect a too-even cluster of shadows near the horizon? A crisscross of low mounds there scored the plateau, giving rise to the only regular pattern in that otherwise harshly tortured region. Illusion? Mockery? Or hint? Was I looking at the buried traces of primordial nuragic village?

Descending from that ledge, I took the only way through. The defile leading to the vast wavelike expanse passed between walls of cracked stone, walls that were cleft vertically. Going down, I made some slight noise. From a crevice a thick-barreled rifle was shoved in my face. I saw the clawed finger squeezing the trigger, the blood-shot eye, the sweaty granite cheek matted with hair and dirt, a stranger, and I heard him scream. I screamed, too, but I heard only his scream—a savage, passionate bellow that tore me apart, and then his black gun went off, yanked aside.

I had come upon him without warning. For someone who has been dodging pursuit, shooting is a reflex, but in the agony of recognizing me, in the instantaneous despair of being unable to stop that reflex of finger on trigger, he'd jerked the gun and in the same instant shrieked to release the dammed-up terrific tension of blowing off my whole face. It was a howl from the chest that kept going after the detonation had temporarily taken my hearing: I could see him screaming, wide-mouthed, soundless.

I don't think I ever again saw Puddu lose his composure, but what he did next was so unbalanced that had I been capable of any further emotion, it would have paralyzed me further. For now, because he had very nearly killed me, he began battering the guilty weapon against the sides of the rock with tragic, maniacal force. A ram of a man, he splintered and split the stock from the barrel and, with his gun half destroyed, began bending the amputated steel barrel and smashing the metal against the stone in a hopeless attempt to destroy it utterly.

Then he embraced me.

I was rigid with terror.

In the gathering dusk, we made it back. "The police are everywhere. But it isn't over yet," was all he would say when I questioned him about his escape, his prospects, his plans. His face had changed noticeably. The quality of bark was gone. His features were more ponderous, thicker and drier, and his entire expression was peculiarly hardened with specks like the glint of mica, a thickening crust of a face. Like stone, I remember thinking—not the first time nor the last, certainly, I was to think it. Under the star-fogged blackness I hid him in my tent.

The Sardinian dinner hour is late. The men, a circle round the fire, were still eating when I sat down. Foreman Urru informed me in peculiar tones of the manhunt for Mungianeddu, who had broken out of prison again, he chuckled, and quaintly inquired of me if I'd heard a shot. No, said I, I'd been in to Mamoiada with the truck.

With the truck? Predu asked. They knew I was lying. With the truck, Totoneddu answered for me. Before eating, I openly carried half a loaf of bread, a pot of soup, and a platter of meat over to my tent with me. Jacheddu helped me carry. He stood outside and walked me back. Then I ate. No one said anything.

Inside my tent after dinner it was utterly black and smelled foul. It was still there after I removed the dishes and came back. It hung in the void. I lit a match. He was on his back under the sheepskin cover of my cot. His eyes stared upward, unblinking.

"The men outside all know that you're here."

"No one will speak," he said. He put out his tongue and made the gesture of slicing it off.

I blew out the match. Standing there, I wondered about the rumors of his torture in prison. I didn't dare ask.

Solemnly he said, "No one will come looking for me here. To-morrow, after dark, I will leave."

"You'd better rest up," I pointed out. "You can pose as one of the regular workmen, we can get documents for you, Urru will vouch—"

"I have other work to do," he said. "And there are still men in the mountains. Have no concern. They're waiting for me. I'll be safe."

"I'll join you."

"There's nothing to join."

"I'm coming with you."

"Later maybe. When we have regrouped. Not now."

"Money—"

He made a peevish, throaty, satiric noise. "Tomorrow you will go to Nuoro for me and bring her to me. Before I go into the mountains again, I want to see the child." So completely had I put her out of mind that for the space of a black instant I didn't realize that he was talking about . . . "Mavi," he whispered, "wants to see me."

Was she in Nuoro?—how long had she . . . ? I stood in murk, hoping he'd go on. He did. "And do not be offended by what you smell. The prison doctors say it is skin disease. The skin on me is turning to stone."

Afterward I came to learn that he'd been suffering from the sickness known to physicians as scleroderma. But hearing it from him like that, with everything else on my mind, the seriousness of his condition was hard to digest. In the thickening silence as I undressed for the night it occurred to me that Puddu, who with the practiced fingers and eye of a shepherd had once delivered Mavi, knew as well as or better than anyone of my double sex. And today, having very nearly blasted my head off, he had for the first time embraced me passionately. We were inclined to solemnity.

Under the sheepskin the stench was sulphurous. Eyes closed, heart closed, desire closed, legs closed, anxious and exultant, I felt I had entered the gaseous cone of a live volcano. I drew deep sucking stinking breaths for panicky joy. But it wasn't enough.

I wanted to *be* the volcano.

He took my throat. He bit it with his gums, chewing it unpleasantly. The reek from the pit of his groin swirled up and I found his curving, bulky horn. I touched it with the back of my hand only, not fondling it but pressing it so that it struggled forward, straining against the back of my hand for more, while with his own grainy fingers he climbed down the landscape of my breasts, over and over from the tops of my breasts down over the softness softening, all his weight on me like sun-hot acres of boulders and blinding rockface, insectless and dry, where the soles burn as they hurry across wrinkles, now running, searching fast for a shadow that's always provided, the tenderness of cliffs, when under his chest I heard the sliding of small pebbles down a granite slope, and I listened and couldn't tell whether it was his heart or mine making noises, the tiny earliest tremors, or whether two animals I knew were in hiding, listening, had stirred, betrayed by anxiety. My thighs sweated, burning against his stone. And I swung my legs around his horn in a roiling tremor of my own womb's lava. I wouldn't loosen my legs. Instead, I held him tight there, his point forcing my groin. His sweated hands pulled at my thighs, my hips, the slopes of my volcanic mountain of magma and seething joy, and I wouldn't let him in. His fingers slid into my cone, and yet I wouldn't open, only my lips opening, puffing with loving heat around his expedition to the brink. And still the lava rose. Yet for some reason I couldn't open for him, some crushing pressure held me down, and he put his hand to the back of my mountain and let his fingers' force down into my hot molten cone from the cliff behind, advancing into my tiny enormous opening, he lifted mountains, moving them, he turned me over, around and over, he struggled over, head into heat, while his hands retreated cautiously to rocks and briar, one hand leaping from crag to crag, the other protecting my furze from the flame, testing the radiant earth, watchful for lava, as I surged upward, resisting resistance, as I burst upward into a heaven-high furnace of sparks and cinders and flowing metals pouring dark pushing rocks glowing red thrusting earth shoving sky knocking islands cracking me while all of him pulsed and pulsed and pulsed to, pulsed into, pulsed all into, pulsed always into, pulsed always all into always, always, always, always, almost always, almost, always, all.

The house looked pleasant enough, three stories of reddish stone, the one livable exception on a cobbled street of hulking houses and musty courtyards. With care I studied the street and its approaches. The police, I was to hear later, had come and gone frequently in the last days, to interrogate his wife and to get her to identify his remains. Divided as they were between hope and belief—that Puddu was dead or that he was in Corsica—the cordon had been withdrawn from her house by now: typical blundering, the kind I was familiar with. Nevertheless, I approached circumspectly. I rang and introduced myself to Signora Puddu discreetly. I handed her the folded message Mungianeddu had given me.

The woman was shaped like a bull, bejowled in the neck and thin in the loins. That huge bulge of flesh under her jaw shook. Jet-black hair piled in two elaborate coils on either side of her head shook, too. "The imbecile! To send a messenger!" Charging behind her voice, her frontal attack on me was supported by a battering-ram bosom as meaty as the minotaur's. "*Here!*" she stamped, incredulous. "The sentimental, strutting imbecile! Tell him he must leave tonight! For France. Tell him 'Bosa,' remember." Her flared, bull-shaped nose quivered. It was hard for me to look at her. That heavy face must once have been handsome. But somewhere along the line her features had grown not merely unattractive. They had become unappetizing. Each of her eyes sagged differently. And they were rimmed like two healed cuts on a tree trunk.

She instructed me to wait for Mavi while she went upstairs. "To prepare her," she said. I waited, watching a small discolored dog who appeared out of an inner room and snarled at me from a safe distance, and a cat who came circling my feet before pawing up the stairs. The cat was paunchy. I recall wondering if it was pregnant. "To prepare her" must have meant telling her about her father—it could hardly have meant me—all I'd said was that I was an American archaeologist, an old friend of the lawyer and patriot, Carlo Satori. A message-bearer. Certainly nothing in Puddu's note had revealed who I was.

She came down alone. "The child is absolutely beside herself with excitement. I told her for both of us that we will not expect her to come down here until she has caught hold of herself." She quieted the snarling dog. "And since you are American, sir," she added with pride, "she will speak to you in English."

I had all I could do to catch hold, myself. When she appeared at the top of those steep stairs, I repressed an insane desire to rush up. Excited? Down she came with frosty dignity. She was the most self-contained fifteen-year-old I've ever met. Extending her hand, she addressed me in halting, mistaken, but carefully prepared English. "Have a pleasant journey!" was what she said.

The silence. From my lips not a single word would come. Her peculiar phrase of greeting confused me for only a second. That wasn't the reason I couldn't speak. I was speechless because she seemed soulless. I don't *know* what that means, and I didn't know what it meant when I thought it, but that's what I couldn't help thinking. Though she was graceful and lovely, there was something wilted, terribly dried-up about her. Her face was peaked, her eyelids had a frayed droop, and from her temples to her chin ran those indescribable lines of hard-fought years—the incisions of age. Worn-out, skinny, mature, stately, beautiful, and encased in a heavy gown, she looked past her prime at fifteen. And yet, and perhaps more disturbing, Mavi looked distinctly like Sandy! My brother and I resemble each other, but she had his longer thinner face and ribbon-like lips. Quick, lean, and watchful, though wizened, she brought back memories of him at just her age, completely familiar to me, this complete stranger with Sandy's grey eyes and her own braided lemon-and-straw hair, holding my hand, unknowable.

As for me, I imagine that the bloodless pallor of my jaw, the bloodstain on my cheeks, the chill greeting of my speechless handshake must have been attributed to my worried, urgent anxiety about Mungianeddu's safety.

Signora Puddu suddenly arrived with a sealed thick envelope for her husband. She severed our handclasp and drove us apart.

Again, "Bosa," she snorted. For a long while this message of hers which I was to bear remained incomprehensible to me. "Remember. Tell him."

We drove. Hardly a word, though I made a couple of stabs at the question-and-answer business. The whining and groaning of the truck substituted for contact, for acknowledgment, almost for memory. Even the first rush of overpowering vague familiarity had already ebbed away into strangeness. Absence. Vacuum. Certainly I experienced for Mavidda Puddu nothing I could call a maternal feeling. Puddu's child. The pang of birth, the dilation and opening of the self by the tongues of pain, and the doll-like suckling afterward, these had nothing to do with the dignified adolescent beside me on the high front seat.

I think I may have wanted to love her, I'm not sure. But she was denied to me. I grasped that. Fully. However—and it was a big, overpowering reservation—I wanted to come to know her. To learn who she was, that was all and everything. As for affection, the only really distinct hollow of tenderness came to me from that single thick blonde braid she had, plaited right down to the small of her smallish back, brightening her darkness of mood, a blondeness of hair singular in Sardinia, but a braid common and (it seemed to me) serene and authoritative. I did not know then how braided was the mind, how full the solitude, of this extraordinarily silent child. Nor am I entirely happy that I have called her dignified, because her dignity was in fact a balance on the brink of inferno, a self-possession against the waning of life, a counterweight to the void.

When we were halfway to the site, I ventured to say to her over the hypnotic sound of the wheels, "He's leaving tonight. Would you like to go with him?"

So thin, too thin. Looking straight ahead, she shook her head, no, answering me thoughtfully but without a word. It was the beginning, and it was the continuation, of the vacuum between us.

My kid. The long multicolored Sardinian gown she wore, festive with brocade, made her skinniness seem ornate. Only her braid was fat. From her elegant grey retinas one rapidly intuited the quickness of her being, her very muscles seemed conscious and endowed with feeling. She was harshly beautiful, all right; somewhere, somehow, I kept feeling, withered inside and out. I couldn't account for it. Her bloom, her complexion, her stance had all shriveled to protect herself. She hadn't faded—she had dried in order to be hard. Sardinians can be pretty guarded about revealing themselves, but never, anywhere, had I come across someone whose bodily shell, whose epidermis and skeleton, so immediately gave an impression of total reserve. A detailed self-knowledge like blood vessels with one-way valves . . . in, only. Sphincters of personality whose established reflex held back everything important, everything I wanted to know.

Puddu must have been asleep in the tent as we climbed to it, but we were hardly through the flap before he was on his feet. First he embraced Mavi, who leaned silently into his shoulder, then he tore open the envelope. There were keys inside and a plump roll of bills. I remembered to tell him "Bosa," but pocketing the money, he thrust the keys back at me. "The keys go back to the she-goat," he snapped. And suddenly close to laughing, he shook Mavi victoriously by the shoulders. "Shall we go to Bosa and the Balearics, you and I?"

Sudden venom distorted her brows, her lips, and in the frayed voice of a crone, with a controlled, monstrous rancor I could not have imagined in a child her age, she said, "No, you will stay here and be killed."

I left them alone.

All that day my men exerted themselves as never before, the sweat running into their mouths. They knew who was in my tent. When the afternoon's digging was through and our watch fires illumined the depilated private scar of the cave, Mavi and I left again in the truck, with Puddu now concealed in the back. I dropped him off where he wanted to go, twenty miles farther around the desolate rump of Gennargentu. I made him promise to keep in touch with me, to drop me some word when he could. As he stood by the ragged edge of the road, I saw once more that look of his, the grief-smile I'd seen on his face when I first met him.

With Mavi I returned to Nuoro. There Signora Puddu took the keys from me again mutely, the barest breath of a sneer on her nostrils. But at the door, pausing to pick up the small growling dog, she said to me, "The Lord provided even animals with more than brute courage, with sufficient intelligence for self-defense. My husband, with all the courage of a simpleton, lacks the intelligence of a dog."

When the news of Mungianeddu's escape had first spread, the island had been electrified. But though the uproar continued, everyone knew, and knew correctly, that there was no chance of a comeback, practically speaking. The only questions were when he would be found—some said whether—and where. A week or ten days later the police tore through our site, but there had been no sign of Puddu anywhere in our neighborhood and it was still generally believed he had fled to Corsica.

The sun toasted us mad by day; at night, nevertheless, frost pinned us to our campfires and pinched us inside our tents. In the mornings we would find owls huddled in the gouges of our excavation, nestling there in Gennargentu's bowels for warmth. Picking up staples and supplies in Nuoro, I paid a couple of calls on Signora Puddu. The police, she said with ambiguous intention, had been alternating their visits with mine. Mavi was nowhere visible, only the shadowy cat, the snarling dog—it was the second time before I had the courage to mention that though I'd grown tolerably accustomed to sleeping in a tent, still, for a bit of comfort and civilization, a room in town . . . in short, I asked her, could she rent me a room?

Her alacrity startled me. But there was no friendliness in it. Up on the third floor, up two squeaking flights of stairs, she showed me a small room. "As a favor to my husband," she said with goring sarcasm, "who deserted me to go whoring with Sardinia." It occurred to me that he might have chosen to sleep with Sardinia in order to desert his wife. What did *not* occur to me—and should have—was that ever since then she had been taking it out on the child; making Mavi pay for Puddu. The third-floor room was small, almost empty. For a price, she said, I could have it that way. For a higher price she could put a bed in it for me, a rug, chairs, a bureau, curtains. I might take it if it suited me. Payment would be by the week.

But the moment I accepted her figure, she came at me, bargaining from a peculiar angle. "Mavidda studies English at school. Badly. You can imagine. An English-speaking person in the house is an occasion not to be wasted. You know, the world everywhere, even here, is changing. Do you realize what will happen when the present government falls?" She looked at me clear-sightedly. "I'd prefer a bit of Russian of course. More practical. But then," she sighed. "Can you provide English lessons? Naturally, at a small reduction in your rent." She named a new figure, almost the same.

"Daily," I said with delight . . . unfeigned elation, "an hour of conversation?"

"Written composition," she insisted. "Translation. Dictation. Grammar. Formal lessons—you must understand me—lessons that are not a casual favor to the child. Something that you will owe me, while you are here, above and beyond your rent."

What had I hoped? Though I lived in the same house with her, though I gave her lessons an hour a day before dinner, I was no closer, I found it bafflingly hard to make contact, I learned more from the grocer down the street than from the curved spaces of Mavi's eyes. Confronted by the feelable repulsion in Signora Puddu's voice, my speculations soared back at me like a boomerang. But downstairs at the corner grocery where I'd begun buying the staples we needed out at the site, a couple of times a week I got to talk to the owner. Signora Puddu was his landlady, too. "You didn't know? But yes certainly." My grocer's eyes and ears went up together, a child's fat face with a loose gold tooth, and he told me he hated her frothily: standing amidst his lettuce and leeks, into the sawdust he spat. I gathered that my landlady was a rent-gouger. And a miser. That despite all appearances of modest circumstances and niggardliness, she had a grand fortune salted away. Her second husband had left her extensive real estate holdings. Yet she was charging me, he assured me without asking what I paid, three times the rent I *should* have been paying. "Ah, she's well off, but you can get nothing from her, not if your walls crack or your ceiling rips. But her husband, her third, I mean, the one they're out hunting for, he managed to pry money loose from her, ah you should have known the man, a jewel, and for all of us here, a friend. Not the good shepherd, as they say in church, but still a great leader. Have you heard of the escape? Well of course, yes, in the Secession, captured and tortured by the secret police. But now for the fourth time he's escaped! And wait, just as before, he'll *more* than pay them back for whatever they did to him. Or if he can't, God will. But she, *she's* worse than the Fascists, you don't know the half, I assure you. The way she treats the little girl, for that alone, they ought to hang the bitch."

By then I had already begun to hear noises downstairs, whimpering noises I couldn't identify.

I told myself that these were not Mavi, they were not human, those sounds, and they were certainly not for my ears. Moreover, let me say here that by no word or sign during her lessons, by no unguarded, special look at me, did Mavi ever once betray to me a single family secret. Our lessons were managed in one corner of an austere first-floor sitting room, within earshot of her mother. Since Signora Puddu understood not one word of English, we had the possibility of a perfect code between us, had Mavi wished to avail herself of it. But my queries were deflected. Even my cautiously contrived, conventional writing assignments, like "My Mother" or "My Fears," produced from her only her equally contrived and evasive compositions. So when she'd sit at the table and lean forward to look into her dictionary, I'd study the cursive script her blue veins traced on the scrolls of her eyelids. When she'd catch my stare by glancing up unexpectedly, I always thought I might suddenly learn what it was like to be her mother; what was going on between her and her adoptive mother; and what it had to do with her father. I kept thinking about Puddu. Mavidda had eyes like medals already earned for unknown acts of heroism. Was this nothing more than the customary and pretentious sentiment of an adolescent: the pose of pain? Surely there was more to it. I looked at her eyes' large surfaces to discover what willpower, what hand-to-hand combat, what sacrifice, and I learned nothing—or rather something else—that I'd been staring too hard and that she regarded me with mistrust. But I took the hand that held her pen and guided the cluster of her fingers over the page so that her ink might flow in flawless English.

At the site new test shafts had begun to seem promising, and I began to push a series of parallel cuttings into the slope of the inner cave. The work was demanding. Patient in uncongenial depths of rocklike soil, my trusted front-line men deserve special commendation here. Predu and Tidu had been trained by Satori. They were pickmen extraordinary. It was very joy to watch them work. Accurate in every stroke, their picks probed and explored. In all the time they were with me they never nicked a bone. They smashed no pots, they rarely chipped even an edge of flint. The points of their picks were fingers, they could feel in mother earth. When their picks pressed something, they knew it and raised a ruckus and running I'd come. Bent at their feet with brushes and rags, I'd dustmop the specimen with gratitude, even when the hullabaloo was only for a broken tooth.

Regular as clockwork after a day of spadework and soil analysis, I'd head back for Nuoro in the truck in time for Mavidda's lesson. Still in my boots and covered with grime, I'd tramp into the sitting room. When Mavi went in for her dinner (and I was never invited to eat with them), I washed, changed, and left the house.

The restaurants in Nuoro remained open late. After dinner I generally took a stroll. I'd either return then to scribble verse (disturbing fragments later reworked and published under the title *These Bare Bones*) or else sip a glass of *vernaccia* at a nearby cafe, listening quietly and absorbing the full extent of the political disillusion with the Separatist Movement. Some now maintained that the guerrillas had all along been hardly better than the Mafia in Sicily, nothing less than a Sardinian version of Murder, Incorporated. All those avowed aims of reform and independence had concealed the motives of a violent gangsterism: personal and malignant ambition. I disagreed cautiously, with difficulty refraining from bitterness. But most of the Nuoresi took the line that the guerrillas, while patriotic sons of Sardinia, had been sentimental and simply unrealistic. "If the nation of Sardinia were born again next Monday, we'd all be invited to the funeral on Friday." No one seemed inclined to fight, even over opinions.

By the time I had my dinner, a walk, and a drink, it was almost midnight. To get to my room on the top floor of the house, I had to pass a door on the first landing of the stairs, and that heavy door, I discovered, had a way of suddenly snapping partway open . . . the stairs would squeak, and Signora Puddu would catch me more than half the time. "You're going to bed—" with that chopping innuendo —"now?"

With every snap of her voice she seemed to be snapping her long-nailed thumbs, imperatives flashing round me this way and that with a controlled hiss. "Turn it so, insert the key softly, incredible hour. Please remove your shoes." Even matters of information were delivered with hints and barbs: "Rushing in again, no, not you, your countrymen, the news looks bad tonight?" And in her simplest phrases something vaguely indecent. "You're going to bed? You're going to sleep? Everything all right?" Seductive, inquisitive, insinuating—yet she never invited me in. She'd just begin by complaining about the noise on the stairs, then ask me if I thought they would take her husband dead or alive this time, and finally switch to the international situation, her favorite topic—swaying there in that yellow door slit of hers in her opaque nightgown at midnight or one A.M. and asking me if I'd heard the latest news bulletins.

In bed, insomniac, I'd try to guess what callous trampling or what heavy knowledge of evil had left Mavi looking like a field of crushed flowers. Sometimes as my lost wits wandered toward sleep I imagined that Signora Puddu was herself in the pay of the secret police. In a hazy and senseless depression I wondered if it had been Puddu's wife who had ratted on him the first time . . . whether she might do so again now if only she knew where he was. Sometimes I lay there half-dreaming that the bull, Mavi's mother, asleep in a warm bed, kept the helpless child in a cage, suspended down there below me at a wide-open window. In sheer mercy, it seemed, I had no alternative but to crawl down the outside wall and unlock that cage. Or sometimes near dreams I saw that I myself, denounced to the authorities by Signora Puddu, had many years ago been condemned to serve like Jean Valjean in the galleys, that I sat chained now and sweating at the oarlocks, and that proud free Mavi, who came at last to rescue me, couldn't, because my limbs were stuck, warped, and clotted with a luminous mold, the color of blood.

Directing the work at the site despite these nightly distractions, my eyes twitched underground with vague intimations of an above-ground disaster, either for Mavi or myself, and in broad daylight my old Adam and Eve ribs palpitated with a heartache founded on nothing I could be sure of, grounded in everything I felt. For a while, sick with a nervous stomach or a mild dysentery, I lost my grip, and sulked like a scientific Achilles in my tent, while Urru took over. And then, recovering fully, I directed all my anxiety cruelly back into the uncomplaining and vulnerable earth. That month I had my workmen force two new probes into the mountain creature. For as I had pressed down into her, her walls had turned, then gradually sloped apart, and the width of the natural cave had expanded for me. Left and right now, battering in fresh rows of wooden stakes, I forced two additional parallel shafts in and down into my womb, my center, my self. Growing impatient, I adopted my own shortcut modification of the orthodox but tedious Pitt-Rivers method. I was still learning the necessary calm, forbearance in the face of time, which is one mark of the archaeologist. Time, which had toddled for aeons before our dig began, could not be made to run now without endangering the scientific value of our investigations.

Immediately beyond the position of the figurine and to the left, in our first parallel probe the stratification lines sloped again, quite discernibly. Though we did not guess it then, we were approaching pit number two. What we did know, however, was that we had penetrated through several millennia to an obdurate layer—red and peevish. This was not only tough stuff, it wanted to fight back. Picks could barely prevail against it. Primordial springs, now dried up, had permeated everything with calcium, toughening the original soil to something now nastily close to rock. Red rock. Excavation was arduous. But here, working against odds, we hit upon our first human material! Embedded in this calcified deposit was a glossy tubular bone.

There was more of the skeleton: it took painstaking, teasing effort with chisels and brushes before I had it all out, before I was sure. At my feet I had an adult male, with both his long hard thighbones and the delectable smoothness of his pelvis. That was all, there was no more of him, he was not in the best condition, but I loved him. I bathed him in acetate, I sponged his luckless limbs with alvar, I massaged his dear pelvis with ambroid.

I wooed him for the purposes of science of course, I fondled him as Baron had taught me. Your Neolithic bones are lightweight and feel oily to the touch, whereas your Paleolithic are sleek hefty things. Paleolithic. He was Paleolithic, this chap. Not a relatively recent man of the Iron Age. The only question was, which glaciation! I was exultant, I was awed. Ice Age Man!

Where had he come from? Since mankind could not very well have originated on the Island of Sardinia, he and his people had come from somewhere else, clearly. But where? And were they the precursors of the much later nuragic people? Tantalizing questions, impossible as yet to answer.

And not two feet beyond him, a human jaw. Not his. Adolescent teeth. The men were feverish. I was nervous myself. Everyone wanted to dig. I thanked them, but it was impossible. A dig must be kept orderly and uncluttered. My insistence paid off.

Before we had gone much farther we reached the skeletal remains of a human leg: the intact metatarsal, humerus, and femur. My guess was that it was female. But as more of the skeleton emerged, I concluded it must be that of another male, this time virtually intact except for the tinier bones that time had crumbled. We were all on edge, but the good fortune of our finds became overwhelming, it was really too much to take, when we realized that we were unearthing not one, but two distinct, reasonably well-preserved skeletons. They were, however, confusingly intertwined.

She was on her back. He was on top. I didn't blame the men for jumping to unscientific conclusions. Gathered around, they muttered and stared. Tension was high. Feelings were raw. Urru's eyes crinkled in contemplation for some while before he tapped me on the shoulder brusquely and announced firmly, "They are praying."

Boricu chuckled.

Tidu rolled his eyes.

Jacheddu snickered. He said crudely in the local dialect, "They are fucking."

Totoneddu hit him. "They are worshipping."

Perhaps so. Man and wife? Anyhow, they'd been interred together. Bustianeddu mopped his brow. Jacheddu made a smutty sign with his finger. Totoneddu struck him again. I had to restore order before we could proceed. On we went.

Down we went. We were in what appeared to be a second pit. It had not been hewn or carved in any way. But at this point the cavern had a naturally domed, almost oval ceiling with irregularly sloping walls. In this very chamber, near the east wall, well preserved in the compacted soil, we uncovered the dolichocephalic skull of a young lady. Without a shred of flesh to her bones, she nevertheless managed to look very feminine indeed, with a wide-open delicate lower jaw and teeth curiously fine, like a child's. Then the rest of her. She emerged not at all grisly, but quite graceful and natural, her long lustrous arms close to her spine, her thighbones apart. Cuddled in her pelvis was the brachycephalic skull of a young man. Chin to her groin. He, too, was disinterred intact. I took pictures. Urru hovered anxiously over the pickmen. And underneath, under the bones of the young man, was yet another skeleton—female. She was slightly flexed. Cheekbones down, hipbones up. Curled as she was, her posture was graphic. There was no question now about what it appeared the three of them were doing together.

It was a find beyond my most extravagant expectations. I left everything in place. For the sake of science I photographed this three-some from every conceivable angle. Murmuring was resumed. Urru kept the peace. Digging was resumed.

Multiple inhumation is a commonplace of archaeology—religious, ritualized mass burials. In all, we gradually disinterred thirty-six skeletons: arranged in striking clusters of two, three, four, and five . . . in one case an intricate wreath of twelve skeletons. Linked in phantasmagoric sexual postures, they had been assured an eternity of bliss. Had their ritual death been administered during a tumultuous and orgiastic celebration of life?—for the purpose of sanctification? —after some dynastic succession?—to secure a procreative afterlife? Had they been so arranged only after slaughter or had they waited for the end like that? A few were in what we should consider everyday erotic positions. One amorous female, no larger than a child, her teeth already showing her permanent incisors and canines but her molars still unerupted, had her open jaws nestled in the lap of a seated male. He had no flesh, it's true, for her tiny jaws to clasp or teeth to hurt or tongue to thrill. With his elbows wantonly spread in the dirt, however, and arched over her spine, he appeared to be still enjoying it.

A tall female skeleton was pinned in one corner by a huge male pelvis. I must say *she* looked rather too heavy; she must have been an unattractive woman. Chinless and brutal. Between both sets of their spread thighbones lay the glabrous bones of another adult male. For these two gallant and indomitable vertebrates there had once been two openings . . . but she was all openings now . . . in vain might one speculate. And on that supine second fellow's open eye-sockets rested the seated pelvis and huge thighbones of a female adult.

Further description here would exceed the canons of taste. (My drawings, photographs, and a descriptive analysis may be found in the *Proceedings of the New York State Archaeological Association,* Volume CXXXIV.) Yet one point should be stressed. The large single group of twelve was arranged in what is known today as a daisy chain. The men were face down, the women on their backs, awkward as this appears to us. Six men, six women. Twelve in all—not thirteen, as was erroneously reported in the *American Journal of Archaeology,* a mere misprint there, yet without the slightest foundation in fact, repeated outrageously in the *Proceedings of the Prehistoric Society (Cambridge).* I can confidently affirm that in this crudest crypt, even taking into account the variety of postures possible to skeletal remains, a decorous heterosexuality was observed. Frankly admitting the complexity of interpreting such a scene and freely granting all the mathematical permutations permissible to Paleolithic man, the ritual must be seen as one of mystic self-fulfillment in eternal human fertilization.

Why was I so successful? It is a question worth pondering. Was I smarter, more cunning, more gifted, more scientific than the most highly trained and widely renowned archaeologists? Not a bit of it. Was I then plain lucky? No, sir. I was just simpler. From the word go, I knew I had hit upon the cave of caves. Of course! Even the most primitive of primitive men, the shaggiest, hoariest, coarsest, most thick-skulled low-browed shallow-brained brachycephalic Man, must have seen in this very cave what I had seen. No primate worthy of being called Man could have failed, looking at that cleft, to have seen the same thing. No wonder numberless generations of men in millennia past had sacrificed all those animals in there; no wonder they had returned their dead to the earth through that receptive opening and commended them to the afterlife in orgiastic positions; no wonder it turned out to be one of the richest sources of archaic logic ever excavated. And no wonder I was now more than ever convinced that it would bear witness to the very origins of human civilization. I knew it all had to be there. Somewhere. I wouldn't quit, not till I'd drilled her clean, every last possible cavity.

There is one footnote to this excavation. The strain of climactic discovery had evidently been too much for my men. As I was getting into bed one night they surrounded my tent to serenade me first, and then had the effrontery, with lots of jokes and lots of shouts, to come in and pull me out of my cot in my nightgown. Tugging at my hands, they insisted on leading me, over my protests, over my laughter, with lots of flashlights and song, to the nearby Cave of the Throat. I was irritated at being dragged into an unlighted cave at night by so many aroused old men. But for group morale I decided to be a good sport about the whole thing and confined my objections to nervous reprimands. When we reached the cave, they hauled me in all the way under the arch to that inflamed pink-and-purple-and-red stalagmite poking up out of the floor, engorged and glistening. They pulled my legs apart and rudely lifted my nightgown out of the way. Even Totoneddu. I was paralyzed with the shock: worse, I was plain speechless. With all of them cackling together, intoning some unctuous local chant, and holding me up by my spread thighs over the ancient protruding deposit, rather gently they wedded me to the rock.

As their boss I was outraged. As a poet, however, I was impressed to the core and upon reflection realized that I had experienced a rape that deserved reverence. How else was I to interpret it? Some obscenities are sacred, certain violations sacramental.

Nevertheless, I fired them. I had no alternative. My status as their employer had been offended and my authority over them too seriously impaired. Celebrants, yes; workmen, no. Out they went. All but Urru, who had made a futile attempt to dissuade them at the start and had remained behind when his shouts were ignored. Urru's loyalty to the men, however, was older than his loyalty to me. He asked me to dismiss him, too, so that he might at least appear neutral. I did, for form's sake, though I made use of his services later.

I considered hiring a new crew, but beyond the second pit the bedrock and ceiling had so narrowed that only one man could safely dig anyhow, and I had some idea that I might be able to continue the actual work of excavation myself, alone. For the time, however, I had my hands full caring for thirty-six skeletons. As for the men I'd fired, I was a little anxious that in retaliation they might go to the police with the story of my identity. But I doubted it. What worried me more was that they might blurt and gossip widely about their experience, and that the police, picking up the mere scent of my concealed sex and false identity, might themselves put two and two together.

It wasn't very likely. But it disturbed me and for a time, I remember, the prospect of arrest and imprisonment preyed on my mind.

The *carabiniere* in the upstairs parlor startled me. "It's all right," Signora Puddu said. "You've done nothing wrong."

As usual, I was dressed in my workclothes, very sturdy and very male. But suddenly I felt not well enough concealed. In the dry air the points of my hair stood out, disheveled and electric like my thoughts. "My husband has not been found yet—" she began, but she was interrupted.

"Signor—" the officer inquired, "Signor *what?*" His voice wavered extravagantly in its pitch, suggesting that my real name could hardly be whatever I was about to claim. He held open menacingly at his waist a thick black book, chained to his trousers' belt, only a few inches from his gun. "Perhaps we can walk upstairs to your room?"

"Please, not at all," Signora Puddu insisted. "Stay right here." Mavi said nothing, absorbed in her schoolwork. "You can discuss the matter here."

I thought of objecting. But the officer had already begun writing my answers before he began asking me questions: "Very good, you are an archaeologist? You are American? Age, please." He had been oiled: a half-empty bottle and a couple of glasses rested on the table. *Nel mezzo del cammin,* I reflected, *lo punto sommo di questo arco.*

The two pets were asleep in the room. The pregnant cat I had often seen on the stairs lay curled in a basket; on the chair alongside Mavidda slept the little dog. "And you have occupied a room in these premises, renting from Signora Puddu—since when, exactly?" Seated at the smaller table, Mavi dipped her sunflower face from book to book. I hesitated over the date. Signora Puddu supplied it.

The *carabiniere* quietly asked to see my passport and began checking it against a list he kept in his thick black book.

While he checked, I turned, horrified, and said to Mavi in English, as calm and casual as you please, "Mavi, what country am I a citizen of?"

She didn't answer. She looked up—yellow-white eyes—sucked her underlip in, then looked away . . . features immobile, pale braid pulled very tight, and thin throbbing throat. For all the yellow blossom of her face and those breasts which were already swaying flowercups, she was skinny everywhere else—stemlike, stalklike, her inflexible arms, her infolding shoulders, the hardly-any bumps of her hips. "Your exact rent, please?" the officer demanded, glancing sideways at me. "Per month."

My landlady said loudly, "Eighteen thousand lire." She paused, then repeated that figure firmly.

This was one-quarter of the correct amount . . . a rent-control check! I dissolved with relief. I smiled with sudden rapt friendliness at everyone in the room. It was she, not I, who was threatened . . . a rent-control check!

Was it a mere formality by now . . . had the cop been bribed? . . . What would the grocer have answered? I saw now why she had carefully avoided giving me weekly rent receipts, but I had no intention of calling her bluff. Mavi was translating busily. I nodded.

"May I see your receipts?" the officer asked while writing.

Signora Puddu's unevenly rimmed eyes arched separately.

Mavi with one slow parchment arm began to stroke the dog. When it stirred, I stirred, the stroke on my heart. "I always throw them away."

The officer dipped his head slyly; we were all now in collusion. He finished the rest of his drink. He closed his book and his pen officially, patted Mavidda's head genially, and closed the door: gone. "It is evident," Signora Pudda said, "that you know how to handle the police." Her mouth was rosy and gold-flecked. "And now we will have a little drink together."

Her sagging eyes rose to a pointed pause . . . nothing happened . . . and "*Mavi!*" Mavi rose calmly, obediently, refilled her mother's glass, and filled a clean glass for me.

We talked about the political situation in Sardinia—hopeless; the political situation in America—hopeless; the international situation—without hope; I said to Mavi in English, "How's your English homework? Hopeless?"

She shrugged her thin neck. She motioned for the dog. "Sss!" The dog stalked obediently past the basket in which the pregnant cat lay dozing, and growled. The cat's eyelids flickered; its jaws opened and it seemed to sigh. Mavi caught the dog—a dirty mop of a dog, it wasn't much bigger than a cat—she scooped it up with a sudden, shy bend and played with its ears. She said in English, startling me, "Do you wish I say the name of the dog? She is Puppa." And pointing to the cat, "She is Cucca."

I felt gratified; she rarely spoke to me at all, to say nothing of speaking in English.

"Mavi has never performed very well at school," her mother informed me. "A pity. Mathematics and languages are particular weaknesses, they require the kind of discipline for which she has no aptitude. But an American in the house is a golden opportunity? And perhaps when the Soviet Occupation comes, she will have occasion to learn Russian from a Russian—eh, Mavi?"

It was a pointed remark, with a flick of malice behind it. I said only, "You expect war again in the near future?"

"Yes certainly, soon, very soon," she assured me, "though I guarantee we will not wait for it here." She drank, then leaned forward and said in her most compelling, mocking tone, "Did you know that during the last war Sardinia was occupied by the Germans? Did you know—how could you know?—listen, at Bosa on the sea, in my summer house, I have a small, seaworthy craft, which I keep always stocked with provisions and loaded rifles. At the very first signs of trouble between the great powers, of which there have been many during the past years, I have always fled immediately to Bosa. There at Bosa I listen continually to the radio. Should there be a more serious sign, I would immediately flee with Mavi in the boat, to the inconsequential island of Ibiza in the Balearics. It is a crossing I have already practiced—to a tiny village there which I know well. I will not wait."

"You really expect to know in advance if there's an outbreak—?"

"I don't ever wait to find out. Mavidda and I and the animals have gone often to Bosa, eh, little beast?" For an instant I thought she meant Mavi, but she clicked her fingers and the dog wriggled loose from Mavi and came to her at once.

She put it on her lap, saying, "Though of course we shall all be blown to bits, not even the Balearic Islands will be safe. Tell me, be frank, what do you think, are men beasts? Are they capable of reason and foresight? Or will fear make them intelligent—like my little girl here? Have you seen her tricks?" Shocked, I thought she meant Mavi, but with one hand she took the dog by its collar. With her other hand she reached under her own collar, and the nightmare began.

"Please, Mother," Mavi said, tilting her head.

There was a long pause . . . I cleared my throat. . . . "Pastry," her mother said. "Quick." I remember I was sitting in a rocking chair and I began to rock in it, unaccountably nervous. My pupil disappeared into the kitchen and came out again in moments with a plate of little cakes heavily coated with icing. She offered me a piece, offered her mother a piece, then put the plate down near me. Deliberately, she avoided looking at me.

I said, "May I offer Mavi some?" I lifted the plate.

"Mavi has no desire for pastry, I assure you."

She stood by her mother's chair. I wanted to resist . . . though I had no idea yet what I was resisting . . . I said, "Why don't you ask her?"

Unruffled, quite sweet, Signora Puddu shook her high-piled hair, then craned her neck round so that the flesh there wrinkled like a braid. "Mavidda, there, you see, there are some extra pieces of pastry, would you like one?"

Her tone was inviting. There was a split second in which Mavi tried to decide which way her mother wanted the tipping situation to right itself. She bent and touched the dog's fur with her lips. "No, Mother." She took the dog.

"Give me that dog," Signora Puddu said. The dog was returned. "Eat that." Mavi took the plate. It all happened rapidly and was said softly. "Now eat."

Self-conscious, with restraint, Mavi began to eat. She kept her medal eyes pinned to her mother.

With the dog on her lap, Signora Puddu took a sewing needle from just under the inside of her elegant lapel and said to me, "Watch. I suspect you have failed so far to appreciate this fine animal." Holding the dog down, she placed the point of the sewing needle against the animal's black snout. She pressed, and the dog began to whimper—no squeal, no bark, only a high-pitched, faraway complaint. "You see," she continued, "not to cry out, that is the lesson, to endure this life without rising up in protest, to bear as others do even the most unbearable existence, that is the hard thing." She withdrew the point, the dog wrenched its head, she forced the point again into the snarling snout—the black lips lifted into a snarl, nearly soundless except for the remote whimper.

She said, "You can inquire of my husband."

Mavi had stopped eating.

In her basket, the cat's tail swept and twitched in an arc against her sleeping body.

The needle approached again. The dog's helpless eyes, already vast and rheumy, opened wider—the pincushion nose could take it no longer—and suddenly the bitch barked. The noise was stunning. Her head jerked sideways, then shot forward, teeth snapping at her mistress's hand. The needle fixed itself in the animal's upper palate, visibly.

The noise—the rapid motion—were instantaneous and repeated. Terrified squealing *with* terrifying barking—the sounds of two separate dogs locked teeth to throat—the jaws bared, another lunge at the needle, and another, and always the teeth closed over the shaft and the point sank into the half-open palate. Until finally no motion, no sound, and Signora Puddu could put the point into the dry snout at will. Puppa remained rigid. There was not even whimpering now, only the red-rimmed watching eyes.

"My husband stood up and cried out," she said.

At the surge of barking, even Cucca the cat had begun to stretch. She had risen up in her basket on two legs at the sound, then stretched again. Too pregnant to bother, she curled heavily around, meaning to retire perhaps. But she came instead, evidently by long-established habit—many-teated, sagging, and shaking her paws as though wet— to the foot of Signora Puddu's chair. "If he had not cried out," she said.

There was no attempt to finish the phrase. She lowered the dog to the floor.

Mavi's yellowish cheeks were now white, veined over the jaws and red at the bones, as if she were out in the cold. I had begun a strange slow rocking in my chair—with what feelings, I don't know —terror? guilt? compassion? hatred?—I had ceased to exist, I think, just as if from the very beginning the dog's torment had wiped me out. I don't remember myself there; I just remember It: It whimpering, It rocking, It mouthless, It freezing, It pushing a needle.

On the floor Puppa lay on her back, quite still, even her eyes still. Obediently, Cucca's left paw shook with that wet motion again, then the cat's bored claws came through their sheaths and sank with electric viciousness into Puppa's undefended snout. Well trained.

The dog made no sound—in memory I see her staring at me alone, but probably that's only a trick of memory—eyes without a plea in them, without a hope, and paws folded rigidly against her gaunt protruding breastbone. I still see the cat's paw, always the same one, the left, the claws thin and spread like a spider's legs—the strike so fast it can hardly be seen. But felt, yes. And I am rocking faster. The rungs of the chair creak slightly. Besides that, there is only one sound in the room—a whimpering. Not Puppa's of course. Mavidda's mouth is closed, she is slowly chewing her pastry, the sound comes from there. With all the life left in me I want to rise, to mother her, to marry her, to caress her, to love her. But I don't rise. Her eyes are yellow like Puppa's but smaller, and she is moaning. I hear it still.

Should I have kidnapped her? Should I have consulted Mavi about it? One thing I knew now. I wanted my child back. But how? I suppose that had it concerned only her and Signora Puddu, I might have stolen her away to the States and faced the consequences. But she was Mungianeddu's, too, and no telling what he wanted. Impossible as it may have been—how I grieved, how I fought my grief!— he *should* years ago have taken my little girl out into the Barbagia with him. I accused him of cruelty, indifference . . . though of course he had no idea, I'm sure, of what had been going on at home.

Far from recovered next morning and desperate to get the child away from her mother, I invited Mavi to accompany me to the site. I knew she was on vacation: at least working would serve to distract her from the compression and torment of this house. I asked her in her mother's presence, assuring Signora Puddu that I would pay, that the work would be pleasant and comfortable, that the child would be safe. I wasn't surprised by now to find that her mother was unconcerned with matters of safety, comfort, or propriety. "What will you pay her?" We arranged that.

"Do you wish to?" she asked Mavi.

There was no reply. Mavi knew better than to reply.

The loose folds of flesh under Signora Puddu's jaws nodded. "An experience, eh?" And then, permission granted, she added, "Tomorrow."

To me Signora Puddu turned, saying, "Not in science either, as you will see—no aptitude whatever. And what is the prospect, sir, for a girl without aptitude, here as in your country?" She let one of her raw eyes sag. "Perhaps she can marry a rich American?"

Mavi bristled, turning through a blur as my own vision shuddered. And still the woman continued, shaking her jowls and goring me, "My husband, according to his friends, is sick, cared for in the mountains by a pack of bandits and, if his friends can be believed, suffering from a probably incurable skin ailment. He was better off in prison, eh?"

Putting a phone call through to New York from Nuoro is something of a trick. I spent the better part of that day trying to reach Sandy. When I finally managed to get him on the phone, I told him what there was to know, my gratifying searches and new sorrows, and asked for his help. He'd see what he could do, he said, and suggested I mail him his passport.

Mavi came out to the truck with me early next morning, carrying the dog. She held it on her lap the whole way. The day after that she took the cat as well, and thereafter both animals accompanied us daily to the site.

I found her, as I expected, an apt pupil. She was skillful, but she could hardly have been called enthusiastic. She remained as mute as the dog hanging around her chair and the cat hovering in the shadow of the cave, but she grasped my instructions quickly. I showed her the trenches, down to the end. The depths of the cave and its contents held no terror and no interest for her. Neither skulls nor soil changes evoked a flicker of curiosity. I put her to work outside.

There was so much that still required sorting and cleansing—the most delicate soaking and washing, followed by careful bagging—that I was genuinely grateful for her assistance. I explained the process and she took to it rapidly. While I labored back in the cave, she spent the days outside, with her hands in a bowl of tepid water, organizing and cleaning my finds, sorting out whatever seemed to be dross for me to check through later. She kept a fire going all day out there in the open, on the flat part of the slope near the cave entrance. In her long heavy dress she seemed warm. With her one thick braid she seemed ancient. With waxen lips and thin nose she seemed wise. And with eyes quivering closed, she seemed blind, learning by touch in the muddied waters the textures of my shards and bones, my pots and ornaments. I could have sworn that her hands—not she—knew they were in contact with elemental forces and inaccessible adventures, with abysses of time and sacred energies. I trusted her. I had entrusted to her hands my most precious booty, confident that she, too, must soon love and learn what her hands intimately touched. But judging from all she would say ("Yes," "I will," "It's all right,") her scrupulous care for the mysteries of this earth was founded on utter indifference. I had her string together for me the pierced mammoth-tusk fragments. I placed the incomplete necklace round her throat. She patted it vaguely, hardly more than that. Her indifference was relentless. She would not glance my way. I noted how she turned her face up to the sun and took the uncomplicated heat on it and seemed to enjoy the formless light. For a few days the dog clinging under her chair still bothered to yap at me from time to time, and the cat—belly hanging low and dugs poking out—wandered deeper into the cave. She was very heavy now. I wondered if she would give birth in there.

Beyond the farthest extremity of the second pit, my third trench had already passed beneath the level of the cave's apparent rear wall. Exploring bedrock under there just before all excavation had ceased, my trenching operation had been forced up an incline. I resumed my digging in a tiny tunnel that seemed of its own will to open a way upward into the womb of this indulgent mountain.

Till now I'd required a team of men to sweat for me in the bowels of my dig, and I'd accepted paid help, as any man does—in the main with thanks and good grace—but partly regretting that I could not go in there and do the whole job of penetration and excavation, reach in with my own two hands and rip loose the final secret, the needle in the womb, the primordial tool. The solution to my problem, I could not doubt it, must lie at her inmost core. If so, it lay buried there for me. I was filled with a sense of mission, calling, and grace. The cavern's slopes, the converging walls, floor, and ceiling, were now so close together, their once parallel lines now practically meeting at my infinity, and the possible area for any further discovery so confined, that the end was unmistakable . . . I was determined to fight my way through those last remaining feet to it alone. Grubbing in her calcified and slowly loosening soil with my two bare hands and my short pick, probing all her secret places with the scratch of my fingers and my tiniest tools, I rooted inside her vitals. Work within her most intimate organs soon required the ultra-sensitive manipulation of fine dental picks and a specially curved trowel, a dull-edged knife and a blower. Here, in a small natural cavity just beyond that eerie burial chamber, after uncovering first the tibia, then the ulna of an eohippus, between a few inches of breccia and the sidewalls I began to unearth implements—archaic things, unwilling to be pried loose, the most primitive artifacts I'd ever seen, except perhaps those from the Dordogne. When they were out, I handled them with sufficient reverence, though it was only later after they had been analyzed in laboratories, that I realized their priceless value to the science of archaeology and the study of prehistory. They were among the earliest hand tools and eoliths ever to be found anywhere in Europe: subsequent potassium-argon tests confirmed that they dated from 440,000 B.C. ($\pm$ 5,000 years), that is, from the first interglacial age, older in fact than Pleyel's discoveries in the Dordogne caves of France.

Nor were they all tools. Scraps there were aplenty in there, and chipped items barely recognizable as possible implements. Even discounting these, however, I realized that I was in possession of a considerable treasure of the most primeval blade tools, in the main volcanic: coarse chipped obsidian. These included one carinated scraper; a probable burin; what appeared to be a backed blade; two crude cleavers, possibly; two worked cores; a unifacial chopper; a single cracked stone that may have been a rude kind of hand ax. And one thing more. What interested me most was a channeled and fluted, rather elongated item that looked like what I was after, but which had probably, I concluded, actually served as an awl.

While she washed outside, I tried to go over all of this with Mavi, who listened to my excitement not merely patiently, but almost somnolently. Nevertheless, I was sure she understood. And for me, there, little by little as I explained it to her, detail by detail, the picture—the sequence—emerged. For me, too. I had now an extraordinary progression of animal and human bones, objects of adornment and worship, and hand tools, these implements going back from fairly sophisticated blade tools to the earliest and crudest implements ever fashioned and clutched by human fingers. Missing, however, was the first link in the long chain—the leap from sexual consciousness to human craft—the source of all toolmaking and technology and more, the unbroken chain of the human urge to manipulate, reconstruct, and recreate the world—the impulse I could still feel in my *own* bones when I recalled the leap of procreative energy that had driven me into business for abstract pleasure—the historical link and the personal link—the erotic bond between poet and businessman and scientist. Hard evidence.

I was bent on digging till I'd found it, determined not to give up till I'd reached the ultimate bedrock of Gennargentu. For surely here if anywhere, in this cave of all caves, the clue would turn up.

I kept on probing, pick in hand. On succeeding days, forgetful of Mavi, I worked in the earth long stretches at a time. I worked with a chisel and a drill. I was quarrying in cramped quarters now, and I suffered from a new oppression. Claustrophobic pressures. Apprehensive, I felt with dread at every moment that if I were scientifically in error, or if I now made one mistaken turn, the whole of the immense weight of Gennargentu would collapse on top of me. But she didn't, she didn't. With a lurch that sucked earth noisily beneath me, with a surge of air that jolted me off balance, my fingers and drill together poked their way right down into emptiness—a perforation in the crust below. The crust there crumbled inward. My tiny drill had punched a hole into a vacuum. A small hollow. Hitherto sealed—an utterly black empty void? With both hands I reached in, scooping and scraping.

There was . . . something. Some . . . thing in there . . . several things . . . small . . . I investigated with fingers first, touching gingerly and then delicately maneuvering a long searchlight in through the aperture, trying to get the shadows off whatever. . . .

I ran out of the abyss and into the light of day to shout to Mavi, to tootle hysterically, to announce, to explicate, to celebrate . . . she was not at the fire, not at the basin . . . I found her at last . . . and I shrieked my science at her.

But let me not speak loudly or rashly here. Yes, I exulted. But for the record I prefer to describe my last finds objectively and conservatively. (Additional detail will be found in *PNYAA*, CXXXIV, 12–39.) Preserved by the vacuum in which they had been trapped for hundreds of millennia were two elongated tools of dull, coarsely flaked obsidian, nineteen and twenty centimeters in length. One of them lay cracked in three fragments, the other was virtually intact. One stump was missing from its tripod base. Analysis of the particular method of pressure-chipping subsequently confirmed these artifacts to be in lineal evolution with the primeval implements unearthed nearby, but older by a gap of centuries (if one accepts the fission and potassium-argon dates provided by the rest of the material). I did not hesitate to surmise as much immediately, and to conclude that these tools, whose function seemed to meet the eye, were *not* functional—as evidenced by the deeply cupped and flanged support on which they had once stood erect; and by the absence of any edge for cutting or tip for puncturing. I had wrested from the earth the ritual objects of a sacrament older by far than the adoration of the Mediterranean mother-goddess, older than the worship of fertility itself, we may suspect. The workmanship was still elementary, but not without its own severe grace. Executed with a primitive and stylized artistry, the bold tumescence of shaft and glans was unmistakable. Though worked with care, these artifacts had surely served neither as dildos nor as implements. The cup at the base, discernible even in the broken phallus, and the support provided by three squat legs, made manifest their religious intention. Both small cups were empty, but inches away, deposited in a large fragment of once polished bone (unidentified as yet) and stored in this airless womb for hundreds of thousands of years, lay more than a dozen seeds, each about the size of a button. They reminded me at once of the cactus buttons I had seen at the tower of Barbagia sos Nidos fifteen years earlier on the eve of Mavi's birth. Though here again I had to wait for laboratory confirmation, it did not take much ratiocination or inspiration to conjecture, with pride and awe, that these archaic seeds must have played their part in an unthinkably distant rite of worship—mystic . . . phallic . . . primeval . . . yet clearly human.

It struck me forcibly that the seeds might be the key to that remote sanctuary. I had come looking for tools. Fragile black powdery seeds preserved in a vacuum were beyond anything I had anticipated. Perhaps they were even a clue to all the material I had uncovered in the uterine cave from the start. There remained one thing to do—it was beyond science and scientists—it was not beyond me.

Devoutly, I took one of the little seeds and put it to my lips.

I wanted to understand *more*—more archaeologically, of course, but also more poetically. I was hoping, in fact, for a kind of participatory enlightenment. I wanted to reach down further, farther back through time than even archaeology envisions. So kneeling before the alien sanctuary I had pierced, I acknowledged it directly, I sought to include myself in its meaning. And in a flow of veneration for the divinity of the mountain that had permitted me to approach this sanctum, I did the most reverent thing I could think of.

The seed shriveled to dust in my mouth, turning instantly to fine powder when slightly pressed. Its dryness and bitterness did not appall me. In prayerful thanks, my saliva flowed, and flowed copiously. I kept swallowing, though the taste numbed my palate. I lowered my head in simple respect, but nothing happened. A minute or two of disappointed expectancy, then a minute more of homage, it was all I could manage before I ran out of the cave to shout the news to the world—to air, to sun, to Mavi.

Can you imagine my feelings? In explaining all this to Mavi, when I found her, I was not at all calm, I simmered and boiled over with enthusiasm. She heard me out. I had found her standing against the truck. She was quite impassive. In her own rigidly contained way, however, she seemed to be excited, too—so skinny, tired, trembling—but not excited, I began at length to perceive, by anything I was saying. In fact . . . was she not even interested?—had she not heard a thing?—she was leaning peculiarly against the back of the truck, her shiny elbows tight against her waist, her flowerbell breasts pressed between her arms. I became aware of the cat wailing over the steady whirring sound of the generator. Below the double doors at the back of the truck, Cucca, stalking back and forth up on the rear bumper, arched and rubbed her back strangely.

"Do you understand?"

"What."

"What a day this is for science?" I said.

"Go away," Mavi said. "Please."

It was one of the most disconcerting moments of my life. Clearly I was unwanted, my discovery for her was an irrelevance—yet in some way I couldn't fathom, she did somehow seem excited . . . and exhausted. Her cheeks were pulsing. I soothed the strain there, caressing the pulse in her cheek. Instantly the cat's wail modulated to a new pitch. My movement must have done something—increased Cucca's urgency—the gyrations against the door of the truck changed to frantic clawing. Her claws scratched audibly and visibly into the polish and paint on the metal. She must have just had her kittens —I hadn't noticed any change in her heaviness, as a matter of fact. It was Mavi's face I'd read: emptied, sagging with fatigue and joy, as if she'd given birth in pain. I asked as calmly as I could, "Did you lock her kittens inside the truck?"

She didn't answer.

Slowly horrified at her expression, I said, "Did you drown Cucca's kittens?" I was aware that I wanted not to have to think about it, wanted to get back to my discovery without the fuss of understanding her or burying them.

Her eyes were fixed on the door of the truck; she hadn't been crying. Except for an irregular swallowing, except for an almost imperceptible rubbing of her childlike wrists against her thighs, she was very still, she hadn't moved since I'd found her here. I doubt if she had actually looked at me more than an instant. But now—I was startled—she gently pinched my arm. It was slight, but evidently important. She had decided to share something with me. It was the first time she had shared anything with me, and though it was a trifle, after it came everything else.

"No," she said finally, "they are alive. Six. Four black kittens and two grey-and-white. I have given them to Puppa. It's my decision."

I thought I hadn't heard correctly. I thought I was imagining it . . . the seed I'd swallowed . . . "You gave the kittens . . . to the dog?"

"Don't be afraid. She wants kittens, too, yes, and she will love them as much as Cucca. But I have disciplined the cat now, which she deserves." She was very happy. "I've decided."

I tried the door handle. Locked. Mavi was already on her way up the slope. I went round to the cab of the truck to get the keys out of the ignition. Keys weren't there, she must have used them to open the rear doors but she hadn't put them back, I looked around, dropped them? hidden them? taken them? I almost lost my voice. . . . "Mavi!" She was heading for the mouth of the cave. "Give me the key!" I desperately picked up a screwdriver from the floor under the seat, went back round to the truck door, looked first to see if by any chance the keys were still lying on the bumper or nearby. The cat stood on her hind legs, straining for the high handle as though to help me—I tried to force the door.

The new noise must have wakened them inside . . . the dog began to bark . . . a piercing maternal yapping sound . . . a bark of triumph . . . and the six newborn blind bits of kitten flesh began to pipe . . . shrill, faint, so many, with such energy . . . the cat went wild at the door handle—and inside the truck I heard Mavi's terrible loving vengeance, her motherly delight, the dog's brute throat exploding through the metal, proclaiming that there was justice on earth, that love followed patience, that after mutilation came six puppies.

I made my way after her up the hill and back down into the ground and through the trenches and pits, past one floodlight after another, and found her at the end where I'd been scraping. She was huddled in the shadows of the rock walls. "The key," I said peremptorily. The ceiling was so low I had to crouch to get in there. "Let's have it."

She was expressionless. "Maybe I still have it," she said, and added, playing with me, "or maybe an hour ago I threw it down the hill outside somewhere."

I was fully aware that the anguish of the child was greater than the pain of the animals outside . . . nevertheless, "I want that key. Right now," I said, reaching out. "Hand it over." I shook her by the shoulder.

Her shoulder darted away under my touch and at the same instant her other hand came at me, at my face, all five nails extended to caress me. I jerked to one side and to avoid striking my head, swerved to my knees. But she hadn't missed her aim. And she was on me by that time. Seizing my neck, she clung there, half tearing my flesh and hugging my head, half petting my throat and choking me. Berserk, she seethed at my dumbfounded mouth, sweeping it with a lover's tongue and no mistake.

I shoved at her and pulled myself out of her range. Jerking up, I hit my head hard and hot-brained, a sting that ran from the crown of my skull into my jaw like a bright awful flavor. And then my eyes clamped on darkness.

Seconds later when they opened, my first fear was the seed . . . my first hope . . . hadn't I hallucinated that mix-up of love? . . . surely I could deal with my own daughter, reach, comprehend, and win her back to me? Hadn't I always come out on top? I felt the wet on my nose, jaw, neck, blood where her fingers had registered her first protest. The floodlights came rippling back into position, in and out. And I saw Mavi's face, serious and watchful, in and out, her distance from me shifting, something dizzy about my sense of distance, as I raised my head and said with thickening speech in English, "No God there isn't in life Mavi you don't know. About me—" and realized what language I was talking and shifted immediately to hers, "Mavi, you don't know. I'm not—"

"Of course I know," she replied with incredible and calloused love. "You're not a man."

Had I given myself away somehow? I thought, feeling my head where the swelling . . . and then what she was saying came over me and I wanted my eyes to close again.

She was coming closer. I wobbled away. To stave her off, I announced without fuss and bluntly, "I'm your mother." My feet were weak.

"I know that," she said, half-sneering. "Did you think I didn't know that?"

The walls of the cave were too close. I hoped prayed wished I was imagining it, every word. Maybe I was. Goddamn seed, goddamn rock, I had a couple of reasons to be dizzy and hearing things. "Did Mungianeddu tell you? In the tent?"

She laughed without sound, without showing her teeth, more savage than with teeth or sound. "He didn't have to. I have been waiting for fifteen years. From the minute the she-goat came upstairs to tell me you had arrived, I knew who had come for me."

Behind her eyes, where the shadow of her head blackened the rock, the low ceiling swayed, troubling my thoughts with nervous fear, ruining my concentration with sickening claustrophobic . . . she-goat. . . . "Your mother . . . does she . . . "

"Yes, she *knows*. And perfectly well. Of course she knows. Exactly who you are. She has been letting you stay, she has been keeping you there in order to put me to the torture, to torment me further, a little more every day." She came closer. "And you. To torture us both." And she began to undress. "But I've decided."

Vertigo, nausea, fear of being touched, broken. When her fingers approached my eyes and nose with the needle, I winced. Needle? What—there was no needle of course, I told myself. I warned myself that my sense of reality and proportion was hopelessly warped. I wasn't even sure she was undressing, or had been saying . . . what? There was no point in trying to reason with her at a time like this. The crucial thing now was to get help: someone to lean on to get myself out of this cave. I said quietly, "I need a little help, Mavi. I ate one of the seeds."

In her slip, she turned away, and the look of disdain curtaining her eyelids curdled my mind. A few feet away from me she crouched, examining the hollow I'd found, the vacuum I'd unsealed. The walls everywhere were in motion. My stomach . . .

She reached down into the hollow. "Don't touch anything," I instructed her gently. I got to my knees to crawl. She had taken the scooped bone out and . . . "Put that—"

She had picked out one of the seeds and holding it up to me for inspection, holding it out to me—"One of these?"—she suddenly flexed her arm to her mouth and swallowed it.

I got to my feet shuddering with renewed strength, bent under the cramping rock, horrified beyond telling.

Opposite me, hunched over, she stood and with elbows spread and both hands raised, stronger than me, she touched the roof. She palmed the rock over her head, holding it up for a minute or two. Then she stooped once more, slowly, and slowly offered me another one.

I took it from her hand, mesmerized.

She nodded.

I swallowed it. The same instant pulverizing and numbing bitterness, the same rush of saliva . . .

She nodded again and one of her eyes lost its luster and turned into a dusty seed. Her face, nevertheless, had a transparency and flush I had not seen in it before. Her cheeks bobbed and sparkled like thin red leaves turning in the sun, her closed mouth shook loose for my eyes new messages I couldn't quite get, and then her braid came coiling over her shoulders, a friendly snake. I knew that snake. I guessed it wasn't moving at all. "I want my father and mother," she said distinctly. I understood. No one had spoken, no one was moving. I looked at the walls all around me and noticed for the first time a pronounced grain on the rock surface, a pattern in the stone I'd never seen, and then the grain began to writhe for me. It gyrated slowly with increasing energy until the entire pattern seemed to come up several inches off the surface of the rock and grow luminous with unsuspected colors, hues that advanced and shifted into other hues, and then . . . flooded with color . . . the entire grain of the rock came sliding right off the wall and enveloped me. I had a sudden impulse to look after Mavi, was she all right? was she wrapped safely in colors? was she with me? I turned to look. Mavi? Her smile was a braid. Her shoulders and her bosom and her hips had grown, and they heaved, they swung, they danced.

They danced, and I was scared. I took a remarkably slow breath.

Something sturdy in me resisted, something vigorously workaday, self-conserving, cautious, moral, and sane. Resisting, I grew all at once curious and scientific, I thought of crawling past Mavi and examining—perhaps breaking—the one phallic image that was still intact to see if I could break the trance and stop Mavi from growing and dancing her life and death, to stop all torture and desire, and with them joy. The urge was powerful. But something in me of still greater power, much greater, resisted my resistance . . . dispelled it . . . and something oddly sad in me, confiding and quiet, told me that images of sex had nothing to do with anything that was now happening or had ever happened. Nor did anyone's genitalia, never. And the moment I understood, the mountain gave way and fell on me. Crushing me—I thought—peculiarly resigned—but no, it came down around me gradually and maternally. Not like an avalanche, the incredible weight drifted in like a hug to my very bones, a blanket of stone. It enfolded me, time slowed down, and I took another, longer breath.

My heart beat.

a long time later another breath, rasping until

braking to a halt, time slowed down in me further and then listening

the incredible interval from my next labored breath to my next was so long that

each rasp of my breath so unutterably slow that

the interval lingering so nearly forever that

prolonged for years, the empty interval of time from one beat of my heart to the next was so forsaken, and the one heartbeat that came long-lastingly thundering through me after centuries, and the next when it finally drifted in after vacant thousands of centuries so slow, so much slower, all time sliding to a pause, that

enduring heartbeat

one

and after an emptiness close to infinite, a nearly

infinite space of listening and waiting for two, there came only absence

no beat

and no time

I was nothing

and It was gone

an eternity

un-

and very slowly

It

un-
began
believably
overpowering sweetness
and the most extreme tenderness of all tenderness blessed time-
lessness and encircled it, blossoming around space, it came into me, and
filled me up, brimming
I had never known
brimming
When a voice
of judgment withheld
of limitless reassurance of inexhaustible patience of sadness edged
with the slightest possible satire enfolded in personal love of someone's distinctive turn of voice never before heard
in cadences of unimaginable tenderness for me
nodded slowly
telling me
"You knew, Millie-Willie,
"You knew."

Time once more
without me
Begins the world
All over through me and I am whirring positrons and neutrons
and antiprotons and I am slowly dancing
Because It is energy and music and It keeps on coming out of
the void, it keeps on coming through me out of nothingness, dancing
me back into existence because I am inside the beat, and time blowing through me, time was blowing itself up, unfurling me as I danced
moment within moment not sweeping forward in a long line of moments but each one concentric and expanding, each one energetically
expectant, a swelling spreading spherical time, the nearest instant and
the farthest reaches of time, any part of time, my lifetime, the time

elapsed since Man appeared on earth, the geological evolution of seas and mountains, each one a concentric bubble of the same duration.

Keeping time the cosmos has been sweeping it was sweeping now to its fullness in time and contracting it would contract back back to zero then of its essence energy beat dance the play of it arise and in a single beat expand to fullness a single beat and so on forever every tiniest instant every breath or act pulse and consume itself to zero and a new breath or new act pulses expands then dies and the energy beats forward mountains rise flowers open trees shoot up then shrivel into the ground of the universe while through infinite extension the vast cycle breathes and beats people are giving rise to other people who born and aging age and die and sink all their energy again into the ground of energy which is the universe and the little cycles of spring and the great cycles of cosmic time are no more no less than the same single concentric beat

I am

an infinitesimally short-lived pulse

I am

an eternal pulse

I am

whirling around the earth at stupendous dizzying whirling around the sun at inhuman stupefying whirling through the galaxy at supreme shattering rushing through the universe at disintegrating howling speed approaching light too much stopstopstooo-o-o-

But the mountain has been lying on me non-stop. The cave has been eating its way through me non-stop. I cannot die. I? I am a fleck of It. And It arises continually. Through me or through anything else. Has it ever mattered through which?—the death of the energy that danced me is strictly speaking not possible. It dances me, a double shimmering, a shimmer flashing in contrary directions, visibly whirring around an invisible center.

From which the sensation of embodied space follows, the world appears to exist, and spaceless bodies appear to rub, just as someone now is rubbing me.

Sandy? Mavi? For a long time he or she or someone or a number of them have been trying to bring me back. That's my guess. About thirty years, I'd say. Trying out on me all sorts of fascinating apparatus and benevolent methods of care. Working hard, all of them, Satori and Tieger and Puddu and Mavi and Carlo and Flaminia and all

of those specialist quacks. But especially Sandy—I love your face—
Sandy, *you've* been working harder than anyone—and I want to
tell you, I want to tell you all how much I appreciate your efforts,
but yours especially, Sandy. And I do love you all, but it's impractical,
it's hopeless, you see. But thank you, anyhow. I appreciate your taking care of my body, no matter how unreal it is. For nevertheless, it
has to be fed. Now that's a curious illusion, isn't it, as matter-of-fact
as it seems. My illusory body must swinishly crave its spectral
food, it's obliged to copulate not mechanically but with immense conviction, it must needs urinate discreetly and defecate apart, and how
dutifully it suffers its ghastly pains!

I do see your face, Sandy. I have always seen it. You know I see it.
But would you hold it still? What are you making faces for?
Stop twisting your cheeks and eyes at me. When you churn like
that, it isn't your face, it's more like Baron's ugly mug, only somehow
more—more like Puddu's granite and leather and mica—is it?—is it
Puddu?—come again to prove me real?—but he is monstrous—the flesh
over his muscles is hard, ugly as toenails—so horn-skinned he brings
to mind the—caveman, Peking Man, the Dermalene illusion, almost
alive he too once seemed, but this being is more alive than Tieger or
Puddu or anyone alive has ever been, is it a being, am I imagining him,
his face flickers and shifts with grief and curiosity, he moves with an
interior fire subdued, he contains a flame of life greater than his own
shape, and so ancient I tremble and can't stop trembling before him,
his eyes fixed on me, agitated yet focused, he is big-boned and hot-
fleshed, heavily creased in the brows and matted with a tangled shag
snaking from the movement of his muscled shoulders, and his entire
being—his visible spirit—is possessed of incredible energy—his
shoulders flex, his arms ripple, his eyes breathe—and I know him, I
know him from the heat emanating right out of the sockets of his
eyes, I recognize him as the Ancient Man of the Mountain—and he
is coming at me. There is life in the Old Man yet. The skins he is
wearing flow and burn like lava over his slowly advancing, rising
limbs. I can't close my burned eyes as he comes at me, coming to me
from where I started, thousands and thousands of generations back.
He is in me, he has always been in me, he is still coming at me. He has
been working through me his extraordinary fervor and energy and
passion, he is coming right on through me, whether I know it or care,
and he will keep on coming through me to my child or children and
their children, without limit, with or without our consent, this

fierce stupendous life, a god beyond himself, because once, and once forever, he had been called by name, he heard his own name called aloud, and replied forever, "Here I am,"

I said and saw Mavi. It wasn't the Old Man of the Mountain or Puddu or anyone else, it was my child, and she was naked. All her features writhed, her hair stood out from her head and flexed its muscled braid at me. Where he had been, she stood, calling me. She had been calling me, and though I replied for her sake, I knew she was me. With two names, we were a single flesh elongated through time to stand apart, four-legged and two-brained, I Millie, I Mavi, I here, I there. For I had simply been stretched through time, my flesh had been drawn out along with the bubble's dilation, we were a vine of flesh, she and I. All men, all women, were that vine. A million-year creeper, creeping and budding, creeping and budding, the energetic length of it reached all the way from the Old Man to me to her, an ancient flesh spurting and seeding, an ancient flesh bearing and giving birth, one living glory of protoplasm thickspreading and tangling in the sunlight of millions of years. By the spreading of time one being had been forced to crawl down millions of branches, to push out billions of buds, and all of them me, however brained and muscled. The Old Man and Tieger and Puddu and Satori and Carlo and Flaminia and I had been forced by expanding time, which blew the cosmos up as it puffed, to occupy different slots in space. Cobweb creation, accordion rhythm, I Millie, I Mavi, I here, I there. Out of me whitened and bloody she had budded, me out of the center of me, and despite the explosion of time, we were connected physically through that time, a time-stretched vine. "Here I am," I said and saw myself calling me, named Mavi. Her muscled braid swayed to me, her sex offered a cluster of genitals like grapes, she had offered me something to eat, I recalled, dust, an ancient seed, and I had eaten, but since she was me, I had offered myself some seed to eat, but the seed and the bone and the soil and the rock and I there, I here, we were all of me flecks of It, so It had given Itself its sacred perishable imperishable dust to eat, It had given Itself to eat, I had taken my sacred flesh. And chewed.

And swallowed the disintegrating seed of dust as the mountain of dust had swallowed me. I felt the sacred wall, I touched each crinkle and fold, the pocks in the surface, and as I caressed them, they caressed me back. I went down on my knees, I paid attention and homage to rubble, each tiniest spot was a gorgeous unrepeated landscape of pulverized rock and soil. I was astonished, but not at the beauty of it. At the tenderness. I was astonished to know that I loved *things*. The dust. I felt inexpressible tenderness for the dust and put it to my lips. Gratitude for this dust. Gratitude . . . for everything . . . unending, boundless gratitude.

Someone was in the dust with me. I saw her new, I saw her suddenly, I saw her sacredness, I woke, I kept waking as she crawled toward me, and each time I saw her coming, I saw exactly how hideous she was, but also how holy she was. Gratitude kept passing through me like explosions of love through wounds. She touched my hand, slowly entwining her fingers in mine, and the dry, heavily scored wrinkles in her knuckles seemed, each deep wrinkle, overpoweringly sacred to me. I swayed with a tidal feeling of compassionate love for flesh, the swaying and heaving of ocean for moon. For my own flesh . . . for all created flesh. She bowed her crone's white-haired head on my shoulder, and I stroked the puffy and suppurating sores on her deformed face. The perishability of flesh, as now she withered and charred back into the ground of creation before my eyes, under my touch, made it especially to be loved, needy of love. Tenderness. Everything was tender.

Her crust of skeletal shoulder, her termite's ear. And her wizened hands were rubbing my spine, all covered with my own hide, and the gristle of her lips was placed on the scab of my mouth, calling me, Here I am, consuming me, Here you are, enwombing me, Here she was, entombing me, Here they were, they have been here always, thirty-six copulating skeletons, and I thought to myself with amazed lucidity, That isn't it. Not sex. Not the phallic idol, a mere implement, the tool of love. Irrelevant discovery. Sex isn't it at all, not at all. It's getting to the center, that's it, I'm getting to the center of It, we're getting to the center. I can feel It working through me, through us, driving us back to that center, navel, womb, I was reaching her belly through her vulva, the zero-point out of which—again, each time for a space again—life pulses, and It arises, the vine crawls and It buds, It arises.

She was taking something, an ancient seed, she was discovering something, irrelevant tool, we were creating something, a squirming vine, its roots to the dust, her fruit on my stalk, her vegetable life, her pit, her rind, her seed. Whose stalk stalks her, whose dust dusts me, whose core cores her, whose skin skins me, whose root roots her, whose pulp pulps me, whose seed seeds her and here I am, there's life in the Old Man yet. In the one posture possible, in the one impossible posture, we are grafted together into a protoplasm writhing on through convulsions of space and time. She has given herself something at last. She has given herself me. It has taken Itself as always.

Immaterial bodies rub and suffer their pains and are carried howling through space on an engorged bubble of time, illusions approaching the speed of light too much stopstopstooo-o-o-

How I

When I first saw him, I didn't think I was alive. I saw his transparent grey eyes. Sandy's eyes! Then Urru's eyes like slate just behind his shoulder. And Mavi's sulphurous eyes off to one side. If I was alive, I didn't think I could go on living. What I remembered —was that conceivable? The world so touch-me-not precious with light and knock-on-wood solid to touch brought tears to my eyes. But what I remembered—had that occurred?

What is perversion anyhow in this perverse century? It took me weeks to think it through. After the essential form of existence I'd known—life on the vine—did it matter? But I was halfway between that other life and this, and settling fast again, and I didn't have the courage to confront Mavi with love, nor the strength of mind for questions. Cowardly, I hinted at what slowly began shattering me from my bonehead crown of consciousness to my primal taproot of selfhood. And I got for my pains one of those elaborate and mistrustful glances while at the same time five clustering fingers twined themselves in mine.

Hallucination? Those seeds? Was that all? There was no denying the exultation in her fingers. She too had taken a seed. And what had she experienced? Was her touch an answer? Her mother and father . . . our lost unity recovered and fulfilled in chaos?

When I recovered my wits sufficiently, I confided in Sandy. After flying out from New York, he had managed to get hold of Urru through Signora Puddu, and Urru had taken him to the site. Exhausted, I appealed for my brother's advice.

He regarded me for a long while before he asked me thoughtfully what I wanted *besides* Mavi.

Everything I could think of suddenly began once more with "M." Mastery. Maturity. Mystery. Moon. I told him.

Nodding, he clarified all those "M"s for me mystically as the closing of my lips around the primal syllable, "OM." I accepted this at the time, though later I came to think it was crass capital commonsense "M" for Millie.

"And Mavi?" I asked.

Patiently, he reminded me that the difference between male and female was after all only a biologically crude distinction—genetic, psychological, functional, but relatively unsubtle. That at more fundamental levels the crucial polarity was never the distinction between male and female, but always the division between Self and Being. And that at a deeper level still, just as all seeming sex was one and androgyne, so the self and its own creation both desired, in sacramental imitation of Self and Being, to be united.

I listened. I wanted her. And I saw the way at last. Daring all the old gods, we'd be the first complete couple in history.

But the vilification to which I was subjected afterward, the harassment of my later years by snotty politicians and public prosecutors eager to kick my unsavory reputation: how petty is the vulgar reflex to cry "But I'm innocent" out loud in one's personal reminiscences. Worse still is the way the acid works its will from the heart to the poem. Dante in exile, Milton in obloquy, Blake in cahoots with the Devil. Look, I refuse to demean myself. What about those charges of obscenity, incest, and treason? The reader can relax, relieved to hear from M. W. Niemann's mouth that I'm guilty. Not as charged of course. But in my own terms still more culpable.

And impenitent.

Time and space, not matter and energy, make it inexpedient to complete this autobiography within the compass of a single volume. Amid the various demands of a still busy life, I hope to find leisure to trace the remainder of my career. In any event, my half-life has been radioactive. The clicking and clucking of prose is a warning of contamination. There are telltale traces of future fallout on every page thus far. For the rest: How the kittens, though mothered by a dog, grew up to be normal animals; How long it took me to recover from ingesting those seeds in the primordial sanctuary; How Sandy, who had brought over with him the latest American antibiotics, worked hard to cure the stricken Puddu with these broad-spectrum drugs, using in addition hypnotism, meditation, and subcutaneous electrolysis; How Puddu nevertheless turned to stone and near the end was shot to bits because he could not move when attacked; How Signora Puddu fled to the Balearics and what vengeance pursued her there; How the scientific world pooh-poohed my Sardinian cave discoveries and then had to stifle its laughter and eat archaeological crow; How the CIA approached me, hoping to use me as an agent in Sicily, how I refused, and how they always nursed a grudge against me; How Baron Tieger married Flaminia; How I helped solve the economic problems of Sardinia and became in consequence a greatly respected figure throughout Italy while, dishonored in my own land, I was looked upon as a moral leper; How Carlo came to my aid in the nick of time and produced unshakable evidence to clear my name; How though I had been dragged unmercifully through the courts, I changed a hanging jury to a hung jury, emerged from the contest in triumph, and lived to serve my country well at last; How I finally realized the dream of my childhood and rocketed in glory to the Moon; How I forged new and stronger poems, year in, year out, for my private joy in spite of public abuse, and received the highest acclaim; How Mavi and I had a child; How I found in the end the last line of my first poem; all this and more will have to wait.

A NOTE ON THE TYPE

The text of this book was set on the Linotype in Janson, a recutting made direct from type cast from matrices long thought to have been made by the Dutchman Anton Janson, who was a practicing type founder in Leipzig during the years 1668–87. However, it has been conclusively demonstrated that these types are actually the work of Nicholas Kis (1650–1702), a Hungarian, who most probably learned his trade from the master Dutch type founder Dirk Voskens. The type is an excellent example of the influential and sturdy Dutch types that prevailed in England up to the time William Caslon developed his own incomparable designs from these Dutch faces.

This book was composed, printed, and bound by The Colonial Press Inc., Clinton, Mass.

Typography and binding design by Christine Aulicino